ECHOES

A goose has walked over my grave

JOHN FRANKS

What readers are saying about
ECHOES

"You know it was a good book when you spend the afternoon wondering what the characters are doing."

Sandra Boyd, editor

"John Franks' remarkable debut novel, *Echoes*, is primarily a modern story of love, challenge and relationships. Interwoven through this contemporary tale is an intriguing historical narrative, the significance of which left me guessing right up to the book's ending. *Echoes* is beautifully and sensitively written without ever being sentimental or saccharine. A lovely debut novel – touching, poignant and effortlessly readable!"

Pam Garfoot, author
Capricorn Drover and the
prize-winning *Making Them Real*

"Franks is an engaging and idiosyncratic writer whose first novel *Echoes* balances a modern-day love story with a secondary 19th century tale of colonial Australia. *Echoes* is a smooth and well written tale that many people will relate to the realistic interplay between the main characters. The ending makes the journey worthwhile, and the author's style should have a widespread appeal."

Ned Stephenson, author
Sutcliffe's Alchemy series, and
2023 Newcastle Herald short story
competition people's choice award

"*Echoes* tells stories of colonial Sydney, Threlkeld's Lake Macquarie mission and post-war Poland. They form the background to an engaging modern love story about identity and how history and the land shape us."

Claire Williams
Author and historian

ECHOES

A goose has walked over my grave

JOHN FRANKS

Title: Echoes / A goose has walked over my grave
First published in 2023 by Kani Consultants, Newcastle, Australia.
Copyright © 2023 John Franks

Disclaimer: The role played by the characters in the modern
sections of this narrative are entirely fictional. In the historical
sections, the role of Lili is entirely fictional, but others are based
on research conducted by the author. The author has been able
to correlate the fictitious narrative with generally known facts of
their real lives.

 A catalogue record for this
work is available from the
NATIONAL
LIBRARY   National Library of Australia
OF AUSTRALIA

Cover Designed by Dez Robertson of Realized Design, Newcastle
Edited by Sandra Boyd
Illustrations by John Franks
Photo by Bronywn MacRitchie
Published by Kani Consultants www.kaniconsultants.com.au

Typeface: Modern content - Times New Roman 12 point
Typeface: Historical sections - Poor Richard 14 point

ISBN: 978-0-6450672-8-6 Echoes (paperback)
ISBN: 978-0-6450672-9-3 Echoes (hardcover)
ISBN: 978-0-6488089-1-6 Echoes (e-book)

Author: Franks, John
Subjects: Fiction / General; Fiction / Historical / General

Gideon Owen Davis
Sydney, New South Wales
1840

I

Gideon Davis stared in bewilderment at the vast expanses of the tree-lined coves and headlands as his ship slowly made its way, under reduced sail, towards the cluster of buildings that made up the destination known to him only as Sydney Town.

As the ship drew closer to a smaller inlet within the expansive sun-washed harbour, he could see through the forest of masts and furled sails clusters of wooden buildings, with several more important sandstone constructions scattered between them. He felt there was something invigorating about the developing town in a vast country whose entire population, after fifty years of white settlement, was less than fifty thousand souls.

Leaning both hands on the deck rail and gripping his hold-all, which contained his worldly possessions between his feet, he was all too aware that within the hour he would set foot on a land that struck elements of fear and doubt mingled with anticipation and excitement, deep inside him.

He'd been inspired during his many discussions with Presbyterian Minister Lewis, in Pengam, his hometown in Wales, who had spoken about 'doing God's work' in the missions of the new Pacific colonies, including Sydney Town, New South Wales. Mr Lewis' eyes shone with fervour when quoting biblical references, particularly Matthew 28:19: "Go therefore and make disciples of all nations," and Romans 10:12-15 "There is no difference … for the same Lord overall is rich unto all that call upon him. How beautiful are the feet of those who preach the good news?"

Specifically, Mr Lewis' view was that there was a need to bring the heathen unbaptised Aborigines, 'from darkness into Christ's light'. The fact that he was the third son in his family, with limited inheritance opportunities in a predestined village life, reinforced his determination to answer what he believed was his 'calling'.

Seven months ago, on the morning of his departure from his home in a coal mining community in the Rhymney Valley north of Cardiff, Gideon had waved goodbye to his parents, then walked for six hours to Cardiff, his port of embarkation. Looking again at the harbour he was now entering, he could not help comparing its broad, open sparseness with the busy Cardiff port teeming with the activity of coal loading operations for ships bound for the Americas and other exotic locations.

He watched as his ship eased its way to a berth, and observed the crew bustling around the deck, hurling ropes onto the wharf where dockside workers scurried to secure them to bollards. Here on board, other crew members were preparing for the passengers to disembark, yelling instructions at the top of their voices. Gripping the railing firmly, with more than a hint of nervousness, he waited his turn, summoning the resolution to begin what he believed was his 'new world' vocation.

Through Minister Lewis' Presbyterian contacts with the London Missionary Society, he had learned of a hard-working missionary with the stirring name of Lancelot Threlkeld who had established a mission sixty miles north of Sydney on the shores of Lake Macquarie. Minister Lewis had pointed out that Threlkeld, christened Lancelot Edward, was named after Lancelot Andrewes, a scholarly English bishop who had overseen the translation of the King James version of the Bible. Surely a good omen.

He intended to make his way to Threlkeld's mission, despite having been made aware of the harsh, often contradictory, reports about the difficulty of converting the 'ignorant heathen', steeped as they were, according to many, in pagan practices. He believed it was his mission to bring a Christian God into their lives.

Those reports included assessments by the Church of England minister, magistrate, stockbreeder and farmer, Samuel Marsden. Added to these considerable responsibilities was his role in overseeing the work of the London Missionary Society.

Unbeknown to Reverend Lewis in Pengam, Marsden despite being recommended by the humanitarian activist William Wilberforce for his position, was known to have an irascible personality who claimed to have tried without success, to civilise and convert the Aborigines.

Ultimately, Marsden had concluded that the natives had no concept of a divine being and were impervious to the notion of heavenly reward. He believed that their complicated social order and few wants, other than for basic day-to-day survival, were an insurmountable barrier to conversion to Christianity. He came to the commonly held view that the Aborigines were, with few exceptions, impossible to convert.

Gideon waited, allowing other passengers to disembark, as he tried to take in the surroundings. The town had certainly grown beyond the descriptions he had read. During the long journey, he had been told that chief among the reasons for its rapid growth was its original purpose as a prison colony, where many thousands of convicts had been transported.

Of added significance was its strategic location in the South Pacific Ocean as a safe harbour, for British naval ships, as well as occasional French naval, and American whaling vessels. A predominantly male population with a ratio of men to women of more than six to one, had resulted in very poor moral standards and violence, particularly directed towards the Aboriginal women.

Having lived so far from the sea, Gideon could make little sense of the frenetic dockside activity. When he was abruptly told, 'Eee! Young lad, get tha' a move on," by a crew member, he tentatively made his way down the gangway, all the while looking for someone who could direct him. Minister Lewis had told him to seek out the Scots Presbyterian Church. It was presided over by John Dunmore Lang, a man whose pamphlets promised a better life for England's poor in the expanding colony.

Gideon was also aware of Lang's extensive political interests which, in his mind, raised the dilemma of how he could achieve both his spiritual and political goals. In other discussions with Mr Lewis, Gideon was made aware of the discord between the protestant denominations within the colony, mainly united only in their intolerance of Catholicism. John Dunmore Lang was a vigorous and principal protagonist in most debates, frequently in opposition to the Reverend Samuel Marsden.

It took Gideon almost an hour in the heat of the day to find his way to the Scots Church. The occasional sight of gangs of shackled men hauling building materials, farm produce and all manner of goods, occasionally accompanied by threats, shouts and commands from overseers wielding whips, was both fascinating and shocking. He was being awakened to the problems of transition to a new way of life for the inhabitants thrown together: the convicts, their gaolers, migrants, ticket-of-leave men and women, as well as assigned convicts and the dispossessed Aborigines, the former inhabitants of the land.

On arrival at the Scots Church, he was devastated to hear from a pale-faced deacon dressed, despite the heat, in a black frock coat with a high collar, that Reverend

Lang was away on a visit back to England. After he explained his intentions to make his way to the mission established by Reverend Threlkeld, the deacon was at pains to advise Gideon not to mention the name of Threlkeld in Lang's hearing or indeed, to any of Lang's close acquaintances, because they had serious differences of opinion on Threlkeld's management of his mission. He made it clear that Lang would offer no help to Gideon on the matter.

Furthermore, Gideon was shocked to hear that Threlkeld's mission was in decline. The deacon explained that, more recently, Threlkeld's time was divided between religious commitments and his coal mining ventures in Lake Macquarie.

He added that, at present, Threlkeld might be found somewhere around the docks as his ship was in port having just arrived from Newport, Lake Macquarie.

Gideon felt a slight thrill to think that he was headed for a place with the same name as the rapidly developing Newport just fifteen miles from his hometown, Pengam. It was changing very quickly from a small seaport to one of the most important places in the country for coal export.

Dismayed and more than a little disturbed, Gideon returned to the harbour to make inquiries about finding either Threlkeld or his ship. Once again, his inquiries were mistimed. He found the ship, but the Master, Mr Jarrow, told him Threlkeld was ashore somewhere on business. Mr Jarrow didn't know when the Reverend would return but that he was due back on board before the ship sailed to Lake Macquarie in two days' time.

Gideon quickly considered his next move.

Foremost was where he could stay while he waited for Threlkeld's return. The sun was setting and, with his funds almost exhausted, he couldn't afford accommodation in the town. In a moment of inspiration, he asked the master if he could stay on board while he waited.

After subjecting Gideon to close scrutiny, Mr Jarrow offered him working passage to Lake Macquarie. Despite still recovering from his voyage, he accepted, albeit with a nagging sense of apprehension.

Late the following day Threlkeld returned to the ship and Mr Jarrow introduced the newest team member. On an impulse, he gave his preferred name as Owen, his middle name, instead of Gideon, his Christened name. He did so in his belief that as he was in a new land, a new name seemed appropriate.

Minmi, Newcastle
NSW 2005

"Same again, gents?"

Marek shook his head and Darren answered for them both. "Nah, thanks all the same mate. Better not. Got a few jobs to do later this arvo."

Darren Merrigan and Marek Benning slid from their barstools in the old Minmi pub and sauntered out, offering a brief wave as they went. "See you next time. Cheers."

After casting his gaze over the village of Minmi, Marek let it wander over the semi-rural landscape, situated as it was, on the outskirts of Newcastle, New South Wales, just a couple of hours' drive north of Sydney via the freeway. Away from suburbia, it gave the impression of it would be a peaceful, relaxed place to live.

Maybe it was the pub meal, or the beer, which made it a feel-good day for him. He adjusted his stained and battered old broad-brimmed cricket hat, which his mother had given him years ago. He had a mildly curious sensation that the land was pleading for his attention.

Overhead, puffy white clouds drifted listlessly from the north-west in a pale blue sky. The stillness accentuated a sense of timelessness. Occasional lowing of belted Galloway cattle, identifiable even at this distance by the white band around their bellies, grazing within rough-cut post-and-rail fenced paddocks, suggested the remnants of the cattle grazing history of this much neglected village. The only other visible stock were a few horses, with their heads down, cropping grass and lazily flicking their tails at ever-present flies.

As they were heading back to their truck, Marek saw a sign advertising land for sale and his interest was immediately piqued.

"Are we in a hurry, Darren? I'd like to have a closer look around."

"Sure thing, go ahead. I have a few calls to make. I'll wait in the truck."

The land for sale was a generous portion he guessed at less than a hectare and out of earshot of traffic. Its gentle north-facing slope rose to a flat area, ideal for a view of the distant hills to the west, presently a muted bluish shade.

Houses, both farm-style and modern, were scattered irregularly across the landscape. He scanned the middle distance and counted about twenty dwellings and out-buildings.

Dragging his feet through the patches of tufty native grass provided a comforting sense of contact with the earth. A grasshopper, disturbed by his presence, flew off in a frenzied whirr, only to be targeted by an ever-vigilant swooping kookaburra. Invasive clumps of lantana did not enhance the aspect, but they could be cleared.

Farther away, the main road served travellers moving between Newcastle and districts to the north-west in the upper reaches of the Hunter Valley.

Marek, nearing thirty, was contemplating a long-held ambition of buying land for his first solo spec-home project.

The decision was all the weightier because although he had built previous spec houses, which had been financially rewarding, they had been built in partnership with Darren

Merrigan, with whom he had worked since beginning his apprenticeship more than a dozen years ago. Now he was considering taking on a 'speculative building project home', as they were sometimes formally referred to, or informally as a 'speckie', on his own, because Darren had recently told him he was retiring from the trade.

The announcement, although unsettling, had come as no great surprise to Marek. Darren had several health issues typical of long-term carpenters and builders, including bursitis in a shoulder that often caused a sharp pain when lifting timber, sawing by hand or even swinging a hammer.

Over lunch, Darren had made it clear. "Marek, it's time I got off the tools. Something's got to give before my body packs it in completely. My doctor's been giving me warning advice for a couple of years and, after talking it over, at home with Maxine, we've decided that a recent job offer in an air-conditioning installation firm is too good to refuse. I'll be fifty-seven next birthday."

Darren looked down, kicked at a tuft of grass for no reason other than the obvious: he was giving up on a job he loved. "It's a job that could take me up to retirement if all goes well. As you know, with Maxine's job as office manager for Select Accounting, the reduced income won't be a big problem and the responsibility from running even a small building firm like this will be a welcome relief. It's a young man's game this is but, if you decide to go it alone, I'll do what I can to help you get set up."

As his critical eye moved over the land, Marek knew any such purchase, and the building project itself, would cost more money than he had. Finance would need meticulous examination, but he recognised the location as an opportunity to develop a property in an area that he thought would appreciate as demand for housing increased. In his mind's eye he saw it as something which could make his reputation as an independent builder.

He trudged over the uneven surface and was reminded of some of the photos and captions displayed in the pub. In the late 1800s, Minmi had become a developing coal mining area but before that it had been cattle grazing country. He wanted to get a feeling of what it would be like living here by seeking out desirable locations and an outlook for his dream home.

A small stand of paperbarks, some of which still showed late-blooming creamy, nectar-rich, bottlebrush flowers, on which rainbow lorikeets were noisily feeding, attracted his attention.

As he made his way closer, he stumbled on the edges of a long-dried stream bed. He stopped to check but saw nothing obvious which might have caused a misstep. He mumbled aloud to himself to watch where he was going.

Unexpectedly, given the mild weather conditions, a cold chill prickled the back of his neck. He looked up, noting the stillness of the leaves. His spine tingled, causing him to shiver, disturbing his peace of mind. He recalled one of his mother's Polish sayings: '*A goose has walked over my grave*'.

Unbidden, his imagination flashed back to a lost period some time in the mid-nineteenth century. The image conjured was something akin to a palimpsest, the scene before him morphing with an image from the past.

He wondered whether he had spent too much time looking at the old pictures in the pub; or shouldn't have had the beer. For a few moments, all sound and motion were frozen.

Again, he felt compelled to examine his surroundings but saw nothing untoward. With a shrug of his shoulders, he turned and walked back to the truck.

Two weeks later he was invited to a small retirement party for Darren at the Merrigan home. It would correspond with Darren's last ever Business Activity Statement, the dreaded BAS, for their partnership.

Maxine had invited a few of Darren's and Marek's building mates and some of her colleagues from Select Accounting. It was supposed to be a casual affair but the employees of Select arrived after work, creating a stark contrast in dress standard well above that of their builder workmates.

Darren had advised him to continue essential financial advice from the same firm but under his own trading name.

When he was introduced to the bean counters, as he privately thought of them, he tried to make small talk with a few, with discomfort evident on both sides.

The most intriguing person to whom he had been introduced was Gwynne Alwen. He guessed she was somewhere in her mid-twenties, the youngest by far in attendance. She had positioned herself apart from any particular group and seemed more reserved, to the point of looking uncomfortable.

After chatting with a few of his mates, Marek drifted back to Gwynne. Hopeful of getting to know her, he reintroduced himself. "Hello again, I'm Marek, Darren's partner … building partner that is."

The twitch on Gwynne's lips indicated she understood the inference of the clarification. "Yes, I know. Maxine has told me, and Darren mentioned it ten minutes ago."

"Sorry, I thought you might have forgotten."

As they made small talk Gwynne mused, "I'm not really sure why Maxine invited me today. She probably thought I would benefit from socialising with colleagues and clients."

The dismissive tone in her voice suggested she was slightly underwhelmed. "So, you work with Darren in a building partnership."

"Yeah, that's about it. But with Darren retiring, I have to decide if, and how, to set out on my own. I think I'm in a similar position to you. Just here to make up the numbers as Darren's sidekick. How about you? What's your role at Select Accounting?"

Taking a sip of her drink, she lowered her voice and answered. "Well, I'm the junior, completing my Chartered Accountant's qualifications; getting practical experience for the next couple of months. It's a great opportunity for me. Currently, the part-time hours suit me by allowing me to look after my three-year-old daughter."

Marek hoped he covered his surprise at this last piece of information.

Not sure if he was brave or foolish, he asked, "And is there a Mister Alwen?"

Almost theatrically she straightened her stance and lifted her head and shoulders to maximise her slightly above-average height. Meeting his gaze squarely, she responded edgily with her own questions: "Why do you ask? What's that got to do with my work?"

Marek realised he had trampled over a privacy issue and, in a back-pedalling recovery manoeuvre countered, "Nothing. Just making conversation."

Trying to dig himself out of a hole he compounded his mistake by asking, "By the way, I couldn't help observing you have very attractive hands."

"Thank you," she replied, with a warning look and a 'don't start' tone.

Failing to recognise the import of her response he added, "And in doing so I noticed you're only wearing that one small ring on your ring finger." As soon as he said it, he knew he shouldn't have. He was digging himself in deeper, but it couldn't be un-said.

"So?" Her sharp response had a chill to it, and he became aware he was in danger of being buried.

"Look, sorry I asked. I didn't mean to intrude. Okay?"

He hesitated before finally and cheekily composing his best boyish grin and asking, "Well is there a Mr Alwen, or anyone else?"

"How pushy you are! Yes, there is a Mr Alwen if you must know."

He was only slightly crest fallen but restrained himself from voicing his inner thought: *What a shame!*

Before he could say another word, Maxine interrupted to whisk Gwynne away to meet some of the other guests. As Gwynne turned from him, she boldly and sassily quipped back over her shoulder: "Yes, there is a Mr Alwen. That would be my father."

He watched as she walked away. His curiosity was aroused but he wasn't sure whether it was in a good or a bad way. On reflection, after a few minutes, he realised he had allowed himself to be distracted by her appearance as well as her barbed and evasive retorts. She was, he guessed, in a not too dissimilar position as himself: both of them were about to enter a new career phase. She projected a cool and aloof demeanour, and clearly had an off-beat sense of humour.

Someone to keep an eye on ... or avoid?

The following Friday afternoon he rang Select Accounting. "Hi Maxine. I'd like to arrange to speak to someone about going it alone as a sole trader. Can you suggest someone who can give me a heads-up on what's involved?"

"Hello Marek, I'm glad you called. I've been thinking about that ever since Darren told me you were considering that option. How about Gwynne Alwen? It would be a challenge for her. She's not yet a certificated accountant but I think she could outline the basics required of a sole trader. It would be a good case study for her, and we have other senior members of staff to advise her if required. However, the boss will make the final decision."

"Are you sure? We didn't hit it off when we met at your party the other night. She seemed a bit aloof, almost indifferent to me."

"She might have been putting on her professional face, trying to appear disinterested. Or maybe she had been looking into your eyes and got put off."

"Yes, well that worked in reverse. It's put *me* off."

"I meant, disinterested in the sense of being impartial and objective. I can tell you, she has done very well at Select and knows the ropes. And … her fee would be less than a fully qualified accountant's. Think about it. It could work for you both as you find your feet."

"Yeah, okay, if you think so. I'll play it cool, but she can't blame me for my eye colour. Is next Friday afternoon available for an appointment?"

2

After a difficult day, Marek arrived late at Select Accounting. He was directed to an office where Gwynne sat working at her computer.

Without stopping for more than a second, she held up her hand and indicated that he should be seated quietly while she finished.

Not a great start.

Then he realised how he didn't like being interrupted when he was doing something requiring full concentration. *Swings and roundabouts?*

The task was completed with a noticeable sigh. She spun her chair to face him and began the corporate welcome from the 'how to' manual. It was an obvious PR spiel.

Marek wasn't up for it. He'd had a tough week with Darren, trying to get a grip on the myriad practical details of becoming a sole trader. He felt his lips twitch as the spiel droned on and when it ended, he noticed even Gwynne had a look of relief when it was over. They settled down to the business of discussing his financial position and tax arrangements.

"I've discussed this with Tom Wright, my supervisor. He thinks it would be helpful for the firm to have a client profile of your work background. For example, qualifications, certificates gained, specific areas of expertise. Some personal background can be useful. No rush. Any time before our next meeting will do."

"No problem. It might take me a while to put it all together."

Marek wasn't overly pleased with how the consultation progressed; sensing Gwynne's professionalism was leading towards a dictatorship rather than a consultative process. He realised he'd made a mistake in timing the meeting for a Friday afternoon and hadn't mentally prepared for it. Either that or he was simply in a grumpy mood.

His concentration started to waver, and his basic instincts began to focus on some of her specific and admittedly, disturbingly attractive, features: dress sense; make-up; honey-blonde hair in a bobbed style, which framed her face; and particularly, her hands. Again, he fixed on that small, glittering stone in the ring on the third finger of her left hand. He had an urge to find out more about it but with a little more subtlety than his first attempt.

He snapped back to the task at hand when he heard Gwynne say, "When you provide the information I've asked for, I'll collate it, consult with my supervisor, and get back to you. We'll then make another appointment. How does that sound? Of course, you'll need to consult your solicitor regarding the formal dissolution of your partnership with Darren Merrigan."

"Sounds fine by me. My solicitor is on to it. He's a mate I went to school with," Marek confidently replied. "Thanks for your time. I'll get onto those things you suggested. G'bye."

He walked out of the office feeling as if something was missing; wondering whether he should call Maxine and ask for a different consultant. He didn't feel this one was going to work for him.

Most of the following week his thoughts pin-balled around his uncertain future. Any previous major decisions in his life had been made after talking to his father and mother.

But his mother had died from breast cancer five years ago and his father had decided on a return visit to family and old friends in Poland.

He decided to ring his father.

After their greetings, he listened patiently, and was comforted by the sound of his father's voice as he filled him in on some of what he was up to in his old hometown of Zakopane.

When his father had finished, Marek broached the matter weighing him down. "Dad, you know I told you Darren was retiring. Well, it's happening, and I'm thinking of going it alone as a sole trader. I'm talking to Ross about the legalities, I'm in contact with Select for financial advice and Darren is giving me a lot of operational help. What do you think?"

"Son, I've been here for almost two years, and you've done extremely well up to now without me looking over your shoulder. Yeah, it will be a risk, but good advice from Darren and your own common sense will help. What's your main worry?"

"Well, on the down-side, I'll be personally liable; bigger operations may not deal with sole-traders, and I'll have to rely on my own initiative."

"You know, your grandfather took a risk leaving Kraków to start a new life here in Zakopane. Your mother and I took a bigger risk leaving Poland to go to Australia. We were ambitious. You can do it, but it won't be easy. What's on the up-side? What other options do you have?"

"I get to be the boss; I keep the profits, if there are any; I can use the experience as a test for my business nous and I can always bail out if it doesn't work.

"That is true."

"On the other hand, I could work for another builder or get a job with a home construction firm."

"You want to do that? Or you want to be your own boss? Marek, you're young, you can give it a go. Just take your time and be patient. I think you can do it."

"Thanks Dad. By the way, I won't be seeing much of Briony, that girl I've told you about. She's moved to Albury to take up a promotion. We've agreed we won't be seeing much of each other from now on."

"Hmm! I'm not surprised. She is ambitious, which is a good thing. She knows what she wants. I think your mother would have said that Briony was on a different journey to you. I agree with that. That clears the way for you to do what you want. Go for it. Choose your own destiny."

"Dad, when are you coming home? How are you getting by?"

"Don't worry for me. I get work two, three days a week. Sometimes more. Enough for rent, food and living expenses. You find a nice girl so I can come home and be a *dziadek* to your children."

"You make it sound simple. No sign of you becoming a grandpa yet. It takes two people for that. I'll try to keep level-headed on both counts. You taught me that. Good talking to you Dad. Love you. G'bye."

"I love you too. Your mother and I were always proud of you. Let me know how you get on. On both counts. *Do widzenia.*"

When he'd told Darren about the meeting with Gwynne Alwen and his father's comments, his response had been wary, punctuated with a litany of *don'ts*.

"Gwynne's only doing her job. Your challenge is to do yours. You know the routine: don't overcommit yourself physically or financially. Check everything: materials, labour time, council conditions, mine subsidence, surveys – twice! Just like we say in the trade, 'measure twice, cut once'. Let your clients know you're being thorough. Good ones'll appreciate it."

His solicitor, Ross Brennan, whom he had known since school days, was dealing with the dissolution of his partnership. Over the years, Darren and he had done Ross' firm a few good turns with property maintenance issues.

During a phone conversation a few days later, he mentioned the Minmi land he'd seen. "Ross, there's something else I wanted to bring up. I saw some land for sale when we stopped for lunch in Minmi and I started thinking that if everything works out business-wise, I might look at buying it and build a spec home. Any thoughts?"

"Take it easy! One thing at a time. I'll speak to a mate of mine in the real estate business over that way and ask him to check it out. Email me any details. If he thinks he'll get a sale out of it, it won't be any bother to him. Don't rush it though. Don't overload yourself."

"Yeah, that's what Darren would say, but thanks."

Eventually, Gwynne rang. "Hello Marek, I'm sorry it has taken so long to get back to you."

"That's okay, what are we up to?" was his neutral response.

"We've been as busy as all get out here and, only yesterday, I managed to consult with Tom Wright on your case. We're now ready to proceed."

"That's great news." Marek felt the excitement swelling within.

"Will you have that material we discussed available for our next meeting?"

"Yes, almost done," he replied, slightly stretching the truth. "I'm working on it, but yes, it'll be ready."

"Good to hear."

"Thanks for the call. See you Friday?"

"Yes. See you here at three o'clock. Goodbye."

Compiling the necessary information was more time consuming than he had supposed. Paperwork wasn't where he thought it was. Obtaining statements of his working life with Darren was awkward. As senior member of the partnership, Darren had handled most of the documentation and he had to ask him for copies. It was a bit like asking him for work references for a new job. Which, in a way, he was.

3

Late morning rain halted work on the day of his meeting at Select. The early finish allowed him to shower, dress and check the required paperwork was in order. It also gave him time to check with his bank that a business loan was possible if he was to pursue the land purchase at Minmi. The business loans manager had been encouraging, with the usual proviso, 'under certain conditions', regularly repeated. If all the ducks lined up, Marek thought it was possible he might be able to put in an offer on the land.

He was acutely aware he was on the brink of two major decisions in his working life. But first there was Gwynne Alwen to confront.

When he walked through the door at Select, he again experienced that unbusinesslike disturbance in the pit of his stomach. He had to quell a sensation of resistance to being bossed; being talked down to. She disturbed him, and it wasn't just her business manner that got at him. It was an undefinable distance she seemed to convey. Fortunately, as soon as he was seated, her professionalism focused his thoughts. "Let's have a look at what you've got there."

He handed over his folder and she flicked through it, eyes quickly scanning each page while his gaze alternated from comparing his own *un*manicured fingernails with the perfection of hers. A stark contrast to her creamy delicate fingers caressing, almost massaging, the keyboard.

Hands! Do I need to get out more?

She closed the folder and looked straight at him. "Thanks, it looks comprehensive; well done. Sorry, does that sound patronising? I didn't mean it to be."

Yes, now that you mention it.

In a flat tone he replied, "Not terribly."

Gwynne rolled her chair back and sat with a concentrated look on her face for a few moments. He had obviously thrown her off kilter.

"I do apologise, I'm a bit nervous."

"That's alright, so am I. Look, I haven't thought it through fully, but Darren's retirement and advice has made me think about the long term. I like what I do, and I reckon I'm good at it. But, as with many long-term plans, there may be unforeseen difficulties forcing other options. As with most things, including builders' health, I guess such decisions down the track need to be considered on their merits."

He watched as Gwynne tapped the pen she was holding against her chin before she responded.

"Just out of curiosity," she asked, "have you got anything in mind?"

"Well, freelance building consultant; a building inspector for real estate agents; council building inspector; valuer for banks. Stuff like that. Look, I'm not saying I'm going to quit building immediately. I like it and I've been told I do good work. It's just something to consider in maybe fifteen, even twenty or more years."

Gwynne drew a deep breath and let it out slowly. Her facial expression, especially her pursed lips, indicated she was puzzled. "Hmm! This meeting isn't going the way I expected. I can't see any immediate impact on what we're doing here today, except maybe superannuation. I'll consult with my supervisor. I'll be in touch. That's all for now I think."

"Look, sorry if I've put a cat among the pigeons. I didn't come in here to make any revelations. I just wanted to be up-front about any future ambitions."

"I appreciate that. We'll leave it there, shall we?"

Gwynne stood up, indicating the meeting was at an end. When she put out her hand, he took it and held it momentarily before giving it the gentlest of shakes, almost a caress. What wasn't so gentle was the electric shock he experienced. Her hands were not only lovely to look at, but they were also sensuous to touch.

That evening Marek was pleased when Darren called. "Hi Marek! How's it going?"

"Not too bad thanks. I had that meeting with Gwynne Alwen. I'm not sure how it's all going but it was better than our last meeting. What's up?"

"I've got wind of a job. Maxine mentioned that Gwynne Alwen has a friend, or someone, who wants some additions done. By the sound of it, it might be a good one for you. Not too big to manage on your own. Can I tell her it's alright for her friend to contact you?"

"Yeah, sure. She didn't mention anything at the meeting today. Where is it? Is it local?"

"Don't know. Whoever it is can discuss all that with you. They seem keen to start. Okay for me to pass on that you're interested? That's it. Let me know how you get on or if you have any questions, but I think you'll manage just fine. Keep in touch. Cheers."

"Thanks Darren. Will do. G'bye."

For the first time since he had met her, he was slightly more than content to hear Gwynne's voice when he answered his phone a few days later. "Marek, I've got your business profile ready for you to consider. You can pick it up at the front desk and look it over and get back to us if you have any comments or concerns."

The way she spoke was quite formal as if, once again, she was reciting from the company's 'best practice' manual.

"Very good. Thank you. I'll pick it up after work tomorrow. Thanks. By the way, those comments about other job options were just my imagination working overtime."

"Always a good idea to plan ahead, so I've heard."

"That's the sort of thing my old dad would say. G'bye."

"Have you got a moment Marek? "

"Of course. What's up?"

"I hope this doesn't sound unprofessional on my part. Please tell me if you feel under any pressure. The fact is, I'm thinking of having some work done on my house.

"That's exciting."

"Would you be able to advise me on one or two aspects of it? I can't discuss it at the office for reasons which will become obvious. Could we discuss it some time?"

"Darren rang me, but he didn't say it was you who wanted work done. This is sounding a bit mysterious. What did you have in mind?"

"How about a meeting on Saturday morning at a café somewhere? I can get Mum to look after Merren, so we aren't interrupted."

"Sure, I'm intrigued. Text me the time and place. See you Saturday."

Well, what a turn-up! *'Curiouser and curiouser!'* he quoted from Alice's adventures.

The business profile report was well set out and Marek took time to work through it in some detail, as per Darren's instructions. To clarify some of the particulars he contacted him and went over the trickier sections. He was now able to appreciate Darren's and Maxine's management roles while he had spent most of his working life dealing with the *hands-on* part of the partnership. One question Darren asked got him thinking: "Have you come up with a name for your business?"

"No, I haven't. Got any suggestions?"

"Yeah, keep it clear and simple. Something people can read and remember when they glimpse your name on the side of your truck. Something like, 'Benning Building' or 'Benning the Builder'."

"Thanks for the heads-up, Darren. I'm glad my name isn't Bob. I'll think about it. What I *have* been thinking about is how much work you and Maxine were doing behind the scenes. I think I'm beginning to get the hang of it."

"What? After two weeks? Cocky bugger! Problems come in all shapes and sizes. Take care."

"I will. Oh, by the way, good luck with your new job. G'bye"

4

After a hesitant greeting and settling at a table secluded from street view, Gwynne got straight to the point.

"Thanks for this Marek. I'll be frank. I'd like this to be confidential, strictly between us at this stage."

He didn't know what he expected but Gwynne's opening line wasn't it. It put him on guard. She had captured his interest in more ways than one, but a confidential tête-à-tête wasn't on the list. She sat looking straight at him; her hands resting on the table, her fingers interlaced. His gaze alternated from her face to her hands: *unblemished; creamy; alabaster; ring on third finger left hand.*

"I want to get some ideas regarding possible extensions to my house, to add a room or two, and I need advice about who might do the job and how much it would cost."

His brain automatically flicked to the question on why she wanted more space. He had the impression from Darren that there were just Gwynne and her daughter Merren living in the house; no mention of anyone else. *Interesting. Have I misinterpreted her comment about the existence of a Mr Alwen?* The possibility couldn't be dismissed.

He raised a questioning eyebrow. Taking her query at face value he asked, "Can you tell me what exactly you're after?"

She hesitated, exhaled as her shoulders slumped and then, as if making a confession, said, "The fact is I'm thinking of adding a home office, but it's early days so I would appreciate your keeping it confidential." She paused to let that sink in.

He frowned, not quite understanding. "That could be a bit awkward, given it was Darren who told me to expect your call. I don't want to be caught up in some office squabble. I've got my own sh…, sorry, stuff, to deal with. And he's my friend."

After a slight grimace at his near-miss choice of word, she said, "I'm sorry too. I was just thinking of myself. But it could be awkward for me too. The bosses at Select might change their thinking about my employment if they knew what I'm planning. Also, they might have a cynical view if they found out I asked you to do the work because you're a client. Do you know someone, a reliable builder, for this sort of job? How do I go about getting a quote?"

He looked intensely at her for a few moments. What she had just told him was a surprise and he took time to form his answer. "It all depends on the details of what you want. I know lots of builders but, depending on the job, some might be more suitable than others."

She started to fold and unfold her paper napkin, indicating either uncertainty or impatience. "I'm not talking about redesigning the Opera House! It's just an ordinary suburban house."

Pausing to calm herself, she apologised, "Sorry, that was me being flippant."

She was obviously someone who could dig her heels in when push came to shove. Marek tucked that characteristic away for future consideration.

Taking a deep breath, she explained, "I need a few pointers on how and where to start. What I'm asking for is advice to help me organise my ideas on some extension possibilities. I'm sorry if it looks like I'm taking advantage of you as a client, which I probably am, but I can't pass up the opportunity for an honest opinion."

"How do you know I'll give you an honest opinion?" he asked, barely concealing the sarcasm in his voice.

Then, after observing her startled reaction, he said, "Don't worry, you'll get it. When do you want it?"

He waited while some of the pink left her cheeks. By now the napkin in her hands looked like a tragic origami failure.

In a calmer tone she asked, "When would be convenient for you?"

"Because of my work schedule, Saturdays are best. Sundays are possible but are usually devoted to paperwork, working on quotes and so on. Plus, home stuff and what passes for my social life."

He looked up.

Was she batting her eyes at him? Am I seeing a playful side of her personality?

"Today's Saturday." Again, she refolded the scrunched napkin. "Would now suit? I live only a short distance away. My mother is looking after Merren while I'm here having coffee, ostensibly, with a friend. Sooner today, rather than later, would be preferable to avoid a clash when they return."

In what he hoped came across as a look of thoughtful deliberation while he considered whether he was being railroaded, and hoping to convey the pressures of time, he looked at his watch, and counted to ten.

Despite already having made up his mind to agree he conceded, "You seem to have it all worked out. Okay, it's fine with me. It makes no difference if your mother turns up, does it?"

This time, she chose her words more deliberately. "I want some sort of plan in my head before discussing the idea further with Mum. If she turns up with Merren while you're there it could raise all sorts of speculation, which I don't need at this early stage. Also, Merren would almost certainly start asking lots of questions possibly, dare I say probably, at the wrong time."

He felt like he was being drawn not only into a business intrigue, but a family one.

As luck would have it, he had both the time and the curiosity. "It's not too late. We can have a quick look and I'll see what I can come up with," he paused, and added with a grin, "possibly even an honest opinion".

She offered a sardonic smile and nodded her head, acknowledging his *touché* retort.

Marek followed her to a well-maintained suburban weatherboard 1940s style cottage. He was surprised by the location and wondered about its suitability as a business premises for an accountant.

Not my problem!

When they walked around to the back of the house, he was even more pleasantly surprised. There was a small garden with some flower beds and a not-so-well maintained vegetable patch. The rest was lawn.

Experience told him there was room for an addition, depending on Council regulations – and Gwynne's requirements.

She described what she wanted. "I'd like a space for an office plus an ensuite accessible from both inside and outside the house. Windows overlooking the backyard and solar panels on the roof, budget permitting, would be nice."

As she outlined her wish list, which he noted was functional but basic, he walked across the backyard. There was a driveway giving access to the yard and he asked, "Which side of the house are you thinking about for the additions?"

"The side opposite the driveway would be best because it won't interfere with access."

He nodded in silent agreement and continued his inspection. He got down on his hands and knees and looked under the house. He stood, brushed the dirt from his trousers and walked down the backyard and, standing on tiptoes, looked at the roof.

"Wait here a minute, I'll be back in a sec."

He went to his truck to get a tape to measure how far the rooms might extend down the side of the house as well as across the back. After about ten minutes, he said, "OK, let's talk."

Gwynne led him into the sunroom at the back of the house where he sat, collected his thoughts for a minute and began. "As far as I can judge, there is room for an extension. There are no obvious ground surface issues and plumbing down that side of the house looks feasible." He paused for a moment to choose his words carefully. "The extent to which the addition would extend across the back of the house needs some thinking about. Some additional alterations might be necessary. For example, this sunroom might be partially shaded. Natural light might be reduced but that could be offset by skylights."

"What you're saying is that I need to work out exactly what I want before I can get an accurate costing."

"That's about it," he confirmed. "Once a preliminary sketch is drawn up, you can approach builders to provide a more detailed plan and a quote for the job. Think about it and get back to me if you have any questions."

Believing he had covered the topic and not really expecting much of a reply, he asked, "Is there anything else you'd like to know?"

She stood, crossed to the back window to look out at the yard and with one arm held across her body and her other hand raised to her chin. "I'll need to think about it."

Her body language clearly showed him that she was attending to the proposition in a clinical fashion. Typical accountant, he thought, digging into the fine print.

He watched as she confidently returned to the table, suggesting she'd come to a decision. "Thanks awfully Marek. You've been a big help. Time is getting away. I'll get back to you when we, - *I've* made up my mind."

She led the way to the front door. He had followed, perhaps too closely, and when she turned abruptly, she almost trod on his toes.

Marek retreated half a step and uncertainly raised his hand as if to shake hers.

Hesitating only slightly, she took it and held it, and looked straight at him. "Do you wear coloured contact lenses?"

"What? Contact lenses? No! Whatever made you ask that?"

"Um, sorry. It was something that just came into my head. Outside in sunlight your eyes looked different, a pale azure blue, but inside they're a shady dark blue; cornflower to cobalt in two minutes. Sorry, forget I asked."

He shook his head, perplexed, trying to figure out why she would ask such a question in the context of what they were discussing. One minute she was being clinical, the next cryptic.

The mood and the moment were lost at the sound of a woman's voice outside saying.

"Wait a minute Merren, will you? I'm getting out the key."

The voice was followed by the sound of a key in the lock and the front door being flung open by a small blonde-headed child heralded by the call, "Mummy!"

5

Monday morning on his way to work, and he was still trying to make sense of his meeting with Gwynne. He was in a buoyant mood as he drove to the site of the last new partnership job for which their quote had been accepted. His mind flicked randomly between the sequence of tasks: drainage, ordering materials and so on – and the whirlwind arrival of Merren with Gwynne's mother, Audrey, in tow.

Audrey, somewhere in her late fifties, cut a fine figure, but definitely not a matronly one, dressed as she was in designer jeans and a fashionably loose t-shirt. She had uniformly grey shoulder length hair and wore a single-strand coloured necklace, possibly lapis lazuli, tied in a loose knot. Simple, but classy and elegant.

A glance at her hands and fingers, the latter glittering with several rings, told Marek from whom Gwynne inherited her delicately sculptured hands. Although polite, in a formal sort of way, she had given him the impression she was assessing him from head to toe and filing the data in her system for future reference.

Merren had proved to be an absolute delight. A free-spirited three-year-old who seemed to not have a care in the world. She sprang into her mother's arms, gave her a resounding kiss on her cheek then scrambled down.

Skipping over to the overnight bag Audrey had carried in, she returned with two soft toys which she immediately held up to Marek, and shook them at him. He'd felt obliged to shake a paw of each. All he could remember saying was, "Who do we have here?"

"This is Squinty, and this is Binko," she'd confidently said, thrusting each forward in turn.

"Very pleased to meet all three of you," he responded in a more formal tone than he'd intended but which he'd immediately tried to soften with a smile. Momentarily satisfied, Merren had then skipped back to her mother's side.

Gwynne had reclaimed the situation by picking her up, turning towards him and saying, "Don't let me hold you up. Thanks for dropping in. I'll be in touch to discuss further details". He clearly understood the subtext of her statement: *Don't say anything while my mother is here!*

In a not-so-subtle effort to change the subject she'd asked her mother, "What's Daddy doing today?"

Audrey's response was vaguely dismissive. On reflection, he'd thought she was one of those people who couldn't understand anyone who couldn't keep busy on their own initiative. Her off-hand, almost trivial response had been, "Oh, he's off golfing with some of his old business chums somewhere or other."

Gwynne turned back to Marek, shepherding him to the door. "Well, thanks again. I'll get back to you soon."

At the time, he had felt he was being dismissed until further notice. "Pleased to meet you, Mrs Alwen."

As Gwynne opened the door, Merren suddenly appeared between them with her infectious smile and doing an improvised jig. He couldn't help responding in a playful manner.

After hesitating momentarily, he said, "And pleased to meet you, and Squinty and Binko as well."

In a flashback recollection he'd then recalled the ritual greeting he'd shared with his cousin Helena when they were young kids. He kissed the tip of his forefinger, held it aloft, and gradually brought it closer to Merren's hand. Fixing his eyes on hers, he'd nodded, pointed with his other hand to her forefinger, nodded again and said, "Your turn."

Surprisingly, and to his own delight, she had responded in like manner and kissed her own forefinger and held it up. He gradually lowered his hand until their fingers came into contact, whereupon he had made a "Bzzzzzz!" sound.

Merren had giggled uncontrollably and skipped away. Only slightly embarrassed, he had briefly noted how the two women had looked quizzically at each other.

"Goodbye Mrs Alwen."

In a quieter voice, as he moved towards the door, he'd said, "G'bye Gwynne. Let me know how you get on."

The door had closed sharply behind him.

He hesitated on the doorstep long enough to hear Audrey's sardonic question of Gwynne: "That was coffee with a friend, was it?"

Late the following afternoon, she telephoned Marek to thank him for his time and advice. "I'm sorry I had to cut you off when Mum arrived. As I said, I don't really want to get into details with her until I've thought it through. I've already hinted at the idea to Dad, and we decided it would be better if we got our ideas sorted before letting her in on what's happening."

Interrupting the apology he said, "That's fine, I had all but finished and we can discuss the matter further whenever we can agree on a time. As I said, weekends are best, preferably Saturdays."

There had then been one of those awkward silences where neither could think of anything to say. Then she began what was clearly a prepared statement. "Marek, I have to say this:

I'm nearing the end of my qualification period as a certified chartered accountant. She then corrected herself, I mean *certificated* accountant. It's a bit like being on probation. As you now know, I want to explore opportunities to branch out on my own if Select Accounting can't allow me the flexibility I need with Merren when I'm certified, *certificated!* You know what I mean. The best I can think is to work at least part of the week here at home where I can have greater control over my working hours."

Marek was impressed. He judged her comments as being honest and up-front. He was slightly disappointed that she assiduously avoided any comments of a personal nature. Her voice hesitated as if she'd been about to continue, but as he waited the moment passed. Apparently, realising her best option was to keep it businesslike by turning the conversation back to their next planning meeting, she was closing that particular door. Again, there was an awkward moment.

Finally, he broken the silence, "I think I appreciate your position, at least where the extensions are concerned. I think … never mind, see you Saturday."

After a brief silence Gwynne asked, "You said, 'I think'. What were you going to say?"

"It'll keep. Forget it."

6

The following Saturday, the arranged meeting began with a discussion of what, where and how the extension could be managed.

They sat at the same table in Gwynne's sunroom and Marek showed her a sketch of what he proposed. She hadn't asked him for it but was clearly pleased he had shown his interest in the project.

Forefinger tapping the sketch, he began. "There is an obvious location down the side opposite the driveway, as you rightly suggested, where plumbing can be more easily installed. At present, the laundry is the back room on that side. Plumbing could be extended for an ensuite with the office further along."

Marek then laid out another sketch on the table. "Have a look at this."

He drew her attention to an additional feature. "What do you think of the idea of having a timber deck across part of the back of the house? Tinted polycarbonate or other roofing can be installed which will reduce the shading effect here in this sunroom. It will add an entertainment area, and a play space for Merren, admittedly at additional cost, but I think it's worth considering."

Gwynne looked at the sketch, picked it up and walked to the window to relate the sketch to the proposed site. Marek watched her, trying to read in her body language what she made of his ideas.

After deliberating for a few minutes, she turned and said, "I accept that the deck would have the advantages you've mentioned but the added cost will be a serious consideration. I can see the deck could also serve as a waiting area for clients. I like it. I'll have to talk to Dad when I've got some clue of the additional cost. Can I get a quote with and without the deck?"

"No problem. We're often asked to separate out some of the costs. In this case, I think it'll add capital value to the house. Something not to be dismissed."

The conversation then turned to having a more precise sketch drawn up on which the builder could conduct his own inspection and prepare plans and a quote.

When Marek offered to draw it, she looked apprehensive. She sat back in her chair with hand raised to her chin.

Given her conditional support for the deck and feeling upbeat about the project, Marek pressed his luck by asking: "How's Merren? Where is she now?"

She fixed him with an uncertain look. "She's with my parents for lunch and will be home later."

Without further comment she refocused on the sketch and asked, "Have you a particular builder in mind?"

He cleared his throat and explained, "Yes, a few actually. A couple of them will probably think it odd that I'm passing on a job which is a normal part of my work."

Without waiting for any comment, he quickly added, "If the Council approves it the way it is now, the job isn't a major undertaking. If you like, I could provide ongoing advice, but it isn't a good idea for me to interfere directly with the builder. Nobody likes having too many bosses. Your choice."

She turned to face him and said, "Thanks Marek, you've been very helpful. Some colleagues may think it unscrupulous of me but, '*in for a penny* ...' as they say. A more detailed sketch from you would be much appreciated."

Marek arranged for two of his builder-mates to give quotes based on their own inspections and the sketches he had provided. Ultimately it was to be her decision but after both quotes were received, she again sought his opinion. It was the third time she'd asked him to her home.

Demonstrating her practical nature, she dragged a chair next to him and they sat shoulder to shoulder at the table with the quotes spread in front of them. Occasionally she had to reach across him to point out specific features. Marek found himself consciously breathing in her perfume's subtle scent. Whatever it was, it made concentration difficult. He forced himself to focus. Although there were some technical differences regarding roofing and plumbing, the basics were similar. Even the costings were close enough to not be a determining factor.

"This one," noted Gwynne, "has an availability date to begin work. The sooner the better suits me. Do I just ring him and tell him he's got the job?"

"Well, yes, you could," he supposed, implying there was an alternative. "Whoever you choose will want you to sign a contract. Once that's done, there will be a delay while the plans go to Council. Nothing will happen until building permission is granted. Be prepared for the inevitable disruption to the household. The backyard is going to be a worksite and will get messy as work progresses."

"You said I *could* ring the builder I choose. That suggests there was another possibility."

"Yes, there is. You could tell him to his face."

"What do you mean?"

"You do realise I'm a builder, don't you?"

"What? You're saying you could do it?"

"It's what I do woman! I've worked on bigger jobs than this, so yes, that's what I'm saying. But it's your choice."

"That could set off a few alarm bells at Select. I'll have to think about it and discuss it with Dad."

"Fair enough. In the meantime, would you like me to confidentially ask Darren to run the proposal by Maxine to check out how Select might view the arrangement?"

"Would you? I don't want to put my job at risk. I'm beginning to feel excited that it might actually happen. I'm very grateful for all you've done."

"Let's see. Don't get too carried away. You haven't got my quote yet."

Gideon Owen Davis
Sydney, New South Wales
1840

II

Despite his uncertainty of meeting the very man he had crossed half the world to see, Owen stood comfortably on the gently rocking ship.

It had taken courage and determination to have made it this far, but he needed to choose his words carefully if Threlkeld was to accept his freely-given assistance at his mission.

Mr Jarrow and Threlkeld withdrew to a relatively private area of the deck, away from crew members. The two men briefly discussed sailing conditions and he heard his own name being mentioned.

Owen could catch only some of their conversation. It seemed the Master was supportive of having Owen on board but curious to see how he would respond to the older man's taciturn nature.

The Reverend Threlkeld, Owen observed, was a white-haired man clearly not in his prime. His face had a worn, dogged resolute expression. His speech and gestures exhibited an almost belligerent determination to fulfil a divine sense of duty and commitment to his enterprises and especially his ministrations to the Aborigines.

"What exactly do you want of me?" was his stern query after the master's introductions.

"I have come here at the suggestion of my minister back home, to help with your mission, to bring the word of God to the Aborigines," he faltered, almost apologetically.

Threlkeld turned away from him, gripped the railing and seemed to stare vaguely around the harbour. His look of dissatisfaction was manifest. "You've made a hard decision Owen Davis, and I fear you've underestimated the task. The poor black people have suffered irretrievable loss at the hands of unscrupulous white people. I fear you have embarked on a lost cause."

It was plain Threlkeld deemed the Aborigines incapable of being converted or making their way in a less than perfect world where white people appropriated their land, often by violence, in an atmosphere of mutual misunderstanding; a world in which Owen was later to learn Threlkeld's own ambitions had been thwarted at almost every turn.

He could see the old man was initially undecided whether to accept his offer of assistance at his Ebenezer mission. "Who is this minister who sent you here?"

Owen told him about his home in Pengam, a coal-mining village in the Welsh Valleys and Mr Lewis, the village minister.

Threlkeld, still casting his gaze around the harbour, not looking at him directly, made Owen uneasy. In a tone of forced resignation, he said, "I hope you don't come to regret it, but your help with God's work may be rather more different than you expected."

It was not a fulsome acceptance by Threlkeld, but after more than six months at sea thinking of doing little else other than missionary work, Owen remained steadfast in his determination to give the mission his full support.

The ship weighed anchor early on a brilliant summer's morning and headed towards what Mr Jarrow referred to as 'The Heads' then out to sea to follow the coastline north.

Mr Jarrow had mentioned that they would be sailing against the prevailing south-bound current. He had explained the vessel had a shallow draft to enable it to navigate the bar in the channel at Reid's Mistake, the entrance to Lake Macquarie. It also meant that the partially laden ship was more affected by swell and the prevailing winds.

The voyage lasted until late afternoon owing to the relentless north-easterly wind which buffeted the ship as it thudded into the heavy seas. Salty spume constantly swept along the deck, drenching anyone not able to take cover. The crew was hard pressed responding to Mr Jarrow's bellowed commands.

After the confinement of his berth on the long trip, Owen relished the opportunity to complete what Mr Jarrow asked of him. In doing so, he noted Threlkeld seemed to keep a keen eye on him and he sensed his approval of how well he applied himself to the allotted tasks.

He was to learn later from Mr Jarrow that Threlkeld always tried to detect the divine hand of Providence in his work and that he believed Owen had been sent to him, perhaps too late, to assist them both in whatever God had in store.

Midway on their journey, with the ship making slow but steady progress despite the conditions, Threlkeld asked Owen how he came to be so fervent in his desire to become a missionary.

Owen told him about his family, and his life in Pengam and more of his talks with Mr Lewis.

During one such conversation, Mr Jarrow interrupted their conversation asking, "A word with you Mr Threlkeld if you please?"

"Of course, Mr Jarrow. We seem to be making fair time in the conditions if I may say so."

"Yes, you are correct. However, as the ship approaches Moon Island marking the entrance to the lake at Reid's Mistake, I propose we exercise some caution. The worst conditions for crossing the bar are when the wind is a nor'-easter as it is now. The swell isn't too heavy and I recommend we stand-off Moon Island to assess the conditions, before proceeding."

"Do you think that's necessary Mr Jarrow? The ship's not heavily laden. I'd like to be home before nightfall."

"Even so, our keel will be crossing the bar less than a fathom below the surface of the water. There's a risk to us if a trough comes through at the wrong time. We'll have sufficient time before the tide reaches its peak. We may also learn something which might be of benefit when we're returning fully laden."

Threlkeld conceded the point, "Very good Mr Jarrow, do as you see fit." As he moved around the ship the

Master warned the men to keep alert and be ready for any difficulties.

When they reached the entrance known as Reid's Mistake, the tide was running into the Lake and, as the wind gusts were abating, Mr Jarrow decided that it was not necessary to launch a boat to pilot the ship over the bar, through the channel and into the lake.

In the eventuality, Mr Jarrow's experience, and perhaps even Threlkeld's prayers, the entry was without mishap and the ship was able to make its way in the easing conditions. This allowed Owen to take note of the comparative solitude and peace of the lake. To the west he could see a horizon of substantial hills. In almost every other direction the coastline was thick bushland seemingly untouched by any human hand. Only the sound of the wash as the ship sliced through the sparklingly clear water, the sound of a plop as a fish jumped to elude the approaching ship, and the piercing calls of passing gulls could be heard.

The ship continued on a north-westerly course to what seemed a finger-point of land jutting out to meet them. It was the most northerly of three heavily wooded points of land, where the ship eased its way to a none too sturdy jetty. As Threlkeld and Owen were disembarking, Owen thanked Mr Jarrow, who shook his hand and offered him working passage if ever he should choose to return to Sydney.

Threlkeld directed Owen's attention to a horse in a nearby enclosure and asked him if he could hitch it to the cart near the gate while he spoke to Mr Jarrow. Harnessing was a task with which Owen was quite familiar, having done it countless times for Minister Lewis back home.

After completing it, he had an opportunity to assess the laborious process by which coal was transferred from the mineshaft to the ship. In his home village, because the Rhymney River was not navigable, coal was being transported to Cardiff ports by rail, not horse-drawn wagons. The coal was then transferred into modern ships, many of which were fitted with both sail and steam power.

When Threlkeld returned, they climbed onto the cart and set off for Ebenezer, the site of Threlkeld's mission and house. "We'll be home in less than an hour barring mishaps," He grumbled. It became apparent to Owen that Threlkeld was not a conversationalist. His own attention was fixed on the unfamiliar surroundings while clinging to his seat as the wagon jolted its way over the rough bush track.

Newcastle
NSW 2005

"Hi Darren. Thanks for bringing that job of Gwynne's to my attention but there's a hitch which you might be able to help me sort out."

"Oh, yeah? What's that then?"

"It's Gwynne who wants the job done. She's a bit windy about me doing it because she thinks there might be a conflict of interest or some such thing, with me being a client of Select. Do you think you could have a discrete word with Maxine about it? I agree, the job's a good one for me, but Gwynne needs reassurance Select won't kick up a fuss."

"Sure, I'll have a word with Maxine but I'm pretty sure there won't be a problem. Things like this happen all the time. Word of mouth, who you know, and all that. Hang on, Maxine's here, ask her yourself."

Before Marek could think what to say, Maxine came on the line.

"Hi Marek, what's up?"

Marek went through the story again, ending with, "What do you think? Is it ethical? Will she get into any strife if I do the job for her?"

"I doubt it. This happens occasionally. What she should do is go to her supervisor and lay it all out for him. She can say that it's her parents who want the improvements on their investment property."

"Okay, I'll tell her. What you said is nearly the truth."

"I wouldn't be surprised if her boss gives her credit for asking before committing to the work. It shows respect for the firm. I won't say anything at work until I'm officially informed."

"Thanks Maxine. I'll let her know and she can take it from there. Cheers."

"Tell her to keep calm about it. G'bye Marek. Good luck."

Marek telephoned Gwynne and explained Maxine's advice.

After thinking for a week about how to word it, Gwynne approached her supervisor, Tom Wright. His reaction was unexpectedly calm.

"Thanks for bringing this to me before you went ahead Gwynne. This sort of thing does happen and there's nothing wrong with it. The only requirement is that all the paperwork *must* be legit. No kickbacks, nothing underhand. A straightforward commercial deal. Okay?"

"Certainly. I'll make sure all the paperwork is in order. Thank you."

"Gwynne, you did the right thing coming to me. I'll pass it up the line. Well done. Good luck with it."

Six weeks later, Council's approval was granted, and on-site preparations began in the form of setting out the perimeter markers for the job.

The string lines were a source of amusement to Merren. "Mummy, they look like the 'lastics game the big girls play." Gwynne had to use her sternest 'mother's voice' to warn her not to get tangled in them.

Building materials were delivered regularly and the backyard began to turn into a no-go area for Merren and to a lesser extent, for Gwynne. Accessing the clothesline turned into an obstacle course.

After putting up with it for a few days, on Friday Gwynne approached Marek before he'd knocked off for the day.

She launched into the matter without preamble: "Is it possible to move the clothesline away from the worksite to a sunnier location in the yard when the job is finished?"

Before answering her question, he walked over to the clothesline to inspect it. "It's set in concrete, and it will have to be dug out. I'll do it tomorrow if that suits you, then I can start the foundation work on Monday."

Gwynne noticed how serious he was when considering work matters on the job. "That's very generous of you to offer. I've already taken advantage of your kindness several times. It's becoming a habit. I feel guilty that I am exploiting your goodwill for the second, or third … or whatever number of times it is. I'll make it up to you by providing lunch, small compensation as that might be. Thanks. Again."

Her voice trailed off and after a longer pause she asked, "How long do you think it will take? I've just remembered, there's something I am supposed to attend tomorrow evening. It's a birthday barbecue at Lana's place. She's one of my oldest and best friends. We have history. It's a birthday number ending in zero; one not to be missed. I've promised her."

On hearing her, Marek felt relegated to the tradesman's role. *Get used to it, he thought.* "If we get started early enough, it should all be over by mid-afternoon. Does that suit you?"

"Thanks Marek. Yes, that'll be fine. I don't know what I'd do without your help. See you then."

Plans went awry from the start when Saturday morning dawned with a light fall of rain. Gwynne telephoned Marek to ask if he was going to postpone the job.

"It's sprinkling here. What do you think? Do you want to go ahead? I have to take Merren over to Mum and Dad's, but we can call it off if it's a problem."

Marek replied, "I've got most of what I need in the truck ready to start. I can at least get the hole dug where the clothesline is going. We'll just keep an eye on the weather and decide as we go."

On arrival, after a quick chat when they decided on the new location, he made a start. One advantage of the rain was that it had softened the surface ground and he was able to make good initial progress. However, the topsoil was shallow, and he hit a layer of clay and progress slowed. He continued digging until he thought the hole deep enough.

Knowing the rain would make Gwynne's access to the existing clothesline even more difficult over the next few days, he pressed on with the job. Next, he started to dig around the concrete base of the clothesline. As he dug, the water seeped into the hole turning the job into a gluggy mess.

Fortunately, the clothesline was a modern folding type and eventually he was able to extract it from its base and drag it over to the new hole. He retrieved its base and packed it into a vertical position with bits of rubble and clay to hold it vertical.

With Gwynne hovering on regular visits to see how he was progressing, plus the rain, his patience began to fray.

"For God's sake, go back inside. You're like a kookaburra waiting for me to turn up a worm." Then, seeing the affronted look on her face, added, "No need for both of us to get wet."

Lunch was delayed. As a compromise, with signs of a break in the weather, Gwynne suggested a coffee break and a tactical chat saying, "This has turned into a much more difficult job than I ever imagined. I feel terrible that I have taken advantage of your generosity in such horrible weather."

Although soaked to the skin, Marek countered saying, "Lunch can wait. I'll have the coffee as I go. You get back inside, or you'll catch a cold and pass it on to Merren."

Gwynne's stance, with hands on hips, showed how agitated she was. He thought it might be because she was used to doing things for herself or because she didn't like being told what to do. Or even guilt, not being able to give more practical assistance.

In frustration she said, "You're being stubborn. You're covered in dirt and it's starting to drizzle again. I'll give the barbecue a miss. I couldn't possibly go in the circumstances."

"Don't do anything yet. Once I've concreted the base, I can cover it with a sheet of brattice I've got in the truck. No problem."

"Alright, have it your own way!" With that she turned her back on him and strode inside.

It took another half an hour to concrete the base and cover it. He stood at the back door and called, "Finished. For today anyway."

When she came out to inspect the job, he was slightly unnerved by the stubborn gaze she directed at him. Then it relaxed and he noted a pink flush on her cheeks.

To avoid a possible toe-to-toe standoff, she relaxed the set of her jaw and seemed to sense a need to concede, if only to get through the day without further argument.

She broke eye contact and after she did so, he looked down at her and grinned. His grin quickly developed into an unrestrained chortle.

"What's so funny? I've never heard you laugh like that before, or any other way, come to think of it."

He pointed to her. "Wet and half covered in muck! You look like a navvy."

She looked down at herself and joined in the laughter and replied, "Well, thanks for the compliment. You don't exactly look like royalty yourself. More like Lord Muck! Sorry, that's a bit unkind since you look that way because you've been doing me a big favour."

Major repairs to their appearances were required, and quickly, if she was to attend the barbecue. Trying to reclaim control she said, "Listen to me! You finish off here and put your tools away." She added in a tone that was not to be contradicted, "You can't leave here in such filthy condition. When you're finished, you must have a shower."

It was obvious she would not accept any excuses. Besides, when he looked down at the state he was in, a shower was exactly what he needed. Objection was futile. Besides, to be honest, he wasn't the one in a hurry. Sadly, his night would be spent at home. Marek watched as she disappeared into the house, and then started cleaning his tools. Unlike most of his mates, keepong his tools and his truck as clean as possible was a priority.

When he'd finished, he realised he couldn't go into the house in his wet and dirty state, so he sat on the back step to remove and clean his boots. The drizzle had stopped, and a mocking ray of sunshine broke through. Inexplicably, he felt not just pleased with the job but happy with himself. Why, was a question he chose to ignore.

From the back door Gwynne called, "Right, into the shower you go."

"I've taken off my boots but even my clothes are too dirty to go inside like this. I'll leave a trail wherever I go."

"Don't worry. Here's an old towel. Just shuffle and slide your way along. Drop your clothes outside the bathroom door. I'll wash them and put them through the dryer. No discussion! I'll find something for you to wear while they're drying."

He shuffled to the bathroom as carefully as he could and once inside, stripped off. He took a moment to check his briefs and was glad he'd worn a pair fit to be seen, then dropped everything outside the door on the towel.

Ten minutes later he called, "Finished! What am I supposed to do now?"

"I'm sorry," she said, opening the door very slightly and calling apologetically, "All I can find that I think might fit is hanging on the door handle. You can try it, or you can tie a towel around your waist, and I'll get something for you to wrap around your shoulders."

Marek reluctantly, and more than somewhat nervously, given her unconvincing tone, reached around the door to grope for whatever Gwynne had left for him.

When he held it up, he didn't know whether to laugh, or throw it back out the door in disgust. He was staring at a brown onesie with the head of a bear for the hood.

Dismissing it outright, he hung it on a hook behind the door and tied a towel around his waist. He was out of his comfort zone in his present state, with Gwynne nearby, *with Gwynne near…*

One thought followed another and when he looked at himself in the mirror he realised that even with a blanket around his shoulders, he had a problem.

The onesie might make him look ridiculous but at least it would be modest. In his present state, the towel around his waist indicated anything but modesty.

He stood, waiting, trying to think of something … anything: brussels sprouts … trigonometry … Nelson's Column … *no, not that!*

Thinking didn't help. Again, he heard Gwynne's voice outside the door, "What are you doing? What's taking so long? Lunch is waiting."

He made some excuse hoping his 'condition' would ease but her voice and his unrestricted thoughts of her so close, seemed to make it worse … as things stood.

Against his better judgement, he struggled into the undersized onesie and zipped it up as far as he could. It camouflaged his *problem* and he decided that there was nothing else to do.

With his embarrassment evident, both on his face as well as by his stooped waddling posture, he made his appearance.

One step out the door and it was too late. He was standing, or rather stooping, beggar-like, in front of her. An added nuisance was that his height meant that the crotch of the onesie was below his hips shackling his progress and preventing him from walking at anything more than a shuffle.

Gwynne took one look and, after a few seconds, burst into fits of laughter. There was nothing he could do or say but wait for her to settle.

He realised what a sight he must look and wryly joined in. "Finished? That's a fine way to thank someone who has been slaving away for you all day."

Gwynne made the most of his situation by saying, "You must be a very brave bear to appear in public that way."

More sheepish than bearish, he walked to the table, relieved to be able to sit down.

He didn't know whether he felt like giving her a bear hug, choking her, or … *what*? Instead, he picked up a sandwich and bit into it in a way that left no doubt about his state of discomfort.

When he'd finished, he asked, "How long will it take for my clothes to dry?"

Her answer didn't settle his unease one bit. It was going to be a very long 'hour or so'.

On hearing her reply, he decided that his best course of action was to go home, still wearing the onesie, and change into something … manly!

"Look, I'll leave you to it and pick up my clothes tomorrow. Once I'm out of the way you can go off to the barbecue."

In a tone of exasperation, she said, "You have not once been in the way today. You have been extremely generous, and I am enormously grateful."

This time, his decision prevailed. Eager to remove himself from a recurrence of his discomfort and be on his way, he interrupted her as she repeated her appreciation for what he had done saying, "The pole can be reinserted in the base tomorrow. I'll call you in the morning and arrange a time. It's been a very … interesting … day. G'bye."

She opened the front door and furtively looked out to check if any of any neighbours were in sight. With no one about, she gave him the 'all clear'. He shuffled out the door, stopping to slip on his boots.

As he was shuffling to the gate, Gwynne called to him. When he turned, she shouted, "Smile!" and took his photo on her phone, then quickly ducked back inside and slammed the door. He couldn't help but shake his head. Inwardly he was amused at the spectacle he must be making.

He was less amused however when, just as he reached his truck, a vehicle drove past and the driver honked the horn several times. He was about to give a middle-finger salute but decided against it. At least he couldn't be recognised.

He drove off in such a state of confusion about the day and, without thinking what an exhibition he would make, decided to stop and get a few groceries. As he climbed awkwardly out of his truck he thought, *What the hell!* and in an overwhelming attack of *joie de vivre*, waddled into the supermarket anyway.

In a more relaxed state, and taking no notice of the stares of the other shoppers, he got what he needed, went through the checkout po-faced, ignoring the smile on the face of the checkout-chick.

He spent much of the night churning over the events of the day. *Did I really spend my Saturday doing a job for someone I've met only recently?* He told himself it was because of the schedule he'd set for the job.

Really?

He tried to list reasons why he felt the way he did. Gwynne had style, charm, a sense of duty and commitment and … *sex appeal*. He was even intoxicated by her laughter when he wore the onesie. He worried that the reasons were superficial, lame even. So, what if she had beautiful hands? *Did he have a fetish?*

Whatever the reasons, his feelings had transformed into something deeper. The logic escaped him.

The disturbed sleep that night provided little benefit. When he awoke in the morning, he felt woolly-headed, unable to decide what to do. Ultimately, he thought the best thing to do was what he mostly did with private problems – get on with work. First task: collect the gear.

Second task: *Keep his emotional responses on a tight rein.*

8

When Gwynne answered her phone just after ten o'clock, without preamble Marek asked, "Is it okay for me to call in to check the job, pick up my clothes and return the onesie?"

Hesitating momentarily, not wanting to inconvenience him after his untiring efforts the previous day, she chose her words carefully. "Sure, that's fine, but Mum will return Merren sometime this morning."

"No problem as far as I'm concerned. See you soon. G'bye."

He was about to hang up when she murmured, "You almost received a phone call last night."

"Why? What do you mean? You haven't changed your mind, have you?"

"No, I haven't. When I told Lana and my friends about moving the clothesline, they were amazed how very generous you had been. They thought I was inconsiderate, stingy even, for sending you home and not inviting you to the barbecue."

Marek's grip on the phone hardened and he inhaled deeply as he waited for her to continue.

After a brief pause, Gwynne asked, "Would you have come if I had?"

In an audible gasp he exhaled. "What does it matter? It's all history now. But I will say this: I helped you because I wanted to. I want to get started on the job tomorrow." Once he had begun, the words came tumbling out. "I'm looking forward to this job because it's my first solo contract. I must learn to cope with all sorts of clients. Thinking it over late last night, I reckon we coped well enough."

"You sound like you agree with my friends. Makes me feel like I'm being hard to get on with. Selfish even."

"Sorry, I didn't sleep well. Hope what I implied doesn't spoil our business arrangements, such as they are. See you in about twenty minutes. I won't stay longer than necessary. G'bye."

Stunned, Gwynne stood looking at the phone in her hand as if it was contaminated. She threw it onto the lounge and walked to the sunroom window and looked at the work Marek had done, inwardly acknowledging his generosity in its several phases. She became vaguely aware of an odd feeling in her chest.

Just as she began to dwell on it, the front door opened, and her mother walked in with Merren in hand.

The look on Merren's face was that of a child not at her brightest and happiest.

Before she could say anything, Audrey explained, "She's had a restless night and seemed a little off-colour earlier this morning. She's brightened up a little on the way home."

Gwynne picked up Merren and placed her hand on her forehead. "She does feel a little warm. Hopefully it's a minor thing which'll pass."

She continued to brush her hand soothingly over Merren's forehead and cheeks. In reaction, Merren laid her head on Gwynne's shoulder.

While they stood considering what special attention Merren might need, there was a knock on the door. Gwynne, still carrying Merren, crossed the room and opened the door.

"GRAAAAGH!!!!"

She jumped back at the shock of it, clutching Merren.

Standing in the doorway was a man-sized bear making menacing growling noises with arms raised. To add to the bizarre sight, the bear had work boots on its forepaws.

Merren squealed, climbed down, and ran to hide behind her grandmother. For the second time in half an hour Gwynne was stunned, this time by what she was seeing rather than what she had heard on the phone. For the moment, words failed her.

As Marek struggled out of the onesie, she regained some composure. Foremost was the awareness that Marek's sense of humour had overcome the events of the previous afternoon as well as this morning's telephone comments. His clownish way of presenting himself was a dimension she hadn't seen before, nor even thought existed.

She dared not look at her mother but regained some of her composure, took him by the arm and gave it a shake saying, in a more than half-serious reprimanding tone, "What do you think you're doing, scaring my sick daughter half out of her wits?"

It wasn't until Marek had fully extricated himself from the onesie that he looked around and saw Audrey standing with a bemused expression on her face. He didn't know what to say, but on seeing Merren emerge from her hiding place, he quickly transferred his attention to her.

Walking over to her, crouching down and taking both her hands in his, he said, "Aren't you feeling well? I'm sorry. I was trying to be funny. Did I scare you?"

Unconvincingly, Merren shook her head and murmured, "Only a little bit."

"A little bit funny? Or a little bit scary? How are Squinty and Binky? Did I scare them too?"

In an affronted tone Merren corrected him, "Not Binky, *Binko*!"

"My apologies to *Binko*."

Merren, showing almost no sign of being unwell, ran to her overnight bag and dragged the toys out and held them up to him.

He kissed his forefinger and slowly brought it down on the paws being presented, as well as Merren's upraised forefinger, complete with a 'Bzzzzzz!' when contact was made.

Merren immediately broke into her giggle which brought a smile to both women's faces.

Gwynne looked at her mother and both shrugged and slowly shook their heads in bewilderment.

Marek made a diplomatic decision to excuse himself saying, "I'll just duck out the back and do a final clean-up of yesterday's job."

He padded through to the back door, put on his boots, and went out.

Merren, disengaging herself from her companions, followed as far as the back window and watched him.

Audrey noted the look on Gwynne's face, how much calmer and more relaxed it was. Audrey's frown and pursed lips clearly told another story.

Looking at Gwynne she said, "He's a bit strange, isn't he? What was that all about?"

As she watched Marek tidying up the yard she said vaguely, "Oh, nothing really. Just a bit of an add-on to a joke after he'd finished yesterday. What do you think of the job we did?"

"Good idea. It'll work well when everything's finished," was Audrey's brusque reply.

With tension and frown still lingering, she said, "I knew you and your father had cooked something up between you. You took your time letting me in on the secret."

With greater conviction than she felt, Gwynne said, "Well, now that you know, when it comes to decorating, you'll be able to give us the benefit of your advice."

She knew Audrey's advice would be forthcoming whether asked for or not.

The family pussy-footed around Audrey when she got wound up over an issue. On occasions like this, she reverted to her former administrative role in the Commonwealth Department of Social Security.

Having begun in the late 1970s she had risen through its ranks, earning an excellent reputation, and was informally known as 'AA'. The nick name was less to do with her initials or the national credit rating, than a barbed jibe relating to her adherence to regulations only moderated by a strict sense of social justice and concern for those in need.

As soon as he had finished loading his gear into his truck, Marek returned to the front door.

As Gwynne opened it he said, "That's everything except for my clothes."

Audrey's jaw dropped. It wasn't often she was lost for words. Shock and incredulity, suggesting mistrust of Gwynne's judgement, was clearly evident.

Without a word of explanation, Gwynne left the room and returned with a bag containing Marek's washed and folded work clothes. "There you go," she said matter-of-factly and then added, "And thanks again for what you did in appalling conditions yesterday."

"No worries." He then reminded her, "I've set everything up but don't use the clothesline for forty-eight hours while the concrete sets."

"I'll try to think of something to make it up to you soon. I'll be in touch." She was beginning to feel flustered imagining her mother's ears burning and her eyes almost spinning even as they drilled into her. She knew if her mother had antennae, they'd be twitching.

What he had said on the phone earlier still preyed on her mind, as did his appearance on arrival, but she didn't know where to begin to explain.

On impulse, without looking at, or referring to her mother, she announced, "Sunday week our family is having a lunch to celebrate my aunt Colette's birthday. She's Mum's younger sister. Would you be able to come? Would you like to? It'll be a fairly simple lunch for about six or seven of us. You can explain to everyone about the extensions. Get it over in one fell swoop."

He turned back to face her, not quite comprehending what Gwynne meant. It was obvious she hadn't planned, or even thought it through. She was prattling in a way he had never heard before. Gwynne continued, "She, Colette I mean, regularly looked after me as a child and we're still very close. This might make up for me not inviting you to Lana's barbecue. You've done us all a big favour ..." she concluded, her voice fading in her uncertainty.

The confusion running through his mind registered on his face. Looking at Audrey, he could see she had a similar reaction.

He was beginning to say he was unavailable on that day when Audrey, recovering more quickly, and realising Gwynne's invitation couldn't be withdrawn, endorsed it with convincing enthusiasm. "By all means, you will be most welcome. Besides, your company will add a fresh take on the usual topics of conversation. It'll give Huw someone else to talk to about his banking career and your thoughts about the scheme you've all been plotting."

Still recovering from the surprise, Marek stammered with as much conviction as he could muster, "I'm not sure I'll have much to contribute but thank you. If you think I won't be intruding."

In obvious haste to end her embarrassment, Gwynne began to close the door. "I'll be in touch about the arrangements."

When Marek focused his gaze upon her, he saw her blush, which coincidentally, was exactly what he felt he was doing.

Only Merren, tugging to release Audrey's hold, broke the determined set of Audrey's jaw in reaction to what she had observed.

Just as Audrey was about to close the door, Merren squeezed in front of Gwynne, kissed her forefinger, and raised it. Marek responded and as their fingers touched, both buzzed and gave a shiver. Merren ran back to her grandmother, her infectious tinkling laugh in stark contrast to the bewildered look on the face of her mother and her grandmother's steely-eyed stare.

Gwynne slowly closed the door, still not daring to make eye-contact with her mother. From experience in conversations over the years, she knew this was exactly the sort of event which rekindled the role Audrey had had in the DSS, especially when she became overly protective because she believed an individual was teetering on the edge of a momentous, but dubious life-changing decision.

9

Gwynne's phone call about the lunch party was expected but with reservations, probably on both sides, Marek thought.

"Hi Marek, I'm ringing about the birthday lunch on Sunday. I want you to know your presence will be most welcome."

"Thanks Gwynne. I've been hoping you'd ring. I'm a bit concerned I'll be out of place being an outsider in a family gathering. Are you sure about this? I must say though, I am curious about your family. After all, your mother produced you and you produced Merren and well, you're all a bit ..."

"Better stop there, I think. Look, think of it however you like. Perhaps as a business lunch with clients?"

"I think we inhabit different business worlds, but yes, all right, I'll be there. I probably need to learn more about your world than you need to learn about mine."

"I'm not twisting your arm to attend. It's your choice." Her tone suggested uncertainty as she immediately changed the subject saying, "By the way, I used the clothesline and was pleased not to have to complete the obstacle course someone set up getting to it. It seems fine. And more building materials were delivered late yesterday: two stacks of bricks and a huge bundle of timber."

For something to say, Marek said, "The timber is for the bearers and joists; the bricks are for the piers. I've asked to make sure the sand is not dumped in the driveway. If you're home, keep an eye on it, will you? I've suggested the spot near where the clothesline had been. When the job is finished it will camouflage and level out that bit of ground."

"Great, yes I will. Thanks for that. Oh, one last thing, do you want me to pick you up from your place on Sunday or do you want to drive here, and we'll go in my car? Parking might be a problem if you take your truck, it's a narrow street. Anyway, I need the booster seat for Merren."

"What if I drive over to your place and we go from there?"

"What a good idea! Why didn't I think of that? Does eleven o'clock suit you?"

"Fine by me. See you then. I'll wear my best overalls. G'bye."

Marek pulled up in front of Gwynne's house a few minutes after eleven o'clock. When Gwynne opened the door, she looked him up and down and commented, "Well, don't you look different? Last time I opened the door to a man there was a weirdo in a bear onesie standing there growling at me."

Marek, commanding considerable restraint replied, "Well, I might look different, but I can also confirm, I feel different. This time I'm not here for work or business. Bit out of my comfort zone. And you're the cause. Again!"

You make it sound like you're entering the lions' den. Just be ... um, yourself."

After Merren and Marek exchanged their fingertip greetings, he helped Gwynne wrangle the wriggling child into her child-safe seat without the least bit of cooperation. Twisting and giggling, she obviously thought the struggle a huge joke as she waved Squinty and Binko in their faces.

"Marek, stand back. You're not helping. She's showing off." Gwynne said, showing her impatience.

Marek shrugged, "Showing off she may be, but she's quite amusing. At least she thinks so."

Once on the move, Marek was aware of being in close proximity to Gwynne. Again, her perfume had him captivated. It was a clean, fresh fragrance which he found enticing.

He knew nothing about perfume other than his mother loved lavender. This perfume was seductive, and suggestive … or something.

He angled himself on the seat so he could study her profile as she drove. He was conscious of the fact that his relationships with the now almost forgotten Briony, and other girlfriends, were different.

This was something else: she wasn't his girlfriend, and she wasn't giving any sign of encouragement.

More mood swings here than a footy ground turnstile.

On arrival at the Alwen home, Gwynne introduced him to Colette and her husband, Keith. It took only minutes to realise the younger Colette was clearly much more flamboyant and confident in her behaviour, conversation and dress than her older sister.

Initially he thought Keith seemed wary and hesitant, making him suspect Keith was assessing his reaction to meeting the family.

As they chatted, Marek discovered Keith was slightly younger than Colette which, for some reason, didn't surprise him in the least. Colette's vivacity indicated she needed a partner mentally and physically agile.

Engaging in some nimble private observations of his own, Marek judged the adult ages ranged from Gwynne in her mid-twenties to Huw in his late sixties. Neatly stepped as they were, the range had the effect of allowing wider generational views as the free-ranging banter developed.

In a brief lull, Keith brought the conversation around to the building trade by asking, "How did you end up in the building game? Is it a family thing?"

Feeling more comfortable, Marek replied, "I'd always been interested in industrial arts activities and construction, even as a kid at school. Lego has a lot to answer for. I guess I inherited it from my father's side, but no, building is not a family thing; manufacturing things is. And work in the open air seemed vastly preferable to office or factory work."

He wanted to leave it there, but it was obvious everyone was listening and expected him to continue.

"After finishing my trade apprenticeship and getting my licence, I opted to accept the offer to carry on working with Darren Merrigan. So, a few years later, when Darren offered me an opportunity to buy into the partnership, I jumped at it. We settled on the legalities, and we've been in partnership now for six years. Darren's more on the organisational side and I'm more hands on. When Darren decided to retire, we had to sort out some accountancy stuff. That's how I met Gwynne."

Shooting a wry grin at Gwynne he added, "I guess you could say it's all Darren's fault, and Gwynne's, that I'm here today!"

At his final comment, meaningful looks were exchanged between Audrey, Huw and Colette. Only on Keith's lips were there traces of a smile.

"What about you Keith? What's your line of work?"

"It's a tortured trail really but, most recently, I've been involved in property, particularly in light industry and developing commercial land sites. The market is always changing but the firm allows me a long lead, including flexible work hours. When a deal comes off, I do alright but there can be ups and downs. We manage okay, Colette and me."

The lunch was an informal affair, buffet style. The gas barbecue had been lit and, once the meat was cooked, with almost all the adults except Marek and Colette having taken a hand in the preparation, everyone served themselves and sat around the patio table.

Marek silently contrasted the arrangements with his usual workday lunch breaks where he ate his homemade or, less often, bought sandwiches or pies, sitting on whatever was available: an upturned crate, even a stack of bricks or timber.

Merren was in her element being the only child and once she had finished, she wandered around to each of the adults, sometimes sitting on her mother's lap, occasionally her grandmother's or grandfather's or Colette's. At one stage she came over to Marek with Binko, shaking him at Marek saying in a squeaky voice, "Hello, Marek!"

Marek replied in a deep, gruff voice which made Merren laugh, and she climbed onto his lap, trying to make a three-way conversation between herself, Marek and Binko while he tried to eat. Between mouthfuls he asked, "Where's Squinty?"

She explained that he had eaten too much and was having a sleep. He nodded agreement. "That sounds fair enough. I sometimes feel the same."

Merren remained seated on his lap as the conversation drifted onto a range of topics: social, occasionally political, or commercial. She amused herself by ruffling the hair on his arms then twisting it into spikey points she called, "Pixie hats." His cries of feigned pain were a further amusement to her.

It suited Marek because he did not want to get too involved in anything political, knowing how some people, including his own immigrant parents, held very strong personal, and all too frequently, controversial views, generating heated reactions. His parents had made extreme choices in a difficult political climate and then had to live with their decisions.

During a slight lull, Keith returned to his earlier theme. "So, Marek, what jobs, before this one, have you been working on?"

"Before I started on Gwynne's extensions. I'd just finished some renovations which were the tail-end of my last job with Darren. Now I'm considering putting in an offer to buy a piece of land on which to build a spec-home."

"Oh, really? Where's the land?" Keith's interest was more than evident.

When Marek mentioned that it was in a developing area around Minmi, Huw, who had been listening attentively, expressed some misgivings. "That sounds a bit risky. That's a fair way out and away from current business and residential areas." Ever the banker, he went on to query the financial arrangements.

Unexpectedly, Gwynne intervened and explained, "Dad, land values out that way are currently very favourable to buyers. It's a target area and land value is likely to appreciate. Marek has been exploring the prospects. Things are always changing in the market. Interest rates are quite reasonable. And there are lots of people seeking land in a more rural outlook too."

Her enthusiasm in coming into the discussion prompted ominous looks with pursed lips and raised eyebrows between Colette and Audrey.

Keith's bemused smile went unnoticed.

Colette then changed tack completely and asked in a thinly disguised casual manner, "You've never married?"

There was a brief stunned silence in which all present, except Marek and Merren, thought how typical it was of Colette to crash into a conversation with such a gauche personal question, directed at someone she was meeting for the first time.

Colette brushed off Gwynne's obvious looks of alarm, saying, "What? Why are you all looking at me like that? I'm only making small talk."

Gwynne muttered, "I'd like to know what sort of question you'd ask when you aren't making *small talk*."

Marek replied cryptically, "No, although I almost thought about it a couple of times."

Huw's sage reply, "Good idea to think before you take such a step," was met with a dubious look from Audrey, which forestalled further comment from him.

When Gwynne noticed Merren was starting to tire, she began to clear the table.

She returned from the kitchen carrying a birthday cake, complete with lit candles, although not the number indicating Colette's age. All except Marek and Merren knew her age, even though it was something Colette zealously guarded.

Happy Birthday was sung, the candles were blown out, with Merren's help, and the conversation resumed.

When Huw started on one of his banking life-history stories, Audrey and Gwynne, observing Marek's interest, let it go for a while.

They could see Huw felt he had found someone who was fascinated by his experiences and that he looked very pleased with the turn of events.

Eventually, Gwynne gave her mother a nod and Audrey interrupted saying, "Time's getting on. Some people have to work tomorrow."

And with that the party began to break up.

As soon as Merren was buckled in and they were on their way, Gwynne began to apologise for her aunt's nosey interrogation. "I'm sorry if Colette's question seemed intrusive. Her forthrightness does get close to the bone occasionally."

Marek admitted, "It was a bit of a shock. I'm not used to giving out so much personal information, especially to people I don't really know."

"You were very polite listening to Dad's work stories. Thank you."

"That's okay, I was curious. It's an area about which I know very little but need to learn more. As I said, Darren used to deal with most of the financial stuff. Most of my mates in the game are tight-lipped about their financial arrangements, possibly with good cause. And I don't know many people with financial acumen." Tongue in cheek, he added, "Do you?"

The look on her face told him he had hit the mark. "Would you like to rephrase that? I'll give you three seconds."

10

Gwynne lapsed into silence as she drove, preoccupied with Marek's answer to Colette's question on marriage. She understood that he might have come close on at least one occasion, although how close wasn't clear.

Was he just being provocative? Coy? Why did she feel irritated? But so far, he had not been snared.

What a cryptic response! 'I almost thought about it.' *What does that mean?*

If it wasn't for the fact Colette had already put him on the spot, she might have pursued the subject herself, hopefully, more subtly.

When they arrived home, she asked Marek to wait while she settled Merren. She returned, intent on changing her mindset by asking for an update on the extensions.

"It's early days yet but I think it's going as we planned. If it isn't, you'll be the second person to know."

"Thanks. I suppose you'll be the first?"

"You got it in one."

"Enigmatic but reassuring." As she said the words, she slid her arm through his and gave it a friendly tug. She was drawn back to Colette's question and had to ask, "Are you sorry you came to the lunch today? You had to parry a couple of tricky questions. I was beginning to feel sorry for you."

"Yeah, well, I'm a big boy now. Colette caught me unprepared. It *was* interesting watching and listening to your family. It seemed almost everything was up for discussion.

What's the go with you and your mother clamping down on your father's stories? I thought they were kind of interesting. It's something I guess I've got to get a better grip on. After a while I felt more comfortable. Families can be like that. Come to think of it, my cousin Helena can ask some quite personal questions."

"Let's not talk about my family. How about yours? You have never spoken about your family before. I can't imagine you as a child. To me it seems as if you've been hatched fully formed as an adult. A bit like some Greek mythological creature – and almost as inscrutable at times. Although your appearance at my front door wearing my bear onesie shows me you have a sense of humour which I hadn't seen before. Merren loved it too. Sort of."

"Too? You mean as in *also*? As well as? Merren is such a happy kid. She is a credit to you. And the family, I suppose. What's she doing now?"

Looking intently out at the backyard worksite, wanting to gloss over any motive for Marek's comment, Gwynne let the first comment pass and instead said, "She's in her room. I'll run a bath for her shortly then set her up with a video. I think she'll be settled by bedtime, after a light tea. You know, I never really thought you would actually *wear* the onesie. I put it out half-jokingly. I thought that you'd choose the towel and blanket option."

"I did try that first but decided against it."

"Any special reason?"

"Yes." His demeanour showed some reluctance to explain.

"Well, are you going to tell me what it was?" Gwynne probed.

"No."

"What? Why not? You really can be exasperating at times."

"Huh! You'd know more about that. I'm just not and that's that!" He shut his eyes and lifted his chin in a childish stance of stubborn resistance.

She gave his arm another more forceful shake, rapidly removed her arm from his. "All right! I'm sorry for asking. Am I seeing a more dogged side of your character? You can be a bit off-putting you know," she said, only half joking. "I mean, you don't even talk like a builder."

As if a touchy subject had been prodded, he let forth. "Yes, well, I've been told that before. But *me* off-putting? That's a bit rich coming from you. Are you an expert on how people should talk or think? How do you want me to talk? Or behave, for that matter? D'you want me to be effing and blinding my way through every sentence like some of my mates?" Pausing to draw breath, he continued more calmly, "And what's more, if I did speak and act that way, would we be here having this conversation? If ever I mutter something in Polish, you can guess at what I'm saying. But okay, maybe I'll tell you why I wore the onesie ... one day; if we get to know each other better."

"Well, now I really am intrigued; but it's your decision, mystery man."

"I'd better go. I've got a full day tomorrow. I'll be back here working early in the morning. Thanks for the invitation to your family lunch. Let me say this: it may not be obvious to you but the main reason I accepted was because – well, just because. End of."

As he was about to leave, he rested his hand on Gwynne's arm and leant forward. He saw her eyes widen in surprise and her head tilt back. He checked, removed his hand and, fixing her with a penetrating gaze said, "It was an opportunity and I think I'm glad I went." As an afterthought he added, "Keith seems a bit of a dark horse. And now I'm off."

Without another word he turned and walked away.

She raised her hand to her face in amazement.

What just happened? Or didn't happen?

His drive home was troubled by recollections of his teenage years. Gwynne had touched on a raw nerve relating to his social experiences with mates. He had always felt different from the other boys, whose chiaking and boisterous behaviour was something he often considered either too embarrassing, or plain stupid. It underlined the separateness he felt. It had resulted in him only ever being on the fringes of their adolescent antics. He put it down to the stories of the harshness of teenage life with which his parents had to deal.

"Think about it," his father used to say. "Don't go rushing into things. Don't just be a follower. There may be consequences about which you know nothing. When you do make up your mind, stick to it. Do your best but be aware things can change. Nothing lasts forever."

Only his mother's death was forever.

Halfway home, the bleep of his mobile told him he had a message. Once home, he looked at his phone and saw it was from Ross advising him there was some sort of hitch with the Minmi land he had been looking at. He made a mental note to return the call.

11

Later that evening, Gwynne was unsettled by thoughts about the day ... and her past. She went over her contacts with Marek, reviewing some of the things he had said and now, this afternoon, what she imagined had almost happened.

His physical presence had activated repressed thoughts and feelings. Was it Marek's recognition of her own confusion which had thwarted his intention at their parting? Her mother's and Colette's admonitions whirled around her head, but something in her inner being was acting in opposition to them.

Her reaction now, drilled into her by her mother, was to try and focus on her immediate challenges. Foremost of all was Merren, followed by work, including her chartered accountant's certification and now, the office extensions. For those final decorative touches, she intended to co-opt her mother, who was chafing at the bit to be in on the fitting-out. She had to admit her mother's suggestions were invariably both tasteful and practical.

Choices would have to be made for paint, tiles, curtains or blinds, electrical outlets and switches. In the least expected moments, thoughts of what Marek, as the builder, might think of their selections, crept into her consciousness.

Gwynne sat in her sunroom, sipping a glass of chilled moscato, absentmindedly comparing its almost golden colour with a dying ray of sunlight slanting across the room, occasionally looking out at Marek's work transforming the backyard. Because of her mother's cautions and her own wariness, she had deliberately moved all thoughts of serious relationships out of her mind.

Such thoughts contrasted achingly with those of her one life-changing romance which had resulted in the birth of Merren.

It haunted her and undermined her confidence. Any thought of the 'pre-David' person of those days now came under the heading, 'that *other* Gwynne'.

She had always felt loved and protected, and not overly constrained by her parents. They had provided so well for her physical and mental wellbeing that she had been able to enjoy school and social activities, including having several boyfriends. Scarcely was there a need to do anything too rebellious. As an only child, she was treated almost as an adult from her mid-teens.

Another of her characteristics, doubtless inherited from her mother, was her forthrightness; always up-front, she was not one for playing secrets which – to her cost – was something some of her friends did.

In her later teens there had been pop concerts, parties which were rowdy, uninhibited, and frequently alcohol-fuelled. Gwynne's innate self-restraint had set her apart. What she saw when any of her friends became intoxicated was not something she felt inclined to imitate.

And yet, her values and attitudes were accepted by close friends. They playfully told her she was quirky, sometimes weird, with a peculiar personality. It manifested itself in her creative dress combinations and her quick and lively, sometimes cutting, sense of humour.

What really made her welcome at parties was her knowledge of the words of so many pop songs and her ability to mimic singing them in the style of the artist.

An uncomfortable question now wormed its way into her consciousness: *Where has that girl gone?*

At twenty-one, she was transferred by the bank for which she worked, to Sydney. There, she had moved into a pokey inner suburban flat with workmates Lana and Shelli. The absence of all the conveniences of home were outweighed by the additional freedoms and independence she gained by not having to account to anyone but herself for her lifestyle choices and any consequences.

As the friendships strengthened, they'd hatched a plan to share a unit for a week of their holidays on the Sunshine Coast. They were encouraged by Lana, whose older sister had done something similar a couple of years previously. She convinced them it would be a great adventure.

After searching the internet for accommodation, they rented a unit, booked their flights, and began what was for Gwynne, a pivotal life experience.

As soon as the girls had settled into their unit, they'd set about exploring the retail and social scenes: shops, cafés, pubs and clubs. Their budget wasn't huge so they decided clubs might be the most economical – and safest – entertainment options.

On their third day, Lana had met a girl in the lift of their unit complex who had told her about the local surf lifesaving club which had, "Great vibes and a pretty good band." Lana, ever the enthusiastic one, passed on the information and the girls unanimously agreed that night was to be '*party night!*'.

Dressed-to-impress, they were intent on a good night out and three attractive girls were never going to have any difficulty gaining attention at the disco.

The vibrant atmosphere was made to order: subdued lighting, loud but not eardrum-splitting music, and a crowd more twenties than teenies.

They particularly noticed one group of boys whose style and appearance didn't quite fit with either the surfer types or the city yuppies. When the band started playing, the girls moved to the dance floor. A short while later, they found themselves sharing their space with a couple of the boys they had noticed. The night was picking up.

After dancing together to the end of the set, they stopped for a break. The three boys hustled extra chairs and joined them at their table. Over the course of the evening, some pairing off resulted. Gwynne learned that the boys were on twenty-four hours' leave from the RAAF base outside Ipswich, one hundred and fifty kilometres away. The boy sitting next to her, David Richards, told her he was from a property in Western Australia.

Whenever the band started up again, Lana and Shelli hit the dance floor and Gwynne noticed they got plenty of attention. As the night wore on, she and David danced less and talked more.

In the small hours after midnight, Lana jogged Gwynne's elbow and indicated they should soon be on their way. Gwynne hesitantly agreed and lingered over saying goodbye to David. At the last minute they exchanged phone numbers. Shelli, for some unexplained reason, gave Ben the address of their holiday unit.

During the taxi ride back, they all agreed it had been a great idea and that it was a pity they hadn't discovered the club earlier in their holiday. Lana, usually careful with words, asked, "Shelli why did you give Ben our unit's address?"

"He asked. So, what if I did?" She replied dismissively.

They all shared bits of information gleaned from the boys. They were from a RAAF health services wing squadron, but what work they actually did was unclear.

The next morning, Shelli answered a knock on their door and there stood Ben and David, both grinning and looking very pleased with themselves. "Ladies," they announced, in mock-courtly manner, "We've come to take you to breakfast. What do you say?"

Gwynne, in her best imitation of a lilting U.S. southern drawl, answered for all of them. "Why, how could we refuse such a kindly offer from such gen'l'men as y'all?" And then, in her normal voice, added, "Give us fifteen minutes. You'd better wait in the car while we dress."

"Aw, shucks Ma'am, do we have to?"

"Yes! Move!"

Once the girls were ready, they climbed into the car and headed to a beachside open-air café. Conversations from the previous night were revisited and vague promises were made about keeping in touch.

Eventually, the boys explained they had to leave to get back to the RAAF base on time.

It was all totally rushed and unplanned. They returned the girls to their unit and then noisily departed with car-horn hooting and farewells shouted.

Their holiday had slowly drawn to an end. On their last full day, Shelli and Lana wanted to do some shopping. Gwynne had tagged along with little enthusiasm, merely re-arranging the stock on a couple of clothes racks in a few boutiques.

Nothing particularly interested her, but she bought an egg-shaped golf ball as a novelty-joke for her dad and a scarf for her mother as well as a beach bag, which she didn't really need, for herself.

That evening, when her mobile phone rang, she was amused and pleasantly surprised to find it was David. He'd said he just wanted to hear her voice and wish her safe travelling. He also mumbled something about getting together again some time. She'd felt flattered and murmured agreement.

When the call ended, she'd felt pleased, even if there wasn't much likelihood of meeting again.

His calls had kept coming every few days and three weeks later he called to say he was scheduled to come to Sydney and asked if they could meet. Gwynne wasn't sure what David was suggesting but agreed she could meet him at a café at Central Station on the Saturday morning in question.

Now, after four years, as she sipped her wine, she still felt her face blush. She recalled the anticipation and uncertainty of what to expect and how it almost made her a nervous wreck.

When the day finally arrived, she had painstakingly dressed in her best outfit, checking everything from toenails to any stray strand of hair. She checked the train timetable four times before setting off for the station. With mixed emotions and expectations, the overall feeling was one of sheer exhilaration.

Fortunately, the train was on time and once seated, she was able to calm herself as she stared unseeingly at the close-packed tenements and terrace-houses flashing by.

She recalled the tingle of David's lips on hers as they nervously greeted each other. They went to a nearby café and, after a coffee and free-ranging banter full of smiles and hand touches, they decided to go to a movie.

Thirty minutes later they were seated in a small cinema which showed its age by its rather drab, worn out and close-packed seating; but they hardly noticed, or cared. They were together. The movie, *In the Cut*, which neither of them knew anything about, was a psycho-thriller, written and directed by Jane Campion, who had directed *The Piano,* a movie they had both seen and which had intrigued them. The tension of this new movie had caused her to take a firm hold of David's hand. At one stage, he had prised her fingers loose because her nails were digging into his palm.

Gwynne put her glass of moscato down and examined her hands, flexed her fingers and smiled, remembering how David had made sure he continued to hold her hand for the rest of the movie. It hadn't been a romantic film but somehow, at the end, they both felt closer to each other, as if they had just shared a meaningful, if undefined, personal experience.

Still holding hands, they found another café and had a late lunch. They talked about what each of them had been doing since they'd last seen each other and let it be known they had been eagerly anticipating this catch-up. David had explained that he was in Sydney to complete the first of three mandatory trauma clinics for paramedics.

Eventually, it was time for Gwynne to catch her train. David walked with her back to the station and they both clung to each other in a passionate kiss. Gwynne had been shocked by its intensity. Even now her chest constricted, and she still recalled how her heart had been pounding.

Little more had been said other than David asking, "Can we do this again next time?"

"Oh yes! I hope so. It's been wonderful. Let me know as soon as you can," had been her gushing and breathless reply.

Once seated on the train, she'd waved goodbye to David and for the next half hour, with eyes closed, she reviewed the events of the day, especially the pressure and pleasure of his lips on hers.

Similar meeting arrangements had been made for David's follow-up clinics. As the time drew near, she allowed her expectations free reign. Her imagination and desires had magnified the first experience and, at their second meeting, their hugs and kisses were less restrained, more fervent.

During lunch, David informed her that the next clinic would be his last and that afterwards he would be flying home to Western Australia for two weeks' leave. "I'm staying over and my flight leaves on Sunday afternoon."

The statement hung in the air in the intense silence that followed, allowing their imaginations free rein at the opportunities. Once again, she felt a lump in her throat. They both knew what the occasion offered and its inferences.

She'd asked where he would stay in Sydney. It was a leading question and when David asked, "Would you like to stay over with me?" her breathing faltered.

There, he'd said it! It was out in the open. She'd reached across the table, looked into his eyes and, seeing nothing but a reflection of her own love and desire, she nodded agreement, "Yes, I'd like that, if you'd like me to."

"More than anything else in the world. I'll ring you as soon as it's confirmed and let you know the details."

It was settled as easily as that and, brazenly contradictory as it appeared, she has never had the slightest regret.

Leaning back in her chair, with eyes closed and moscato finished, she relived her disappointment when, ten days before the overnight visit was scheduled, she had come down with a heavy dose of the flu.

At first, her reaction to the symptoms was little more than annoyance and she consoled herself by thinking that it wouldn't last more than a few days.

Unfortunately, even after taking aspirin and a decongestant syrup and staying home from work, the symptoms worsened, and she finally went to her doctor. He had diagnosed acute bacterial bronchitis and prescribed an antibiotic. The medication proved effective, and she gradually improved.

Late on the Thursday before the weekend, she'd convinced herself she was well and began to regain her excitement.

She'd awoken on that anxiously awaited Saturday morning in a heightened state of anticipation. She'd had only the vaguest idea of what to expect but her anxiety, ratcheted up to the possibilities, became all-consuming. She'd packed and unpacked and re-packed an overnight bag but was almost beside herself worrying if she'd chosen sensibly. In a burst of romantic anticipation, she had bought new underwear and sleepwear. On the train she'd been unable to concentrate on anything other than spending a night with David.

When they met at Central Station, they embraced more passionately than ever. Too early to check-in, they decided to walk to the hotel and leave her luggage there before strolling down Pitt Street Mall to Sydney Tower where, on a spur-of-the-moment decision, they decided to go up and view the sights.

David decided to make the most of the occasion and have lunch at the restaurant. Their conversation touched on anything other than what was foremost in their thoughts for the afternoon and night. Afterwards, neither had felt like sitting through a movie so they window shopped, something Gwynne felt David only endured to quell his unconcealed eagerness.

Eventually they meandered through Hyde Park where the sight of couples sitting or lying together became exquisitely tantalising. By mid-afternoon they could contain themselves no longer and headed back to the hotel.

Once in the room, they had nervously begun to unpack their things, after which David had taken her hand and gently drawn her to him. They kissed, gradually letting their emotions and actions run ever more freely. Every touch had sent a new sensation through her as David became bolder with his caresses. His hands found their way to buttons and zips.

Before long, she was standing in her new underwear and David was murmuring about how beautiful she was, how wonderful she smelt and how much he loved her. They were words she delighted in hearing, while she in turn began to return his caresses with increasing confidence and boldness.

At some point, conversation faded. He'd swept her up in his arms and carried her to the bed and gently laid her down. He kissed her again then unbuttoned his shirt, removed shoes and socks and laid down beside her. His kisses and caresses resumed as he fumblingly removed her bra and cupped her breasts, fondling and lightly pinching her nipples. In her boldest move, she began to loosen his belt and, with unrestrained haste, he removed his trousers.

Moments later he removed her panties then his own briefs, enabling them to explore each other's naked bodies more completely. They kissed, touched, caressed, and fondled every part of each other in a state of lust-driven frenzy.

He continued to kiss and nip her breasts, and, with unexpected boldness, she held his penis for only a few moments before the physical hunger for each other became unbearable, culminating in passionate, but somewhat hurried and inexpert lovemaking.

Afterwards, as they lay in each other's arms, she had felt slightly deflated. Their inexperience had encumbered the encounter, resulting in something less than her imagination had promised. They curled up with the tension of the moment reduced, if not entirely released, and resumed their love-talk before drifting into a blissful semiconscious state.

Sometime later, Gwynne was woken by David's kisses. Scarcely any part of her body was left unexplored: her lips, ears, eyes, neck and then downwards, lingering deliriously at her breasts, before continuing lower, nipping and kissing all the way.

She recalled how, once again, she had felt her passion build and overflow as she had responded in kind. That second time they were more adventurous with no part of either body left untouched by lips or fingers.

Eventually they had come together wildly, franticly, resulting in waves of ecstasy for Gwynne and animal groans of satisfaction from David. They held each other in that final embrace before they separated with a deep sigh of contentment and released sexual tension.

She recalled again David's words of love for her, the feeling of his hand smoothing her hair, his lips kissing her ears and eyes and saying how beautiful she was, even as her eyes had blurred in their post-coital release.

And then, drowsily, David had broken the trance asking, "Are you hungry?"

To her surprise she answered, "I'm starving."

"Me too. Let's eat. There's a small restaurant not far away. I don't want to go too far."

They dressed and walked to the café, arm in arm, barely aware of the bustling city life around them. Their meal was plain but neither cared as they devoured every morsel.

She remembered nothing of the walk back to the hotel. Once there, they stripped off and climbed back into bed, curled up in each other's embrace and again allowed their passions free expression.

Gwynn smiled now at the recollection that she had worn her new nightie for less than two minutes. The memory of the following day, after the ecstasy of their lovemaking, was one of descending from an emotional high.

They'd had to vacate their room early because David had a plane to catch. They had coffee and a croissant for breakfast on the way to the station and both had felt the anguish of parting.

She vividly recalled how she had been on the edge of tears feeling both sorrow at their parting and unbridled joy at the time they had spent together. From the rasping tone of David's voice, she'd known he was in a similar state.

At the station, prolonging the parting moment, they'd stood, she with her hands clasped behind his neck and he with his arms firmly around her waist, pressing her to him. A tableau of two lovers embracing in their passionate goodbyes.

As the train had pulled away from the platform and after waving a final goodbye, she had turned her head to the window and let the tears flow. Only occasionally did she brush them away as the train negotiated the humdrum inner suburban network accentuating the heartrending sense of separation.

The days at work after their passion-driven weekend had been something of a torture. David had rung from his home in Western Australia which had filled her with joy. While he was staying with his parents, she had waited for him to call rather than ringing him because she felt his time with his family was precious to him.

The days passed in an eternity of wrenching anticipation of the next phone call with news of his return. Gwynne hadn't quite known what to expect when David had eventually rung from the airport on the evening of his homecoming. He had been full of news about his family and catching up with friends from pre-RAAF days.

Both expressed their desire to see each other as soon as could be arranged. Her pulse quickened as she recalled his words: "I'm not sure how it can be managed but I can't wait to see you again. I'll let you know once I've worked something out."

The next Gwynne had heard from David was a brief call to say that he had landed in Brisbane and was waiting to collect his luggage from the carousel.

Phone calls continued every second day for two weeks and on each occasion, he sounded so pleased with himself she had wondered if he was holding onto a secret. But then came a period of days when she heard nothing.

Her anxiety built until she became frantic. She had been unable to control the feeling of dread that something wasn't right.

Even recalling it now after four years made her shiver and her stomach churn. Grasping at possibilities, she had wondered whether RAAF duties had interfered in their lives or whether it was personal; something, or someone else, he was unable to talk about. She felt as if she was being drawn into a tumble dryer descending into the vortex whereby her erratic thoughts, sensations and emotions came briefly into focus, then were blurred and lost.

Nine days after his last call, she had been unable to contain herself any longer and, while she was alone in the flat, she had rung the RAAF base and asked the operator if she could speak to David Richards. After a rather long period in which she could hear voices talking about, 'someone wanting to talk to David Richards', the speaker asked who was calling. Gwynne had immediately become alert to the tone of voice and, in a hesitant voice said, "My name is Gwynne Alwen. I'm a friend of David Richards. I've been expecting a call from him for the last week."

The girl had then said, "Please hold while I transfer your call."

After half a dozen rings, a male voice had answered and identified himself. Gwynne recognised the name of one of David's senior officers. "May I ask who's calling please?"

As she answered, again giving her name and a reference to her relationship with David, her heart turned to stone. She'd had to resist an almost overpowering urge to hang up in fear of what she might hear. Her frozen hand gripped the phone, her knuckles whitening as she held her breath.

The next words she heard were the most terrifying she had ever heard in her life. "I'm sorry Ma'am, David Richards was involved in a single vehicle traffic accident almost a week ago. Prior to the accident he had been granted forty-eight hours special leave for an unspecified personal reason."

The disembodied voice continued, "I'm sorry for your loss. All I can say, from a local newspaper report, is that David was in New South Wales travelling south on the New England highway when his car left the road and crashed down a culvert. When he was found, he was rushed to hospital where he was placed in an induced coma from which he never regained consciousness."

Now, in the darkening gloom of her home, Gwynne shut her eyes tightly as she recalled how devastated she had felt. How she'd been overwhelmed, as if drowning; wanting to scream but unable to speak. Again, as she did every time she recalled the events, her eyes stung with salty tears.

She recollected the words but barely comprehended them as the officer continued, "David died last Wednesday morning. I suppose the delay from the time of the accident to the time of death resulted in the accident receiving minimal media coverage. I repeat, I'm very sorry for your loss …"

She had heard nothing further. Her mind went blank as her brain ceased to function. A kaleidoscope of thoughts and images had flickered through her imagination as if on super fast-forward. Her tongue had felt withered and dry, incapable of speech. Her throat constricted, her breathing deteriorated into gasps for air, and she'd felt firstly a wave of dizziness, then nausea. The phone had fallen to the floor as she shuffled to the toilet where she had puked the entire contents of her stomach. Later, when she had felt capable of standing, she made her way to her bed, climbed in, and pulled the blankets up as she sobbed herself into unconsciousness.

Now, her stomach still churned at the vivid recollection of the mindless state of depression into which she had sunk. It seemed to last forever as time had ground to a halt. It was incomprehensible that David had died four days before she had found out. His body had been transported back to his home in Western Australia for burial and there seemed to be nothing anyone could do to help her emerge from the black abyss.

When she didn't emerge from her room that evening, Lana and Shelli realised something had happened. They waited until the next morning before knocking on her door and asking if she was alright. They entered, but before she could say a word, they knew something terrible had happened. Through sobs and tears, Gwynne told them David was dead and what scant details she knew. They tried with little success to comfort her. She missed five more days from work on the pretext that she was having a bronchitis relapse.

Three weeks later, she found out she was pregnant.

12

Gwynne retreated into a dark world where the past faded into distorted obscurity, one in which a thousand unknowns cascaded down upon her.

How would she cope? What about her career? Could she face the future alone as an unmarried mother? Three questions haunted her every moment: Abortion? Adoption? Single mother?

She said nothing to Lana and Shelli, but they had noticed her moodiness and general decline. She'd passed it off as grief and a relapse of the flu saying, "I'm ok. I'm just feeling a bit off."

Eventually, unable to bear the mental anguish, she had told Lana of her pregnancy. Between tears and anger at falling into an age-old trap, with breaking voice, she briefly recounted her story. Lana had done all she could to console her. They'd both known it was most girls' worst nightmare – how to deal with it was terrifying.

"Gwynne, what are you going to do?" The question hung like a bad smell in the flat.

Gwynne had simply said, "I don't know. I don't even know how to tell my parents or even if I should tell them. Or just go away somewhere."

Lana reacted angrily. "Don't even think that! We're friends, here to support you. Promise me you won't make any rash decisions, especially running away. It's your decision but *please* don't push us away. We want to help."

The following day Shelli had repeated her offer of support but with one major difference: she openly advised Gwynne to seek a termination. "Gwynne, I had a cousin who got pregnant and had the baby. Her life was never the same. As a single mother, she had no social life and her career prospects were all but ruined. You deserve better than that."

She'd also mentioned a decline in other more prosaic personal relationships with men, some of whom steered clear of single women with a baby and others who thought she was fair game.

Gwynne had listened but her brain was overwhelmed by white noise, amid her own swirling fears and misgivings on what her parents would say and what her future held.

Her recurring maddening thought had been on how she had fallen pregnant. When she visited her doctor, she asked, "What happened? How did I fall pregnant when I've been taking the pill since I was eighteen? I know the pill is not one hundred percent guaranteed effective, but what went wrong?"

Her doctor had removed his stethoscope, placed it on his desk and spun his chair to face her. "Some medications can make the pill less effective. They include some antibiotics which were prescribed when your flu progressed to bacterial bronchitis. Side effects may include menstrual changes. It's possible that you may have been one of the unlucky and rare cases whereby the antibiotic, bronchitis and the flu itself, combined to render the pill ineffective."

She reprised another turning point in her life. It had occurred over a long weekend on a return visit to her parents' home here in Newcastle when, having suffered morning sickness for two weeks and trying to conceal it while she was at home, her mother had insisted on taking her out for coffee. Shortly after they'd sat down Audrey, perceptive and as straight forward as ever, commented, "You haven't been in contact much lately and you seem a little off colour since you came home. Are you well?"

The arrival of the waitress to take their order precluded an immediate response and gave her thinking time. When giving their order to the waitress, the thought of her usual *café latte* almost made her gag, so she asked for a mineral water.

She'd ignored her mother's interrogation but after some prevarication, Audrey had simply asked, "Gwynne, are you pregnant?"

Gwynne had gasped at the abruptness of her mother's question. It was one of the few occasions in which Gwynne recognised her mother's sibling similarity to Colette. She hung her head. Audrey hadn't needed further confirmation. She reached across the table and placed her hand over Gwynne's and, in a sympathetic mothering tone Gwynne had only rarely heard, Audrey quietly said, "Tell me."

In a halting, anguished voice, barely above a whisper, Gwynne gradually related her story as simply as she could, ending with the news of David's death.

"Oh Gwynne, why haven't you told your father and me this before now? You've had a devastating experience losing someone you love. How far along are you?"

On hearing her reply, "Just over eight weeks", it was Audrey's turn to show surprise, marked with a degree of anger. "Eight weeks! How could you keep this from your father and me? Did you think the problem was going to just disappear? You're our daughter and you're carrying our grandchild!"

Gwynne hung her head in total confusion. "I've been trying to decide what to do."

Audrey knew what Gwynne was alluding to and said, "If you've been dithering and keeping this secret for that long, you have already decided what to do but haven't admitted it to yourself. You're going to keep it, aren't you?"

Gwynne's response was somewhere between a nod and a shrug. "We only saw each other a few times. I'm certain David is, *was*, a very loving and considerate person. I honestly believe that had he not died we would have managed together and got married as soon as was practicable."

Even to herself, her response sounded like a lame justification for her indecisiveness. "This baby was conceived with love and that knowledge is imprinted on my mind. It's a living being. It reminds me of what we had together. David's death will never change that. It isn't the baby's fault that it exists or that its father is dead."

Audrey had sat looking at her and then rather suddenly stood up. Gwynne thought she was about to storm out in a state of fury and so she also stood. Feeling alone, empty and on the edge of abandonment, she was again on the verge of tears.

However, Audrey, completely unexpectedly, reached out and hugged her as if she were still five years old, saying, "Gwynnie, whatever you decide to do, whatever you want, your father and I will back your decision."

She'd been shocked at this open show of support and affection. Her mother hadn't used her childhood name since she'd reached her teens. She hugged her mother and felt a flow of emotion surge through her. Oblivious to the fact that other patrons were looking on, she clung hard, feeling some of the strength her mother had always shown flow into her, and not wanting it to stop.

After that emotional outburst, in which a glimmer of hope was sparked in Gwynne, her mother had released her. Audrey went to the counter and paid the bill. When she returned, she hooked her arm through Gwynne's and asked, "Do you want me to tell your father, or will you tell him?"

Gwynne hadn't thought about it but after a few moments, she said, "When I have worked out exactly what I want, I'll tell him in my own way. I promise I won't take too long".

Audrey's reply was both precise and stern, almost back to her old self. "Make sure you don't."

Once the decision to have the baby had been acknowledged, the next step she had taken was to secure her long-term future financially. Her pregnancy, and the anticipated responsibilities of motherhood, had influenced her decision to resign her position at the bank. A re-think of her future had been her immediate challenge, given the inevitable conclusion of her bank career prospects.

Two weeks later Gwynne made up her mind to tell her father. With morning sickness on the wane and a risky morning coffee that no longer tasted like dishwater in front of her, she had theatrically lifted her chin and squared her shoulders. She felt a wave of determination to take control of her life wash over her.

She rang her parents. Having made the decision, she wanted to tell them while her resolve was firm.

"Mum, are you going to be home for me to visit this weekend?"

"Is this about what we discussed? If the answer's yes, we'll *definitely* be here."

Audrey had picked her up from the station and driven her home. Greetings were exchanged albeit in a slightly stilted, guilt laden atmosphere on Gwynne's part.

When they sat down, she looked at her father and mother across the kitchen table and she knew, by their expressions, that her father knew. Neither said a word; they just waited.

Gwynne began her story. She had gone over it so many times in her mind that it felt like an off-the-shelf script in a soap opera. She avoided looking directly at her father, instead fixing her gaze on her hands as she let the words flow.

When she had finished, she raised her face to her parents with a mixture of misery, guilt and resignation, as if to add, *There, that's it! Say what you think.* What she did say was uttered with an element of defiant challenge. "I'm sorry if I have let you down."

Her mother gave her a brief nod. Gwynne looked at her father who, after looking back at her in a way she had rarely experienced, reached out and grasped both her hands firmly saying, "Gwynne, love, don't even think it! You haven't let us down. It'll be alright. We can help you make this work. It isn't the end of the world, nor is it the end of your life. It is the beginning of a new life for you and your baby, and we're here for you. Now, come here and give me a hug."

Hearing her father's words, she stood and, breaking into another flood of tears she wrapped her arms around his neck and kissed his cheek before resting her head on his shoulder. It was the first time in many years she had done such a thing and the gesture was magnified by a sense of protection, reminiscent of her childhood. It was also the first time in almost three months that she felt positive about anything to do with her life.

After the coffee, her father asked how she intended to manage her pregnancy with respect to her job at the bank. She had thought about that but hadn't acted on her decision, mostly because she hadn't known what to expect from her parents until that moment. Her mother had then outlined some downside possibilities that might make continuing at work difficult for a working mother-to-be beyond her second trimester.

After an ominous silence, Huw suggested, "When you feel the time is right, why don't you move back here? This has been your home for most of your life. Your old room is still there for you, and we can help when you feel you need it."

Gwynne had thanked him, saying only that she would think about it. She realised that her independence would be affected firstly by the pregnancy and then motherhood. Adding to this was the guilt of encroaching on her friend's space by filling the small flat with the trappings of a baby.

Now, thinking back on that time, she had not realised the extent of mental, emotional and financial adjustment which had lay ahead of her.

She remembered with a deep sense of gratitude, the huge relief at having unburdened herself, and her decision to keep the baby. Their unqualified support had buoyed her beyond all expectations.

Gwynne was brought out of her reverie by the sound of Merren singing a Playschool song. Three-and-a-half-year-old Merren, the product of her one and only serious love affair. She had to almost shake herself free physically from her daydreaming to concentrate on her here-and-now, real-world priorities: Merren, work, and her ambitions to expand into her home office. In that order.

She could never have imagined that, after all that had happened, she would have a bright, healthy daughter, was about to become a certificated accountant and paying nominal rent on an investment house her parents had bought, ostensibly for her. They were paying for the extensions because they realised the additions enhanced the capital value of the property. Those additions were almost complete and being overseen by a client for whom she was trying to ignore sentiments she had not experienced since before Merren was born.

And now? *How should she deal with the reawakening?*

13

The finished extensions were handed over four weeks later for Gwynne to complete the furnishing. As she knew would be the case, Audrey was in her element.

Once selections had been made for paint, a job which Marek routinely passed on to contractors, and soft furnishings in place, the family decided to celebrate the occasion by asking family and a few friends over. Gwynne convinced herself Marek had to be invited because of his many contributions, both paid and unpaid, and some other less clearly defined reasons.

When she rang, his phone went to voicemail. She was unprepared with any message and after a slight stammer, simply asked him to call when convenient. She was annoyed with herself for being so inept and almost rang him back straight away, but she held off with the excuse that he might be too busy.

Most of her friends were working people and so Friday or Saturday evenings were the obvious choices for the party. It wouldn't be a big affair and an early evening starting time would be best. While she was listing a few names and ideas for food and drink, her phone rang.

"Hello Marek. Thanks for calling back. How are you?"

"Hi Gwynne. This is an unexpected pleasure … er, call. I'm fine. What's up? The roof blown away?"

"No, not yet anyway. Nothing serious is up. I just wanted to invite you to a small party I'm hosting to celebrate the completion of my new home office. What do you think? Given your part in the whole thing, the least I can do is ask when you will be available."

"That's very kind of you. When were you thinking of having it? Will I have to declare it as a fringe benefit?"

"Be serious. Without your contribution I might never have started. It's only fair you get to have a say when to have the party. Probably early on a Saturday evening. Weekdays are out for most people. When would suit you?"

There was silence for a few moments before Marek spoke. "I'm flattered. I'm free Saturday week. How does that suit?"

"Great! Sounds good to me. It gives me time to ring around and organise things. I'll see you around five o'clock Saturday week. After the additions themselves, you'll be guest of honour."

"Oh, please, don't say that. I'm happy to keep a low profile. What can I bring?"

Gwynne replied emphatically, "Just yourself. You've already made a huge contribution."

"Well, I have to bring something."

"Alright then, surprise us when you arrive with whatever you like. And perhaps a bottle of something."

"Alright, I'll bring a bottle of red cordial for Merren! Oh, and maybe a different one for us big people. Should I bring something savoury or something sweet?"

"Forget the first bottle and make the last one part of the surprise. It's up to you but you really don't have to bring anything. You've made your contribution."

"Thanks again for the invitation. How many people do you think will come?" he asked, in an effort to prolong the conversation.

"What? Why? I'd guess no more than twenty. Ok? What does it matter how many?"

"I just wanted to make sure everyone got a chocolate crackle."

"See you Saturday week. Don't forget."

"Cheers. Looking forward to it. I'll iron my best overalls to wear. Unless you want to lend me your onesie. Thanks again."

"Bye Marek."

He considered taking pierogi, and even having a go at making them himself. He'd seen his mother make them so often, but even so, he quickly changed his mind. Watching his mother start with boiling the potatoes, was one thing but knowing the proportions needed for the fillings of cheese, onions and spices was another.

Plus making the pastry, rolling it, cutting it into little round cut-outs, and inserting a little ball of mixture and sealing it all seemed too much.

He realised it was beyond his skill range.

He knew exactly what he wanted to take: a *makowiec*, a type of strudel cake with poppy seed and yeast dough made into a roll. It tasted something like a rich spicey doughnut for grown-ups. His mother used to make a joke about it being a play on his name: '*Makowiec* for Marek'.

Hopefully, he thought, people won't ask how he knew about it, and he wouldn't be asked too many questions about his background, of which he was justifiably proud. People were often inquisitive about his parents' story, but there's a time and place for disclosing such things.

The good thing was, he knew exactly where he could get a *makowiec*. What's more, he knew he would have to organise it soon.

The person in question was his second Cousin Helena, the daughter of his mother's cousin. Her parents had helped his parents when they first arrived in Newcastle. Helena had kept her mother's recipes and it was from her he would beg the favour.

He'd have to allow plenty of time for the call because he knew from experience that Helena had the Polish gene allowing her to turn a simple phone call into a three-act drama.

After knocking off work the following Friday, he made himself comfortable and rang his cousin. He'd barely got out a few words before she took control.

"Hello stranger. We haven't seen or heard from you for ages. How are you Marek? When are you coming over to see us?"

"Hi Helena. Yes, I know it's been a while. I've been really busy dealing with a few changes happening at work. Helena, I'm ringing to ask a big favour. I've been invited to a small party, and I'd like to take a cake. But the one I'd like is a *makowiec*. You're the only one I know who can make it the way our mothers made it. Can you make one for me? Please?"

"Hmmm! I sense something cooking and it isn't in any kitchen. Of course, I'll make a *makowiec*, but only after I know exactly who it's for. It must be for someone special, or you owe someone a special favour."

She sounded disappointed when he offered only a few details, but he knew she was astute enough to suspect there were more to be extricated. "Yes, I'll do it, but only on one condition: you must come over to collect it Thursday night, stay for dinner and give us the full story. I know there's more to this than you're letting on. Take it or leave it."

He smiled to himself but they both knew she had him cornered. "I'll take it, with pleasure. Thanks, that would be lovely. It'll be a welcome catch up. The thing is, I need it for Saturday week. Is that ok?"

He knew it would be one of those occasions when he'd have to choose his words carefully or she would jump to unwarranted assumptions.

He knew too that they would reminisce over 'the old days', culminating in the death of his mother five years ago from breast cancer. Her death was the most devastating experience of his life. Furthermore, it had led to a decline in his father's general drive and enthusiasm, his mojo, as some people say, which caused his life to take an unexpected turn: an extended visit back to his hometown of Zakopane, Poland.

The closer he got to the Ellis home, Marek's state of mind lightened. His second cousin Helena was his only relative in Australia. They had enjoyed a shared family upbringing which included a strong Polish link.

Occasionally he felt guilty that he didn't always understand the bonds his parents shared with Helena's family and Poland. When their parents launched into Polish reminiscences, they had often wandered off to play in the garden.

Alan Ellis, Helena's husband, opened the door and welcomed him. "G'day Marek. Come on in. I was just about to open a beer ... or two?"

"G'day Alan, how are you? I'm driving, but yeah, thanks, just the one would be good. Here's a bottle of wine to contribute to the meal. I'll have to be careful."

He followed Alan and they sat chatting in the loungeroom. He stood when Helena bustled in and greeted him with a gushing hug and a kiss. "Oh, it's good to see you Marek. Dinner's almost ready. I'll be back in a minute. Have a seat and chat with Alan."

The conversation went as predicted over the course of the meal. Alan and Helena wanted to know how his father was getting on back in Zakopane. As predicted, they reminisced about the arrival of Helena's mother and Marek's parents in Australia, their early lives in Newcastle and most painfully, the shock of his mother's premature death.

Alan had a few more questions about his new work arrangements and eventually, at Helena's probing, the story of Gwynne's office additions. By the time he had finished answering their questions, he felt as if he had been interrogated by the Bezpieczeństwa, or *Polish SB* as it was less than affectionately known. The Polish secret police had a reputation for their vigorous interviewing techniques.

Finally, the *makowiec* made an appearance. It looked delicious and he suspected it would raise a deal of interest. He thanked Helena profusely and, at her insistence, promised a full account of its acceptance at the party.

On the drive home, with the cake safely ensconced on the floor of the passenger seat, Marek admitted to himself how pleased he felt with the evening. They had eventually agreed that his father deserved and needed a new incentive in his life after the devastating death of his mother and Milosz's soulmate, Alicja.

Driving home, almost on automatic pilot, he recalled how Milosz and Alicja would regale him on their uncertain life in Poland.

From an early age, the terrible conditions had been drummed into him. How ethnic and religious 'sanitisation' measures were introduced in the 1930s; the failings of a democracy imposed on a politically divided and uninformed population; the subsequent restrictions on freedom of the press; centralised authoritarian rule and the rise of the military in enforcing contentious policies.

He'd been shocked when his mother had told him one day, 'Even in churches, a blind eye was turned towards anti-Semitism. People started to become restless and very worried.'

On another occasion, when talking about refugees coming to Australia by boat, his father had heatedly reminded him that in the 1960s, extremes of fascism and communism were gaining popular support throughout Europe. Thousands of people fled their homelands to find safer places to live. Concluding by making it personal, his father had reminded him, "That is the main reason why your grandfather moved to Zakopane. Besides, Zakopane was becoming increasingly popular as a winter sports tourist destination – a more exciting and cosmopolitan town for a young man; and a chance to earn money."

His parents had often reminded him how his grandfather married his grandmother Katarzyna, and Milosz was born, and then his Uncle Jan. They'd told him how they grew up to be idealistic teenagers.

A decade after the war, Milosz and Alicja had met, and shared their hopes for a better future. They'd joined a youth group and been introduced to new ideas and dreamt of a freer lifestyle. Marek remembered feeling embarrassed when his father revealed, 'We were in love from the day we met.'

When there was another clampdown on press freedom in the late 1950s, we began to dream of a way to escape. It took two years to develop a plan and another to work up the courage, but in 1961 we put our secret plan into action.'

His parents' story then took on the tone of a clandestine struggle for freedom. 'After fleeing our home with only Baptism certificates, showing our names, birthdates and proving we were not Jewish, we walked and hitchhiked over twelve hundred kilometres, avoiding capital cities, where political unrest was greatest, to get to Genoa. There we got married and used our baptism and marriage certificates to get passage on the first available boat. We both spoke a little German, Russian and English having worked in the winter tourist season in Zakopane and that was a big help. However, the first available boat was not to the United States, but to Australia, our second-choice destination.'

Marek had been stunned to learn they lied and claimed their original birth certificates had been destroyed in Kraków during the war. An example of his own mother and father risking everything for their freedom.

Their lives in Newcastle, Australia had then changed into something approaching normality. Marek was born in 1975, shortly after his parents had taken up Australian citizenship. His name was registered as Marek *Benning*; not *Benningowicz*. He realised how their determination and resolution had been absorbed into his own character from birth.

'An Australian name for an Australian boy', his parents had proclaimed and his parents had constantly reminded him, 'You are an Australian by birth, but you have Polish blood in your veins.'

When his mother died, Milosz became the last surviving Polish-born link in their family. Marek and Helena were the new Australian-born generation.

His mother's death resulted in a major change in his father. On the brink of retirement, and without his loving wife beside him, Milosz had begun to brood on an increasingly bleak future.

Marek had watched his strongly willed father sink into a world of grief which somehow translated into an overwhelming desire to visit his homeland, despite having called Australia home for almost forty years. Australia, where he had never been out of work; where 'rule of law', even in an imperfect world, offered security and opportunity unavailable in many countries; where together they had bought and paid for a home and had become proud parents.

Milosz's intended visit caused one of the few major adult arguments he ever had with his father.

Marek had emphatically countered saying, "But you have Australian citizenship now!"

He was only partially convinced when his father replied. 'Yes, Australian citizen with Polish core and Polish thinking. I can't change that. I want to see what's happened there.'

Milosz had continued in a pleading tone, "I want to return to see the people of our youth. The places where we grew up, and the political and social changes I've read about since the 1990s. I want to see where your mother and I went together and fell in love; where we dreamed of a better life, which is what we achieved and passed on to you."

Despite infrequent contact with his younger brother Jan, Milosz had written to him asking if it was possible to visit. The reply, via his son, Marek's cousin Anton, was positive, if not effusive. Jan was now living in a nursing home in Kraków and suffering from lung cancer. Anton agreed to pick Milosz up from the airport in Kraków and arrange for him to rent a flat in Zakopane.

Whenever he thought about it, Marek became aware of a persistent knot in the pit of his stomach. He himself wasn't obsessed to know about the demise of Soviet domination of Poland, the social and political changes, as his father was.

Begrudgingly, he helped with planning to make his father's visit as safe as possible, but he worried whether his father was quite capable of enduring the long hours of travel, and even more apprehensive of how relatives and friends might react after so many years.

That had been two years ago. Who would have guessed that, at his age, when he returned to Zakopane, Milosz's industrial skills acquired in Comsteel, Newcastle, Australia would afford opportunities for employment? Their regular telephone calls surprised Marek how quickly his father was able to settle in, catch up with old friends, and make new ones.

Now, at a time when his own career was hanging in the balance, he admitted to himself that he missed his father's company and his counsel.

On the spur of the moment, he rang Darren, the man who was second only to his father for sharing events in his life.

"Hi, Darren, how's it going?"

"Yeah, not bad thanks. What's up?"

"Nothing. Just a catch-up call. I got an invitation from Gwynne to a small gathering she's putting on for the completion of her home office. It's next Saturday evening. Not something I expected."

"Take it as one of the rare perks of the job."

"Yeah, I did. None of it would have happened without you though. I'm really grateful and am beginning to appreciate even more what you and Maxine did for the partnership."

"Thanks mate, but you're on your own now. I reckon you'll do alright, but it isn't all a bed of roses."

"No, I think I'm beginning to find that out. I'll keep it in mind. But seriously, thanks for everything you've done for me Darren. The new job working out for you?"

"Yeah, not too badly thanks. The team is mixed with a few inexperienced young blokes. Reminds me of a certain apprentice a dozen years ago."

"Huh! You should be so lucky. As I recall that kid worked out okay."

"Cocky bugger though!"

"Not so much anymore. The game has got a lot more serious lately."

"Hang in there Marek. Don't start getting too flash like some young blokes do. Remember what I've said."

"Will do Darren. Although you said quite a lot over the years. And you're still doing it."

"Some people take more telling than others. Besides that, I still feel I have a vested interest."

"And rightly so. Thanks again Darren. Talk to you next time."

"Yep. G'bye Marek."

14

The door was opened by Colette, accompanied by Merren, whose curiosity at the arrival of every party guest was not to be denied. Colette welcomed him with an almost friendly smile, shaded with uncertainty.

She took the cake he held out to her. "This looks lovely. I'll put it with the other goodies, shall I? What a lovely bunch of flowers. How thoughtful. Go through. The others are admiring your work out the back."

"Thanks Colette. It was my first solo job and I'm quite pleased with it. And I'm keen to see it all fitted out."

Jigging from one foot to the other, Merren's reaction was one of unrestrained joy. They enacted the greeting ritual for the first time in weeks, complete with sound effects.

Colette watched, bemused, as if seeing some secret game, or perhaps something from one of the cartoon shows of which Merren was so fond. She stood back to allow him to pass, her lower lip held between her teeth, suspicion ruffling her usual confident demeanour.

Merren skipped ahead and called to her mother, "Marek's here!" and disappeared up the hallway and into her room. Seconds later she reappeared with Squinty and Binko, waving them in front of Marek for him to greet them.

Marek, awkwardly juggling the flowers, obliged and gave each a paw-shake. He then followed Merren through to the kitchen where he self-consciously handed over the flowers. "These are for you."

"Oh Marek, you didn't have to do this, they look lovely. You've already done so much. Thank you."

When Colette placed the *makowiec* on the table Gwynne asked, "What's this? Flowers and a cake? You're too kind."

Marek lifted his chin in a mock-pompous style intended to forestall any inquisition into the cake's history. "It's a special Polish order intended to provide a multicultural dimension to the celebrations." He then gave her a wink and the hint of a smile to forestall further comment.

Colette chose a vase, arranged the flowers, and placed them at the centre of the table.

Admiring the display, Gwynne turned back to Marek, "You really shouldn't have, but thank you again for your thoughtfulness." She looked at him and reached up to brush his cheek with an air-kiss and a hug, saying, "You really are very sweet." She held the hug a little longer than intended and when she released it, blushed with self-consciousness.

Colette's disapproving look was in stark contrast to Marek's, who was both disturbed and excited by Gwynne's reaction to the gifts but held his composure and asked if he could look through the finished product now it was fully furnished.

"Go right ahead. I'm busy here in the kitchen. I'll catch up with you in a few minutes. Mum, Dad and Keith are out there somewhere."

Marek gave a wave to Keith as he found his way to the main event of the party.

He quietly checked over the furnishings, nodding in approval, noting how stylish, comfortable and practical it looked.

At that point Gwynne bustled into the room asking, "Well, what do you think? How do you like the way we've set it up?"

"It's great. Looks like a functional and nicely fitted out working area, very tastefully decorated."

"I'm glad you think so. I wouldn't like to think that a project in which you had such a big hand fell short at the final hurdle. I think it'll be a great workspace. I must be honest and admit Mum had a big hand in the decorating."

They were interrupted by a call from Colette in the kitchen. "Gwynne!"

"Sorry Marek, but I have to go. Hostess duties call. I'll catch up with you a little bit later."

As she disappeared, Huw casually strolled in as if he too was checking out the workmanship. As he sidled up to Marek, he observed, "It looks good don't you think? Audrey and I are very pleased."

Marek sensed Huw was prevaricating, taking in little of the detail. He seemed distracted as he remarked, "Even if Gwynne were to move, the extra rooms could function as a bedroom with ensuite or even as a granny flat or teenager's retreat."

Marek nodded and murmured his agreement, sensing Huw wasn't speaking directly to him but rather airing his own thoughts.

Huw then changed his expression. He turned only slightly to address Marek without having to look directly at him. "Audrey and I are very proud of Gwynne and what she has achieved since Merren's birth," adding obliquely, "And Merren is an utter delight."

Marek was somewhat surprised by the unexpected twist in the conversation but could only wholeheartedly agree. "From what I can see, Merren, like her mother, seems to have a good idea of what she wants out of life, even at her young age. And Gwynne should be congratulated for what she's achieved."

Huw then came out with something which momentarily confounded Marek. "Audrey and I would not like to see Gwynne emotionally upset or disappointed by extraneous events."

"What? No, of course you wouldn't," the confusion evident in his tone. He had no idea what Huw was talking about.

Huw began to leave the room but turned at the door and added, "We wouldn't like to see her messed about. By anyone!"

Marek watched as Huw walked away – still wondering what on earth he was referring to. 'Messed about? Emotionally upset?' What's he on about?

He shook his head in bafflement then drifted out to mix with the other guests, totally distracted, trying to fathom what Huw had just implied. *Or threatened?*

The first person whose eye he caught was Keith, who brought him back to reality by asking him his opinion on the fitting out.

Marek briefly tried to clear his head and endorsed the furnishings but in such a distracted tone that Keith said, "You don't sound convinced. Don't you like what they've done?"

Bewildered, Marek shook his head. "No, nothing wrong there, but I just had a strange conversation with Huw which ended rather bizarrely. I think I've just had a warning shot fired across my bows."

Intrigued, Keith asked, "What are you talking about? Huw is a serial non-combatant. I don't think he's fired anything but blanks for years. Exactly what did he say?"

When Marek explained, Keith's reply was hardly reassuring. "Hmm, I sense the women's involvement in this. I think Huw was the messenger but, pounds to peanuts, I'll bet Audrey and Colette loaded and primed the message."

"Now, what are *you* talking about?" asked Marek. "Why is everyone talking in riddles?"

"Well," explained Keith, "Huw, and particularly Audrey, who worked for Social Services, have helped Gwynne through an understandably difficult time over the last four years. She is now set fair for a bright future – as much as anyone can be these days. They don't want to see that future threatened by some bloke looking for an easy life from a well-positioned wife."

Marek's jaw dropped at what Keith was implying.

After a sudden intake of breath, he clenched his fists and felt a wave of anger wash over him. He had to use all his self-control to not lash out, either verbally or physically.

"Explain yourself. '*Some bloke*?' Who're you talking about? I can understand his fatherly interest but is he, or they, having a go at me? On what grounds? What have I done?"

Keith's matter-of-fact reply only made Marek feel worse. "Colette has told me in a round-about way that she and Audrey are concerned that the strong focus Gwynne has maintained in getting her life in order may be shifting. Until now, they've thought she has placed personal relationships out of bounds. Now that the struggles of the past four years are almost behind her, they don't want Gwynne to ease-off on her guard."

"Keith, I can't believe what I'm hearing. Isn't she entitled to do that? For God's sake, she's an adult, not a puppet, or a hot-house specimen. They can't keep her under glass forever."

"That's the issue, you see. Audrey and Colette think that Gwynne is showing signs something is brewing and they think it's too much, too soon. What's more, the tealeaves they've been reading have indicated that the person in the picture is you. Hence the comments from Huw. Just saying."

Marek had to force himself to breathe steadily but he could not hide his anger. "Are you kidding? There has been nothing between Gwynne and me that could give them that idea. I've never so much as had a date with Gwynne let alone laid a finger on her. The whole idea is preposterous. It sounds like they've got her in witness protection. They're crazy."

"They don't think they're crazy. Like I said, it's in the tealeaves, or women's intuition or secret women's business, whatever way you want to put it. Sometimes the Wi Fi on their crystal ball drops out … or something. I'm giving you the heads-up, so you'll know the lay of the land. Personally, my advice is 'go for it'! But take it easy. Remember, 'Softly, softly, catchee monkey'."

"I think you're as mad as they are. I admit, I find Gwynne very curious and, well, attractive too. Who wouldn't? The thought of asking her out has barely crossed my mind. She has made it abundantly clear she is fully committed to raising Merren, her certification and setting up her home office. I have done nothing whatsoever to cause any such speculation."

"Yes, well, keep your shirt on. Look at it objectively. The office is finished, her certification is in the bag, and Merren is … Merren. I think if they heard the way you've just spoken it would only fuel their imaginations. Any other bloke would have made a move by now. The fact that you haven't suggests to them that you are more of a threat than someone looking for a quick one-nighter. They've been playing the long game and they think you're doing the same."

Marek looked at Keith as if he was a court jester spouting insults disguised as riddles. His final comment was, "You know, it's a long time since I wanted to punch someone! Tonight has changed that. Suddenly there's a queue I want to throttle one by one. This party's turned into something I never expected in my wildest imaginings. I can't get a handle on it all. Should I thank you? I'm not sure I should. I might get back to you later. From what you're telling me, it might be a good idea for me to wash my hands of the lot of you. I don't need this sort of complication in my life. Right now, I'm going to finish this beer, then I'll get out of here."

Marek stewed over what had been said. He thought about storming out but the urge to resolve, and not run from the situation, prevented him. He finished his beer and vented his frustration somewhat by crushing the can and dumping it into the bin.

After calming down slightly, and out of sheer curiosity, he began mingling with some of the guests, chatting about nothing in particular until a woman to whom he was talking, asked him his name. When he told her she exclaimed, "Oh, you're Marek! You're the builder. Well, it seems to have paid off because Gwynne is very pleased with the results. She spoke well of you."

Barely restraining his relief on hearing her comment, he asked, "Did she? No one else seems to. How do you know Gwynne?"

"We've been friends for a few years. I'm Lana. I worked with her about five years ago. We really got on well. She came on a holiday with me and Shelli, another friend, to the Sunshine Coast. It was great fun but, well, you know, sometimes things don't always work out the way we'd like. Poor Gwynne."

Marek noted the dramatic change in her voice and asked, "Did something happen?"

"You might say that. She deserved better, despite having the gorgeous Merren. She didn't even get to the funeral." Marek understood that something terrible had occurred during or after their holiday, but Lana didn't share the details.

Just as he was about to ask her to explain, Huw sought everyone's attention by clinking his glass with a spoon and announcing, "Ladies and gentlemen, may I have your attention for a few moments please?"

The conversation slowly dwindled.

"Welcome everyone and thank you for coming this evening. For all intents and purposes, this occasion is to view the new additions to the house, beautifully completed by Marek Benning, here tonight." He gestured towards Marek and paused for a smattering of applause.

On hearing Huw mention his name favourably, after his earlier salvo, Marek almost choked. Given Keith's recent comments, he clamped his jaw shut and smiled as a few of the guests glanced his way. He tried to camouflage any signs of his inner resentment by focusing on Gwynne, trying to read her thoughts.

Huw continued, "However, another reason for this gathering is to congratulate Gwynne on gaining certification as a fully qualified chartered accountant. Gwynne has received notification she will graduate this year. This home office is a step in the right direction to help her realise her ambitions. It will allow her to be her own boss."

"Yeah. Right!" interjected one wag, followed by, "At last" from another, with a few chuckles and murmurs of agreement.

Eventually Huw's speech ended with, "Given the circumstances, this is a marvellous achievement, and we are all very proud of her." This last comment generated another smattering of applause. "Audrey and I wish everyone an enjoyable evening and I'd like to finish by proposing a toast to Gwynne. Ladies and gentlemen, to Gwynne!"

"To Gwynne!" the group responded as one, and the toast was enthusiastically drunk before talking continued.

When Marek turned back to Lana, he saw she had drifted over to Gwynne to congratulate her personally. He wasn't sure he had regained his calm disposition sufficiently to do the same.

Again, he felt at a bit of a loose end and was about to offer his apologies via Keith and quietly depart.

Just as he stood in two minds, Colette casually strolled up to him and said in her bright and breezy way, "Well, you're a bit of a surprise. Where on earth did you get that delicious dessert cake? Don't tell me you're a cook as well as a builder."

Marek wasn't sure what to say, after his earlier heads-up from Keith. Holding back the venom he felt towards her, he decided it wasn't the time and place for a showdown and simply responded saying "No. I didn't make the cake."

"Did you buy it? You must tell me where."

"It was made by someone I know," he reluctantly admitted.

"You know someone who can cook Polish desserts like that? You really are a mystery man."

In his current frame of mind, the brashness of Colette's comment was enough to tip him over the edge. He could restrain himself no longer and he erupted.

"Do you mind if I speak frankly? You seem to be able to make value judgements and generalisations about people with very few facts."

"I beg your pardon! What on earth brought this on? I didn't know the *makowiec* was such a sensitive subject. I'm sorry I mentioned it!"

"I'm not talking about the damned *makowiec*. What I'm referring to is you and Audrey jumping to conclusions about me and any imagined relationship I may or may not have with Gwynne. And then priming Huw to have a go at me. There is no relationship other than a business one between us and although I might wish there were, it's no business of yours."

"Don't get upset," countered Colette, ever ready to accept a challenge. "All we are trying to do is look out for Gwynne's well-being. I saw you talking to Keith, and I suspect he has said more than he should. We're just interested observers."

"Bullshit! More like undercover saboteurs muddying the waters! Any intentions I had, or have, regarding Gwynne, are between her and me. But now, thanks to your meddling, you have prejudiced any possible developments. You've put me in the category of *all men are bastards* and presumed, therefore, that Gwynne needs to steer clear of men, including me."

Getting more heated with every word, and through clenched teeth he added: "Well thanks very much. I might make an equally offensive generalisation that, women are interfering bit ... busybodies. Your attitude will certainly be noticed by Gwynne which means she'll be more likely to put up barriers every time I, or any other man, so much as looks at her."

Colette stood staring at Marek, obviously affronted, and responded in her own haughty manner, defending her position, purportedly on Gwynne's behalf. "I think you're overestimating our influence on Gwynne and underestimating her own self-determination. She will make her own decisions as she has shown by her achievements which Huw, in his fatherly pride, referred to just now."

"I can understand your family concerns and I'm sorry if I have crudely expressed my opinion. Let's say you're right and that I do like her and that I might think about asking her out. Now I find you and her parents running interference, supposedly for her wellbeing. On what evidence? We all have a background, which might include things of which we may not be proud, or want made public, which have made us sensitive, even defensive." The venom in his voice was evident. "Gwynne's past, whatever it is, is exactly that: past. That doesn't give you the right to use it to interfere and deprive her of determining her own future. You should all butt out! And you can tell Audrey and Huw what I've said. Goodnight!"

With that he made his way to the front door. As he walked past the kitchen, Gwynne caught sight of him and called out, "Oh Marek, you're not leaving, are you? We haven't had much chance to talk all evening, I've been so busy. I've been a terrible hostess."

Marek stopped and replied heatedly, "I don't know about that, but I do think you've got a defence committee which is a bit over-the-top in their supposed support."

"What on earth are you talking about?" Throwing the tea-towel onto the bench she followed him to the door.

He turned back to her. "Ask your family. Three of them have each had a word with me which I can make neither head nor tail of. Gwynne, I have to say this now; it may be my last opportunity. I know you have expressed some reservations on this matter, but here it is. I have been thinking about asking you out for coffee, or lunch, or dinner, whatever you prefer, for some time. If Merren is an issue, which I totally understand, I'm happy to have a picnic at the beach or wherever you like for the three of us. Your family has indicated I should back off. I generally watch my step and don't intrude where I'm not wanted, but now, I'm asking you: would you like us to do something along the lines I'm suggesting, or am I wasting my time?"

He saw the look of confusion on her face as she stepped back and stared at him, obviously bewildered, both by what he was asking and his comments about her family.

With a slight shake of her head to clear it and settle herself, she tentatively and uncomprehendingly replied, "I have no idea what you're saying about my family. What has my family got to do with this? I can't answer right now but can we discuss it another time?"

Not for the first time that evening, his thoughts were thrown into disarray. Her reaction was the complete opposite to the red-light signals he had received from most of her family.

Totally confused, he took her hands in his and said, "Ask them. And then ring me and we might arrange something."

He continued holding her hands fixing her with his penetrating eyes, today a gentian blue, for a long moment, then nodded, as if a decision had been agreed, and left her standing there.

The door clicked softly behind him.

Totally confused, Gwynne slowly turned to return to her guests. She did not see Keith who, standing at the end of the hallway with a very smug look on his face, had observed everything.

Keith eased back into the hallway and watched Gwynne slowly and distractedly make her way back to her remaining guests. Smugly, he noted the flushed, though puzzled look on her face, suggesting she was far from being angry or displeased.

He followed, making his way over to Colette and warily suggested: "You know what, Colette? I think the family might have overstepped its brief in looking after Gwynne. I think it's about time everyone pulled back on organising her life."

Colette's reaction was a characteristic retort. "What do you mean? You were talking to Marek about us, weren't you? All we're doing is looking after her as any family would."

"Gwynne is twenty-five; she's a big girl now. She's a mother for God's sake. Let her get on with her own life. So what if she stuffs up occasionally? We all do. If it happens, we'll be there to help. From what I can see, nothing that has happened to Gwynne reflects badly on her character or judgement. Merren is the product of a loving relationship which, given other circumstances, might have developed into a lasting one."

With a slight tone of concession Colette replied, "Well, all I can say is, the end justifies the means. Gwynne is in a very good position now, largely because of our help."

"Exactly!" Keith exclaimed. "Although I tend to think she herself has done most of the heavy lifting. Whatever … it's now time to step back. *You* would never have stood for the overbearing scrutiny you've imposed on Gwynne."

"Yes, I agree, but I never had a baby."

"No, you didn't, did you? That's another matter entirely. It's not the point here. It doesn't change the essence of what's been happening. What I'm telling you is that you, Audrey and Huw should pull back. Marek is a decent bloke. Under Audrey's supervision, you have handled Gwynne as if she was in danger of becoming one of her old departmental social work cases. You need to get real and let nature take its course … if you know what I mean. Let them work it out. And what's more, when you've thought about it, you'll realise you all owe him an apology."

"Finished?" Colette gave him baleful stare.

Feigning thoughtful consideration of the question, he answered, "Yes, I think so."

After further reflection he added: "For the time being anyway."

Audrey had played no direct role in the encounters at the party, but the family knew she had been pulling the strings. Later in the evening, the family sat around the table while Gwynne attended to Merren. Audrey took the opportunity to concede that, having heard Keith's opinion via Colette, she thought Keith might be partly right.

As jaws dropped in disbelief, and heads swung to stare in astonishment, she explained, "I only ever wanted to help Gwynne regain her confidence and that included her career prospects. We wanted to steer her in the right direction. This year has been a turning point for her."

No-one was game to say anything in calling out Audrey's blatant about face. Huw nodded his head in silent agreement, which was no surprise to anyone. Keith covered his smirk in a pretended yawn while Colette's face darkened, indicating incredulity at being made to feel part of a protection conspiracy which was disintegrating.

Audrey took advantage of the silence by shifting the focus to Merren. "The thing which has most contributed to my attitude is the way he treats Merren. She really likes him. That, plus the episode with the bear onesie after ..."

"What bear onesie?" interjected Colette.

"I'll explain later. It's a weird story," volunteered Audrey. "There's also the photo Gwynne took of him wearing the onesie, and the next day, when he had turned up at the house wearing it again."

"Well," mused Colette. "I'm not so sure. This's all new to me. It sounds like you've been holding out on the rest of us. He's a bit odd, is Marek. I'd like to know more about the kissing of the forefinger followed by the buzzing sound. What's that all about?"

Audrey, ignoring Colette's query, put an end to the matter by changing tack. "If Gwynne asks about anything anyone said to Marek tonight, let's just say very simply and sincerely, that the whole thing was an over-reaction, or a misunderstanding, on his part."

Keith shook his head at the enormity of Audrey's hypocritical backflip. He wondered whether she was afflicted with a sudden admission of wrong-doing but, based on experience, dismissed it as unlikely. No one was brave enough to point out to Audrey that much of the protection racket they had been running since Gwynne's pregnancy, was at her instigation.

No one mentioned an apology. *Case closed.*

When she returned, all conversation halted in obvious discomfort with vague looks everywhere and nowhere. Realising she had been the subject of conversation, she said, "What? What's going on? You're all looking very sheepish."

Colette, ever ready to fill a gap in a conversation, was first to regain her composure and said, "We were wondering what all the finger kissing and buzzing sound on contact, which Marek and Merren do, is all about."

Gwynne laughed, "Oh that. Marek told me all about it. It's a routine that is the result of him and his cousin watching bees around the flowers in their garden when they were kids. They'd seen the bees hover above a flower, gently settle on it as if to kiss it or play in its petals, then, with a buzz, fly off to another flower. It became their childhood greeting ritual."

She looked at the faces staring at her in amazement and added, "At their age they'd known nothing about pollen gathering and they'd developed the charade to imitate what they thought was happening. Rather imaginative of them don't you think?"

Keith leant back in his chair and, in mock innocence asked, "So, is this saga all something to do with the birds and the bees?"

A few days after the party, Gwynne decided she needed to clear the air with Marek. When he answered her call, she began her prepared statement. "Hello Marek, thanks for coming to the party and your cake and flowers. They were both lovely. I've been thinking seriously about a couple of things you said. The first thing is that I've spoken to Mum about your comment regarding a family defence committee acting on my behalf. Mum thinks you are imagining things. She hadn't the vaguest idea what I was referring to."

Marek waited in silence.

"Look, I know what my mother is capable of. You could well be right, but I told her in no uncertain terms that I was capable of looking after myself and she shouldn't interfere with my social and personal life.

"The second thing I want to say is, yes, I'd like to have coffee with you. How about Friday afternoon after work? Merren is being picked up from child-care by the mother of one of her friends and having a sleepover. I mean Merren's having a sleepover, not the mother. I mean yes, the mother is also having a sleepover, she lives there. You know what I mean. Say something! What do you say?"

There was a teasingly protracted pause while Marek carefully unscrambled what she'd said. "Being invited to a sleepover is a bit thought provoking. Sorry, did I say that out loud? Well, if not that, then I'd love to have coffee, but I can't on Friday. Well, I can, but it would have to be brief because I'm having dinner with my cousin, the one who made the *makowiec* dessert cake. She wants to know how the *makowiec* went down. I mean, how it was received; we know how it was devoured. Can I get a raincheck?"

Having worked up the courage to call him, Gwynne couldn't hide her disappointment and assured him another time would be fine.

Ten minutes later he her rang back. When she answered he said, "Gwynne, after our conversation I rang Helena. When I explained, she immediately insisted I invite you to dinner on Friday night. She was quite adamant. I've met most of your immediate family, what do you say to meeting mine? Bear in mind, there are only two of them."

Gwynne hesitated for a few seconds before answering, "Yes, if you think it will be alright. It's a bit of a leap from coffee to dinner with your family," she teased. "But now that you mention it, I am curious, even though I've only known you for a few months. What time? Do I meet you there?"

"No, you don't. It's my invitation and I'll come to your place. Six-thirty suit you? From there we'll get a taxi. I'm not a great drinker and neither of us can afford taking any risks. Alright?"

"It's a deal. Is it a dress-up event? Will you be wearing a dinner suit, or would you like to borrow my onesie again?"

"Is that you trying to be funny? It will be very casual, not fancy dress. If it's a nice evening, we can sit outside. Maybe you should bring a warm wrap but otherwise, wear whatever you think. For myself, if it's warm, I might just come in my *bare* skin! There's something to ponder."

"I'm looking forward to it." The ambiguity of her reply was not accidental. "See you Friday."

"Helena, I'd like you to meet Gwynne. Gwynne, this is my cousin Helena. Well, technically she's my second cousin but as she's currently my only living blood relative in Australia, I've elevated her to number one cousin."

"Oh Marek, you do go on sometimes. Very pleased to meet you Gwynne. You're most welcome. Marek has told me a little about you which, to be honest, is more than he has said about many of his friends."

"Thanks very much Helena. But I'm afraid you have a slight advantage because Marek has disclosed very little about any of his family. All I really know is that you baked that exquisite dessert cake for the party. I'm grateful for the opportunity to thank you personally and return the plate. There wasn't a crumb left on it."

"It was my pleasure. Come in and sit down." Helena fussed with a gushing commentary. "Alan's just getting changed and will be down in a few minutes. Come into the lounge room and sit. We're having a Polish meal tonight. I hope you like it. The entrée is pierogi and then a traditional Polish stew. Can I get you a drink? White or red wine? Something stronger? We have some Polish vodka if you'd like to try it?"

"White wine would be fine, thanks Helena."

Holding out a bottle of wine to Helena, Marek said, "Here's a contribution to the evening but it needs chilling."

"Thanks Marek, but you really didn't have to bring anything. We have Chardonnay or Semillon. Any preference? Alan will have beer so it's just for us."

"Chardonnay, please, would be lovely."

"Chardonnay it is. Beer for you Marek?"

When she returned from the kitchen, she passed him the wine bottle asking, "Will you do the honours? I'll be right back."

When Gwynne was alone with Marek she quietly commented, "Helena seems nice. You're lucky, I don't have any cousins at all."

Marek was hard pressed not to reply *thank God for that; the family you've got is quite enough.*

As he opened then poured the wine he said, "Helena and I are each other's only relatives in Australia. We've always had a bond. She does tend to fuss a bit when we get together."

When Alan walked in with his beer, Marek introduced him. Alan shook her hand and then looked at Marek. "Who's a dark horse then? You've kept this pretty quiet."

Both Marek's and Gwynne's faces reddened.

"Not really anything to keep quiet about," explained Marek. "Gwynne's my accountant. And friend. As I told you when I collected the *makowiec*, I did some additions to her house."

"You're welcome here Gwynne. Nice to see Marek travelling in such lovely company for a change." Alan sipped his beer and, ever the one with some quip, announced, "Here's to Gwynne and her additions. Or should I say, to Marek, and his addition? Cheers!"

Helena came in with a tray on which were a platter of pierogi, sour cream, small plates and napkins. "Help yourself everyone. There are more if needed. Don't be shy."

Gwynne tasted the pierogi, savouring the fragrance, "Mmm! These are scrumptious. I'd love to have the recipe."

"Thanks," said Helena, "I'll email it to Marek, and he can forward it. Is that okay?"

"What if I give you my email address now, and then we can cut out the middleman?"

"Fine by me," said Helena, giggling and pointing to the stunned look on Marek's face.

The conversation then moved on to an edited report on the *makowiec* and the party.

After about ten minutes, Helena excused herself to check on the meal. Gwynne stood and offered assistance and, although Helena said that there was no need, she added, "Come along anyway and we can chat while I serve."

128

Helena managed to keep up a running conversation about how she and Marek had grown up as children of immigrants. Gwynne was quite intrigued hearing bits of Marek's family history.

Curiosity aroused, she wanted to hear more. In a lull in the conversation, Gwynne excused herself, "Would you mind if I rang to check on my daughter? She's staying over at a friend's tonight."

"Of course not. Go ahead. This won't be ready for another five minutes. Oh, and the loo's just there on the left if you need it."

When she returned, she said, "I needn't have worried. She's having a wonderful time. Can I help with the serving? It smells delicious."

Helena carried an earthenware pot into the dining room and placed it on the table. Gwynne followed with plates and a bowl of warm bread rolls. Helena served the tantalising food, with its garlicky aroma, onto their plates saying, "Eat up everyone." It sounded more like a command than a suggestion.

A new round of exclamations of appreciation began. Helena was obliged to go through the recipe for Gwynne's sake. "It's simple really. It's called *bigos*: diced beef, vegetables and a few spices."

During the meal, various references to Marek's upbringing served to embarrass him and make Gwynne more curious.

She was especially intrigued by brief comments about how Marek's parents had bravely decided to leave their homeland, trekked across half of Europe, and eventually arrived in Carrington, Newcastle. She knew this wasn't the time, but she was keen to find out the whole story.

Under Helena's astute questioning, Gwynne revealed a little about herself and Merren. She was grateful that no specifics were asked for, but she realised that the time would come when those details might have to be made known.

In the silence that followed, Gwynne also realised that she would only have to make them known if her relationship with Marek developed. That was a thought she had been avoiding.

So far, that relationship had just drifted, albeit somewhere between their private and professional lives, into a friendly, but cautious, non-committal safety zone.

After the meal, Marek was able to share one piece of good news that he had received that day. "I've had a quote accepted for a major house renovation. The contract was signed today. It's brick with a terracotta tile roof, built in the late 1930s. Sort of a late federation-style bungalow. It's a biggish job and the owners want to retain the outside character but open up the interior. It'll keep me busy for a while. And it will be a good earner for me."

"Well done old son. Good luck with it," said Alan, voicing the general feeling. "I hope it goes well for you."

"Thanks. I got it through a schoolmate of mine who's also my solicitor. Who you know …"

Marek stopped when Gwynne suddenly interrupted as she stood saying, "Will you excuse me while I just make a visit?"

By eleven o'clock, it was obvious that the end of the working week was catching up on everyone. As Marek and Gwynne prepared to say goodnight, Gwynne again went off to the toilet. Marek took out his phone and rang for a taxi.

Alan had noticed Marek's glance at Gwynne and the concentrated look that followed. After a few moments he asked, "Is she just a date for tonight, or someone special? She looks like a good-un to me."

Marek was explaining a little of how they first met when Gwynne returned. He smiled at her and, raising an eyebrow, tapped his wristwatch, feeling inordinately pleased with the night.

They chatted for a few minutes until they heard the beep of the taxi.

As they shuffled their way to the door and made their goodbyes, he shook Alan's hand. As he did so, he held the grip and pulled Alan in closer and said, "She's better than a good-un".

He placed his hand lightly on Gwynne's back as he ushered her to the door.

Gwynne took one step then stopped and turned to Helena and gave her a hug and a kiss. "It's been a lovely night and thanks again for the beautiful food. And don't forget that recipe. Thank you too Alan. It's been nice meeting you."

"It was our pleasure. We must do it again sometime." He replied with a wink at Marek.

"Oh yes. The sooner the better." Helena added.

Again, a horn beeped and Marek kissed Helena goodnight, "Thanks for what you've done tonight. I, *we*, really appreciate it. It's been lovely."

Once seated in the taxi, Marek asked, "Are you feeling alright? You seem a bit bothered or something."

"I'm fine. Nothing for you to worry about."

The taxi ride home was unexpectedly subdued with each of them keeping their thoughts to themselves.

The evening wasn't ending the way he had expected and, to break the silence, he asked, "Are you sure you're alright? You're very quiet."

Gwynne dismissed the comment with a nod and a smile. "Fine thanks. It was lovely night. It was a pleasure to meet them. Thanks for arranging it."

When the taxi pulled up at Gwynne's place, they made their way to the front door. Gwynne unlocked it, stepped over the threshold, and half-heartedly turned and asked Marek if he would like coffee.

Marek took one step inside and wrapped his arms around her. "No, thanks. But I'd like to say how much I've enjoyed the evening. I'm so glad you came."

"I enjoyed it too. They're very nice. I can see the bond you have with Helena. I can't recall an evening in recent times which has been so relaxing. Thank you again. It was much nicer than coffee in a café."

Marek prevented another word passing her lips by drawing her to him and kissing her. The embrace continued with Marek's hand gradually moving lower on Gwynne's back in a gentle circular motion. It was a kiss of passionate release for Marek and as Gwynne responded, they held the moment until they were both breathless.

Suddenly, despite the positive physical reaction to what was happening, Gwynne abruptly stopped and removed his hand and said, "Marek, it has been a wonderful evening but it's time to say goodnight. I'll be in contact but for now … it's goodnight."

Marek felt deflated and held Gwynne at arm's length wondering why she suddenly seemed to be putting him off. Had he over-played his hand? He realised it was her call and he could only nod and say he looked forward to hearing from her soon.

Seeing his disappointment, she paused, tilted her head forward to rest her forehead briefly on his shoulder and again whispered, "Goodnight".

After a moment they looked at each other, resignation evident on both their faces and, without saying a word, both realised they had blurred the line in their relationship. He stepped back from Gwynne, looked into her eyes and said, "Goodnight, and thank you".

He turned and walked to his truck.

Marek only ever worked on weekends when the job demanded it; when progress was delayed by wet weather; when tradesmen or tradeswomen required work done to meet their own strict schedule; or, when he wanted to simply get on with a job.

The reason he was working this Saturday didn't fit any of those. He was working to keep busy, to take his mind off things, to distract himself from the over-riding emotion of frustration with the way the previous night had ended at Gwynne's front door.

He needed something to focus on. Had he misread the situation? He hadn't planned anything for the night but his emotions on their return had suddenly overflowed. Now he felt embarrassed, disappointed with himself. And this home renovation was just the thing. Stripping out the old kitchen would keep him busy for a day or so. Ripping out bits of timber and lining was therapeutic.

By mid-afternoon he'd done enough. He had to stop for some groceries on the way home and wasn't looking forward to a long night alone with his thoughts. He chuckled quietly as he realised his thoughts were erratic, or a word which sounded very similar: one with an 'o' in the middle.

That evening he rang Helena just to thank her again and hear a friendly voice. When she asked him how Gwynne was, he told her in abrupt terms, "I don't know. I expect she's fine".

Helena's Polish intuition pinged, and she not-so-subtly suggested, "It would be nice if you rang her to ask. I thought she seemed a little jaded towards the end of the evening. Was she worried about her daughter? Or tired, do you think?"

"I don't know, possibly. On the way home I asked her how she was and what she thought of the evening. She said she was fine, the evening was very nice, but not much more. I didn't think anything of it at the time."

"Oh well, it was probably nothing. Alan and I enjoyed last night too. We must get together again soon. Don't work too hard, and don't forget to ring Gwynne. Keep in touch. Bye!"

"Yes, got all that. I'll ring her later. It's got me thinking."

Gideon Owen Davis
Sydney, New South Wales
1840
III

As the cart lurched to a halt in the grounds of the Ebenezer mission house, Owen had to admit that he had seen a lot worse in the mining villages around Pengam, his home village. Threlkeld led him to a small partitioned-off area at the back of a barn saying, "This will have to do for the while. There's little space in the house. We are a large family."

Owen was aware that Threlkeld's first wife had died before coming to New South Wales, and he had eventually remarried the daughter of Thomas Arndell, the magistrate in Windsor on the Hawkesbury River who had been instrumental in having a chapel built which was named 'Ebenezer'. He had since added to his family. He suspected Threlkeld wanted him kept at a distance until they knew each other better.

From what he could observe, Threlkeld divided his energies between his coal interests and the remnants of the mission. Threlkeld believed that coal mining was a way to ensure the financial wellbeing of his family as well as providing funds for the support for the remnants of the Awabakal tribe who drifted into the declining Ebenezer mission. Owen's concern was that coal mining was foremost in Threlkeld's mind whereas his own goal was fixed on missionary work.

A few days later, he raised the topic of mission work again with Threlkeld. What he was told, in a tone of dour acceptance bordering on defeat, was that the number of Aborigines had dwindled to less than twenty, which barely justified the existence of the mission in its original form." Of those twenty, slightly more than half reside here permanently; mainly the very old and the very young."

Slowly shaking his head in the inevitability of the course of events he added, "Probably because they are less able to be continually on the move to their traditional hunting grounds, which are constantly diminishing because of the violence directed at them."

Also dwindling was the financial support he had received from the Missionary Society. Owen was dismayed, but understood, that Threlkeld's attitudes were the result of dealing with the deaths of so many Aborigines from problems inflicted on them by white men, notably alcohol and numerous diseases including measles and smallpox.

Threlkeld explained another problem concerning some of the convicts, whether assigned or emancipated, who harboured resentment against authority and turned a blind eye to the bushrangers' activities.

Threlkeld especially blamed both groups, both bushrangers and convicts, for their 'immoral practices', as he euphemistically referred to them, especially their often-violent practices in luring and abducting Aboriginal womenand very young girls. He had been embarrassed to admit that the abuses were mostly perpetrated by supposedly Christian white men over the last sixty years.

He concluded saying, "The decision to abolish the system of transportation is most welcome in my opinion."

Adding to the difficulties being faced was the shocking news that a gang of bushrangers had invaded the homes of settlers as close as Newport, a developing estate near Dora Creek. It was from there, within a struggling community, that coal and other goods were loaded onto barges to be floated across the lake and over the bar in the channel to larger ships waiting near the entrance at Reid's Mistake.

He knew the story of a local Maitland police magistrate, Edward Denny Day, who had tracked down and captured the perpetrators of a massacre at Myall Creek over one hundred and fifty miles north, but that seemed too far away to worry the mission and its residents. Newport was less than twelve miles away. He was only slightly comforted by the knowledge that magistrate Day was again hunting down a local Lake Macquarie gang led by Edward Marshall and John Davis. Known as The Jewboy Gang, they had reportedly fled to the north-west to the less-populated Upper Hunter region after murdering one man and robbing farms and homesteads of much-needed supplies including money, jewellery, food, tools, weapons and even clothing.

The journey by horse-drawn cart to Threlkeld's mine was often one whereby, conversations with Threlkeld covered a wide range of subjects on the problems keeping the mission operating. Owen gained an understanding of the need for the mine to support the mission.

On one occasion, Threlkeld explained that he had begun to understand the commercial value of mining coal when, fifteen years previously, he had witnessed the construction of a new coal loading wharf in Newcastle, known in its early years as Coal River. He had been granted permission to mine coal and soon realised its financial benefit to his mission.

Regrettably, after almost fifteen years, except for a very small number, the Aborigines showed no interest in Christian values and practices. They sought only the necessities of life: shelter, clothing and food, all of which had traditionally been provided within their own spiritual tribal lands. For most of the women, children and older men, protection from white men was their main reason for attending the mission.

Almost as if voicing his private thoughts, Threlkeld bemoaned the fact that, "The Awabakal people have no spiritual understanding of a God as a loving divine being, as our faith tells us, or of a life in heaven after death. They have been robbed of their hunting grounds, driven from their traditional lands by force of arms or trickery and when arrested, afforded little protection by British law because, as unbaptised non-Christians, they are not permitted to swear an oath on a bible in court, and their testimony is therefore unacceptable."

He recounted how he was frequently called upon to offer his skills as an interpreter, fighting against the injustices dealt them by Christian white people. He'd spent much time studying the Awabakal language in order to translate the gospels so he could preach to them in their own language. He concluded saying, "I fear the plight of the Aborigines is on a terrible decline to extinction in this area".

As the days passed, Owen confirmed that very few Aborigines visited the mission for long periods, and he felt his own sense of purpose was waning. He observed those natives who did make an appearance were generally greeted warmly by the residents.

There was much talking and laughing accompanied by brushing each other's shoulders and arms, accompanied by words of welcome. Shaking hands seemed unfamiliar to them.

Attempts within the mission to provide some basic education, mainly for boys, stumbled along at an irregular pace. This was undoubtedly due as much to Threlkeld's frequent absences on trips to Sydney on legal and mining business, as a lack of genuine interest from the adults and boys themselves. Some of the women continued to fulfil domestic tasks in exchange for the safety and protection the mission offered.

One young girl with a shy but happy nature, who answered to the name of Lily, seemed particularly willing and capable, carrying out her allotted tasks with an aptitude for learning greater than any of the others. Indeed, it was obvious she was held in high regard by her people, including Threlkeld, and especially his daughters, who taught her sewing and other domestic skills.

Initially, Owen's work was tending to stock and extensive farming activities around the mission, but within a few months he was increasingly taken to the mine-site. Here, because of his Welsh mining background, he was employed as a supervisor. Threlkeld had been forced to take legal action against the monopoly on coal mining held by the Australian Agricultural Company, and although he had won the right to mine coal, he had restrictions placed on who he could employ. No convicts could be assigned for his mining activities and so he had to pay for workers. Coal mining was a laborious and costly enterprise.

Owen's responsibilities there increased in proportion to Threlkeld's absences. Although Threlkeld was always passionately involved in promoting his religious principles in support of Evangelical Protestantism, Owen learned that there were mounting disputes and opposition from other religions within the colony. He could only justify Threlkeld's mining operations by accepting it as a necessary means of support for the mission. His reasoning allowed him to believe that at least, in part, he was being true to his own calling.

Weeks led to months of steady decline in both the mission and mining. Owen learned the mine was failing due to difficulties with labourers and transportation on both land and sea. Due to so many ships dumping their ballast near the entrance to the lake, siltation within the channel was worsening, despite Threlkeld having gone into debt to purchase shallow draft ships. It was becoming obvious that the weight of his debts and his declining health had taken their toll.

A further impediment to Owen's vocational ideals were the intermittent outbreaks of lawlessness committed by thieves, bushrangers, escaped and ex-convicts and, to an unknown extent, Aborigines. The latter were thought to be employed by white outlaws, to steal food, clothing, equipment and livestock, and often paid with alcohol. Police officers were stationed at Newcastle, Maitland and Brisbane Water, although around Lake Macquarie, patrols by civilian Mounted Police, known as the Road Patrol, were less frequent.

It was with dismay that, within a year of his arrival, he learned that the mine, ships, house and all Threlkeld's property were to be sold. Threlkeld accepted an appointment in Sydney and was preparing to abandon the mission. Owen was left to decide his own future. What was to happen to the few remaining Aborigines who frequented the mission he did not know. The Awabakal tribe or Pambalong clan to which they belonged – he was never sure which, had almost ceased to exist in the area.

He wondered especially about the women and children, but they kept their intentions to themselves. Most spoke some English and only Lily spoke good English, although she was only heard to do so when it suited her. With her intelligence, willing smile, and good nature, she seemed to pop up at unexpected times and places, offering a glimmer of hope for herself and the future.

On one occasion when Lily had been particularly helpful, tending the kitchen garden, he asked, "How did you come to be here?"

Lily hung her head, avoiding eye contact, and whispered, "Mother, father … sorry business. Father help Mr Threlkeld learn our language. Help with police problems in court."

"Where will you go if the mission closes? How will you survive?"

Lily just smiled and, in a sweeping gesture towards the lake, said, "Awaba". She then moved her arm in a wider arc indicating the surrounding lands. She nodded slowly, saying, in a softer voice, "Our place. Awabakal people. Here."

Threlkeld's feuds with bigger and more established coal mining companies, had brought the Ebenezer mine to wider attention, essentially for its unrealised commercial potential, if investment could be procured. That interest included the workers and miners Threlkeld employed, and especially Owen, who came to the notice of other mining officials for his hard work and application to his duties.

Throughout the decline, Threlkeld himself was understandably dejected, but he tried to explain to Owen that he felt a new chapter in his own life was emerging with his call back to Sydney. On the day of his departure, he encouraged Owen to take up the evangelical role he had been unable to complete and thanked him for his help in befriending and caring for the Aborigines. "To help in any venture you undertake, the horse and cart are now yours. It may assist you in finding work." He then handed Owen a small package wrapped in coarse brown paper. "This too may be a reminder of the work God has called upon us to perform." They shook hands and Threlkeld trudged away, apparently resigned to whatever Providence had in store.

It was a life-changing moment and reminded Owen of how Mr Lewis had referred to the words of poet, William Cowper, about how God moves in mysterious ways. Feeling somewhat abandoned. Owen watched as the man who had been a major force in his decision to come to New South Wales, departed, leaving Ebenezer, and him, to their respective fates. He walked back to his lodgings in the barn where he opened the package. In it was a small wooden cross with both their initials carved into the crossbar.

Within days, Owen was approached by a nearby mine operator and offered work in Minmi, a mining village about ten miles north of Ebenezer. The mine was in the early stage of development, but the owner was hopeful of its future. A few days later, one of the older women told him the name Minmi came from an Awabakal word meaning 'place of the giant lily'. He was bemused by the connection of the plant with its tall striking red flower with Lily, the young girl at the Ebenezer mission. The offer of work was of little interest, but without Threlkeld to guide him after the closure he realised he had to make further enquiries to secure his future, by visiting the Minmi workings.

The horse and cart Threlkeld had given him provided the means to complete the journey. On doing so, he found, to his surprise and satisfaction, the village had a thriving Welsh Congregational Church. After the disappointment and loss experienced at Ebenezer, the attraction of a community focused on common Christian values and living among those of familiar heritage was too enticing. He accepted work in a similar capacity to that in which he had been employed at Ebenezer.

When Marek's phone rang, he wasn't surprised. He was expecting a call from Helena. The surprise was that instead of hearing *her* voice, he heard a woman's voice, speaking broken English, but with a strong accent he instantly recognised as Polish.

Hesitantly, the voice asked, "Is that Marek Benningowicz?"

Just as tentative at hearing the family's Polish surname, he answered, "Yes, this is Marek Benning speaking".

The voice identified herself saying, "My name is Ana Wójcik. I'm the daughter of a close friend of Milosz Benningowicz here in Zakopane. He is your father, yes?"

Marek immediately felt a knot of fear developing, and rapidly expand in the pit of his stomach. "Yes, he's my father. What's happened?"

"Marek, I have some bad news. I'm sorry to tell you your father has had a heart attack and is in intensive care in the Zakopane hospital. He is in a coma. The doctors are doing everything they can."

The knot in his stomach expanded to fill his chest, affecting his breathing. He was stunned to numbness and barely heard her continued apologies for delivering the news. He didn't know what to say. Useless questions of when, how and where raced through his mind. Bewildered by an avalanche of thoughts he stammered out, "Should I come to Zakopane?"

"I can't answer that," she said, "But I can say that the doctors said it was a very severe heart attack. Perhaps you should think about it." She then gave him her phone number and explained that her mother spoke very little English. As an afterthought she gave him the number for the hospital. She reminded him of the ten-hour time difference between Poland and Australia if he was going to make contact.

He thanked her for ringing, but the irony of offering thanks for such bad news was stark. He ended the call, overwhelmed by the maelstrom of trying to decide what to do. Options sped through his mind: wait for further news? Ring the hospital and confirm what he had been told? Or try to book a flight to Poland?

The hospital was the obvious first call to get the latest information. He looked at the number for a few moments before he found the courage and the words to ring. In his nervous state it took three attempts to enter the plus sign and the twelve-digit number. Much to the despair of his parents, his Polish was good but not entirely fluent, especially at critical moments. When the call was answered he identified himself and said, "I'm ringing to find out if you have a patient named Milosz Benningowicz."

When asked by the woman if he was a relative, his voice cracked as he choked out the words, "I'm his son".

The woman confirmed that a Milosz Benningowicz had been admitted and was in the cardiac intensive care unit. He asked if there was someone who could give him a report on his condition.

A man's voice eventually came on the line. He identified himself as one of the specialist cardiac team doctors. "Your father has had a serious heart attack and is in an induced coma. The next twelve hours will tell us more. You should ring back tomorrow morning."

Marek checked his watch and calculated when he could ring. He shakily thanked the doctor and gave him his own contact details and ended the call.

After half an hour, he realised he had to ring Helena. Her quavering voice told him how shocked she was. "Oh Marek, I'm so sorry. What will you do? Will you go back to Zakopane?"

"I think I'll have to. I can't stay here doing nothing, leaving him on his own. I'll start checking flights and connections to Kraków. I'll hire a car and drive to Zakopane. I'll look up flight schedules tonight and let you know what I decide tomorrow after I've rung the hospital. It's going to be a long nervous wait."

"Would you like me to come over? Have you eaten? Have you told Gwynne?"

"Helena, I've hardly had time to absorb it. I'm not hungry and no, I haven't spoken to Gwynne. I don't know what I would say to her."

"From what I heard and saw, she would want to know. Ring her. Tell her. She cares."

"Alright, I'll think of something. I'll call you tomorrow. Thanks, Helena."

Marek put his phone down and looked about the house in which he had been brought up. Everything reminded him of his parents: every room, every piece of furniture; everything, not just the framed photographs, but the small decorative objects accumulated over the years. He became conscious of even the smell. Echoes of his parents' voices hung in the air. Questions born of fear bore down on him.

Was this to be the end? Was it going to sever the physical living link between Marek and his parents? Was the family bond which defined his upbringing about to be irretrievably lost?

He sat down at his computer and started the process of checking flights and times from Sydney to Kraków.

Whichever he chose, it would be a long flight. He identified one which had the least stopover time in Frankfurt for the final link to Kraków. It would be almost twenty-eight hours in total plus a couple of hours' driving to Zakopane.

He shuddered at the thought but knew there was no other choice.

It was Saturday evening in Australia, so it was mid-morning in Poland. He looked again at the flight times on the screen and calculated it would be Tuesday morning at the earliest before he could arrive in Zakopane.

Struggling to cope with the calamity, he completed the flight booking process. He didn't quibble over the cost and afterwards, was surprised at how little it concerned him, even though it would markedly reduce his bank balance.

He then booked a hire car from Kraków airport. When he had finished the bookings, he reflected on how ridiculously easy the internet made such momentous arrangements, even as his father's life hung by a thread.

He decided to do as Helena had said and, without knowing where he was going to start the conversation, rang Gwynne. Unexpectedly, the sound of her voice was a lifeline he wanted to cling to. He hesitated before speaking, in which time Gwynne asked, "Marek, are you there?"

"Yes," he said, "I'm here. I'm ringing to ask how you are after Friday night. You seemed to end the night on a downbeat … or something."

"Marek, it was nothing spectacular, just my body doing its thing. I'm not used to dealing with it with people I barely know, and I wasn't sure what to say to you. It's good of you to ring anyway. It was a lovely night. You don't sound yourself. Is everything okay?"

"Actually, no. It's not. I've just found out my father has had a heart attack and is in an intensive care unit in Zakopane. I've rung and spoken to a doctor, and he said the next twelve hours are critical and that I should ring then."

"Oh Marek, that's terrible. I'm so sorry. Oh, you must feel dreadful. Have you told Helena?"

"Yes, I've just finished telling her, and yes to the other. I've booked a flight to go there. I'm leaving tomorrow evening."

"Marek, why don't you come over and have supper with us. We had home-made pizza and there's plenty left over. It'll help pass the time for you. I'm sure you don't want to be on your own at a time like this."

Marek hesitated, thinking how poor company he would be, especially with Merren around. Then he heard Gwynne's voice say, "Just do it. Get yourself over here. What else are you going to do?"

Ignoring whether he should inflict himself on anyone in his present state, he felt a small wave of relief flow over him at having something practical to do. He couldn't face being alone all night. "Alright. I'll clean up and see you in about half an hour."

Gwynne opened the door to Marek and immediately reached out to him, giving him a brief self-conscious hug. Merren, already in her pyjamas, and knowing nothing of the reason behind the unexpected visit, skipped around them with excitement at seeing him. Gwynne gently told Merren to get into bed and that she would come and tuck her in shortly. Merren pulled a face showing her dismay at missing out on Marek's attention but reluctantly obeyed, as if sensing something serious was underway.

As soon as she had gone, Gwynne reached for both of Marek's hands and said again how sorry she was. Leading him by an arm she took him to the dining-room and they sat, momentarily lost for words.

Both then started talking at once, each almost echoing the words of the other, "I'm sorry about Friday night, I ..."

Marek pressed on saying, "You have nothing to be sorry about. I'm sorry! I started getting a bit ahead of myself."

"You don't have to apologise. In a way I was flattered, but the circumstances were not quite right."

"And now this has happened. My flight leaves tomorrow night. I'll leave home around three o'clock. I must go ... I've got to be there ... to see him."

"Of course you do. Family comes first."

"Yes, it does, doesn't it?" The blunt response more than suggested it applied to both their families.

Gwynne went into the kitchen to reheat the pizza. Marek drifted after her, watching, unable to hang onto a clear line of thought. The words wouldn't come. He appreciated the fact that he was able to share a moment with Gwynne without expectations from either of them. Time's pendulum seemed to have been slowed by an unbearable, unmovable weight.

When Gwynne served the pizza, Marek only picked at a wedge; his appetite had fled from the moment he had first heard the news. Now he tried to focus his mind on his immediate course of action: packing, getting to the airport, the flight itself and the land of his parents' birth: Poland. A country he'd never seen which had framed and influenced so much of his upbringing but which, at the same time, was only vicariously familiar to him

They chatted about Helena's dinner party, the food and Alan's blokey comments. When the conversation stalled, although grateful to be in Gwynne's company, he realised he had less than twenty-four hours to deal with all the practicalities ahead.

He stood, obviously uneasy, saying, "Thanks for the supper. I'm sorry I'm such poor company. I need to get home and organise a few things. I'll have to make some phone calls to Darren and some customers in the morning. Sorry."

"Don't apologise. I understand – even though I can only imagine what you're going through. Drive carefully, and no rash decisions. Let me know how you're getting on whenever you can."

Gwynne had forgotten to tuck in Merren and kiss her goodnight and as she was walking Marek to the door, Merren appeared next to them. With a tone of bitter complaint she said, "Mummy, you didn't come!"

Gwynne picked her up to console her and then said, "Marek must go away for a little while. Say goodbye to him and I'll tuck you in in a moment."

Instead of kissing her fingertip in their farewell gesture, she held out both arms to Marek and Gwynne passed her to him. He was very touched by the gesture and gave her a hug and a kiss on her head.

Glancing at Gwynne, then looking at Merren, he said, "I'll miss you, Missy Merren. See you when I get back. Be good for your mum."

When he passed her back to Gwynne, he rested his hands lightly on a shoulder of each of them. "Thank you both." With a look of resignation, he turned and walked out the door. Before it closed behind him, he stopped and said, "I'll let you and Helena know my arrangements whenever I can, by phone, text or email."

The next morning, after a restless night in which sleep and his imagination vied with each other, he tidied the house and packed his bag. Just before he left, he rang the hospital. The news was inconclusive. His father was still in a coma. An electrocardiograph had been done and the heart specialists were developing a treatment plan. Despite the lack of any good news, Marek was encouraged by their professionalism.

Before the doctor could hang up Marek told him, "I've booked a flight and I'm scheduled to arrive Tuesday. You've got my number and you can leave a message or contact my cousin on this number." He then gave Helena's phone number and requested that if there was an emergency, and he was out of contact, she be kept informed.

He rang Helena and told her of his arrangements, gave her the number of the hospital and said, "If the hospital calls while I'm out of contact, can you please forward any messages to me."

Through stifled sobs he heard her say, "Of course. I'm so sorry Marek. Do look after yourself. We'll be thinking of you every moment. I hope everything works out well. Safe travelling, cousin."

16

The flight to Kraków was via Frankfurt with a ninety-minute stopover. It was the best he could have hoped for. From Frankfurt he called the hospital and was told there was no change in his father's condition. He sent a text to Helena advising her and filled in the remaining time pacing the terminal until his flight was announced.

The car hire in Kraków was a replica of the same clerical exercise anywhere he'd been, although, in completing the paperwork, he felt he had just about signed his life away. He exchanged some Australian dollars for Polish zloty and then phoned Ana Wójcik.

"Ana? This is Marek Benning … owicz. Have you heard anything more?"

"*Cześć* Marek. I mean, hello. No, we haven't heard anything more than that he is being closely monitored. My mother is very upset."

"I'll be leaving Kraków soon. You know better than I how long it will take to arrive. I'll go straight to the hospital. Can you recommend a place to stay?"

"You should stay in your *Tata's* apartment." She had then told him the address of his father's flat. "I'll put the key in the meter-box to the left of the door. I'll try to visit after work. Let me know if you need anything."

"That's very kind of you. See you later then. Goodbye."

"Tak, d*o zobaczenia później*, Marek. Sorry, yes, see you sometime this afternoon."

As he neared Zakopane, he stopped to look at the map the car hire firm had supplied. A blue cross marking the location of the hospital was quite clear but the same couldn't be said for the local road system. It was going to be a case of try it and see. Before recommencing his journey, recalling Gwynne's advice, he gripped the wheel with two hands, closed his eyes and took several deep breaths to calm his nerves and focus on arriving safely.

After surprisingly few delays, he arrived at the hospital and headed for the enquiries desk. He was directed to the cardiac unit where he was asked to wait for the specialist to speak to him.

Twenty minutes later, pristinely dressed in a white lab-coat, a doctor approached him. "Marek Benningowicz? I am Doctor Krystyna Danek. I am one of the cardiac team treating your father. His condition has deteriorated slightly but we continue to do everything we can. You should prepare yourself. I am sorry to have to tell you this. I'll take you to him now for a brief visit."

Daunted by her brusque manner, his mind in turmoil, he tried to think of questions he should ask. He was barely able to hold back the tears at seeing the man who had raised him looking so frail. His chest barely rising for each breath. Adding to the shock was the range of equipment monitoring his condition.

He blinked his stinging eyes as he took his *Tata's* hand and held it. Half-formed thoughts bubbled from his lips. "Hello *Tata,* it's me, Marek. Ana Wójcik rang me, and I got here as quickly as I could. She suggested I stay in your apartment. I hope you don't mind. I promise I won't make a mess. Everything back in Australia is fine. I've missed you a lot, especially over the last few weeks. I'll tell you about it when you're better and return home."

Sitting there, he watched the man he thought invincible, once strong, tall; the staunch and devoted family stalwart; caretaker and provider, now struggling for breath. He could see him more clearly in his mind than in reality, as tears blurred his vision and trickled down his cheeks. He knew he was babbling but he felt compelled to speak. He had to tell his *Tata* how much he loved him and appreciated what he and his mother had done to provide for the family.

After a few minutes the doctor's pager sounded, and a nurse's aide came in. She spoke quickly to the doctor who apologised to Marek saying, "I'm sorry, I'm needed elsewhere. Don't stay too long," and left the room.

The aide offered to get him a cup of coffee which he accepted, and she hurried away. Within minutes she returned. As he sipped the coffee she explained, "Your father is being closely monitored. The doctors will keep you informed. Dr Danek will see you on your way out."

After an hour without any sign of change, he found Dr Danek at the nurses' station and asked what was to happen.

"The cardiac team will make an assessment first thing tomorrow morning and should be able to give some information after ten o'clock. Now, if you'll excuse me, I have much to do."

He knew he needed to shower, change, and get something to eat before returning to be with his father, but first he had to find his father's flat. He phoned Ana to let her know he was heading to the flat. Ana apologised for not being able to visit him because her mother was so upset and needed her at home. With her instructions and his map, he found the flat and the key.

After showering and unpacking, he helped himself to a cheese and salami sandwich before returning to the hospital. Despite the jetlag and sitting with his father until well after midnight, his sleep was restless. Early the next morning, he rose and tried to organise himself in his unfamiliar surroundings. He wasn't hungry and it was too early for the cardiac team to have completed their assessment.

He took the opportunity to update Darren with a text message. He knew Darren and his father had hit it off, mostly because they both shared different perspectives on the wellbeing of himself: the son and apprentice. He kept it simple: *Darren, I've arrived in Poland. Dad has had a serious heart attack and remains in a coma. Will keep in touch with any developments.*

He plugged his phone in to charge before setting off on a walk around the town where his parents grew up. Just to fill in time. He followed a main road named after Henryka Sienkiewicza, undoubtedly someone famous, he thought. His father would have known but in any event, he felt inclined to follow it.

After walking along the road for only a few minutes, as if being led by an unseen guiding hand, his attention was taken by a tourist advice sign referring to Josepha Conrada Korzeniowskiego: Joseph Conrad, a more famous and better-known writer than any of the six Polish Nobel laureates for Literature.

This time he felt a shiver, due entirely to his recollection of how his *Tata* had constantly urged him to read Conrad's books.

In what he recalled at the time as one of his father's rants, he remembered him claiming Conrad told the world that, despite the overwhelming and humiliating forces of its neighbours, *Poland had preserved its sanity.*

Currently Marek wasn't entirely convinced about his own sanity, let alone Poland's.

The sign directed him to a small well-kept reserve or *Skwer*, with a stream trickling through it. He followed the path and there, to his surprise and delight, was a dedication plaque acknowledging that Joseph Conrad had briefly lived in Zakopane.

He took some pleasure in thinking his father would be content to know Marek had found a tenuous link to the great writer. He looked around. It was another unnerving experience which generated a cold shiver up the length of his spine to the hair at the back of his head. He immediately thought again of his mother's saying: *A goose has walked over my grave.*

He decided to take a photo on his phone and began searching his pockets before remembering he had left it behind to charge. After staring at the plaque for a few moments he checked his watch: 7:35am.

That action broke his train of thought and, shaking his head to refocus on what he was going to be faced with when he spoke to the cardiac team. He needed to get back to his father's apartment.

Breakfast wasn't a consideration until he smelt, and then saw, a bakery. He bought a couple of fresh bread rolls, one of which, after inhaling the aroma, he ate as he walked.

Once back in his father's flat he checked his phone and saw he had missed a call. The voice mail message asked him to ring the hospital. Marek's hands trembled to such an extent he almost dropped the phone. The message asked him to come to the hospital as soon as he could. There was no further information. As he showered and dressed, the knot in the pit of his stomach hardened. He phoned Ana to let her know what he was doing. She told him she would visit him at the hospital, if she could get away from work, or later at the flat when she'd finished.

He drove to the hospital in a state of mind something close to panic. The feeling of dread increased the nearer he got. He almost choked on the lump in his throat as he blinked back tears.

On arrival he was asked to wait in a sparsely furnished room and was told the doctor would see him as soon as he was free. Fifteen minutes later a doctor appeared.

"Marek Benningowicz? I apologise for the delay. Please sit down." He then delivered the wrenching news: "Marek, I am sorry to say your father passed away in his sleep earlier this morning without regaining consciousness. He was not in pain. His passing was peaceful. I am very sorry for your loss."

Marek gasped and hung his head as tears welled and spilt down his cheeks. He covered his face with both hands, trying to hide them as the gut-wrenching shock overwhelmed him.

The doctor placed his hand on Marek's shoulder saying, "Please wait here and a counsellor will come and assist you. She will advise you of all necessary procedures. Once again, our condolences to you and your family."

What family? he thought in his misery.

No *matka* and now, no *tata*.

He sat hanging his head. Still the tears flowed. The sense of abandonment was excruciating. He wanted to call out to his *Tata* as if doing so would bring him back. He couldn't think of anything other than a sense of separation and loss. He would never see him, hear him, speak to or touch him, ever again. He was gone, just as his mother was gone.

When the counsellor arrived, she explained the procedure, but he could only take in some of what she said. The only thing he absorbed was that the documentation would be available after 5:00pm. *Is that what we are reduced to? Scraps of paper signifying the end of life!*

"Can I see him please?"

"Certainly, I'll take you to him. This way; follow me please."

His legs shook as he stood and followed her to a room, almost entirely bare, except for a hospital bed with the outline of a body covered by a sheet.

When she drew back the sheet, Marek looked down at his *tata* through a fresh flow of tears. He bent down and kissed him on his forehead. Words choked in his throat.

He brushed his hand over his father's cheek, barely stifling a shudder at its unnatural coldness and lack of response. He smoothed a stray lock of his hair back into place. *When did it turn grey?*

He recalled the physical contact from his childhood and noted how different this was. He heard his father's voice as clearly as if they were in their kitchen back home, and ached to see or hear some response, to feel the weight of his father's hand on his shoulder; even feel the playful way he used to sneakily tickle his ear while looking the other way and then deny having done so.

When he regained some self-control, he nodded to the counsellor who repositioned the sheet. It seemed to signify the penultimate stage in the passing of the man he had most loved in the world.

"Is there anyone you would like to contact?" the counsellor asked.

"No, I'm an only child. Well, yes, I have a cousin in Krakow and another back home," he added.

Marek then listened while the counsellor repeated the order of formal events. He could barely absorb the details, but he understood most of the basics. "We'll contact you later today when you can collect the formal paperwork. In the meantime, you should speak to a funeral director."

These matters were enough to bring his mind back into the present. Marek had no idea where to go or who to speak to. He thought of Ana and realised that she should be told and hopefully, advise him.

Slowly and painfully, he focused on who to contact and what to say. Inexplicably, the person who came to mind was Gwynne, but a moment's thought told him Helena should be first.

When he rang, neither his voice nor hands were steady. All he could repeat were the basic facts as they had been told to him. "He's gone. Peacefully in his sleep. No suffering."

He heard Helena's voice break as she tearfully offered her and Alan's sympathy. He could only listen. He was not capable of saying more than, "Thanks. I'll call back later when I know more about what's happening."

When she asked if he wanted her to tell Gwynne, after a moment's thought he said, "Would you, please? I'll text her number to you. I'd ring her myself, but I don't know what I should say. Tell her I'll ring tomorrow. And thanks. I'll call later. G'bye Helena."

Disorientated, he stood with his eyes tightly closed as more tears threatened. Just as he blinked, trying to clear them, a young woman came into the room. She walked straight up to him and took both his hands in hers. "You must be Marek Benningowicz. I'm Ana Wójcik. I got here as soon as I could. I had a feeling …"

Marek felt a slight sense of relief, realising someone else was physically present with him. Someone who knew his father. "Thank you for coming. Dad died early this morning in his sleep. He never regained consciousness."

Ana shut her eyes tightly and momentarily hung her head as she said, "Oh no! What will *Matka* do?" She reached for a tissue in her handbag.

Marek knew 'matka' was 'mother' but attached no importance to the comment other than some expression of sympathy. "Ana, I need some local information to make the funeral arrangements."

"Matka will be able to help. You should go back to Milosz's apartment, and I will speak to her and tell her what's happened. She will be devastated."

"Thank you."

"Are you alright to drive? I'll drive if you like."

"No, um, yes. Thanks. I can't really concentrate on much yet."

On the drive back to the flat, Marek tried to understand what Ana and her mother had to do with his father, but could not make sense of anything.

She parked the car and once inside said, "I'll make you a cup of tea before I go. I'll be back after I've spoken to Mum. You'll have to tell your uncle and cousin. I think Mum has their number. Make a list of anything else you need."

Forty minutes later Ana returned with an older woman who she introduced saying, "Marek, this is my Matka, Magdalena. Mum, this is Marek, Milosz's …"

In a barely audible whisper Magdalena said, "Widzę, że jest jego synem."

Ana told Marek, "Mum doesn't speak much English so excuse us for speaking Polish. She says she can clearly recognise you are his son."

"I understood that bit. My Polish isn't as good as my parents would have wished."

Magdalena stood staring at him, a look of abject despair on her face, the significance of which didn't quite register with him.

Looking anxiously from her mother to Marek, Ana said, "Mum has been Milosz's friend."

At that point Magdalena, handkerchief in hand, which she was twisting back and forth and then dabbing at her eyes, said something in Polish which he understood to be some expression of sympathy. He was moved by her grief and replied with what he thought were the right words in Polish. Ana simply said, "They have been very close friends since Milosz arrived back in Zakopane."

After a slight hesitation he asked, "Ana, can you please ask your mother if she knows how to contact Uncle Jan? I left his contact details at home."

He heard the reply but only recognised the name of Kraków. A moment later he heard her make another longer comment and had to wait for Ana to translate.

"Mum says your uncle is in poor health and rarely goes out. She has a contact number for Jan's son, Anton, and suggests you contact him first. He has a dental practice in Kraków."

"Thank you. I'm sorry, but I have one more question. Do you or your mother know a funeral director. I need to make the arrangements."

He watched as Ana asked the question. Again, the reaction generated visible anguish as Magdalena sobbed aloud and turned to lean on Ana's shoulder. She said something in Polish and Ana answered in Polish. In English she said, "Mum wants to know what sort of funeral; a burial or a cremation?"

Instinctively he knew that the thought of his father, who had lived most of his life in Australia, being buried thousands of kilometres away here in Poland, was not his wish.

"I think it will have to be a cremation because that way I can take his ashes home with me to be with my mother."

When Ana translated that for Magdalena, there was another deep sigh.

Marek was at a loss what to say but couldn't see any other option.

Of course, he wanted his parents back together, back home, in Australia.

Ana then said something to Magdalena in Polish. Her mother nodded and Ana turned to Marek and said, "For the last year, *matka* and your *tata* were more than just friends. She often stayed here overnight, and they spent a lot of time together. Do you understand?"

In stunned response, he stared from one of them to the other. As the realisation of what Ana had said dawned on him, he slowly sat and covered his face with his hands.

Was there no end to this nightmare?

The next thing he felt was a hand on his shoulder. When he looked up it was Magdalena standing there, looking down at him.

In short phrases she said, "Your *Tata* … was a good man; very good. We found comfort in each other. He was looking for something … but I think I was only part … of whatever it was. It was enough for me."

Marek was dumbfounded. He had to take several steadying breaths to take in the implications of what he'd just heard. It was enough to momentarily distract him from the shock of his father's death.

He couldn't believe that his father could form a relationship with another woman after almost forty years of marriage to his mother.

He hung his head again but then stood up and faced Magdalena. "*Dziękuję Ci bardzo,*" he said, although he wasn't sure why.

It was a response which took him back to his childhood training. 'Always say thank you,' his mother used to say, 'when people are being kind to you'. Was this kindness? Ana walked over to join them and put her arm around her mother.

It was Ana who brought them back to the task at hand. She asked Magdalena to suggest a funeral director and Magdalena simply shrugged and mentioned a name. Ana said, "There's one not far away. Would you like me to ring and make an appointment?"

"The hospital said they will have the paperwork ready this afternoon. Is six o'clock too late?"

Ana found the phonebook, searched for and found the number, and made the appointment.

As they prepared to leave, with an undisguised plea in his voice, he said, "Would you both like to come to the funeral director with me? You know more about local practices than I do as well as knowing a lot more about my father's life here in Zakopane."

Magdalena came up to him, looked him in the eyes and said in a voice choked with emotion, "*Tak, bardzo dziękuję, że pytasz, Marek*".

The look on her face told him how grateful she was that he had asked for their help.

On a grey afternoon with a heavily clouded sky, he made the depressing trip back to the hospital. The receptionist to whom he spoke was purely functional and impersonal. She spoke in the past tense about a person no longer living while Marek was thinking about the man who was, and would always be, his *Tata*. That father with his stubbly face, dark brown hair, infectious smile and wrinkles around his eyes, his laugh, and the touch of his hands. The man responsible for his very existence.

Casting his eye over the death certificate, Marek noted the coincidence of the recorded time of death: 7:35am. It matched to the minute, the time he had stood by the dedication plaque to Joseph Conrad that morning. He experienced again the unsettling shiver that had passed through him.

A goose has walked over my grave.

When he arrived back at his father's flat, he felt exhausted and unequipped for the duties required of him, but a short while later his ringing phone brought him back to focus on the tasks at hand.

It was Ana advising him of his cousin's phone number as well as giving the directions to the funeral parlour, and saying she and her mother would meet him there as it was within easy walking distance.

They met just before six o'clock and were ushered into an austere, sparsely decorated parlour. A middle-aged man introduced himself only as Szymon. He spoke in a combination of Polish and hesitant English for Marek's benefit, beginning, "I am sorry for your loss, Mr Benningowicz".

"My legal name is Marek Benning. My parents changed it from Benningowicz to make it sound more Australian."

"Ah, I understand. Thank you, Mr Benning. We will try to make the necessary arrangements without causing you too much distress."

Marek handed over the formal paperwork which Szymon asked an assistant to copy and return the originals to him.

"I will arrange to collect your father from the hospital. Mr Benning, may I ask what kind of service you require – interment or cremation?"

"A cremation. I will take my father's ashes back to Australia."

The next question required consultation with Ana and Magdalena: "When would you like it to take place?"

He turned to them, "I have limited time. I would like it to be as soon as possible. When do you think is best?"

Ana deferred to Magdalena. "*Matka* says Milosz made quite a few friends who mostly live locally. There's your uncle and cousin in Kraków of course. She thinks perhaps Friday afternoon."

He nodded in agreement to Szymon who added a note to the folder in front of him. Szymon then asked, "Would you like a religious service?"

Again, Marek looked at Magdalena but knew his parents had avoided any contact with organised religions of any kind. "I'm sure my father would want a civil ceremony." When Magdalena heard the decision, she slowly nodded her head. It would be a secular service, albeit in a country noted for its Catholicism.

After discussing further details, Szymon concluded, "My assistant will telephone you to confirm the details." As he spoke, businessman to the core, he passed a general schedule of fees across to Marek.

"Thank you Szymon."

Once all formalities had been attended to, Magdalena spoke quickly to Ana, who then turned to Marek and said, "Mum wants to know whether you would like to come back to our place for something to eat. She said you shouldn't be alone at a time like this."

He felt a wave of gratitude, mixed with confusion, flow over him. He realised he had been dreading the night alone in the strange surroundings of his father's apartment, knowing he was never to return there. Delaying the inevitable was hugely preferable, even in the presence of this woman, and the knowledge of his father's involvement with her. Once again, "*Dziękuję Ci bardzo, To byłoby bardzo miłe.*" was his response repeating to himself, yes, that would be very nice.

Magdalena nodded and offered a rueful smile.

17

As Magdalena ushered him into their home, she directed him to a seat which, he noted, caused Ana to look questioningly at her mother. When Magdalena went into the kitchen, Ana said, "You are sitting in the seat your *Tata* most preferred when he visited here. Excuse me for one minute while I help *Mumia* in the kitchen."

They returned with a tray on which were a coffee pot, cups and saucers and a cake. Marek was handed his coffee and a small plate with a slice of cake which Ana explained was, "a *sernik,* or cheesecake, Polish style of course, and Milosz's favourite." He had not known what to expect but it had been a day of experiencing the unexpected … and the unwanted. Nothing seemed normal.

When the coffee had been drunk and the cake eaten, a temporary silence descended over the three of them. Marek broke it by asking, "What do you think should be done with my father's possessions? I must admit, I'm not even sure what they are. What should I do with his clothes? Is there a charity you can name? Does the furniture belong to him, or does it belong to the landlord? I'll have to go through everything but I'm not sure what he owns or even if anything is borrowed."

Ana and Magdalena looked at each other and Ana asked, "When you have had a look through everything, would you like us to offer suggestions about anything you're unsure of? I know this is hard."

With unmistakeable relief, Marek gratefully accepted the offer for the following day and stood up to leave. He suddenly realised he was exhausted physically and, even more so, emotionally.

The walk home drained his last reserves, and he changed out of his clothes and climbed into a cold and unfamiliar bed.

He awoke next morning shrouded in an impenetrable fog; a trite phrase he had glossed over in books that he now understood at a personal level. He felt he was in another, unrecognisable world.

He knew he had important things to do but couldn't think where to begin. As his head began to clear he settled on ringing his cousin Anton to tell him of Milosz's passing.

It was an awkward conversation. He had never met his cousin and now his first contact was to inform him of his father's death.

After he had struggled through that news, he then asked a favour. "Anton, I can't trust myself to speak at Dad's funeral, especially in Polish. If I write it in English, would you be willing to translate and read out what I would like to say please?"

His cousin didn't hesitate. "Yes, I can do that and willingly. Can you email it to me as soon as possible? I'm sorry I can't come to see you right now; I have a full schedule of appointments and I must also arrange things with my father and his nursing home. Our apologies but we can't see you until the day of the funeral."

"That's okay. Thank you. I know it's short notice, but I really appreciate you doing this for me … and Dad." A feeling of relief swept over him. He had completed one awkward, but necessary task.

He looked in the kitchen for something to eat, picked up an apple and, despite knowing there were other things needing attention, set off on a walk, hoping to focus on his promised funeral address.

Something at the back of his mind urged him to retrace his steps of the previous day and before long he was staring at the Joseph Conrad plaque, where he had experienced the unnerving feeling of dread. Standing in the early morning solitude helped him think and gradually his thoughts focused, and the words began to form.

Still feeling disoriented in the legendary and mysterious town of his parents' birth, about which he knew both a little and a lot, he explored further, returning home via a different route. Some features he recognised from his parents' descriptions: churches, the remodelled Post Office, new in 1961, modern apartments and old wooden chalet-style houses. The black and white stories of his parents were taking on colour.

Back in the apartment, he started writing, bearing in mind what he imagined his father's friends might want to hear as well as what he himself wanted to say. He assumed few of them knew the details of how his parents had set off to cross from Central to Western Europe on a journey of more than 1,250 kilometres and culminating in the loss of his soul-companion, Alicja, and finally, his father's recent decision to visit Poland.

Marek re-read what he had written and although he felt it inadequate, lacking the personal loving touch locked within his chest, he decided it would have to do.

The funeral address completed, he returned to his father's flat to get on with sorting through his father's possessions. It was weird. Never in his life had he intruded into his father's personal belongings. Many objects reminded him of his *Tata* despite knowing some of them were not directly part of his Australian existence. By noon he had made neat bundles:

things to take, and things to leave such as linen, knick-knacks and kitchen items. He wasn't sure about some electrical items, so he left them out to remind himself to mention them to Ana and Magdalena.

He looked over his father's books and found a mixture of Polish and English titles. He was surprised at the range which covered historical and political subjects alongside the beloved Conrad novels, some of which in recent times, had attracted criticism based on a modern interpretation and definition of racism. The fact that the wreck of Conrad's last ship, *Otago*, of which he was the captain, remained a rusting wreck in Otago Bay fifteen kilometres up the Derwent River from Hobart, Tasmania, was a graphic example of how far the mighty can fall.

His eye caught a book by Henryk Sienkiewicz, the same name as the street he had walked along to discover the Conrad plaque. He picked up the book and was astounded to learn that Sienkiewicz had been the first Polish Nobel prize-winner for Literature in 1905, one hundred years ago. His works included *Quo Vadis* which he knew had been made into a movie. The title translated ominously as '*Where are you going?*' He had no doubt his father would have known about Sienkiewicz and could have regaled him on his contribution to Polish literature, especially at the time of the peace settlement after World War I.

The thought crossed his mind that his father had been reliving long lost nostalgic events: childhood, youth, friends … courting Alicja? Marek felt he was being drawn into the previous existence of a man he now only partially recognised.

Quo Vadis? he asked of himself.

He found some cans of soup in the kitchen and heated the contents of one for lunch. Sitting at the table as he ate, he flicked through more of his father's books. Between the pages of one he found a picture of his mother taken at home in Newcastle. She looked exactly like he remembered her when he was a child. His throat constricted and he closed his stinging eyes as he replaced the photo in the book and put the precious item with his own things to take home. As he did so, he realised he had not checked his father's mobile phone. He assumed it had been with him when his father had the heart attack and he found it in the bag with his father's items which the hospital staff had returned to him.

He found the phone charger in the bedroom and connected the phone. He had no idea how to unlock it and began trying various dates on the number pad. None of the family birth dates worked and it was pure luck that it unlocked when he entered 1-9-6-4, the year his parents had arrived in Australia.

Looking through the photos on the phone, Marek didn't recognise many of the men, but he did recognise several photos of Magdalena. His stomach churned as they reminded him that his father had recently made a new life for himself, a life from which he felt excluded. Fairly or not, he believed Zakopane and its people were dragging the man, his *Tata*, away from him and the memory of his *Matka*. He had to remind himself his father had come back to Poland to satisfy a personal need which he was fully entitled to do.

He then checked the call log and was not surprised to see that many of the calls were to and from Magdalena, and occasionally, his own name and number showed up. The SMS text log told a similar story, the overall effect of which emphasised that a distance had developed between himself and the father, and man, he now realised he only partially knew.

The ringing of his own phone disturbed his train of thought. It was the funeral director's assistant seeking to confirm arrangements. Did he want a viewing? What clothes did he want his father dressed in? What music, if any, did he want? Would people want to speak and how many? He made a list of the questions and said he would get back to him when he had the information.

At the end of the call, he realised the only people with whom he could discuss some of the questions were Magdalena and Ana.

It was becoming awkward and embarrassing that he had to seek so much help about his own Tata, the man whom he thought he knew best in the world, from people he'd only met in the last two days. For the first time in his life, he began to doubt that was so.

Do we ever really know our parents?

He rang Ana to ask about his father's funeral clothing. After a brief discussion, with Magdalena in the background, she said, "Mum thinks he should wear the casual clothes in which he always appeared his best: black shoes, socks and trousers, blue shirt and his favourite tweed sports coat." They all agreed that they couldn't bear to think of anyone else wearing those treasured items.

The most precious item though, which Marek couldn't relinquish, was the favourite flat cap his father wore. He had already packed it in his own bag.

He went on to explain, "My cousin Anton will speak at the funeral on my behalf. I've written what I want said and I wondered if you could scan it and email it to him, please."

Without a second's hesitation she replied, "I'll pick it up after work later today. Anything else?"

The question of a viewing of the body was more difficult. "Can you ask your *Matka* whether she would like a viewing at the funeral parlour?"

He heard Ana speak to her mother and after a few moments in which he could hear Magdalena's muted voice,

Ana said, "Mum says thank you for asking but she is content to remember Milosz the way he was in life and doesn't wish to view him in death."

Blunt as her answer was, it was consistent with his own beliefs, influenced by what he had heard his father say about funerals, but he couldn't suppress a wry smile at Magdalena's typically direct Polish response.

Next, he rang the funeral director and gave the requested information.

Regarding the music, he had three suggestions: the finale of Chopin's *Polonaise in A-flat major,* which was a favourite of his mother's.

He tentatively asked if they had it performed by Jan Paderewski, pianist, prime minister of Poland and a signatory to the Treaty of Versailles. The funeral director made no promises.

His other music choices were the *Internationale,* preferably not a sung version, just the music. He was mindful of his father's emphatic view that it gave encouragement to ordinary men and women to stand up for their rights.

Lastly, a favourite of both his mother and father, the Seekers performing, *The Carnival Is Over.* The funeral director confirmed one of the younger members of staff would attend to it and that the service was set for one o'clock Friday.

He then rang his cousin Helena and let her know what had been decided, self-consciously admitting, "I've asked my cousin Anton to deliver my address. I don't trust myself to do it."

"Good idea. Thinking and writing it at a time like this are hard enough. Saying it out loud to strangers, especially in Polish, is another matter. As you know, I couldn't do it even in English for either my mum or dad."

Helena expressed her sorrow again, "Alan said to pass on his condolences as well. We'll be thinking of you and Milosz at the time. Do try to look after yourself."

"Helena, this is all very weird. I hardly know what I'm doing from one moment to the next. There's more to the story than I can tell you right now. I'll save it until I get home. I'm looking forward to when it's all over."

"That sounds a bit mysterious. I'm intrigued. Take care love. 'Bye."

"Everyone here has been very helpful but I'm looking forward to when it is all over and I can get back home. G'bye Helena."

Mid-afternoon Ana and Magdalena arrived to look over his father's possessions. It was agreed they could be sent to local charities.

Magdalena, looking ashen faced, lightly brushed her hand over many objects and surfaces, but selected only a very few items: small trinkets and a couple of framed photographs.

Ana said she had a friend who could use a few things, especially electrical items. His heart sank further, if that was possible, as he realised that back in Australia he would have to go through a similar process; *something else he was dreading*.

That gruesome business concluded, Ana then spoke to Marek. "An old friend of Milosz's, Jakub Malinski, has asked me to ask you if he could speak at the funeral. He wants to farewell 'the friend of his youth,' as he put it."

Marek was touched. "Certainly. Please thank him and invite him on my behalf."

"What are you doing for dinner tonight?" Ana asked.

"Nothing. I haven't thought about it."

"There's a café nearby where Mum and I sometimes go."

Marek hesitated.

"It will get you out of the flat for a while. What do you say? Does seven o'clock suit you?"

Marek agreed to meet them after he had delivered his father's clothes. Ana and Magdalena then left him to the jumble of thoughts and obligations that were overlaid with his sense of grief.

Weariness from seemingly relentless decision making overtook him. Adding to this, his father's landlord arrived unexpectedly to settle the issues of the furniture and the lease. He introduced himself saying, "My name is Nikołaj Kamiński, I own this apartment. I'm very sorry for your loss. Your father was a very good tenant. He looked after the apartment and paid the rent on time."

When Marek told him he would be leaving on the following Monday, Nikołaj gave the impression his only concern was losing a good tenant and wanting to let the apartment again as soon as possible.

To avoid any misunderstanding, Marek said, "I found the lease agreement in my father's papers, and I'll check everything is in order. Magdalena Wójcik will arrange for my father's remaining possessions to be removed and she will return the keys to you."

When the landlord left, he continued sorting through his father's possessions, grudgingly admitting that things were falling into place. He showered, dressed and, with stomach churning, set off to deliver the cherished funeral clothes. From the funeral parlour it was a short walk to the café for dinner with the Wójciks.

The meal was inexpensive, basic and filling. The surprise was that only Ana arrived for dinner, claiming her grieving mother said it was too soon for her to appear in public. Their conversation drifted over a wide range, but Ana's interests seemed to focus on his life back in Australia. He was happy to reminisce about his childhood: school, Dixon Park, his favourite beach, and sport. They compared favourite pop-music groups.

In a soul-baring moment, with some embarrassment, he admitted that as an only child, his mother had doted on him. The word 'spoilt' was mentioned and that she considered him her 'golden boy'. And throughout their conversation her unconditional love and the ghostly presence of his father hovered. He concluded with a brief résumé of his life as a licensed builder.

When the café owner started to show obvious signs of closing, he looked at his watch and was surprised at the late hour and how quickly the time had passed.

The evening had been a welcome distraction from the events of the last few days. He thanked Ana for her company and as they left the café, he insisted on walking her home saying, "The walk will do me good and perhaps help me sleep."

When they arrived, Ana asked if he wanted to come in, but Marek declined, asking only that she thank her mother again for her help. They said goodnight and Marek began his walk home.

As he walked, he reflected on their conversation and realised the role Ana had played in lifting his spirits. However, with each step his mood sank as the realities of his situation engulfed him. Life, first without his mother and now, without his father, was unfathomable.

Tired but restless, he wondered if he should ring Helena and Gwynne. He knew it was one of Gwynne's full working days and, as his confidence deserted him, he decided against calling her on the premiss she would be in the middle of her day at work. He went to bed feeling exhausted, but sleep eluded him. He decided a nip of his father's vodka might be in order, even if it provided only a temporary solution.

He awoke with a jolt at 4:30am, not knowing what awakened him. He gave in and rang Gwynne, hoping she would be settled at home by then. When she didn't answer, he ended the call without leaving a message. The wave of loneliness was overwhelming.

His phone alarm woke him to a fine sunny day, in stark contrast to his depressed mood. Once again, he decided to go for a walk to pass the time and hopefully, discover more about his parents' childhood home in Zakopane. He tried to imagine them as children, and then as teenagers in love in such a beautiful location, with the Tatra Mountains in the distance looking, at the same time, mysterious, threatening and magnificent. He saw a bench seat in a small open square, sat and let his mind wander over the scene. As a builder, he was fascinated by the numerous designs and construction styles of wooden houses as well as the grander mansions, ornate churches, and villas, many in sandstone quarried from the local region.

It was only when his phone rang that he was brought back to reality. On looking at the screen and seeing Gwynne's name, his spirits lifted; soared would be only a slight exaggeration. He hung on her every word, drinking in the sound of her voice, a voice from back home, the place of his birth, far from his present situation, while she offered her condolences and other kind words. He realised that he was homesick and that he just wanted his present troubles to simply disappear. His inner voice of reality made it clear that wasn't going to happen.

"Thanks for ringing Gwynne. Good to hear a familiar voice. And thanks for your kind thoughts. How is Merren? What's she up to?"

"Merren's fine. I'm here keeping an eye on her having her bath. She's asking when you're coming home."

"I'm booked to fly out on Monday. Given possible schedule issues on Sydney trains, I can't be absolutely precise, but I expect to be back home Wednesday morning, depending on connections." He then told her about the funeral arrangements. When he finished, he paused, and couldn't think of anything to keep the conversation going. Lamely, he ended with, "Say hello to her for me."

"Wait a minute, I'll turn on the speaker and you can tell her yourself. Ready?"

Marek tried to control his breathing before speaking. "Hi Merren, Marek here. Hope you are enjoying your bath. Have you got Squinty and Binko in there with you?"

He heard Merren giggle and say, "No silly, they don't like having baths, only showers in the rain."

"Oh, yes, of course. I'm sure you're being good for your mother. I'm looking forward to seeing you when I get back in a few more days. I've got to go now but it's been very nice talking to you. G'bye, Missy Merren."

To Gwynne he said, "Thanks Gwynne. I … I'm looking forward to when this is all over. G'bye."

"I'll be thinking of you. I wish I could do more. Let me know how it all goes when you get a moment to talk. 'Bye."

It was still too early to set off for the funeral and, after having just told Gwynne about it, he realised he had to tell Darren as well. Talking about it on the phone was upsetting so again, he resorted to a text message, impersonal as it might be. He just didn't have the stomach to go over it all again.

Back in the flat, he decided to fill the remaining time browsing through his father's books again, to see if there was anything else of interest. His eye fell on one of his father's most talked about Joseph Conrad books, *Lord Jim*. He'd tried reading it in his teens but found it complicated at a time in his life when everything else seemed to be blissfully average.

He left the book on the bed and rang Ana to see if they wanted him to pick them up for the funeral. He heard Ana asking her mother and then Ana said, "Mum said, yes please, that would be very good. We'll be waiting."

The knot in the pit of his stomach tightened when he realised it was time to set off on the second-most unwanted experience of his life so far. Only his mother's funeral was worse, even though he had his father beside him that terrible day. He didn't know how he could bear it on his own, yet knew that he must.

18

He arrived a few minutes early at the Wójcik home and sat in the car to try and settle his turbulent mind. He still found it impossible to accept that this was the day his father was going to be cremated.

Thoughts of his mother's funeral punctuated the process, a bizarre fantasy that shouldn't be happening; but it was. After several deep breaths and drawing on all the willpower he could muster, he got out of the car and approached the door.

It was opened before he could knock by Ana with Magdalena close behind. Magdalena, eyes red from crying, and handkerchief balled in her fist, and unspoken resignation in the set of her jaw as she walked determinedly to the car. There seemed to be an implicit agreement that no words were needed, and the sooner the impending ordeal was over, the sooner the healing might begin.

When they arrived at the chapel, Magdalena pointed out Marek's cousin, Anton, and his father's brother, Jan – in his wheelchair, talking to other mourners. With a jolt, Marek noted the facial similarities between Jan and his own father. Magdalena led Marek to them and made the introductions. He shook his cousin's hand then his uncle's, which seemed almost weightless, merely frail bones covered by tissue-like skin.

"Thanks for coming." Then trying it in Polish he added, "Dziękuję za przybycie," before continuing. "I'm sorry to see you unwell Uncle Jan. And thank you too Anton, for bringing him and being here."

The response from his uncle was to reach up and clasp Marek by his jacket and, with surprising strength, pull him down so he could kiss him on both cheeks saying, *"Witaj Marek, mój chłopcze! miło mi cię w końcu poznać.* Wyglądasz jak twój ojciec w twoim wieku."

Marek understood the general meaning behind these phrases: *Hello Marek, my boy! Nice to finally meet you, You look like your father when he was your age.*

"Witaj wujku, Uncle Jan," he replied, expressing that he too was pleased to finally meet him adding, "I don't know anyone but you who knew my father when he was young." Turning towards Anton and speaking English he said, "I can scarcely believe I am saying hello to my uncle and my cousin for the first time in my life, at my father's funeral. It's good of you to agree to deliver my address Anton. I don't think I could manage it in English, let alone Polish. I hope the translation wasn't too much of a problem." He waited while Anton translated for his Uncle Jan.

Jan simply shrugged as Anton relayed his gracious reply, "What's family for? We'll say hello to some of our old friends here and then take our place in the chapel while there's room to manoeuvre, before everyone gets settled."

As mourners arrived, many came up to Magdalena and hugged and kissed her. She then introduced them to Marek and, in almost every case, they looked him up and down in obvious assessment of the son of the man they had come to know again, and for whose funeral they had now gathered. Marek knew he was on display; being judged.

When an elderly man came and stood in front of him, Ana stepped up and introduced him as Jakub Malinski. The man made no effort to conceal the fact that he too was evaluating

Marek. He felt himself flushing as this stranger seemed to examine him from head to toe. In halting English he said, "Thank you for permit me speak. Milosz and me once good friends before he run off with Alicja."

Marek was slightly taken aback by his frank assessment of those long-past events and waited for him to continue. "We were like brothers and spent much time together, often getting into trouble, especially at school."

Marek was lost for words. He could not imagine his father as a boy, having seen scarcely any photographs of either parent as children.

In what sounded to his own ears as excessively formal halting Polish that others could hear, he said, "Thank you for coming and speaking about my father. I'm looking forward to hearing what you have to say. Dad's life here must have had great meaning, because he came back to see his family and old friends."

Jakub, again looked him straight in the eye, nodded, squared his shoulders, and walked into the chapel. Marek half expected him to click his heels.

Polish old school.

When the commencement time approached, Marek, Magdalena and Ana took their seats in the front pew, alongside Anton and Jan.

A family united in death.

He was quite surprised at the number of people present and dismissed the idea that they might only have been prying, nosey onlookers, in favour of well-meant curiosity, even respect. They were Gorals, as the ethnographic citizens of the region around Zakopane were known, and they had come to attend the funeral of a man who had grown up among them, left, and returned to them. They were ready for a story. Whatever their reasons, he was grateful for their presence.

He wanted his father to have a send-off.

The service began with the soft ethereal final two minutes of Chopin's *Polonaise in A flat*, gradually building to its dramatic conclusion. After the final chords faded, the celebrant opened formalities introducing himself and welcoming those present. He then began speaking in general terms of Milosz Benningowicz, the man who had sought a better life elsewhere in the troubled political times of 1960s Poland.

Thankfully, even though Marek couldn't catch every word, the celebrant spoke confidently and without the singsong, overly pious tone, sometimes heard at funerals. After a slight pause he announced, "Anton Benningowicz will now speak on behalf of Marek, Milosz's son."

As Anton stood and walked to the lectern there was shuffling in the congregation. They were making themselves comfortable for a story, not just a eulogy.

"Good afternoon ladies and gentlemen. For those who have forgotten, I am Anton Benningowicz, nephew of Milosz, and Marek's cousin. For reasons I need not explain, he has asked me to deliver his words in Polish. He has tried to be brief but few, if any of us, knew Milosz and Alicja's story in any detail. It is one of courage and determination – and most of all, one of love."

In a steadily paced voice Anton related how Milosz and Alicja decided to leave Zakopane: "As had so many young people at that time, Dad and Mum struggled in a changing world to accept the restrictions and limitations of an oppressive communist regime, living in what they believed was an outpost of a world passing them by.

"They left in Autumn 1961 and in January 1964, their ship berthed in Sydney, Australia. With little money, some basic English, and only a vague plan where to find work or live, they were determined to make this new country their home. Immigration officials suggested they would do well to go to Wollongong or, better still, Newcastle, where the BHP company was always taking on willing workers. Newcastle was chosen because Alicja, who many of you knew, had a cousin living there who had married an Australian."

Marek tried surreptitiously to look around at the faces of those present and was again surprised, this time by their concentrated looks, obviously absorbed in the proceedings.

Anton continued: "Mum had the address of her cousin, Marta, and it was to there they made their way, completely unannounced. Passage to Newcastle by train was arranged by an immigration official.

"As luck would have it, Graham, Marta's husband, worked, as a metallurgist for Comsteel, another steel making company, and he helped Milosz find work in the German built forge making train wheels.

"As a willing worker, determined to make a success of their life-changing decision, they made the most of every opportunity, including working overtime, even double-shifts when available. His efforts were rewarded when Comsteel sent him to technical college to gain the qualifications needed for promotion to higher positions. He quickly found acceptance and success.

"As might be expected, Mum's death resulted in a major change in Dad's life. The nature of that change was not expected. Retirement was imminent and Dad sometimes said he felt that without my mother beside him, a lonely future loomed. He struggled to cope and sometimes in those last working months, he occasionally reminisced about his life in Poland.

"Dad had followed newspaper reports of the political exploits of Lech Wałęsa and the Solidarity movement through the 1980s and '90s. He was overjoyed when, after years of activism and strikes in Poland, the ruling communist party voted to legalise the banned Solidarity movement.

"As you all know, by February 1989, Solidarność was in talks with the government. It swept to power and the seeds of democracy were being sown as the country struggled with constitutional and electoral reform. But that was only the beginning of the road to democracy and Dad was driven to see for himself where it led.

"For him, Poland joining NATO in 1999, and admission to the EU in 2004, indicated the country was finally breaking out of the Soviet mould. It could finally redefine its past historical, political, social and geographic grievances in the pervasive atmosphere of the global economy."

After stopping to draw breath and looking up, Anton noted the attention people were giving to the tale they all so wanted to hear.

He smiled inwardly and continued reading: "Dad's transformation eventuated in a decision to come back to visit Zakopane. A decision in the full knowledge that migrating to Australia had been so successful, where steady work had enabled him to live the freer life he and Alicja had dreamed of, buying their own home, and becoming proud parents."

Straying from Marek's script, and gesturing towards him, Anton added, "I'm sure he would be extremely proud of his son sitting here today: an Australian, born and bred, but with Polish blood in his veins."

Anton folded the speech, and placed it in his pocket, allowing the last comment to hang in the chapel before continuing. "I'll now introduce the next piece of music chosen by Marek. It's by The Seekers, Milosz and Alicja's favourite Australian singing group in the 1960s and 1970s. I think many of you know that this song, *The Carnival Is*

Over, is based on a Russian folk song. The words speak of an undying love between two soulmates. After the music, Jakub Malinski, a boyhood friend of Milosz will speak. Lastly, on Marek's behalf, we members of the family would like to thank you all for coming."

As the music began, Anton returned to his seat and as he reached Marek, he stopped and embraced him.

He then returned the speech to him saying, "You should keep this for your future, whatever it may be."

For the duration of the song, the audience sat transfixed, some murmuring the Polish words to a well-known tune. As it ended Jakub made his way to the front.

He stood blinking, clearly moved by the occasion, as he looked out at the people. Before he said a word, he took a handkerchief from his pocket and dabbed his eyes. In a scratchy voice he began to speak in the distinctive Podhale dialect spoken by the Gorals.

Ana whispered a translation to Marek: "… How … he was when Milosz and Alicja … the most beautiful girl in the town … a girl with whom he himself had been secretly in love … left Zakopane. He had been jealous of Milosz …"

As he continued, the audience responded with apparent delight at some of their childhood mischievous exploits, the essence of which were juvenile but amusing pranks.

He then detected a change in Jakub's expression as he went on to recount his joy and pleasure when his old friend returned to Zakopane.

At the conclusion of Jakub's address, he visibly took a deep breath, walked over to the coffin and placed his hand on it saying, "Vale i żegnaj stary przyjacielu."

Marek looked first at Magdalena who sat with a wistful smile and tears in her eyes, as did many others. She then translated softly, "Vale and goodbye old friend."

Jakub then introduced *The Internationale*, saying that Milosz thought – for his own reasons at that time – that it represented their youthful optimism for all Poles. There was a general shuffle as several people, both men and women, rose to their feet. The rendition was of music only, but they sang with fervour in the crackly voices of the elderly, heightening the emotional effect. As he returned to his seat, he too stopped next to Marek who stood to thank his dad's old friend. Jakub grasped him by the shoulders and kissed him on each cheek.

No words were exchanged. *Polish old school!*

As the proceedings ended, the celebrant invited anyone who wished, to attend the spreading of his father's ashes in the reserve near the dedication sign to Joseph Conrad on Josepha Conrada Korzeniowskiego Road at 3:00pm the following day. Finally, he thanked everyone for coming, shook Marek's hand and walked from the chapel.

The announcement caused quite a reaction. Marek guessed they were surprised more by the fact there was to be a cremation rather than a burial in a predominantly Catholic country.

Marek and Magdalena led the way from the chapel, followed by Ana and then Anton, wheeling his Uncle Jan. Outside, most of the mourners either shook Marek's hand or kissed him, or both, while offering sympathy before moving on to offer her their condolences to Magdalena. When Jakub once again stood before Marek, neither could speak, and they simply wrapped their arms around each other in that universal emotional gesture of mutual understanding and support.

As the crowd dwindled, Ana came over to Marek and told him that her mother had invited several close friends back to their house for something to eat and drink. Ana offered to go back with a family friend straight away to welcome the guests and asked him to bring her mother when she was ready to leave. Anton apologised for being unable to attend as he had to get his father back to the nursing home in Kraków. Marek went over to his uncle and was again blessed with a kiss on each cheek and a warm hug. It took almost forty minutes for the crowd to drift away before Marek could drive the teary-eyed Magdalena home.

All eyes turned to Marek when he entered the Wójcik home. Seeing how uncomfortable he looked, Ana came over and whispered to him, "They're all looking at the son of a man who dared to do what they had only dreamed of doing. Don't worry," she said, "they're just curious, and possibly a little bit jealous."

"Ana, I have arranged to collect my father's ashes after 2:00pm tomorrow and for them to be divided equally into two portions. I would like to invite Magdalena to spread one portion around the Joseph Conrad reserve, because of the … er, high esteem, Dad retained for Zakopane and its people." After a few seconds he added, "Including your mother. I think he would like to leave something of himself in such a beautiful peaceful setting. Will you ask your mother please?"

Ana immediately shut her eyes and gripped his hand, to maintain her self-control. She walked over to her mother and took her aside to tell her. Magdalena's reaction was a gulping sob and she held her handkerchief to her eyes while she clung to Ana.

Conversations stopped and heads turned, wondering what had happened. Magdalena walked across to Marek, stared intently at him as if searching for something, then hugged him so tightly she almost stopped his breath. Everyone looked relieved. It was evident she, and therefore they, approved. Ana announced to everyone what had just been decided and she again invited friends of Milosz and Magdalena to attend the following day.

For the next hour, every man and woman hugged him, kissed him or shook his hand until it felt the flow of blood to it had stopped. Although finding out about his father's Zakopane life had been a huge shock, he was overwhelmed at seeing how people felt about Milosz, the man. He felt that it was fair that some portion of his ashes should remain in the country of his birth – and now his death – and the remainder in his adopted country where he had made a home for Alicja and himself.

After struggling through conversations in a mixture of Polish and English, Marek became aware of the emotional toll the day had taken on him. He said as much to Ana who passed the message on to her mother. This time Magdalena came over to him and in halting English said, "Your *Tata* was very proud of you. Today I can see proof that he was right to be so. Tomorrow, when I am not so sad, I will also be proud. *Dziękuję*."

Marek surprised both Magdalena and himself by leaning forward and kissing her on each cheek. Ana showed him to the door and, as he was about to leave, she reached up and kissed him on the cheek saying, "*Dziękuję*", from me."

Back in the apartment, Marek changed into more comfortable clothes, sat in his *Tata's* comfy chair, and began to read *Lord Jim*.

Ten minutes later he was asleep.

19

When he awoke, he was in a strange bed: his father's, in Zakopane, of all places! His sense of physical and emotional dislocation was profound.

As soon as he was fully awake, he started to worry that he had so little time to settle all his father's remaining affairs. He had no idea if he needed any further documentation for legal purposes when he arrived back in Australia. He knew his father's will was lodged with his long-time school-friend and solicitor back home in Newcastle but, given his father's new life here in Poland, he worried whether he had made a new will.

It seemed a very cold, legalistic thing to be contemplating. He thought of ringing his solicitor mate, Ross Brennan, but resisted, knowing it was very late on a Friday night back home. Instead, he rang Ana to ask her to check with Magdalena. "I'm sorry for ringing so early but I have another question which your mother might be able to answer. Does she know if Dad had any legal matters of any kind while he was here?"

Ana's replied, "I have no idea, but I'll ask Mum and ring you back."

Five minutes later she rang. "Matka doesn't know for sure, but she doesn't think so. Milosz never mentioned anything about lawyers to her."

Through Ana, Magdalena suggested that he contact the public notary in Zakopane to confirm any legal requirements and lodge the details of his father's death. Ana gave him directions to the notary's office and then invited him to dinner that night.

Again, he was grateful for the invitation. "That's very kind of you both. I would like that. I'm feeling panicky about anything I might have forgotten and there's so little time."

It was Saturday and the public notary was not available in person, but Marek was able to lodge notarised photocopies, including his father's passport details, the documents the hospital had given him and funeral arrangements for their records. He advised that he was leaving Zakopane to return to Australia the following Monday.

It was too early to collect his father's ashes, so he went home to finish checking over his father's belongings and begin packing his own.

He found it difficult to make decisions about many of the items. He kept thinking: *This belonged to my father; I must find a place for it.* The pile of belongings, with which he had no idea what to do, kept growing. He forced himself to continue sorting and culling his father's effects until lunch time. Another can of soup would have to do.

As requested, when he arrived at the funeral parlour, his father's ashes were handed over in two small ceramic urns, one sealed and certified, to meet Australian import conditions.

He rang Ana. "I've got Dad's ashes. Do you want me to pick up you and your mother?"

"Yes please. We would both like that."

When he arrived, Magdalena's red eyes told him she was stoically battling with her self-control. Ana was also very subdued. The three of them barely spoke a word on the way to the reserve.

"Good God, look at all the people!" Marek whispered to Ana, as they pulled up.

Overhearing his comment, Magdalena said, with more than a hint of impatience, "We keep telling you, your father was much respected and admired. And loved. It is fitting they should be here."

Almost as an aside, Ana added wryly, for his ears only, "We like an excuse to get together. We're here for the final scene. This story will be retold; we're very sociable … and inquisitive."

Marek had not prepared a speech for the occasion. After nods and glances of recognition and approval were exchanged, he stood, holding the urn, head bowed for a few seconds, to focus his mind.

Dominating his thoughts was the knowledge that he was about to distribute some of the last remains of his father, but memories of his mother intruded on the moment. It was enough to alert those assembled to recognise his anguish at this final parting and they remained respectfully silent.

He began simply by saying in the best Polish he could, "Dziękuję *bardzo*, everyone for coming this afternoon. I feel certain that my father would be honoured to know how many of his friends are gathered here in the town of his, and my mother's birth, and in this reserve dedicated to his favourite author. Ladies and gentlemen, for personal reasons, I will ask Magdalena Wójcik, one of the people who most welcomed and befriended my father, to disperse this portion of his ashes."

Marek then turned to Magdalena and, handing the urn to her said, so all could hear, "Magdalena, would you be so kind? I think it would mean a lot to my father … and to me."

Before accepting the urn, Magdalena again stood in front of him for a moment. It was a very personal habit she had, as if she were reading, or reaching into, his soul. She then reached up and kissed him on each cheek in a formal gesture.

Taking the urn, as if it was the most precious object in her life, she walked over to the Joseph Conrad plaque and began sprinkling the ashes. She moved on to a small garden with a patch of snow drops and scattered a handful around them. Next, she did the same around a bed of crocuses and lastly, she slowly sprinkled the remainder into the stream that flowed through the reserve.

When she tried to give Marek back the empty urn he asked, "Would you like to keep it? As a memento?"

Magdalena first hung her head, patted her eyes with an already damp handkerchief and, with a smile of resignation on her face, nodded. *"Dziękuję Marek."*

Out of the corner of his eye Marek could see nods, and even hear comments of approval. In the unplanned circumstances, no one quite knew what to do or say. They stood around in small groups talking quietly.

Marek tried to get around to each person or group and thank them personally for coming. At one point in doing so, he realised he had never before been hugged or kissed as much, or had his hand shaken, as in the last few days. He had even become used to their garlicky breath, an incontestable staple of Polish cooking. And being crushed against the ample bosoms of so many Polish matriarchs.

Eventually they said their goodbyes and began to depart. As they did so, Ana said to Marek, "I'll wait for you and *Matka* in the car. Take your time, they appreciate it."

When she had gone, Marek put his arm through Magdalena's and they both stood with bowed heads making no attempt to shield their tears. Both knew the physical finality of the moment.

For different reasons, it was a separation from the place, but not an ending to the memory, of the man they had loved above all others. On the way to the Wójciks' home,

Magdalena recovered sufficiently to remind him he was expected for dinner that night.

"I have not forgotten. I cannot think of a better ending to such a stressful day. I'll bring a bottle of wine from Dad's collection. I think he would have liked to contribute to the occasion."

After dropping them off, he returned to the apartment but could not focus on anything.

Finally, as the afternoon faded, he settled himself into his father's favourite chair with *Lord Jim*.

The book was an old battered green 1958, *Everyman's Library* edition, with a BIOGRAPHICAL NOTE. He was astounded to read that according to Conrad's wife, '... *a sort of homing instinct was on Conrad towards the end of his life.*' The similarity to his own father's decision to return to Poland was astounding. Just one of many decisions with which he had to come to terms.

In another remarkable coincidence, Magdalena's meal that night was a near replica of one of his favourite meals which his mother used to cook: *kotlety*.

There were minor differences with the ingredients, particularly the spices, but the basic dish was Polish meatballs.

Marek hadn't thought he was very hungry but once he started, he realised he had eaten very little.

Much to Magdalena's approval, he acquitted himself well. He was able to say, "Magdalena, that was delicious. Your selection of spices made it a meal to remember. My mother used to make *kotlety* back in Australia. She used beef mince but the minced pork with onions and oatmeal was every bit as good. Tonight, it had more of a Polish flavour."

He refrained from saying that the flavour difference was most notable in the quantity of garlic used.

After a few moments, Magdalena asked Ana to clear the table and then, ominously, looking directly at him said, "Will you come into the sitting room? Sit in your *Tata's* chair please. There's something I have to say to you."

When they were seated, with her handkerchief in hand, she began what turned out to be something of a confession in the form of an account of her life in Zakopane from when she was a girl. She spoke slowly, constantly checking Marek's face with her characteristic searching gaze, to be sure he understood what she was saying.

"My older sister was Alicja's best friend. It was through my sister I first met your mother and then Milosz." Magdalena paused, but her gaze never wavered. "I developed a teenage crush on Milosz. When he left Zakopane together with Alicja, I was heartbroken." Again, that s*tare*. "I later married and was happy. But I always held a place in my heart for Milosz. We have a saying here, *to nie ten, który dostajesz, to ten, którego nie można zapomnieć*. Marek struggled to translate it into something like, 'it's not the one you get, it's the one you can't forget'.

"The one I couldn't forget was Milosz. The day he appeared back in Zakopane was perhaps one of, if not *the* happiest days of my life. When I saw him, my heart leapt into my mouth. I was like a teenager again. I was shameless, for once I saw him, I vowed I would not let him go. He was slow to respond but, in some ways, he needed looking after and eventually we became lovers. I have to tell you this, so you understand."

Upon hearing Magdalena's story, his own feelings were in turmoil. How should he respond to such a soulful revelation? She was so serious and yet his overriding reaction to this newly discovered stage in his father's life was one of having heard one side of a heart-rending love story.

He leant forward, elbows resting on his knees, hands clasped tightly, looking at the floor. Despite the emotional discomfort he felt he said, "Magdalena, I cannot hold any ill feelings for someone who obviously loved my father and cared for him. The way I choose to understand it, my father's life here was separate from his life back home. Maybe he was a man I never completely knew but I believe what he shared with you was separate from that life which he had with my mother and me, for so many years. For him, Zakopane has been another time and place. That is the way I choose to believe it."

The sigh from Magdalena made Marek suddenly lift his head and look directly at her. It was a primeval, profound gasp. She stood up, again with her handkerchief dabbing at her eyes. "It has been a tiring and difficult day for both of us. As we Polish say, *Dziękuję za zrozumienie*, thank you for your understanding. If your father was here today, he would be a very proud man. Goodnight Marek."

Before he could respond, she walked slowly from the room, replaced by Ana who simply added, "So, now you know all."

Bewildered, he repeated Magdalena's words to Ana, "*Dziękuję za zrozumienie!*" adding, "I'm not sure if I do completely understand even half of what's been happening."

He had no further response and was grateful when Ana again spoke. "Marek," she said, "Tomorrow, the choir in which I sing, is putting on a small performance of Polish traditional songs in the town hall just a short distance from your place. If you are free, would you like to attend? It will only be for a little over an hour and will be followed by refreshments. Please don't feel under any obligation. I thought that, as it will be your last day in Zakopane, you might like to experience some Goral culture."

Marek recognised that Ana's invitation was said with a sense of both regional Goral and national pride which included measures of empathy and support. It would be a more than fitting way to end his stay in Zakopane.

"Thank you, Ana. That sounds perfect. Do you want me to pick you up?"

"No, I will call on you at the flat about 1:00 o'clock. We can walk there together."

He then said that he, like her mother, felt completely washed out and overwhelmed by the day and that he should be going. He asked Ana to apologise for him for not having thanked her mother for the meal. "And thank you both for all you did in arranging the funeral, and for helping me translate my poor Polish."

Looking into his eyes she said, "I did it because of what your father meant to *Mumia,* for the way you showed love and respect for your father. Besides, we may have improved each other's language skills: your Polish and my English."

He was lost for words. He took her hand and, for what seemed like the thousandth time, said *"Dziękuję bardzo, Ana"*.

He managed to drive home but, once there, even *Lord Jim* couldn't keep him awake.

20

When Marek finally dragged himself out of bed after a restless night, he had a long hot shower trying to wash away the lethargy weighing him down. He glanced out the bathroom window and saw the morning had dawned cloudy and dull.

That was exactly how he felt: dull, foggy and listless; drained and depleted. The tank was empty. He yearned for a bright Australian sunny day which he believed would re-energise him.

Most of the last week seemed to belong to an avatar or clone of another Marek Benning, not himself, the only son of Milosz and Alicja Benningowicz. Not this Marek Benning, who had to accept that his parents were both deceased, and he was in Zakopane, Poland; far from his home in Newcastle, Australia, trying to come to terms with the void caused by the loss first of his mother and now of his father.

At what age does one stop feeling orphaned?

Time dragged. He was reminded of a Beatles song his parents had played, *Lady Madonna*, which contained the words, *Sunday morning creeping like a nun*. He had never been sure of what it meant but he thought he was experiencing it now, on this Sunday.

Near lunchtime, he decided he had things about as well organised as he could manage and so he gave up. His take-home luggage had expanded with those of his father's possessions with which he could not bear to part. It would be a tight squeeze in terms of luggage weight limits for the flight.

He couldn't stomach another can of soup and for lunch he toasted some stale bread, finished off the butter, and ate the last apple. It helped to pass the time and fill some of the void. A void which had nothing to do with hunger. More like a yearning.

When he'd finished, he showered, dressed, and sat with *Lord Jim* waiting for Ana to arrive.

It was only when he heard a firm knock at his door that he realised he had dozed off. When he opened it, Ana immediately said, "When you didn't answer the first time, I thought you had forgotten and gone out."

He assured her he had done no such thing. "No, I hadn't forgotten. I sat down to read and fell asleep. My body clock is out of sync. I'm actually looking forward to getting out of the apartment."

When he realised how ungrateful that sounded, he apologised, "I don't mean that 'getting out' was the only thing I was looking forward to. Truly. Sorry. I had a restless night and I'm a bit gloomy this morning, but I'm definitely looking forward to the concert."

Ana pursed her lips, partly closed one eye, and gave him a doubting, side-eyed stare – *a variation on her mother's* – before smiling and saying, "Chodźmy! It's time."

All seemed forgiven as they set off and she put her arm through his. Over her other arm she carried a garment zip-bag. Marek reached across and took the garment bag without any comment from her other than a grateful look which seemed to say volumes.

"Well Marek," she said, giving him a bit of a shake and a playful bump of her hip. "Let's see if we can brighten your day for you. Or, at least, what's left of it."

The hall wasn't far, and when they arrived, she advised him where to sit to get the best view and sound. She then said she had to go back-stage to get ready.

There was much to observe. The hall was decorated with old, romanticised paintings of scenes of *husaria,* cavalry wearing armour and bizarre, winged helmets, from Poland's troubled Middle Ages. He studied in more detail, the heroic murals, frescoes, and religious iconography; triumphal scenes of kings he'd never heard of: Casimir III, Augustus III, Sigismund I the Old, the son of Emperor (*Good King*) Wenceslas, a doppelgänger for Santa Claus. Only a photo of Lech Wałęsa greeting Pope John Paul II did he actually recognise.

Decorations were predominantly in the national colours of red and white, plus the city's blue and white flag, designating Zakopane as, 'Poland's winter capital'. As intended, the combination of red, white and blue brightened the atmosphere.

As the audience shuffled in to take their seats his anticipation was heightened considerably by their animated voices, flamboyant national dress and particularly the hats some men wore. The audience clearly covered a wide age range that made him think that the *Gorals*, occasionally known as Polish highlanders, were a proud part of the entertainment, ever willing to display their heritage, despite *Goral* being the name of a goat-like antelope. Comparing his own clothes to those of most of the audience, he felt as if he had arrived at a fancy-dress party in his *King Gee*s and a blue singlet.

Right on cue, the choir filed on stage to a smattering of applause and assembled. When in their formation, their traditional Polish costumes looked spectacular and drew another round of applause. The women wore billowing white lacy blouses, colourfully beaded and embroidered vests and flared skirts. The men had donned black Cossack-style, baggy felt trousers. Together, they created a spectacular tableau. Many sported white hats while others wore a cap or beret; and all wore black lace-up boots. It could have been a publicity photo-shoot for a tourist advertisement. He now knew what 'getting ready' meant.

The audience again applauded as the choirmaster took his place centre stage, faced the audience and bowed. Turning to face the singers, he held his hands in a typical conductor's pose and waited. A hush fell throughout the hall.

From the first song to the last, Marek experienced the merry-go-round ride of emotions: the joy, cheerfulness, playfulness and, in some cases, the sadness, which the choir's well-chosen repertoire expertly conveyed. He could not catch all the lyrics but the tunes, harmonies, and clever arrangements were varied and thoroughly entertaining. The choir echoed calls from the audience in between their stamping, whistles and exclamations. Along with everyone, Marek applauded vigorously at the end of each song.

Before what turned out to be the penultimate song, the choirmaster stepped forward and announced: "A special request has been made on behalf of a visitor to Zakopane who has returned owing to a family bereavement. For him and his friends here, it is a time of sadness, of parting. This is a song close to all our hearts." Marek's scalp began to tingle as the choirmaster concluded: "I hope you will enjoy, *Karnawał się skończył.*"

After hearing his parents say the name of one of their favourite songs so often, even Marek could translate that title: *The Carnival is Over.* The version was sung *a capella,* featuring the deep opening chords of the men's bass voices contrasting, then blending and harmonising with, the soprano and contralto voices of the women. He sat transfixed with his eyes welling at the beauty of the rich texture of melody and harmony, supported by the emotive lyrics.

At its conclusion, the audience applauded wildly with some standing and calling, "*Brawo!*" All Marek could do was sit and clap, which he did slowly, as if beating time, in echo to the song itself. A lingering, fading *marche funèbre* in homage to his parents.

Throughout the finale to the concert, a bright playful song which the audience obviously knew well and expected, Marek sat, head bowed, barely restraining his tears, transfixed by the haunting phrases of the song Ana and the choir had gifted him.

As the applause died away, it was replaced by the scraping of chairs as people stood, collected their belongings, and shuffled their way out. Marek sat and waited to regain his composure, and hoped Ana would appear soon. He was oblivious to the stares of the people who knew, or suspected, him to be a stranger in their midst. When Ana did emerge, without caring who noticed, he hugged her and kissed her on each cheek in a wave of gratitude and affection, acknowledging her beautiful and generous gift.

Eventually Ana gently broke the hug and stared into his eyes, clearly affected by this public display, but unconcerned by onlookers.

Magdalena's stare again!

"Would you like to meet a few of the choir members who knew your father? I know they would very much like to meet you."

With only a slight hesitation he agreed. "Yes, alright. I would certainly like to meet the choirmaster and thank him personally for including *Karnawał się skończył*. It was a beautiful rendition."

And then, he asked, disingenuously, "I wonder how they knew its importance to my parents … and me?"

Ana simply responded with a wide-eyed shake of her head and a shrug at the mystery of it all.

After a few minutes spent meeting some of the choir members who expressed their condolences, Ana introduced him to Karol, the conductor who, Marek thought, had a singularly appropriate name for a choirmaster. He thanked him saying, "The arrangement was even more moving in *a capella* style than I could have imagined."

Karol's response, "The Seekers might have been Australian, but that song is pure eastern European in every other way. We Gorals have a proud style of our own."

They stayed for only a few more minutes before he realised how depleted he felt after the strain of the past few days. Both his mind and body seemed to have reached a standstill.

As they left the hall, Ana again slipped her arm through his. They walked home slowly and as they were passing a pizzeria, Ana suggested they get some for their evening meal as few other cafés opened on Sundays.

There was an unvoiced understanding that Ana would keep him company for dinner; a pleasant thought, fazed as he was by the whole Zakopane experience, and its coming to a close.

While waiting in the pizzeria, he ventured the comment, "You know, Joseph Conrad admired much of H.G. Wells' writing. One of his books has a dedication to him."

"*Przepraszam?* I mean, pardon? What are you talking about?"

"Sorry, my mind was just wandering. It's a bit of a twisted connection really, but as you now know, Dad was a huge fan of Conrad. He always claimed Conrad was a writer of his time, writing as he did in the turbulent years of 1890 to 1920.

A time in which previously accepted values, and beliefs were thrown into question. I know that in his novel, *The Secret Agent*, Conrad wrote a dedication to H.G. Wells. That led me to think of Wells' book, *The Time Machine*. I feel a bit like the main character, the un-named time traveller, who gets transported back in time. One week ago, I knew very little about Zakopane and the people who live here."

"And ...?" queried Ana.

"For almost a week I've lived in this perfectly lovely place, in an apartment I never knew my father had, met his brother, my cousin and a group of his friends who have been incredibly hospitable and I've met your mother and found out she and my father were in a relationship. And I've met you, who has been so helpful through it all. I'm dazed."

Ana stopped, turned to him, placed her hands on his shoulders, reached up and kissed him briefly on the lips. "It has been a difficult time for you, but you have done everything possible to give your father the farewell he deserved. You have shown us how much you loved and respected him, and we admire that. Family is everything."

Stunned by the kiss and moved by her comment for other reasons, he said, "I can't think what my life will be like without him being around. He once gave me his opinion of *Lord Jim*, which he considered Conrad's second-best novel. He thought *Jim's* personal philosophy was that one should think first, do one's best, then be optimistic, and take pride and confidence in your actions, whatever happens. I've tried to do that but I'm not sure it's working."

"We can see that you have, and we think it has worked. Now let's go home to your father's place."

The concert had changed Marek's mood in stark contrast from the low he had experienced that morning. When they arrived, Ana put the pizzas in the oven saying, "It's a bit early, we'll have them later. Shall I make coffee, or would you like a small vodka courtesy of your father's mini bar? The bottle is there," she said, pointing to the *Watrawódka* on the shelf. "By the way, that name translates as 'highlander tea' and it seems to me to be an invitation for us to drink a final toast to your dad here in his apartment."

Marek thought for a moment. "Why not? A glass of Dad's vodka seems highly appropriate."

Ana poured two generous shots and as they clinked glasses she said, "To Milosz Benningowicz and his son Marek! *Twoje zdrowie!*"

"And cheers to you too!" Marek echoed, but when holding a glass of vodka, he thought it sounded so much better in Polish. They both downed their shots in a mouthful and, much to Marek's dismay, he coughed and spluttered at the strong alcohol going down his windpipe. Ana was amused and came up and wiped his watering eyes.

She continued standing in front of him. This time it was Marek who bent forward, searching her face and then, as if having made a decision, kissed her.

It was not a 'thank you' kiss but a reactive one, stirred by the emotional roller-coaster ride of the past week. It developed into an outpouring of stifled emotions. He felt Ana responding as she placed her hand behind his head, pulling him to her and pressing herself close against him.

His passion stirred. Or was it lust? Whichever, it was taking control. His hand tenderly caressed her cheek, moved to the back of her head, then neck and down to caressing her back, circling lower to her hips and curves of her bottom, which he gently clasped and squeezed, before moving it back to her waist.

Maintaining his hold with one hand, his other went searching upwards before settling on her breast which he gently clasped and squeezed through the thin woollen material.

Her response was a sigh, which Marek construed as one of pleasure and he lowered his hand and slid it under the knitted top and back to her breast covered only by a silky bra. He found her firm nipple, wanted more and after a moment he lifted the cup over her breast allowing his palm to slide over it and feel its warmth, softness and smoothness, before brushing his thumb back and forth over her nipple. Their lips remained pressed together.

Suddenly she broke the kiss, eased herself back a little, crossed her arms over her upper body and in one sweeping movement, raised and removed her top. With one breast covered and the other wantonly exposed, they resumed their passionate, lust-laden embrace. Moments later, without disengaging, they stumbled into the bedroom and collapsed onto the bed. Frantically, they removed each other's clothing, allowing hands and fingers the freedom to explore. Balancing on one forearm, he leant forward and kissed and nuzzled every part of Ana's face, neck and breasts, as one hand moved lower.

Briefly, after the initial foray, they lay on their sides facing each other. Ana then took his penis gently in her hand, but it was driving Marek beyond his powers of self-control, and he stopped her. She looked startled but then intensely excited as he slid his body further down the bed and began to kiss and nip around her upper thighs before using his tongue and lips to greater, more targeted and satisfying effect. Ana's hands riffled through his hair murmuring her approval, even delighting in the friction of his stubbly face on her inner thighs.

After a few minutes, she indicated it was time and he entered her as slowly as his urgent need would allow.

Gradually, their urgency intensified, their motion coordinated until they reached their peak. Gasping, guttural groans eased into blissful sighs of contentment.

For a short period, they held the moment with neither moving. Both were savouring the contact and the shuddering release of tension as involuntary pulsations emanated from their conjoined bodies and spread to their extremities. Ana continued to grip him with both arms and legs until their passion had fully subsided. Only after that did Marek disengage and stretch out beside her.

He saw with some concern that her eyes were glistening. He went to wipe the tears away, but she held his hand saying, "I'm alright. It was just … so beautiful." Again, they kissed, but this time it was a kiss of deep gratification.

They lay together alternately dozing and caressing each other for some time before Ana asked, "Should we warm up the pizzas now?"

"I'm still enjoying the sensation of having satisfied one appetite. I *could* savour some more delights here, but yes, I could also eat some pizza if you're hungry."

Ana gave him a playful punch and padded naked into the kitchen to turn on the oven. He watched her go and then went to join her.

As she bent to get plates out of the cupboard, he pressed himself against her from behind, holding her hips with both hands, luxuriating in the sensation.

"If you don't stop that, I'm going to drop something, and we'll have nothing to eat."

"Speak for yourself." Reluctantly, he backed off asking, "Would you like another vodka? There's a different bottle here that's almost empty. We might as well finish it off."

He poured the drinks and again they swallowed in one mouthful. Again, they sealed the toast with a kiss, tasting the

Polish *wisniowka*, with its deceptively sweet cherry taste on each other's lips. They laughed.

They took their pizza back to the bedroom and ate it in bed. To Marek it was so far out of his usual practice it felt decadent.

They talked as they ate, and Ana remarked, "We can't leave the sheets in this condition. They'll have to be washed and dried before they can be given away to anyone. I'll take care of them when we clean out the flat."

Marek took their plates back to the kitchen and washed them while Ana stayed in bed. When he returned, she was lying with her eyes closed, looking so calm and peaceful that he thought she was asleep.

He hesitated as he thought again how indebted he was to her for her kindness. When he needed it most, she had been there. She wasn't *the one*, but she had been by his side over the last week while he faced the ordeal of his father's death, funeral, ashes distribution and then, the concert this afternoon that topped it all off so respectfully.

When he climbed into bed, she opened her eyes, smiled, and held out her hand. They embraced, again caressing, kissing and teasing each other from toes to earlobes with increasing sensuality, which led inevitably to another round of lovemaking. Wordlessly, they let their bodies communicate as they explored every sensation in a gentle and more controlled manner, attending in stimulating detail to each other's responses.

This time, with surprising strength and agility, she rolled him over, positioning herself on top, gazing intently into his eyes. Kneeling over him, she teased him by allowing her breasts to brush his face, eyes and eventually his lips. She told Marek to lie still as she guided him with one hand and began the rhythmic motion that gradually built to almost simultaneous climaxes. They held the exquisite sensation of the moment but as pulses slackened, Ana collapsed onto him. They lay facing each other, sated, with arms entwined, before she rolled off him and they sank into an exhausted sleep.

Marek awoke at dawn to the sound of the shower running. He got out of bed, pulled on trousers and shirt and made coffee. He tidied up a few things from the night before and watched as Ana appeared naked from the shower. She went straight into the bedroom and began to dress. Without removing his eyes from her, he followed her.

Eventually he asked, "What will your mother say?"

"About what? Us? Nothing." Ana curtly replied, "Why should she?"

"I just thought she might wonder where you were last night."

"She knows where I am. I kept her life with your father private and confidential. She will do the same for me. It works both ways. We have another saying: *jaki ojciec taki syn*'. In English it's: 'like father, like son'. Only in this case we should say, like mother, like daughter. With one additional peculiar element."

"Oh? What's that?" He asked, puzzled.

"Same bed."

Marek had no comeback. Her reply was so unexpected it jolted him back to mundane reality. All he could think to say was, "I've made coffee. We have to talk."

"Alright, we can talk but we don't have to talk about us. You're going home to Australia in a few hours. End of story."

"But what about last night? Didn't that mean something?"

"Yes, of course it did. How can you ask?" she replied heatedly. "But last night there was no talk of love in what we did. It was basic human emotional need."

"Ana, I can't just leave it there. I feel you and Zakopane have got into my bones."

"Didn't your father tell you Poland was in your blood? Why not your bones? Listen, here's the reality. When you get home, you will have a lot to deal with: your father's will, his estate, not to mention reclaiming your own life. That will all happen fifteen thousand kilometres away from here. It has been wonderful meeting you, despite the tragic circumstances. You are a good, decent man but your time here is over. I know I will never forget you but there is no *us*!"

Marek stood still while Ana's words sank in.

She finished dressing and they walked into the kitchen and drank the coffee.

"Can I walk you home?"

"That's not necessary. At this time of day, I'll be fine."

"But …"

"You can drop the keys at home to *Mumia* when you're leaving Zakopane. We will see everything here is as it should be."

"So, this is goodbye? May I kiss you one last time?"

"I don't think that would be wise; but thank you for asking." She reached out her hand, "*Do widzenia i powodzenia.*"

Having wished him goodbye and good luck, Ana walked out of his life, closing the door behind her. Once again, Marek felt plunged into a deepened sense of loss.

21

Marek closed and locked the door of his father's apartment for the last time, pocketed the keys and stowed the last of his luggage in the hire car. He had left some of his personal things to make space for his father's possessions which held too many memories for him to leave them behind.

When he stopped at the Wójcik house to hand over the keys, Magdalena led him into the sitting room. They stood, facing each other, with very mixed emotions clearly evident on both their faces. "Magdalena, I don't know how to thank you for what you and Ana have done. I couldn't have managed without your help."

She slowly stepped close to him, examining him with a look of unnerving intensity. It seemed as if she was looking, not only at him, but through him, as she processed his farewell words.

Eerily, he felt she was looking at him, but seeing someone else. Still without saying a word, she reached out and wrapped her arms around him, almost smothering him to her bosom, as if she was absorbing him into herself. He felt, rather than heard, her gentle sobs.

It dawned on him that through him, she was saying a final farewell to Milosz and a phase of her life.

It was an excruciating moment. The combination of her relationship with his father and his own embarrassment from Ana having spent the night with him, left him struggling for words. All he could say was, "*Dziękuję Magdalena i do widzenia.*" Thank you and goodbye seemed grossly inadequate in the circumstances.

Magdalena stood back, holding his shoulders firmly at arms' distance for some time before releasing him and in turn saying, "*Dziękuję Mareki do widzenia. Nigdy cię nie zapomnimy.*"

For both, the parting scene was loaded with thoughts for which neither could find words. "No, I'll never forget you either, or Ana, or Zakopane. You're all permanently etched into my being."

Marek turned and walked away. One last backward glance showed Magdalena with one arm partly outstretched and the other to her face. He had to blink his eyes several times to clear them.

He'd allowed more than two hours to drive to Kraków airport and return the car. It gave him time to have a last look at the countryside around his parents' birthplace. In some fields he saw farm labourers tending market garden crops. It was easy to imagine they, or others like them, had been doing the same work for centuries.

Returning the car at the depot was mercifully free of complications. He was provided with a transfer to the terminal where he shouldered his carry-on bag and dragged his check-in bag to the Departures desk.

He was scrutinised at the security check station, doubtless because he was young, male and not a Polish national. Clearance seemed to be grudgingly given without the ignominy of a strip search.

He walked to his departure lounge and sat down. His mood had lifted, he was homeward bound; albeit, to an empty house in which his father would never again be physically present.

Attending to one last loose end he rang Anton and promised to keep in touch and urged him to do the same.

He asked him to pass on his regards to his uncle and tell him it had been a real pleasure meeting him, despite the unfortunate circumstances. They wished each other *do widzenia i powodzenia.*

Marek knew it was very likely a last goodbye and that some good luck would go down very well.

After the call he reconstructed the events of the previous night. It had been totally unexpected on his part, although he couldn't help but think Ana had been right in her assessment that it was a basic human response in a unique situation.

Whatever the case, it had been an intimate, tension-releasing encounter which he would never forget.

When his flight was called Marek shuffled into the queue, boarding pass and passport in hand. He had a window seat which afforded him final views of Poland.

It was a comparatively short flight of three hours to Frankfurt where he had a three hour wait for a connecting flight to Sydney. Total travel time, including time spent waiting, was over twenty-eight hours – plus the train connection to Newcastle.

There was nothing for it but to be patient.

During the brief flight he was able to chat with the *dama* sitting next to him: another ex-pat Pole returning to her adopted home, in her case, Brussels, Belgium.

The discussion focused on what a complex country Poland is. Such a varied, often tortured history being one of the most invaded European countries, but one with which they each had an unshakeable admiration for the resilience of its people.

He filled in time in Frankfurt by strolling through the terminal. It was a major international flight hub and there were thousands of people, many in exotic national dress, milling about.

It suddenly occurred to him to use up his last Polish zlotys to buy a present for Helena. He chose a pendant with an amethyst stone, knowing it was her birthstone.

In what he judged to be an astute bit of bargaining; he also bought a pair of garnet tear-drop earrings for Gwynne which he thought would suit her complexion. He really had no idea about such things, but it was worth a gamble. And then he saw a stall selling national dress costumes and he thought of Merren. He chose a distinctly Polish fairy-style costume in a size he could only guess would fit.

He was very pleased with himself, even though he had to wrap it tightly so he could fit it into his carry-on luggage.

He began a text message to Helena telling her where he was and his best guess of his arrival in Newcastle. Just as he was finishing, his flight was called, and he quickly added a request to forward the information to Gwynne. He knew his phone would be switched off for most of the next twenty hours except for a brief stop in Singapore. His companion for the duration would be *Lord Jim,* which he was determined to finish before he got home.

Boarding was routine but this time he had an aisle seat next to a young girl, a university student from Sydney. She had been visiting Germany for research, as part of her Architecture Master's degree, specialising in reconstruction of historic buildings. He listened but his thoughts drifted onto a reconstruction tangent: how he would have to reconstruct life without his father.

Meals were served, announcements made and the options for entertainment on the screen in front of him were searched but there was no escaping the sheer boredom and discomfort of a long-haul flight in 'cattle class'.

All too frequently, his thoughts about *Lord Jim* and how the book reminded him of his father's love of Conrad and *Jim's* approach to life: Think, do your best, move on. That, and the realisation that he was now an orphan. How ridiculous that sounded. Something unimaginable one week ago. Except in his thoughts, he could never again talk to his parents about life, joke with them, or reminisce; never hear their real-world Polish-accented voices. The consolation was he would forever be warmed by knowing how much they had achieved, and how they had loved each other. And how much they supported and encouraged him. He began to think of Helena, Alan, and his workmates and how much he needed them to fill that void.

And then there was Gwynne!

He dozed into a troubled sleep where the events of his passionate night with Ana were vividly replayed. As he relived them, a strange phenomenon occurred: it was not Ana he was seeing, caressing and making love to, but *her* – Gwynne. It was Ana's body, but the face had morphed into that *other* one, the one whose place had been temporarily usurped.

He suddenly woke and became aware he was aroused. He looked right and left then furtively laid his book on his lap and crossed his hands over it. *What the hell? Am I a hormone driven teenager?* He knew about rapid eye movement sleep from an optometrist he had once dated. During sleep involving REM – rapid eye movement – there is a propensity to dream with realistic intensity, activated by visual and emotional memories resulting in decreased rational thought and extremely lurid dreams.

They were all that, and more!

Now all he could think of was seeing Gwynne. It was only a week since he had seen her, and their last encounter had been disquieting. There had been a 'moment', but it had passed before it led anywhere. Now his foremost desire was to recapture it, but he knew that wouldn't happen until the right circumstances presented themselves. He had no idea when or how, or even if, he could regain the jigsaw pieces of his life back home, let alone form them back into a clear picture.

Half an hour before the scheduled landing he finished *Lord Jim*. He marvelled over what Conrad, born hundreds of kilometres away in what was then Poland but is now Ukraine, had achieved. He wrote in English, his second acquired language after French, which he had only learned in his twenties. It was a phenomenal literary accomplishment: the plot, vocabulary and narrative structure were, and remain, masterful. It evoked his recollections of how his father had spoken about Conrad with such admiration; and he could only agree. He closed his eyes, contemplating Jim's adventure-filled life and his tragic end. He compared it to his own present state, as if having come to the end of a favourite childhood book with its much-loved characters, bound within its hard backed, now sealed, covers.

What now?

Gideon Owen Davis
Minmi, New South Wales
1841
IV

The mine owners who had the coal mining lease for the entire Minmi district permitted Owen to build a small cabin a short distance from the main workings. Whereas supplies at Ebenezer had always been irregular, in Minmi they had the advantage of being closer to Hexham, on the Hunter River from where coal could be shipped. From there they also had access to the rail link to Newcastle for purchasing much needed household goods.

The brethren from the Welsh Congregational Church welcomed him and gradually he was able to settle into a life not too dissimilar to that which he might have lived back in Pengam. The routine of work, evangelical religious observance and social connections within the village satisfied his few needs.

His life continued without any serious adverse events until an extended period of rain caused a nearby creek to overflow. Water flooded into one of the more productive pits and mining operations were stalled for several months.

Men, with families, but without paid work, started to drift away to other mines. Being unmarried, Owen was in a slightly better position. Having the use of Threlkeld's cart, which he could use to transport all manner of goods to and from Minmi to Hexham enabled him to bear the layoff period more easily.

When the pit reopened, work resumed. Long hours spent driving the cart had allowed Owen the time to reflect deeply on his day-to-day existence. Reverend Threlkeld had once told him that Governor Macquarie had believed in Wilberforce's views so much he had named a town on the Hawkesbury River after him. Owen recalled that the Ebenezer mission had been named after the chapel built at the insistence of his wife's father, Thomas Arndell. Wilberforce's perseverance had resulted in the recent passing of the Slavery Abolition Act.

The sentiments held by Lachlan Macquarie through Wilberforce's idealised views on human beings affirmed that every man and woman, including those bearing the convict stain, were capable of reform. Once emancipated, many convicts had distinguished themselves through individual initiative and enterprise. This liberal approach was guided by a spirit of human equality that saw an emancipated convict standing on level ground with their free-settler neighbours, all created in the divine image.

The trials and misfortunes experienced by Reverend Threlkeld, which had resulted in him abandoning the Ebenezer mission troubled him. There was a distinct touch of Evangelical fatalism in his tone when Reverend Threlkeld had informed him that Wilberforce had been instrumental in the appointment of the Reverend

Samuel Marsden as chaplain to the colony. This was in stark contrast to the fact that it was Marsden who was the celebrant in his marriage to Threlkeld's present wife.

Seeking further counsel on his own future, Owen wrote to his old mentor, Mr Lewis in Pengam, describing the turn of events regarding the mission and the terrible plight of the Aborigines. He described how Mr Threlkeld had learnt the Awabakal dialect to preach to them in their own language; even translating the gospel into the Awabakal language. Reluctantly, he finished his letter by recounting how the demise of the mission had thwarted his own vocation. He alluded to commonly held resentment of the Aborigines for not behaving like good 'white' Christians. This, despite the frequently disgraceful behaviour those supposed Christians often displayed.

Owen was overjoyed when the following year, he received a parcel from Mr Lewis. In it was a wordy letter and a book. Besides news from home, the letter urged him to seek out opportunities to help bring Christianity to the natives by his own behaviour, treatment and acceptance of them. He complimented Threlkeld's efforts by comparing them to those of Evangelist Henry Martin, a chaplain in the East India Company, who had translated the New Testament into Urdu.

The book in the parcel, 'A Practical View of Christianity', was by Reverend William Wilberforce. It set out an enlightened view of morality in a world in which God reveals new rights and duties of professed Christians in public and private life. Christianity, it proclaimed, was not a mere morality to be espoused in private. A true Christian should make it part of his everyday existence. The book emphasised the belief that every human being was made in God's image.

In Owen's opinion, Wilberforce's views were not supported in practice by a majority in the colony. He couldn't help contrasting such views with the attitudes which had contributed to the terrible massacres of Aborigines. He heard about one in particular a few years ago in which almost thirty Aboriginal men, women and children were killed. That those perpetrators were brought to justice and hanged did not alter the fact that such attitudes were rife in the far reaches of the colony.

The book prompted him to examine whether he was frittering away his vocation on the tedium of work in a backwater mining village and ignoring his calling. Had he turned a deaf ear to God's call? Had the more benign climate lulled him into complacency? The heat of summer was something he found enervating and exhausting, but the other seasons, compared to those in Wales, were much more tolerable. The greatest variable was water. In dry spells, even the nearby creek was reduced to a chain of waterholes, unless it was replenished by fierce, but welcome, storms.

With so much time to think, he came to the conviction that Wilberforce's message reaffirmed the concept that all men of all colour and religion are made in God's image. It impacted his understanding of the diminishing number of Aborigines he saw around him.

As time went on, he developed an interest in growing a few vegetables which supplemented his meals. Any excess he could trade for eggs or bread baked by a housewife living in the village. Meat was more readily available from nearby sheep and cattle farmers. Occasionally he was able to visit Newcastle where he bought the few items of furniture, household utensils, clothing and linen he needed, as well as one of the rare luxuries he afforded himself: books.

Seemingly unrelated to the weighty issues in Mr Lewis' letter, was his disturbing final comment. It was one which had increasingly exercised his mind. Mr Lewis reminded him Wilberforce hadn't married until he was almost forty years old, and Mr Lewis urged him to seek a partner in life. In another respect, it reminded Owen that circumstances of class and position in the rapidly developing colony were not those in which he had been raised in Pengam. His father-in-law, Surgeon and Magistrate Thomas Arndell, had taken an ex-convict as a second wife.

Newcastle, NSW
2005

22

Marek was tired, fogged by jet lag and struggling to pick up the pieces after the seismic shift in his life over the last ten days. He felt different. Somehow, somewhere, there had been a re-set in his personal compass; the landscape was different. He felt as if he had been set adrift.

Walking into his home, knowing his father's voice and footsteps would never again be heard, was unfathomable.

Partly to blame for his disorientation was his experience with Ana. It had been a departure from his personal code of behaviour, but he couldn't blame anyone, and nor did he want to. It was, as she had said, an instant, unplanned, physical release. He had succumbed willingly to it. And he wasn't sorry. He had never taken sex for granted but he had revelled in the one-night stand. It made him realise that love came in many shades and answered many needs.

The day after his return, he finally rang Gwynne. He wasn't sure how to pick up the pieces. He was afraid that his absence, and what had happened with Ana, would somehow create a barrier between them. But of one thing he was certain: he had to do everything in his power to convince Gwynne that they could make a future together. If she continued to deploy her line of defences, a barrier of Iron Curtain proportions, he was up for the challenge. His confidence was shaken but he wasn't prepared to give up.

Like a ray of sunshine after a storm, her response to his phone call was everything he could have wished for. It was as if the phone he held acted as a defibrillator while his heartbeat skipped a beat, restarted, then steadied.

"Oh Marek, welcome home. Good to know you're back safely. Merren's been asking when we'll see you."

"Thanks Gwynne. Nice to know I've been missed – by someone. I feel as if I've been away for a month. How are you both?"

"We're fine. You sound tired."

"I'm knackered! Sorry, but I think I've been in a parallel universe. The events, experiences and decisions that were needed – and the flight – have all been very peculiar. Now I'm home, I'm trying to pick up the loose ends of my life. But first, there's something I want to ask you and I'm not sure how to put it."

"You don't sound like your old self. It sounds ominous. Go on."

"Helena and I have decided to have a quiet gathering for family and friends to place Dad's ashes next to Mum's, followed by a small wake. I know you're not part of the family, but you know Helena and Alan, and well ... I was wondering if you would like to come. I can't explain exactly. I just thought ... Well, would you?"

"Marek, you've been a big help to me over the last couple of months, with the new office and ... I've been doing some thinking while you were away. I feel I owe you and, yes, I will come."

"Thank you. That's great. I don't know why, I just wanted someone with me and ... I thought of ... er ..."

"It's okay. Tell me when it is, and I'll sort out something. I never met your father, but I can guess how you must feel."

"I think he would have liked your practical attitude to life.

He said that about my last … Sorry, I'm thinking out loud. It's on Monday next week. 11:00am, at the crematorium rose garden. I'll pick you up if that suits you."

"That's fine Marek. Will Merren see you before then?"

"I'd love to but first I've got some unfinished work business and I have to meet up with Ross, my solicitor, and go over the will and all the legal matters. There are a few of dad's mates I have to contact, including Darren Merrigan. Ross and Darren have been my closest friends and supporters and I have to fill them in on what's happened. I'll get back to you with the final arrangements. Thanks again Gwynne. It's been great to hear your voice."

Milosz's ashes were placed in a columbarium next to his mother's after a non-religious ceremony. Marek felt obliged to say a few words and could only think of thanking both for their love for each other and dedication to the family. And for the way he had been raised. "Dad, Milosz, was a family provider and loving husband and father. A man who showed commitment and loyalty to whatever, or with whoever, he was involved. He had a down to earth attitude. At home he had a good sense of humour, even with his Polish fixations and upbringing. He was strong-willed but fair-minded and always tried to do what was right and fair. He is now with my mother here where I know he would wish to be."

There was a general murmur of agreement followed by a few moments of silence after which most mourners came up to Marek and shook his hand.

Several close friends and workmates joined them in a private room at the local Workers Club for the wake. Marek heard again some of his father's old work stories, but in a slightly more lurid banter than his father had related them at home. When the silences between the stories started to lengthen, people began to make their farewells. As they departed, each again shook his hand, often placing a hand on his shoulder showing genuine sympathy for the loss of someone they'd worked with and variously referred to as, 'a good bloke'.

Back at his cousin's home, the conversation was stilted, with both Helena and Marek weighed down by the realisation that the curtain had been drawn on the lives of all their Poland-born parents. Even the appearance of the *Jagnięcina,* barbecued Polish style shish kebabs of lamb with onions and potatoes, barely lifted their spirits. In the sombre mood overlaying the occasion, Helena continued trying desperately to lift everyone's spirits by making a fuss over the fact that Alan had done much of the preparation.

While picking at the food, Marek recounted in an emotionally charged voice, the Zakopane hospital scene details, the subsequent funeral and spreading of half of his father's ashes. It was something he had not felt capable of sharing until the right moment. As soon as he mentioned Magdalena, Helena couldn't restrain herself and the questions came like bullets.

"What? He had a lady-friend? Are you joking? At his age? What about Alicja? That's disgusting!"

Marek's explanation was given within the whirlpool of his own feelings, particularly his night with Ana casting a shadow on his conscience. "Helena, I've gone over this a million times. It upset me at the time, and still does, but when the story eventually came out about Magdalena's teenage crush on Dad, and then his return to Zakopane, I couldn't hate her. She was actually very nice. And she really loved him and was very helpful in making the necessary arrangements, as was her daughter Ana, the one who rang me with the news of Dad's heart attack. Back here in Newcastle, it all seems unreal, but now I think about it, their relationship was one of mutual friendship, care, love and support. I see it as something, entirely separate from anything to do with his life here in Australia."

Alan managed to confine his response to a wink when he caught Gwynne's eye. At one point, in a misguided attempt to lighten the tone, he interrupted briefly to suggest that Marek could tell him all the lurid details later. Marek gave him a baleful look and, when he saw the twinkle in Alan's eye, simply smiled circumspectly. "I'm afraid I don't know all the lurid details and I'm not sure I want to know. Nor will I be sharing them with anyone else if I do find any. The visit to Poland was harrowing and I'm still coming to terms with it all."

Helena remained incredulous that the man she called Uncle Milosz, should have lived, what she could only think of as a double life. She continued to express her doubts but all Marek could add was: "You had to be there." Emotionally drained by the day's events on top of the last two weeks, he didn't have the stomach, or the courage, for further discussion.

He decided this was a good time to lighten the mood by handing over the amethyst pendant he had bought Helena. He tried to make it look like an afterthought as he placed the package on the table and, with one finger on it, slid it across to her saying, "Oh, I almost forgot, this is for you. Hope you like it."

"Oh Marek, you shouldn't have!" She carefully unwrapped it and, exclaimed, "Oh, it's lovely! And my birthstone too." She held it up for all to see and admire.

It worked as a conversation changer as he mentioned some of the legal issues to be dealt with regarding his father's estate. There wasn't much more to be said, and after Helena and Alan gave Marek a brief catch-up on what had been happening locally, they began to clear the table.

Alan offered more drinks but with the drive home ahead, they declined. "That would be good Alan, but another time, okay? Gwynne has to collect Merren. Thanks both of you, for the lunch and your support." With a glance at Gwynne and a questioning raised eyebrow he added, "We'll keep in touch."

Helena and Alan walked with them to the front gate where they said their goodbyes. Dismay and doubt still showed on Helena's face, but the hug and kiss she gave him were a balm to his still raw emotions.

Throughout the day's events, Gwynne had felt she was in the role of supporter, mainly for Marek, but for Helena as well. Hearing Marek and Helena talk about Marek's father, she felt she was being drawn into the family web. What surprised her most was that she was feeling quite comfortable with it.

Something had changed and she wasn't sure what. The news about Milosz's new relationship had caused her to rethink her own position, if only from the viewpoint of basic human emotional need. She struggled, with very little success, to separate it from anything to do with physical needs.

She had also noticed a subtle change in Marek, as if he was holding something back. On the way home she said, "You seem a bit down. It's completely understandable. You've had a lot to contend with. Take all the time you need. I'll think of something to tell Merren."

"I'm still coming to grips with the changes in my situation. I guess I feel a bit un-settled having to deal with Dad's sudden death, getting on with work and so on. But no, I don't want to slow things down, as you imply. Actually, I don't think they could go much slower but that's probably just as well. I'm a bit adrift. You both seem like a safe-haven, but I don't want to impose on you."

"If anyone has imposed on anyone, it's me imposing on you. Call me if there's anything I can do. For now, would you mind if you dropped me at my place? I'll collect Merren later. I've got a few things to do first and it might avoid any scene between you and Mum."

Choosing his words carefully, he responded, "I'm sorry it has come to this. I'm fine with Audrey so long as she stays out of *our* personal lives." He glanced to see if she noticed his use of the plural pronoun.

"She's just guessing about us. There's not much to say really, is there?"

She cast him a sidelong glance, suggesting her comment could be a statement or a question. "She means well. She just gets a bit carried away."

"I live in hope. The farther away she is the better, as far as I'm concerned. Sorry, sorry, I don't mean that. Given time, I'll be happy to catch up with her. Another day."

When they arrived home, while still sitting in the car, he turned to her and, producing the package with the garnet tear-drop earrings said, "I wasn't sure if the time was right at Helena's, but I got these for you."

She was completely caught off guard. "Oh Marek, thank you. You're so thoughtful."

"Open it when you get inside. I hope you like them. It's just something that has a connection with my time in Poland. Um, and this is for Merren," he said as he handed over the wrapped Polish fairy costume. "I don't know if it will fit. I had to guess the size."

"Thank you, Marek. And don't be too put off by Mum and Colette. Keith has niggled away at them."

They walked to her door and stood, each looking completely undecided as to how to say goodbye. In the end, Marek had gently taken her by her shoulders, and given her an almost sisterly hug as their cheeks brushed for a few precious seconds.

Just as they separated, Gwynne kissed his cheek. "That's from Merren."

23

The morning after the placement of his father's ashes with his mother's, Marek awoke to an empty house and an empty feeling. His grief still raw, talking about his father's *liaison* with Magdalena, and Helena's comments, had left him emotionally drained. Thoughts of his mother tumbled through his mind with those of his father.

After drifting through the house wondering where to restart his life, he noticed a compact disc lying on a bookshelf. He picked it up, intending to put it in the cd rack, and glanced at the title. The boldly printed title read, Polonaise *in A flat Major, Op 53*. It was his mother's favourite by Frederic Chopin and had probably lain on the shelf where she had left it for the last five years.

A goose has walked over my grave.

Almost without thinking, he picked it up, opened it, and placed the disc in the player. He sat back in his father's favourite armchair holding the remote control for the player. His thumb hovered over it. He contemplated whether he had the courage, the stamina, the stomach, to press the play button.

The compulsion was overwhelming.

He had returned from Poland only ten days ago and was still struggling to come to terms with his circumstances. Being back in the family home in Newcastle, had been a challenging experience. He'd give anything to hear the sounds of his parents' voices, even their footsteps.

He relived the agony of dealing with his mother's death from breast cancer five years previously. Less than two weeks ago, the ceremony, if that's what one called it, of spreading half his father's ashes in the Joseph Conrad reserve in Zakopane, his parents' birthplace, had reopened that wound. He felt again the hurt of learning what he had first thought of as his father's infidelity: his father's betrayal of his mother's memory.

Some things were too much to absorb, and this was one of them. At his father's funeral, he had made a choice to play the finale of his mother's favourite piece of music. The very same work he had just placed in the cd player. She had adored it for many reasons but the main one was the sheer emotion that it generated in the souls of Polish people. The music evoked images of polish culture, art and of patriotism, through the use of the eponymous Polish dance, the Polonaise.

It went on to conjure nationalistic fervour with military style marching rhythms suggesting a call to arms. All this at a time when Poland was in the grip of change, as were many European countries, with citizens demanding social reform. Civil unrest in the working classes led to demonstrations and sometimes violent skirmishes with authorities that culminated in the 'year of revolutions', in 1848. Chopin managed to encapsulate such feelings in his brilliant 'heroic' polonaise.

As if by its own accord, Marek's thumb pressed the play button and the opening chord sounded, led to the first phrase which was then repeated in rising pitch, with slight embellishments.

He immediately drifted back in time, now hearing his mother's voice softly explaining the introduction as it broke into a polonaise rhythm, the national Polish dance reminiscent of Poland's aristocratic past.

It caused him to recall the murals in the Zakopane town hall where he had attended Ana's concert the day after his father's funeral. The paintings depicted battle scenes in which the famous Polish cavalry rode valiantly into combat striking terror into their enemies, every bit as fierce as the feared Cossacks.

Outwardly, as the music played, he was transfixed. Inwardly, his stomach churned, and his throat constricted.

Through the memories of his mother, he once again felt the emotion of the piece as it morphed into the repeated urgent militaristic rhythms of marching men and cannons rumbling into action.

And then he was lulled by the sequence of calming passages in a gentle interlude before being stirred again by a rousing recapitulation of earlier themes building to a stunning, devastating climax.

The final chords of the thunderous conclusion echoed in his mind as the memories of his mother and father, and what he had known until now as the Benning family, faded. He blinked back salty tears, completely overwhelmed by the music itself and his personal sense of loss.

Frederic Chopin achieved fame through his music which evoked and symbolised all things Polish. His mother and father seemingly invincible to him when he was a child, were now haunting memories. He recalled his father had once said to him, 'You are Australian born and bred, but you have Polish blood in your veins.'

Somehow, because of his mother, he also carried a great love for the musical heritage bequeathed to him by Frederic Chopin.

It too, was in his blood.

The way back to normality rapidly started to unravel when he received his printed bank statement. Even though he had phoned the owners of the job he'd started, his calls had gone unanswered. The disturbingly low balance was caused by three things: his flight to Poland, his expenditure on his father's funeral, and – the most worrying item that was missing, the stage payment from the house owners as per the renovation contract.

Because of the extent of the renovations and the significant materials and labour costs involved, the contract was quite specific in terms of staged payments and missing even one was a serious complication.

Marek rang his bank to confirm there had been no mistake on their part. The bank officer suggested he ring the owners.

When he finally got through after several unanswered calls, the news chilled him.

They explained that one of their major business creditors had gone bankrupt and defaulted on payments owing to them. They in turn were put into an impossible financial position and were temporarily unable to make the stage payment. They advised him that legal action to reclaim their debt was underway but, until that was settled, they would not be able to make good the full payment due to him.

In turn, Marek advised that he had no other choice than to seek legal advice under the terms of the building contract, which defined a builder's rights to progress payments.

A meeting with Ross Brennan was hastily arranged at their local pub. With each of them nursing a beer, Marek listened as Ross explained. "While your contract is sound, financial regulations regarding debt collection are complicated and take time to resolve."

Ross looked uneasy as he continued, "It's clear under the construction contract, you are entitled to receive progress payments but, there are rules to recover payments that have to be followed."

"So where do I stand? What can I do?"

Ross shared Marek's concern. "Not much. I'll set the process in motion, but it will take time. I'll keep you up to speed."

It was cold comfort to Marek, as were Ross' comments on the other matter needed to be resolved: his father's estate.

"I'm making some progress but it's slow going. Besides a notarised translation in English of the death certificate there's other documentation. It takes time; official channels are heavy going."

"Ross, I can get translations made. Dad used the government Interpreting and Translating Centre to get copies of his birth certificate and some other documents before he left for Poland."

"Okay, I'm aware of that service. I'll get you a list. Do it as soon as you can because every box ticked progresses probate on his estate."

He finished by reminding Marek, "Once probate has been granted, as executor of your father's estate, you'll be entitled to recoup most of the funeral costs. In the meantime, I might be able to put a couple of jobs your way: pre-purchase building inspections and so on. I've got two inspections to arrange this week and a real estate agent friend might also have need of similar services. I'll put in a word for you."

"Thanks Ross. I really appreciate it. I'll be sussing out other construction jobs in the meantime; anything I can do to boost my cash flow."

"Before you go, I got some information from that real estate agent mate which will interest you. The land at Minmi you had expressed an interest in buying has been withdrawn from sale."

"Doesn't bother me what happens to it now. In my current position, I'm struggling to cover the essentials," was Marek's cynical reply.

"Listen. You may not believe this, but human remains have been found during a pre-purchase survey of the property. The authorities are investigating the circumstances of the burials and possibly whether a crime has been committed. I'll keep you in the loop if I get any more info."

Marek pointed out, "No hurry. I'll be limited to essentials until my own cash flow is sorted. But thanks anyway.

I'll give Darren a call and run it by him. I think I'll have to cancel all deliveries of materials to the job site. Should I discuss with the owners the need to secure the property with security fencing? From experience, properties left unattended are a target for thieves and vandals."

"Good idea; but do it calmly. Mention it when you have a talk with Darren if you think that will help, but your legal options are fairly limited. It's in the interests of both parties. We need to keep communication channels open. Let me know how you get on."

On the way home Marek wished more than ever, that he could talk things over with his father. This, or anything else, for that matter. He decided that the next best person to talk to was his old boss, Darren Merrigan. He took some consolation in the knowledge that Darren was the type of person who would not say, "I told you so!"

24

Waiting for the grant of probate was an agonisingly uncertain period. When he advised the bank of his father's death, he was informed the bank needed a statement from a solicitor certifying that the attached death certificate, in English, was a certified copy of the original in Polish. At that point he could have screamed. The bank officer advised him that the account balance would be transferred to his account only after all legal requirements were satisfied.

He was able to keep his finances in the black by the slimmest of margins, cutting all but the most necessary expenditure. That included delaying payment on a couple of utility bills for his father's house – based on waiting for probate to be granted. It was a bungee ride in which he bounced up and down at the end of his tether.

The renewal of his builder's licence with the Department of Fair Trading was essential for him to keep working. The timing couldn't be worse and added to his general feelings of resentment, disappointment and fear; something he had never experienced. He felt so embarrassed that he could not tell Helena or Gwynne of his predicament until he had some better news.

That news was slow in coming. He had never felt so constrained by forces beyond his control. The longer it went on, the more isolated he felt from his friends and workmates. He wasn't in the mood to answer questions about his latest job for fear they would make assumptions about the quality of his work or his business judgement. Besides, he thought, everyone had their own problems and wouldn't want to know about his.

More than anything or anyone else, he didn't want to face any questions from Gwynne who, as his accountant, undoubtedly needed to know such details. He knew a day of reckoning was approaching because his tax return would soon be required.

He contemplated doing it himself but, at some point, she would learn the worst. Up to the present, she had only known him as an operating builder in continued employment with a modest but consistent income. Now, without working capital, he wasn't even confident he could seek new jobs and prepare quotes without his business judgement being called into question by himself, and probably others.

He was reluctant to extend his debts on credit, although he knew that's how many tradesmen operated. He had a fair idea of what Gwynne's family would think. Their opinion of him when times were good wasn't all that fantastic. Now that times were anything but, he guessed they would be quite content if he dropped out of the scene altogether – the sooner the better.

During one of his building inspection jobs passed on to him from Ross, he noticed a man, plans in hand, checking the construction of a 'newbuild' next door. Judging by the vehicle parked in front of the house, Marek guessed the man was a council building inspector.

They exchanged greetings in a casual way, but as Marek was leaving, he looked again with a degree of envy at the adjacent building site. He watched as the inspector examined the foundations and footings, normally a fairly routine job. He noticed he was measuring trench dimensions, checking the plan and shaking his head.

"You're looking a bit worried mate. Got a problem?" Marek ventured.

The inspector avoided discussing details but indicated there was an issue. "Maybe. Not sure yet until I go over the approval conditions with my boss back at the office."

Marek glanced at the footings and could see that they seemed alright for a single storey residence. "Single storey, is it?" he queried.

The inspector shook his head, "I think a mistake has been made. I'm just not sure how or by whom. You seem to know a bit," he added.

"I'm a licensed builder myself; just doing a couple of inspections to tide me over." After a slight pause he added, "My job has been temporarily halted. It should be back on track soon. I hope!"

"What area do you generally work in?"

"General domestic building and construction."

The inspector nodded. "What's your name? You got a card with contact details? I might get back to you. We're flat chat at the office."

He had an old card in his truck on which he had to scribble his contact details on the back and handed it over. Marek didn't know what the encounter might mean but, as he watched him drive away, at least he felt that he was still in the game, if only as a reserve player.

Better than being a spectator outside the fence.

25

A week later Marek received the call from the person he had most wanted to talk to, yet dreaded receiving. It was Gwynne, reminding him that the financial year was ending, and his tax return would soon be due, and he should start getting the necessary paperwork in order.

His response was less than enthusiastic. "Yes, I know. It's coming. Just a bit of a delay, that's all."

Sensing a slight hesitation, she asked, "Is everything alright?"

"Yes, more or less."

"From the way you sound it's rather less than more. Come on, what's up?"

He was at a loss. Where to begin? He hedged, saying that settling his father's estate was more complicated and taking longer than expected.

The nearest he came to alluding to his financial difficulties was admitting, "The owner of the house I've been working on has had some problems. He hasn't been able to make the most recent stage payment."

Gwynne's professionalism immediately kicked in, knowing full well how an interruption to cash flow could make life difficult for others in the money chain and she immediately offered to discuss the matter with him.

Marek pulled down the shutters. "I've got Ross Brennan working on it but there may be a need to delay the tax return." He hated saying it.

He did want to see her, but not as a client. That time would have to wait.

She renewed her offer and finished by saying, "You shouldn't leave it too long. It's not going to go away, but you have a bit of time. Let me know if you need an extension."

He tried to reassure her, and himself, by saying, "I'll get back to you as soon as I get any new information." Just to prolong hearing her voice, he enquired, "How have you and Merren been getting on?"

Gwynne gave him a business-like account, "Work; day care for Merren; the usual housekeeping. Oh, I should mention, I've got a new client in my new office. My first."

In the background he heard a call of, "Mummy, I'm finished!"

"Sorry, I've got to go. Motherly duties call." After a slight hesitation she said, "Keep in touch. 'Bye"

"Congratulations on snagging the client and say hello to Merren for me. G'bye".

He felt uncomfortable for not being completely open with her, but he was determined to keep his problems private.

Living and working in a world of uncertainty became the norm. On the bright side, the council building inspector got back to him to arrange a meeting with a council officer to discuss possible employment as a freelance inspector. Something far less certain was a call from Ross Brennan asking if he was free to meet for lunch.

Within the hour they were sitting at a local food court bench, kebabs in hand. Between mouthfuls, Ross was able to say, "Grant of probate is imminent. You'll soon be reimbursed for the funeral and other expenses incurred in executing your dad's will."

"Hallelujah! It won't solve all my problems, but it's a start."

"You should be able to kick-start your career in ten days or so. You up for a couple of building inspections next week? Have you contracted for any new building work?"

"I have a couple of feelers out. Did I mention I met a council building inspector recently? He took my details, and the council has contacted me for a second interview as a freelance inspector."

Ross' reply was encouraging, "Good luck with it. Could be a nice little earner on the side."

"My thoughts exactly."

That was the good news. Ross then cleared his throat and told him the reason why he invited him to meet out of his workplace.

He explained he'd been thinking about any legal battle that might ensue regarding the stalled job. Speaking candidly, he advised that it could be costly, without any certainty of the outcome. "I've got a bit of an idea which I'll outline after I check a few things. I'll know more when we next meet after your dad's estate is settled. Keep in contact with the bank and pass on any progress being made. That way they'll be clued-up when the time comes. And it will."

"I'll do that Ross, and thanks for keeping me up to speed."

They shook hands and Ross left Marek to finish his lunch in a much better mood than when he had started it.

Over the following week Marek completed two quotes for jobs – one small and one medium. He was very particular in checking out the financial circumstances of each and when the medium-sized quote was accepted, he felt a rush of excitement at the thought of getting back to *real* work.

The job wasn't complicated; something along the lines of what he had done on Gwynne's house, but this one was to be a bedroom and ensuite. He could adapt some of his paperwork already on file which could speed up the job.

When Ross Brennan rang with the good news that probate had been granted, Marek's state of mind was boosted several notches, knowing that his financial position should begin to recover.

The clouds were lifting.

Another chat was due with Ross to discuss his legal options. With his prospects improving, he began thinking of a possible pathway through the dilemma regarding the money he was owed and the job itself. He tried not to get too far into the fuzzy economics of it all. He knew that he would need to discuss it with Ross, the bank and his accountant. He was still hesitant to mention it to Darren knowing, if it all went pear-shaped, he knew Darren would be furious with him.

The prospect of that third discussion with Gwynne put him more on edge than the other two combined.

26

Marek warily took his seat in Ross' office. It was to be a meeting that completed another stage of his father's life – in truth, his parents' lives – as well as one which might indicate new opportunities in his own.

Ross informed Marek that his father's estate was legally settled and that all formalities had been attended to for his father's assets to be transferred into his name. That included property, cash assets and the residue of his father's possessions. The thought lodged in Marek's mind that his father's legacy was already beginning to be parcelled-up and consigned to history.

Putting down his pen, leaning back in his swivel-chair and folding his arms, Ross then raised the matter of the payment default on the property he had been renovating.

"To be honest Marek," he said, "there appears little or no likelihood of recouping the loss in the immediate future. However, here's an idea that might be to everyone's satisfaction … more or less. The thing is, because the owners themselves became insolvent, but were not declared bankrupt, they are not constrained by the bankruptcy regulations. Although they have assets, they are temporarily unable to pay their debts. In this case they are in fact victims, almost as much as you are."

Ross then raised the possibility of Marek using his father's house as collateral to take out a loan, or even a mortgage on the house he now legally owned. That could fund the purchase of the stalled renovations property in its incomplete state. He looked at Marek, allowing him time to consider what he had proposed.

"What do you think?"

Marek was totally astonished that Ross had suggested the very course of action he himself had been contemplating. As owner, he would be able to pace the renovations and manage the costs and timing to suit himself. He would be working for himself. He already had the conditions of approval from the Council. The plans and specifications he had would allow him to resume work once he was the legal owner.

Marek's first questions were: "How do I go about this? Do I approach the owners myself or is there a better way?"

Ross answered carefully. "I suggest we send a final demand to the owners for the outstanding payment including a specified time frame. You'll have to be patient. It's sort of a soft way of putting pressure on the owners. We'll see how that plays out before our next move." He waited for Marek's nod of understanding before continuing.

For now, you should consider the buy-out figure very carefully because it is in your best interests for it to be accepted. Don't be greedy. Make a genuine offer, considering the incomplete state of the house and the value of the land. It must be an offer that tempts them. Think carefully what you would need to do to complete the renovations and then weigh all the costs carefully, including labour, against the completed value of the house in today's market."

Marek nodded his agreement. He already had a good understanding of completion costs. A good estimate of the land value was obtainable and so he agreed to Ross' proposal. "As a matter of fact, I have been thinking along very similar lines. Until now finance was the big worry. It looks do-able on paper but there's still a risk."

Ross stated the obvious, "There's always a risk in these cases. When things go wrong, that's what keeps us lawyers in business."

The wry grin on his face belied the slight glow of optimism and Marek couldn't help firing teasingly back, "Sounds suspiciously like preying on the misfortunes of others."

Ross chuckled. "Don't you start getting Bolshie with me! We prefer to think of it as helping the downtrodden, the *Little Aussie Battler*, through their misfortunes. Often caused by some shonky builder exploiting them, mind you. We can't all be as gifted with our hands as some people, who, as I recall from school days, could have waltzed into any university he chose. What I'm suggesting is that we take it slowly and make sure we understand what those risks are. You'll have to endure another tense period while waiting for a response to our, I should say, *your*, offer."

"*Touché*! Okay Ross, I'll try to be patient. Thanks, I owe you one. Be seeing you."

"One! You won't get off that easy. Now get off and start playing with your hammer and nails and all those *Bob the Builder* toys you're always mucking about with. I've got work to do."

"You want me to sharpen your pencils for you? Then I could tell you where to stick them! Seriously, thanks again Ross. I really appreciate what you've done."

Gradually, the documents confirming the transfer of his father's assets were received. The cash was transferred into his account and, for the first time in almost two months, Marek was able to breathe without the tightness in his chest which happened every time he opened his wallet.

His next challenge was to get his tax done. He rang Gwynne with feelings of both anticipation and trepidation.

It was some time since he had spoken to her and there were things he wanted, needed, to say. It would be an emotionally charged meeting, on his part at least, having bottled up his feelings since his return from Poland, and the interment of his father's ashes.

When Gwynne answered the phone, her voice was neutral, lacking the brightness he always associated with her voice. "Hello Marek, I thought you had forsaken us and decided to go elsewhere. Have you?"

He was shocked. "God no! Where'd you get that idea? I'm sorry if I have been so preoccupied that I have given even a *hint* of anything like that. I'm ringing now to try and organise a get-together either at your office or privately. There's a lot I have to say."

"Hold it, hold it! I didn't mean that to sound the way it came out. I have been wondering how things have been going with you and expecting you to call. Merren's always asking where you are."

"Look, I need to see you as soon as possible. Firstly, my tax needs doing. Secondly, I need to run through an idea which has developed following the settlement of Dad's estate. And third," his voice quietened. "There is a third reason."

"Oh? And what would that be?"

"It's got nothing to do with work."

"I'm intrigued. Sounds like it's something to be discussed over coffee. Or something stronger?"

"Yes, I would like that. But first to business. I've got the paperwork ready as soon as you can give me an appointment."

"How about our usual time, after lunch Friday? Say, 1:30? It'll be my last appointment for the day. Does that suit you?"

"That's fine. Looking forward to it. See you then. Oh, say hi to Merren for me. G'bye."

Marek found it almost impossible to be patient, waiting for a response from the owners of the house on which he'd invested ten times more mental energy than physical energy. Like a kid on a car trip, he was tempted to ring Ross' office and ask, 'is it there yet?' He would've dearly loved to have more positive news to tell Gwynne at their meeting.

He found some reassurance in believing that, if the owners were unable to afford to complete the renovations, they might be more susceptible to an offer – if only because of their desperate financial position, for which he felt some sympathy. Hopefully they would see it as a solution to their worries. Time would tell.

Ross' exhortation, 'try to be patient' lurked annoyingly at the back of his mind.

27

As Marek stepped into Gwynne's office, he felt his spirits lift even as his stomach lurched. He was reminded of first dates when he was a teenager.

"Come in Marek. Have a seat."

Was she showing signs of being pleased to see him?

There were a few moments of awkwardness mostly, but not only, on his part before Gwynne settled into her professional mode. She began the formalities by asking for his paperwork, which he handed over without comment.

He sat motionless, deriving ridiculous pleasure from watching her hands glide over the keyboard as she entered the figures for the Tax Office. At one point she paused, looked up at him, but said nothing. She completed the task, looked up again with a puzzled expression.

"I'm dreadfully sorry. I didn't realise what a difficult time you've had financially over the last two months. My thoughts were focused on your father's death and my new office. I feel I've let you down, not professionally but … well, personally, considering um … other matters. The only bright side I can see is that you won't be paying much tax."

"Gwynne, there's not much you could have done. It was all legal stuff, largely complicated by distance, translation of documents and bureaucratic delays. Ross Brennan handled most of that."

He hesitated before addressing the inferences of Gwynne's use of the word, 'personally'.

He was lost for words but bumbled on clumsily.

"I was embarrassed. Until now, I've had a pretty smooth run financially. I haven't made a fortune, but I've made enough to keep comfortably in the black. The unexpected payment default, following on from … well, you know, Dad, Poland etcetera, threw everything out of balance. My confidence took a hit but, with the help of Ross, I got a trickle of building inspection jobs to keep me going. Last week I emerged from the worst of it. Now Ross and I have an idea which might get me back on my feet."

He gave her an abbreviated description of the plan to buy the property and ended by saying, "What I need now is a more detailed picture of tax matters which would impact on the viability of the proposal. I don't want any surprises to scuttle the deal in the home stretch."

Gwynne had jotted down some headings and after a few moments launched into her response. "Firstly, a reconsideration of registering for the GST. This proposition is more suited to GST registration. Secondly, any possible Capital Gains Tax. I'll look into it and give you a run-down when I've got a better idea of the numbers. Give me a few days. I'll need a list of all your costs and expenditure on the property incurred to date, together with the predicted completion costs. It will be harder to estimate a final sale value because it rests on market value. Try to calculate a minimum acceptable sale price."

Marek listened, making some notes himself, determined to have everything ready when required. When finished, he threw his pen down and drew a deep breath. "Thanks. I'm a bit of a babe in the woods in all this. I'll try and sort it all out as soon as I can. How about same time next week?"

He started to collect his things as Gwynne asked, "What's the third reason?"

He looked up, not grasping her meaning. "What third reason?"

"When you made this appointment, you mentioned that there was a third reason."

He shut his eyes, frowned, slowly drew a deep breath, held it for a moment, then exhaled slowly.

"Gwynne, I'm sorry I mentioned it. Can we just forget it? Maybe next week things will sort themselves out. In my head I mean."

Gwynne leant back in her chair. "Do you have time to go for a coffee? By the sound of it, you need to say something that's bugging you. Why bottle it up for another week? Perhaps a cafe where we can find somewhere private to sit? Or a takeaway, or …? What do you say?"

This was the first time she had initiated a meeting on a non-business matter. The suggestion was irresistible. "How about that café we went to last time?"

"Fine, I'll meet you there in half an hour, after I tidy up here. Later, I have to pick up Merren so we can't take long."

Again, Marek's stomach churned as the butterflies fluttered. He wondered how she could look so collected and professional.

He chose the same table they'd sat at previously. Believing this was a 'make or break' moment, but uncertain of the approach he should take. He picked up a coaster, tapped it, twirled it and flicked it back onto the table. He hoped the words would be there when needed.

When Gwynne arrived, he stood up to greet her, semi-formally, feeling awkward, ignoring the fact they had been in discussion half an hour ago.

Still in what sounded like her professional mode, Gwynne started with, "Well, where do we begin? You go first."

He began to move his jaw as if he were chewing a piece of gristle and couldn't spit it out. Nervously clearing his throat, he said. "We've known each other for almost six months. Your professional role aside, in that time I have been thinking … a lot. At the start you bugged me. You seemed to dodge and weave around any topic not of your choosing with cryptic responses which put me on edge."

Oh God, this sounds lame!

"Then, in my mind, I started imagining you as a sounding board. I carried on invented conversations about all sorts of things. A bit like Merren talking to Squinty and Binko. It's been driving me crazy."

"Stop, Marek! You are torturing yourself, and while you're at it, you're torturing me. Do you think I haven't noticed? You need to understand my position, selfish as that may seem to you. I have to consider every move I make, professionally and privately and most especially as a mother."

Marek tried to say something, but didn't want to interrupt her passion.

"I am trying to be independent, to stand on my own two feet, much as you have been recently, only for a longer time. You have only a limited idea of what that means. I could easily consider letting go but these things mean a lot to me. Merren is my responsibility, and even when I see how well you treat her and how much she likes you, I still feel wary. And it scares me. Can you understand that?"

A wave of guilt washed over him but, overriding that, he felt that his own wellbeing, perhaps his own future, was at stake and that he owed it to himself to voice it.

He responded softly, trying to hide the depth of his feelings. "I think I understand, but can I ask how you imagine your future playing out? Are you going to reject every prospect of a relationship because of Merren, until she's off your hands? You're entitled to consider your own happiness, your own wellbeing. You've shown courage and determination in getting to your present professional position. How about extending that attitude to your personal life? I'm not suggesting you throw away your little red book of principles, but surely there is room for someone in your life!"

A palpable silence followed with Marek looking fixedly and determinedly into Gwynne's eyes. "What I have just said has had me by the ball ..., er, throat, for quite some time, but this is the first time I've been game to say it out loud. I want to be a part of your life, however small. At the moment, I think it's not only a case of you shutting me out but you shutting yourself in. Think about it! Personally, I know I can't *not* think about it."

After a long tension-filled silence in which they each digested what had been said, he finished feebly. "Can we leave it there? Thanks for the chat, although I'm not sure it's done either of us much good. It's up to you. Your move!"

As he walked away, he stopped, turned to face her. He snapped a click of his fingers of both left and right hands and pointed at her saying, "Nice coffee, thanks. Your treat! See you next week."

Gwynne stared, tight-lipped with resentment as he left the cafe. And not because of being stuck with the bill. She felt that he had unburdened himself at her expense.

What a hide! *Bully for him!*

She'd found the meeting particularly off-putting, with him staring at her with those damned mesmeric eyes. His organic, mood 'litmus test' eyes! She became flustered as she gathered her things to leave. She had to admit that what he'd said both warmed and agitated her.

At the back of her mind was a voice telling her that what he said made sense.

He had left the next move up to her but whether he knew it or not, he had exposed the gulf between her heart and head.

Was there a bridge?

For the following few days, Marek had to restrain himself from talking out loud to himself about things that bothered him. Mostly he felt he had made a fool of himself with Gwynne and made matters worse. Perhaps irretrievably so.

A couple of trial inspections, unexpectedly forwarded to him after his interview at the council, boosted his finances.

Today, however, he realised he was in a disturbed state as he entered the premises of Select Accounting for another face-to-face with, 'that damn woman!' *That Welsh Morgen evil spirit!*

As usual, Gwynne was seated, working at her computer. She waved him to a chair as he walked in, holding up one index finger suggesting one minute. Silently, he placed the documents on her desk.

This isn't starting well: one twitch of her finger and I obey.

With a sigh of relief, she swivelled her chair to face him. "Finished. Thank God that's done. Sorry, I wanted to get it out of the way before we began. Now, what have you got for me?"

He had to bite his tongue to hold back what he really had in mind for her. He bided his time as she checked through the papers, making several notes as she did so. He was reminded of his school days having to sit through sessions at the dining-room table while his parents examined his school reports.

"Alright, this looks like a pretty good breakdown." He breathed an audible sigh of relief that one obstacle at least had been negotiated. The next, that black cloud over their personal relationship, had yet to be addressed.

He waded in with his opening gambit: "Did you consider that other matter?"

"Are you kidding? It's preyed on my mind all week," was Gwynne's sharp retort. "Marek, you're different to most men. One minute you're more intense, more serious, and then you loosen up and your sense of humour appears out of nowhere. I see it especially where Merren is concerned. Oh yes, and of course the onesie episode. I also saw a different you when we had dinner at Helena's. How is she by the way?"

"She's fine. Alan's fine. Everyone's fine. It's us who aren't *fine*. Can I take you and Merren out to dinner?"

"You don't muck around with small talk, do you? Just listen for a minute. I'd like to invite you to a slightly different event. Would you be interested in attending a trivia night to raise funds for one of the charities Select Accounting supports?"

The question took the wind out of his sails. It was the last thing he expected to hear. Plus, he was taken aback because his general knowledge was largely vague common knowledge. The only specific knowledge he did have involved building and construction.

"A trivia night? Are you serious? I don't know anything about trivia."

"I will agree you are not the trivial type. But this is different." With the trace of a smile twitching at her mouth she explained what it was all about, as well as the charity it was intended to support."

She continued. "Besides, I don't agree you don't know anything about trivia. Trivia's mostly just general knowledge which, out of context, seems inconsequential. The questions will cover a wide range of topics to include people from different backgrounds, occupations and experiences. Most of the questions could be answered by a five-year-old."

"A five-year-old! You certainly know how to flatter a man. You could try working on your recruitment technique. I'm not sure I'd fit in, I'm not a five-year-old."

"No, you're certainly not that. I can't even imagine you as a five-year-old. But that's not the point. It's a charity night. You pay twenty dollars which goes to the charity. We sit with a group of up to eight people and we discuss and answer what questions we can. Haven't you ever been to a trivia night before?"

"No, sorry. I think they must only be for brainy office types. Oh, and five-year-olds."

"Oh, lighten up, will you? It'll be fun. I'll be there. Lots of people of all ages and experiences will be there. It's a night out for heaven's sake."

"Me lighten up? You're the one who's carrying the baggage and forsaking any sort of social life."

"If by *baggage* you are referring to Merren, then I withdraw the invitation and you can take yourself off elsewhere."

"You are deliberately misinterpreting my words. We've had some nice times together and, well, you know what I think about Merren. I'm referring to your barricading yourself away, restricting your life and shutting the door on enjoyment."

"Oh, and I suppose you are the one who can help me enjoy myself. Well let me tell you something, you're not doing much of a job of it at the moment."

"Stop! This has gone too far. I want us to be friends. Well, actually more than friends, but I'm trying to be patient. And you're not letting me! You're exasperating. All right! Enough! You win. I'll go to your trivia night. If I embarrass myself and the team, I'll blame you." Taking out his wallet, he snatched out a note and threw it on the desk. "Here's your twenty dollars. Goodbye."

Two days before the trivia night Gwynne phoned to confirm all the arrangements and generally gee him up for the occasion. Marek continued to express doubts which Gwynne tried to allay by repeating, with increasing emphasis and volume, "It's a trivia night!" she almost shouted, "The questions are trivial; a …"

"Yes, I know, you told me, a five-year-old could answer half of them."

The attraction of seeing Gwynne overrode his misgivings. "Yes, alright, I'll be there. You've got my twenty dollars. See you there in all my trivial glory. G'bye."

On arrival at the venue, Marek was surprised to see a crowded auditorium with people milling around chatting, drinking and nibbling snacks.

Marek looked for Gwynne and eventually saw her sitting at a table which was separated from the other tables. He went up to her and she stood with a half-hearted smile, sliding her arm through his, and then immediately dashing his expectations.

"I'm terribly sorry but I've been conscripted at the last minute to help mark the answer sheets and tallying scores. We won't be able to sit together."

Disappointment and anger surged. He felt like doing an immediate about-turn and walking out. The one attraction to the whole night had been the thought of sitting with her.

As she directed him to a table of eight places where seven people were already seated, her promise to catch up with him at the end of the night was poor compensation. Resignedly, he sat, and the team members began introducing themselves. He wasn't concentrating and remembered only one or two names and spent the next ten minutes trying to understand how the whole thing worked.

It began much as he had feared. His involvement in providing answers was minimal, but he did find much of the banter amusing. He gradually joined in if a question triggered a distant memory, but few questions dealt even remotely with his interests.

He contributed comments on a few sporting questions but one question he answered confidently, which later caused some embarrassment was: 'Name the employee of Select Accounting who has the same surname as a reservoir or *Llyn* in Wales'. When he gave the answer, 'Gwynne Alwen', they were hesitant as none of them even knew what a *Llyn* was. All he could stammer out was that he had seen *Llyn Alwen* somewhere when he was looking at a map of Wales.

The night concluded with some prize-giving, more chit-chat and general comments about the charity concerned and money raised. Gwynne had been fully occupied with the scoring throughout the night. Marek walked over to where she was seated, bundling up the answer sheets. He had a grudging feeling he had been dudded but thanked her for the invitation anyway.

She rose and walked around the table and stood in front of him, before holding out her hand to shake his and thank him for coming. He took her hand in his but instead of a brief polite shake he just held it and looked from her hand to her eyes while she spoke.

"Was it too painful? It wasn't at all the way I thought it would be. I'll try and make it up to you as soon as I can. Maybe that dinner you suggested sounds like a possibility. Do you trust me to get back to you?"

For him, the physical contact of holding her hand was electric. He felt an almost irresistible urge to raise it to his lips, in the way he had seen some of his father's old Polish friends do back in Zakopane.

Looking again into her eyes, her words were lost to him. He saw her eyes widen as if she appeared to realise what he was thinking, and suddenly withdrew her hand.

"Of course I trust you. Goodnight Gwynne. Oh, and for your information, the night wasn't nearly as uncomfortable as I thought it would be. I didn't once feel like a five-year-old. Let me know your thoughts on that dinner." He walked away, feeling that a flag of truce had been raised, forestalling any further war of words.

28

After three tense weeks in a holding pattern of piecemeal inspection work, plus a budget-saving job from a word-of-mouth recommendation to build a roof over a barbecue and entertainment area, Ross Brennan rang with two pieces of information.

The first was that a response had been received from the solicitors of the owners of the property indicating negotiations could commence and suggesting a buy out figure. When Ross mentioned the figure, Marek's hopes were deflated.

"At that price I'll make barely anything out of the project."

Ross' upbeat reply was in stark contrast, "Early days my friend, early days. We're in a cat-and-mouse game. The owners are making an ambit claim. The good news is that they are at least considering the matter; sniffing the bait, so to speak."

Ross then mentioned a figure only slightly lower as a counter-offer. He said that with Marek's approval, he would put it with a subtle reference to the incomplete state of the building and the waiting time to find another builder as well as another buyer.

He reminded Marek, "You have an advantage because you already have plans, the original council development application approval and the consent conditions. You have a working knowledge of the practicalities of completing the job. Factor that into the figure I mentioned. Let's feed out some line and see what happens."

"Alright, if you say so. Thanks Ross. Don't tell me, I know, 'be patient!' I'm trying."

"Hang on, this next bit will give you something else to think about. My real estate mate has told me that the bodies found on the land in Minmi are historical burials and that they could be well over one hundred years old. The word is that forensic analysis indicates one body is that of an Aboriginal woman and that the other is a man of European descent.

"Adding to the mystery is that pieces of dark blue woollen cloth, which matches the jackets worn by policemen at that time, were in the grave. The only other thing found was a small wooden cross with the lettering "LET to GOD" carved into the cross-arms.

"They're thinking it was probably a personal religious reference. On their own, the items could mean anything, but investigations are continuing. I'll put the word out about the land coming back onto the market. Property problems come in all shapes and sizes. Let me know if you hear anything. Cheers!"

It was another slow Sunday afternoon and Gwynne allowed herself to slump into a reflective mood.

In her last conversation with Marek, she had promised to make it up to him for the debacle of the trivia night.

Her thoughts began to drift over the balance, or imbalance, in her life. Nebulous and unformulated ideas which underpinned her happiness, something she had not actively dwelt on for a long time, swirled wraithlike in her imagination.

She started to list the positives in her life: Merren, family, her developing career and financial security. She was still young and reasonably healthy.

Her friends told her she was attractive, witty and that they enjoyed her company. But not today.

Here she was, in a house provided by her parents. She had Merren, but no-one to share daily events. Physical relationships were a thing of the past – locked away – and she now realised something was missing.

She sensed a change within her personal ambitions, her goals and aspirations for her future happiness. What she instinctively felt had changed was her need for adult conversation; someone to share everyday thoughts and opinions.

She was perceptive enough to admit that, despite all her achievements, a seed of discontent had been planted. And she feared it had been planted by Marek Benning.

What to do? She felt as if she were approaching an intersection without signposts. She had reached a not altogether undesirable frame of mind where, unpredictably, she found her concentration drifting.

Recalling an age-old pithy adage, *'A problem shared is a problem halved'*, she came to a decision on the person with whom she wanted to share her predicament. The choice was obvious. In the past she might have spoken to Colette.

Instinctively she now felt Colette was not the sounding board she needed. Lana, whom she had known since her bank-days, was her best hope in giving non-judgemental advice; if that's ever possible.

She rang Lana and asked if they could meet and talk about something that had come up. There were a few moments of silence in which Gwynne believed Lana's gossip-gauge was being booted-up to maximum.

She heard Lana ask, "Is this *secret women's business?* Right, here's my advice: get yourselves over here this afternoon. No excuses!"

Once settled in Lana's kitchen, with Lana's husband Gary watching football on television and Merren playing with Lana's children in the backyard, Lana handed her a glass of white wine. For a few moments Gwynne watched Merren, an only child, playing with other children. *Was that the way of her future?* How and where to begin? Once she started however, the words spilled out. Lana listened without interruption; a near first for her.

When she finally finished, she put the question to Lana, "What do you think?"

Lana sipped her wine, put down the glass, took a deep breath and began. "Gwynne, you have sacrificed yourself since you fell pregnant with Merren, dedicating yourself to her needs and later, developing your career prospects. You have achieved wonders. I don't know anyone who could have shown more discipline. But this sounds like an opportunity of a lifetime, and I mean, your lifetime. Get over yourself Gwynne! There are thousands of women in similar positions to you. I spoke briefly to Marek at your office party. He sounds and looks like a decent guy. You are Gwynne, not Guinevere. Who are you waiting for? Sir Lancelot or Galahad to sweep you away on a white charger?"

Gwynne's jaw dropped. It wasn't the response she had anticipated from her friend. She was about to reply but the words evaporated.

Hesitantly, her innocuous response was, "I'm just trying to get things right, for me and for Merren. I'm thinking of the long term."

Prompted by Lana's reference to the time before she knew she was pregnant with Merren, Gwynne abruptly stood and turned away from Lana. She took a few steps over to a mirrored sideboard and placed her palms on it, leaning on it with arms outstretched for support. Her head dropped as she recalled her dreamlike teenage expectations and having them shattered. When she lifted her head, she saw her reflection in the mirror.

Staring at it, and in a voice coming from deep within her psyche, she said, "Lana, I've been in this space once before with David. Only then, my dreams turned to dust. I had more than a crush on him. I was in love."

Lana smiled at Gwynne.

"I haven't told you of the agonising recurring scenes, nightmares even, I've experienced since his death. His accident was on the New England Highway here in NSW. He'd taken special leave from the RAAF and was heading south. The only one reason I can think of for him being there was because he was coming to see me. That decision led to his death and the death of my dream. I was shattered! And the memory still haunts me."

Lana's face entered the scene reflected in the mirror and she put an arm around Gwynne's shoulders. "Gwynne, I'm sorry. I didn't mean to blank out or diminish those events by saying what I did just now. I can barely imagine the emptiness you must have felt then, but somehow you must look to your future, for yourself … and, from all I know, for Merren too. You have to face life, not turn your back on it. Unlock that empty space you're hiding in. Any relationship, whether with Marek or anyone else, may not develop into anything long-term, although the signs are good, judging by the way you say Marek has behaved to date."

Gwynne turned to face Lana, breaking the spell as she responded, "He's a client at Select Accounting but he just keeps cropping up around other things. It's hard to explain."

Lana led Gwynne back to sit on the lounge and sat next to her. "Well, in my humble opinion, it's the opportunity you need, if only to escape from the seclusion where you've isolated yourself. Why should you go on living the way you have? You used to be so full of life. You're still young, you look terrific, and you deserve, and need, to make the most of this opportunity. Where's that spark? That confident *joie de vivre*? You used to have us in stitches. There's a life out there waiting for you! Loosen up a bit."

"I can't just flick a switch and be someone I'm not anymore. It's got to feel right again."

"You've shown how determined you can be, but it's time to test the waters. You're tougher than you think. Your family has sheltered you but now you need to step out on your own. You can, and should, accept this as an exploratory exercise, a reconnaissance mission. It mightn't be perfectly right, but, on the other hand, it just might be."

"Oh Lana, you make it sound like bungee-jumping, or something whimsical. I'm out of practice; just not sure … you know?" After another sip of her wine, giving her time to think, she said, "Should I suggest dinner, movies, or what?"

Lana was ready with a suggestion. "Gwynne, you're dithering. If it were me, I'd suggest something in a friendly, public setting. Let things proceed gradually. Don't put pressure on yourself in an intimate atmosphere. If this is going anywhere, you'll be in a better position to judge."

Gwynne thought for a few moments. "He did once suggest a picnic. And I need to include Merren. This will affect her, and I must keep the big picture in focus."

Lana picked up her glass, drained the contents in a mouthful and tapping the empty glass against her chin, advised, "Don't make the big picture too big. You're the focus. There may be shadows at the edges of the big picture for any of us. Give yourself a break."

"Yeah, right. But what sort of break? I'm an accountant, used to balancing the numbers."

"Hey, what about The Lagoon? We had our family picnic there last year. It's a safe swimming place for Merren and I heard there's a new playground nearby. It's not far from the beach if you want to go for a walk. A good old-fashioned picnic is a safe way for you all to get to know each other without too much pressure."

Gwynne stood and walked over to the window to watch Merren playing. "I feel like I'm setting up an occupational health and safety risk-management procedure with boxes to tick for Marek. It's so calculating, and he has been, and is, very kind. Odd, but kind."

"Kind is a start. Odd? Nyeh ... that can work both ways. Kind is a good mindset to begin with. So, do it!"

Lana's words were said with finality.

The girls looked at each other and Gwynne crossed to Lana and took both her hands. "Thanks Lana. You've been very helpful. I think."

As they hugged, Lana said confidentially, "You're worrying too much. Just take it in easy stages. Keep your knickers on and see how it works out. You never know, you might even enjoy yourself, possibly without ..."

"Oh Lana, you say some terrible things," she said as she walked over to the back screen door and called, "Merren, it's time to go."

Merren bounced in with Squinty and Binko in hand, they gathered their belongings and prepared to leave.

As Lana was ushering them out, she affected a menacing look and a stern voice saying, "Just remember, I want to hear every word about how it goes. Promise?"

"I promise to think about it. Thanks again Lana for being a good listener, and friend."

29

Ross Brennan rang a few days later.

"G'day Marek. Just a quick call to bring you up to speed. The negotiations are continuing in a positive direction. No deal yet but I'm still hopeful a settlement will be reached. We have an ace up our sleeves. It involves you not pursuing any legal action to recover their payment default. We'll use that as a price-point wedge. You happy with that? It could swing it our way."

Marek knew his profit would be marginal but, from his talks with other builders, he had a feeling that old-style homes with modern interiors were in increasing demand, and even in the short term, he was optimistic prices could rise.

"Jeez, it's cutting it fine. I hope land prices hold up. But okay, go ahead," he agreed, but not without misgivings.

"Will do. Cheers. Keep your pecker up."

It was prophetic when Gwynne rang an hour later to ask him if a picnic might be possible one Saturday. At a very personal level, it was heart-pumping news. He nearly jumped down the phone in his enthusiasm to say, "Yes!"

When he asked if she had a place in mind, she suggested the lagoon in the nature reserve and explained what the location offered, especially for Merren.

He would have accepted any location this side of the mythical 'black stump', and readily agreed. Gwynne told him she would make up a picnic lunch for the three of them and that Marek should bring anything he thought would make the occasion more comfortable. They agreed on a time to meet at Gwynne's house the following Saturday.

He had snared another small additional repair job on the house on which he was currently working. The owners were obviously pleased with what he had done so far. These bits of news were enough to make the rest of his week the most financially viable since his return from Poland.

Ross rang with the news on Thursday afternoon: "You're in! Your offer's been accepted! Our ace took the trick. I'll keep you informed. Contact your bank and have a talk about the financial arrangements: whether to take out a business loan or a mortgage on your house. Get straight back to me if there are any complications."

"Great news Ross. Thanks for all you've done. There'll be a slab of something in your Christmas stocking from me. Besides your legal and brokering fees of course. Thanks mate. Cheers."

Marek floated through the jobs he had to do on Friday.

He felt so uplifted by the news that, by way of celebration, he bought a portable gazebo for their picnic to provide some shade if it got too hot. He'd never had a shopping bug, but it felt great not having to sweat over a non-essential purchase again.

Mercifully, Saturday dawned fine; not too hot, with a cloudless blue sky.

Marek packed the gazebo, a couple of picnic chairs and a cold bag.

He stopped on the way to get a few cans of beer then thought a bottle of white wine might be better.

In the end, he apologised to the attendant and said he'd changed his mind. He'd decided Gwynne might think alcohol politically incorrect in front of Merren, so he went to the supermarket nearby and bought mineral water and fizzy orange drink.

He arrived right on time and was immediately surprised by the sound of someone singing a pop song. He knew it had to be Gwynne and he stopped, hand raised ready to knock, and listened to the first half-dozen lines of a recent hit, *If I ain't got you.* He didn't know who sang it but it was a good rendition, and it lifted his spirits thinking that she must be in a good mood.

His own mood soared when she opened the door and he saw what she was wearing: a sporty figure-hugging blue top with a beaded bird motif and a pair of short pale lemon-coloured shorts which stimulated Marek's imagination.

As if he needed that!

He couldn't take his eyes off her, despite Merren's attention-grabbing behaviour, waving Squinty and Binko at him.

Merren was more excited than even Marek, if that were possible, and showed it by skipping around him wearing a frilly swimming costume and pink-rimmed sunglasses and clutching a beach ball under an arm.

"We're ready!" she chirped as she skipped to the car and climbed in. Gwynne buckled her in. It took several minutes of rearranging the picnic basket, cold bag, and other bits and pieces. The gazebo took up almost all the boot space.

At the last-minute Gwynne ran back to grab her favourite beach bag and a broad brimmed beach hat, as well as one for Merren.

On arrival at the lagoon, Merren immediately squirmed her way out of her seat as soon as the buckles were released. The spot they selected was in a convenient position to keep an eye on Merren while paddling in the lagoon or playing nearby in the playground. Marek set out the chairs as well as the gazebo with almost no resort to the instructions, or Polish profanities. Gwynne laid out a blanket and the picnic things. Merren, wearing her new costume and wanting to get into the water, was dancing around in her pink floaties and sun-shirt, urging them to hurry.

Once they had set up, they followed Merren over to the lagoon to check it was safe. Marek kicked off his sneakers and took a few steps into the water. Merren stamped and splashed her way around the shallow edges. It was slightly brackish water in colour, having both a freshwater creek supply mixed with high tide inflow from the ocean, but it looked perfectly safe. He was surprised how warm it felt, despite the time of year. Gwynne and Marek stood watching, each feeling the tensions of the last few days melt away.

"She'll be fine. We can keep an eye on her from where we've set up," said Marek.

They walked back to the chairs and sat watching Merren. He felt the urge to speak but, more than ever, had to choose his words carefully. He didn't want to fritter away the opportunity of being almost alone with Gwynne.

He began tentatively with, "Ross Brennan rang to say my offer for the property has been accepted."

"Oh, that's wonderful for you. Congratulations!

"Thanks. It's a bit closer to the limit I set but I think it will be okay."

"Fantastic! I'm really pleased for you. You've had a rough trot lately and deserve a break." Her comment gushed out as if she too was relieved to talk about something other than themselves. "How long do you think it will take to finish?"

"Once we settle, which Ross thinks could be a bit over a month, I estimate it will take about six to eight weeks, unless there are complications. I'll be glad to get back to regular work on a proper job. I'll renew the orders I had to cancel for the materials. At least I don't have to start from scratch."

There followed another silence while they watched Merren splashing about in her imitation of swimming. "It looks like I'll have to continue her swimming lessons for a while yet. She certainly doesn't look scared of the water even though it isn't what she's used to at the pool."

Marek took a deep breath and dived in, metaphorically speaking. "Gwynne, I can't help but say again how fantastic I think you are. I mean, with everything you've got on your plate. I wish I could be of more help."

"Marek, we're each of us trying to make our way." Gwynne left the statement hanging, recalling what Lana had said and knowing that the whole point of the day was to try and find out where things stood and where they might lead.

"Also, am I allowed to say how great you look today? That outfit really suits you."

"Thank you, kind sir. You almost always know when to say the right thing."

"Almost?" Marek's forehead wrinkled in a querulous frown.

"I'm just leaving a little room for improvement. I'm not complaining."

"You could do with some lessons in encouragement. In the meantime, I might take the beach ball and join Merren splashing around. Is that OK?"

"Oh Marek! Of course it's OK. You don't have to ask. Go ahead, I'll join you in a minute ... If that's OK?"

Removing his shirt, showing that his suntan ended at white biceps, he said, "Gwynne, you can be a real tease, even when you're not trying."

"How do you know I'm not trying?" she retorted, with a mischievous pursing of her lips.

He picked up the beachball and walked away, shaking his head, somewhere between bemusement and aggravation, at Gwynne's taunting. Just when he thought he was a step ahead, she managed to get a foot in front. Sometimes he enjoyed their wordplay.

Sometimes!

As he approached the water he called out, "Hey Merren, catch!" She held her arms up to catch the ball but missed it by a metre. She splashed after it by which time Marek was in the shallow water up to his thighs.

Merren threw the ball back to him and they continued playing until Merren called, "Here comes Mummy to play!"

He turned around to see Gwynne entering the water. She was wearing an electric blue form-hugging one-piece costume with a low-cut, almost non-existent back. She looked brilliant. His breath caught in his throat. He thought he might have to wade into deeper water.

As the three of them splashed and played, the game degenerated with the adults deliberately throwing the ball near, but not straight to each other, causing them to jump and dive for it.

Gwynne seemed to be particularly inaccurate when throwing the ball to Marek which resulted in him making extravagant leaps to catch it while adding sound effects, much to Merren's delight.

After about twenty minutes they decided it was time for a break. They waded out and flopped down on the blanket. When Marek propped the ball under his head for a pillow, Merren immediately tried to wrestle it from him, all the while giggling and grunting with the effort. Gwynne watched out of the corner of her eye as she began preparing the lunch. It was turning into a simple fun-filled and relaxing day of a kind that took her back to her own childhood.

They idled away more time chatting after Marek allowed Merren to wrest the ball from him. She then wandered off to a nearby sandy patch and tried to build a sandcastle on her own. Eventually she gave up and came back to ask, "When can I play on the playground?"

"Let's have lunch first, it's ready now, and then you can play. After that we might go for a walk down to the beach. What do you say to that?"

Gwynne handed each of them a plate of mixed salad, ham and cheese and a fork. It was tricky balancing the plate, especially for Merren, but they managed without too much spillage. Marek poured mineral water for Gwynne and himself, and orange juice for Merren. Gwynne offered an incentive to them all saying, "If everyone eats their lunch, later on we might have an ice cream for dessert."

Both Merren, and Marek, chorused, "Yeay! Thanks Mummy!"

When they had finished and packed things away, they walked over to the playground. Merren started at ground level and worked her way around, over and up the equipment. Gwynne and Marek sat and talked while keeping an eye on her. At one point Gwynne called, "Not too high there. Hang on tight!"

"Well, what do you think?" asked Marek.

Gwynne knew very well what he was referring to but asked evasively, "About what?"

"There you go again! You know very well. What do you think about the day so far? Do you think that there could be room in your life for this?" He stretched out his arm and gestured broadly towards the lagoon, the playground and the nearby beach. "Room for all of this. Us!"

"Marek, it has been a lovely day. Of course, I think we all need days like this. But don't rush things. Tomorrow, I have an in-house workshop with Select at nine o'clock. Before that, I've got to get Merren up and dressed and over to Mum and Dad's. Like you, I have to manage my work-life around other things."

"Next, you'll be telling me to be patient. At times we have shared moments which were almost intimate. Remember that moment at your front door after Helena's dinner party? I was hopeful. Perhaps more fanciful than anything but everything has a beginning. I'd like to know if we're on the same path.

"What's the workshop on a Sunday of all days, all about?"

"Select is up-grading it's software and the new system comes on-line first thing Monday morning. We've got to get our head around all the changes. Marek, let's just take today for what it is. I think we might be on the same path, but in different places along it. If you don't rush on ahead, I might catch up. In time."

"Well, I hope it's before we get too old. After seeing you in that costume today, my patience is under strain."

"You do have a very Australian way with words for the son of Polish parents."

"I've got news for you Miss CPA; in Poland they have the same inclinations as I have now."

Gwynne looked down, hiding the hint of a blush, and slowly shook her head.

Marek thought he saw the faintest trace of a smile.

When Merren had played enough on the playground, they packed up their lunch things and set off for the beach.

Merren skipped on ahead until they got to the water at which point Gwynne held her by one hand and Marek the other.

They waded ankle deep into the water, stopping at the point where small waves broke, frothed and hissed their way up the beach and back again.

As each wave rolled in, they hoisted Merren over it, complete with sound effects: "Wheeee!" with answering squeals from Merren.

After several wave-jumps Merren wriggled out of their grasp and wanted to jump the waves on her own. She took several quick steps farther into the water, digging her toes into the wet sand and kicking it up into the air.

While still standing on one foot, the biggest wave yet rolled in and completely bowled her over. The backwash began to take her away from Marek and Gwynne and he had to splash after her as she was rolled over and over. He grabbed her under the arms and lifted her up to his shoulders.

Her face showed complete shock at what had happened. She spluttered saltwater and spit over Marek as her nose blossomed with a bubble of mucous. When she opened her eyes, she let out a wail that put a nearby flock of seagulls to flight. Gwynne took her from Marek and tried to calm her, but she wasn't having any of it.

Eventually, after much hugging and cuddling, she calmed down, looking resentfully at both of them and reserving her darkest looks for the breaking waves.

"You're alright now darling. It's just the shock of it. A little salt water won't hurt you. Let me wipe your face." Gwynne continued soothing Merren as they carried her back to the car. Marek couldn't help noticing the unforgiving look Merren trained on the sea. He even noticed some similarities to Gwynne when she had *that look* of determination.

As Marek packed the car, Gwynne dried Merren off and they all climbed in. Five minutes later Merren called out, "Ice cream!"

Gwynne and Marek looked at each other, shook their heads and laughed.

Disaster averted!

30

The drive home was judged by the stages in which Merren regained her good nature. The ice cream had worked wonders even though she seemed to ingest it by smearing half of it over her face.

By the time they reached home, she was just about back to her normal self.

Gwynne ran a bath for her while Marek unpacked the picnic things. Dinner that night had not been decided and Gwynne asked Marek if he had any preferences.

Not pizza! "What about a take-away? Fish and chips? My shout."

"Merren might only eat the chips unless I can persuade her to try the fish."

"Fine by me. Do you have a preference where I go?"

"There's a take-away we passed on the way home, a couple of blocks back on the left. That'll do."

"Righto. Say when you're ready. Do you want the fish grilled, fried, battered or crumbed?" As an afterthought he added, "If you want yours raw, the deal's off."

"Yuk! No thanks. One grilled, one battered. That way I'll have two options with Merren. You get what you like."

As he turned to go, she added, "Thanks Marek, for such a lovely day. It really was enjoyable, despite the last bit. It just goes to show, things don't always work out perfectly."

Marek interrupted, "I've been trying to tell you that for ages."

Not quite succeeding in ignoring his comment, Gwynne said, "I'm sure Merren will be fine in the morning although it might take a while before she's ready for another trip to the beach. I think I will have to pay more attention to her swimming lessons though."

"The picnic was a combined effort. Merren's dunking was just an accident. But you're right about the swimming lessons. I'll bet lots of her friends have pools in their backyard. She's a bright kid. I'm sure she'll be fine once she practices a bit more." He wanted to add: *bright and determined like her mother,* but thought it sounded overly eggy.

When Gwynne gave him the word, Marek went to collect the fish and chips. While he waited for the food, he reviewed the day and decided that it had done a great deal to smooth out some wrinkles in their relationship. If Gwynne couldn't see what the day had meant, his cause was lost, or going to be a greater struggle than he imagined.

Marek was undecided whether to exercise some of the patience Ross had made him practise and not stay to eat with Gwynne and Merren. He decided to wait and see how things were when he got back with the food. His gut told him the next move would be up to Gwynne.

Quit while you're ahead? But am I ahead?

When he returned, Gwynne had the table set and the scene erased his indecision. Merren could be heard as she was watching a favourite sing-along video after her bath. Gwynne took the food and put it in the oven. "I'll delay tea for a bit so that after Merren's eaten, she'll be just about ready for bed."

Marek then asked unexpectedly, "Where are Squinty and Binko?"

"Why do you want to know?"

"Just a little scene I'd like to set up. Can I have a small plate please?"

276

"I'll get them. The plates are in the cupboard, but I warn you, Merren's sense of humour might still be under a bit of a strain."

She unpacked Merren's toys from her beach bag and handed them to Marek with a quizzical, slightly apprehensive look.

"Don't worry, I won't do anything to hurt them," Marek assured her. He then unwrapped the chips and put a few on the plate.

He positioned the toys on either side of the plate, each with a paw reaching for a chip. "Do me a favour will you? Take a photo when she sees them. I'm going to hide in the spare room."

The scene when Merren appeared made her squeal with delight. She immediately sat in her chair and started offering Squinty and Binko chips to nibble, complete with an improvised script. Gwynne was ready and took several photos before Marek popped into the room calling, "Surprise!"

Merren immediately jumped into his arms and hugged him, knowing instinctively it was he who had set up the scene.

Neither paid much attention to the look on Gwynne's face.

They then sat down and picked at their food, reviewing the day's events, all but glossing over the dunking episode.

Merren ate a small portion of the chips but only picked at the batter on the piece of fish and soon started to fade. When everyone had had enough to eat, they cleared the table.

Gwynne picked up Merren and was about to carry her to her bed when she expressed a sudden thought: "Merren, say thank you to Marek for such a lovely day out." She inclined Merren towards Marek whereupon he gave her a kiss on her forehead.

"Goodnight Missy Merren. Sweet dreams."

Gwynne looked at Marek, uncertainty evident by the look on her face. As if a silent question was screaming to be asked. *What now?*

"I'll settle her down and we can have coffee if you like. Make yourself comfortable in the loungeroom. I won't be long."

Marek sat on the lounge and waited, not knowing what to do or say. When Gwynne returned, she said, "She's just about ready to drop off to sleep. I'll make coffee, shall I?"

"Not for me thanks. Will you sit here for a minute? There's something I want to say."

"This sounds serious. What is it?"

"Gwynne, I've had a great day, but I want to tell you I just about said everything I wanted to say today. About us I mean. Today was all I could have wished for, minus Merren's experience of course. Let it sink in. I would really like to hear from you once you've given it some thought. If you'd like a repeat, or something different, it's your choice. Call me."

"This seems a rather awkward finish to the day, but yes, I'll give it some thought. How could I not? No coffee?"

"No thanks. Gwynne, you know how I feel about you, but I don't want to rush you." Marek stood and faced her, "I've got a busy day tomorrow and so have you – even busier by the sound of it. I want to leave here on a high."

"Marek, you really surprise me at times, and this is one of them." She stood, hooked her arm through his and said, "All right, I'll see you out."

Once again, they stood in the doorway, the scene of previous awkward partings. But this time was different. They had reached some sort of understanding. Sufficiently so, for him to wrap his arms around her and draw her to him, firstly for a brief hug and a gentle kiss. Stepping back a pace, he held her at arm's length for several seconds while looking deep into her eyes. At last, he broke the moment saying in an emotionally charged, throaty whisper, "Thank you for a wonderful day. Good night, Gwynne."

"Good night, Marek. And thank you too."

The door closed with a barely audible click.

The following day, despite being a Sunday, Marek again took refuge in his work. Since the buy-out had been given the green light, or at least a flashing amber one, he decided to go over all his paperwork to complete the renovation job.

He knew it would be best to have the job finished and on the market as soon as possible. The sooner the bridging finance period for the project was over, the better. He was hoping that the building inspections would continue being passed on by Ross and council, enabling him to cover his day-to-day expenses. In the current financial landscape, without a regular incoming wage, he would have to depend on them for his cash flow.

He shuffled the papers into chronological stages from council's approval of the plans to the consent approval conditions.

Next, he refreshed himself with the practicalities of the order of progress. Once he was the legal owner, he could physically inspect onsite exactly what was required, even though he already had a pretty good idea. He satisfied himself that, depending on availability of sub-contractors, it would take over a month, hopefully not two. He would have to monitor the brickies, whose idea of punctuality he sometimes thought was gauged on 'never never time'.

By mid-afternoon he felt confident he had done all he could to have the job ready to start once settlement took place. It might not be a plan set in concrete, but he thought he had a good working schedule. He grabbed an apple and wandered out into his parents'– now his – back yard. It showed serious signs of neglect and he decided to do some work in a vain attempt to make it look respectable. Three hours later, the garden didn't look much different, but the lawns looked presentable.

Grimy from head to toe, he showered, dressed and settled down to begin *Typhoon*, from his father's Joseph Conrad collection. The back cover advertising told him it was about the brave but taciturn and aloof Captain MacWhirr, an experienced seaman, reacting calmly under enormous stress in a fierce storm in the China Sea. The destruction of his ship, its cargo and his crew were at stake.

Marek awoke to the distant ringing of his phone, but he couldn't remember where he'd left it. He eventually found it on the back verandah, long after it had stopped ringing. The screen showed three missed calls. The first and third were from his cousin Helena. The middle one was from Gwynne.

He decided to answer them in the order received. Helena answered almost immediately. "Hello Marek, how are you? You didn't answer my call. Are you okay or just busy?"

"I was out in the yard mowing without my phone and didn't hear it. What's up?"

"Nothing's up, we're fine. I was just catching up with you. Last time we spoke you were trying to sort out a couple of legal matters. Have they been settled?"

"Yes, and no. Dad's estate has been settled and my offer to buy out the owners of the property I was renovating has been accepted. But Ross Brennan reckons it will take a few weeks for the legal stuff to be completed."

"That sounds great. I'm pleased for you. How's Gwynne?"

He hesitated before answering. He chose the safe course and gave a brief description of their picnic. It was obvious

Helena wanted to hear more, but he refrained from anything too specific.

Helena barely controlled her exasperation and eventually said, "How about we have another dinner here? It's weeks since you visited. Do you think Gwynne would like to come over again?"

"Thanks for the invitation, Helena. I'll ask her and get back to you. I know she is busy with work, but I'll ask, I promise."

"Well don't take forever. Let me know soon. Look after yourself, cousin dear. Goodbye."

"Thanks Helena. G'bye."

After the call, his mind returned to the picnic. He had tried to set up what might have looked to an outside observer, as a family day out. He had hoped that Gwynne would recognise that the day could be part of her life, of their lives. He was confident that progress had been made and rang her.

To cover his nervousness at perhaps misjudging their parting scene the night before, he rushed straight into what he wanted to say. "I've just been talking to Helena. She asked how you're getting on. I told her about yesterday." Stretching the truth somewhat he added, "She implied we were playing happy families. She's like that. She means well."

He interpreted Gwynne's momentary silence as an indication he might have made more of their parting kiss than she had, so he moved on. "Helena's invited us to another dinner party. I told her you were fairly busy but that I would mention it to you. What do you think?"

Gwynne's enthusiastic reply surprised and confused him. "What if I invite them here? I could prepare something Welsh in contrast to Helena's Polish meal. What do you say?"

"What can I say? It sounds great. I didn't know the Welsh had any national dishes, other than Welsh Rarebit." Marek's spirits were on a high at hearing Gwynne's completely unexpected proposal. "Can I do anything, assuming I'm invited?"

"Are you trying to be funny? Or are you being cryptic? Dad's very Welsh mother from Snowdonia could have put you straight on the Welsh score. I'll dig out one of her recipes. When would you like it to be? A fortnight or so?"

"Sounds fine to me. I'll check with Helena. I assume it would be best on a Friday or Saturday night? Or even a Sunday lunch?"

"Leave that up to Helena and Alan; any time suits me. You can bring the wine or drinks or whatever; but not Polish vodka!"

"I read an article in a fishing magazine at the barber's; apparently seaweed gin is all the go in Wales. How about that? Or should I just stick to red and white wine, comparatively unadventurous as that may be?"

"Now there's an idea. I could use seaweed gin instead of Guinness in the Welsh Rarebit. I'll say it was your suggestion."

"Gin instead of Guinness? What are you talking about?"

"Never mind. Let me know when Helena prefers. How's your week looking?"

"Not too bad. I've a couple of inspection jobs thanks to Ross and I will probably finish the renovations I'm presently working on by Wednesday or Thursday, depending on weather. Those payments will smarten up my next bank statement and might even put a smile on the face of my accountant. It'll be a bit of a squeeze until property settlement. Then it will be all systems go."

"Good luck with that. Let me know what you think of the photo. Goodbye, Marek."

"Sure thing. I was only kidding with the seaweed gin."

31

"Have you heard anything lately from Poland?" Helena's question, although asked in a conversational tone, immediately put Marek on edge. Was it some sort of Polish intuition that she raised the very topic he had been hoping to avoid?

Only the previous day he had received an email from Ana Wójcik. She'd written that Magdalena had not been well recently, and that Ana had to assume more of a carer's role for her mother. She gave no personal details about herself, but did attach some photos and an audio file.

And now, here he was, in Gwynne's house, with Helena asking awkward questions. He wrestled with the idea of saying no to everything, but his silent response was to pick up his phone, open it to Ana's email and show Helena the photos. All he said was, "I got these yesterday. The scenes are from the spreading of Dad's ashes. The girl in the Polish costume is Ana, Magdalena's daughter, who sang in the choir at the concert I went to."

The photos had presumably been taken by friends and sent to her. Three were of the gathering for the spreading of his father's ashes showing Magdalena, Ana and himself together with mourners. They were candid shots which revived the memories of that traumatic experience. Helena examined them in detail.

The fourth photo was of Ana looking straight at the camera, wearing the traditional Polish outfit she wore at the concert. Helena continued her forensic examination of the photo of Ana. "My God, she looks gorgeous, like one of those Polish tourist promotional ads. For all the world, she looks like an exquisitely made doll."

As they examined the photos in turn, Marek recalled his night with Ana. He could not erase the vision of her lying naked next to him on his father's bed with the flush of sex glowing on her face. And undoubtedly his own as well.

His overriding desire was that it wasn't Ana with whom he wanted to relive the experience, but Gwynne. *Why couldn't Gwynne be more spontaneous, like Ana?* A moment later he realised the futility of any such wish.

With difficulty, he maintained a blank expression as the realisation again struck him that these were his people, his family, the ones he wanted to be with despite their quirks.

He watched Gwynne out of the corner of his eye to see how she was responding. She appeared to be struggling to find the right words.

She looked up at him, his phone still in her hand, hesitating slightly, before seeming to withdraw to safer ground and only saying, "It looks like such a peaceful spot. How sad." Reaching over she gave Marek's forearm a comforting squeeze and, after another glance at the photo of Ana in her costume added, "The costume is quite stunning. And she's very pretty."

"She looks a bit of alright to me," was Alan's crass reply. "Fills a shirt out nicely by the look of it." Helena gave him a look of exasperation accompanied by a stagey slap on his shoulder.

Marek then clicked on the audio file. The low quality gave it a nostalgic resonance, of age and sadness underscoring the fact that it belonged to their parents' generation. It produced a hypnotic effect on everyone.

When it finished there was a lingering silence.

"What a beautiful song and a striking version! So heartfelt, so plaintive," Gwynne murmured as she broke the silence. Helena could barely speak and even Alan muttered his approval.

"It was their favourite. Mum's especially, and after she died, if Dad ever heard it, he'd stop whatever he was doing to listen. And here we are listening to it again. Talk about echoes from the past."

They all looked at Marek expecting him to elaborate. With a sigh of resignation he added, "In more ways than one, Zakopane was an experience I'll never forget."

Alan had the penultimate word on the subject, "I suspect there's more to this story than you're letting on."

"Oh, leave it Alan," said Helena. "You're always digging at things." She gave a sharp shake of her head, clearly warning him to drop the subject. "Gwynne, can I help you with anything in the kitchen?"

"Sure. You can help me with the Welsh Rarebit."

In the kitchen, they busied themselves with preparations for the meal. Gwynne asked, "Can you put the bread under the grill to toast? I prefer the toast that way rather than the electric toaster."

Helena did as requested and then smelt the mixture and said, "I've never had *Welsh* Welsh Rarebit. What's that unusual aroma?

"Well detected. I've varied the recipe slightly. It's a small trick I'm playing on Marek. Keep an eye on him. I'll tell you about it later. Let me know what you think."

The girls returned with a plate in each hand.

After his first mouthful Marek said, "This has an exotic aroma and taste, not at all what I expected. It's hard to describe. What's in it, Gwynne?"

"You're not asking me to reveal my family's culinary secrets, are you? Eat up."

The women's eyes turned towards him, with both holding their heads at an obviously fake questioning angle, eyebrows raised. At that point, Marek again felt he was being put on the spot and was desperate to change the subject. Dominating his thoughts was *seaweed gin!*

He wiped his mouth as if about to reply, cleared his throat and said, "You know, about six months ago I was looking at land which was briefly up for sale in Minmi. Shortly afterwards it was withdrawn from sale. According to my solicitor mate, it was because two bodies were found on the site."

Marek's change of subject had the desired effect. "That's terrible. Do they know who they were?" asked Helena.

"They're still working on it but there's not much to go on." He then gave a condensed version of what had been uncovered: the bodies, location and piece of blue cloth. "There was also an old wooden cross with the letters *LET to GOD* carved on it. All a bit cryptic. It's got them all baffled."

As the conversation continued, Gwynne left to attend to the main course. It was a beef *Cawl*, another variation on the Welsh recipe. She carried it into the dining room and placed it on the table in flamboyant style. *Voilà!* Or, as the Welsh might say, *Dyna chi!"*

"Or, as we might say, "There ya go!" was Alan's contribution.

She served it as they continued to chat. Compliments soon interrupted the conversation as each of them savoured the meal.

Picking up on the previous discussion, Alan leaned back in his chair with a thoughtful look and said, "Maybe the bloke wasn't a policeman. Maybe he just *acquired* the jacket. Plenty of stories tell of raids on homesteads by both the Aborigines and bushrangers. It might have been acquired second or even third hand. Or, he could have been given it. All sorts of ways it could have ended up in the grave."

"Yeah," said Marek, "that's true, but in the meantime, the land remains off the market."

Between mouthfuls Alan ventured, "That shouldn't bother you too much, given that you're buying out the owners of the renovation job. How's that going, by the way?"

"It's not *bothering* me. It's just something unusual. The land was in a good position. Regarding the other business, it's progressing. The finances are tricky, but settlement should be happening soon. Although the job's got some bad history, I'll be glad to get on with it. It'll keep me busy; and give me something else to think about."

The last comment, made with a sidelong glance, was a sly reference to Gwynne, and he hoped she knew it.

"All could still work out well," was Gwynne's enigmatic reply.

The rest of the meal went smoothly as the conversation switched to Gwynne's expectations regarding working for Select Accounting as well as working from home in her new office. "It will take a fine balancing act. But the good news is I have two private home clients already and I'm hoping the word will spread."

"Put your picture on a business card and you'll get more clients." His comment was followed by a pregnant silence as heads turned. Who else but Alan would be so tactless?

"Er, I didn't mean that the way it might sound. Sorry Gwynne. Hey, can we have a look at your office?"

"Certainly, I should have thought to offer," she replied, ignoring Alan's *faux pas*. "It's mostly Marek's doing with décor courtesy of my mother. I'll put the coffee on as we go through. If you're all finished here, this way, lady and gentlemen."

As they stood, Helena, not for the first time, and nor would it be the last, gave Alan a look that could kill. He had enough sensitivity to look suitably chastised.

They sauntered through the new rooms, complimenting the work. Blithely carrying on, Alan said, "It certainly looks the goods. I hope it pays off for you."

"That's the plan. But it can also serve other uses in different circumstances. And the deck will be very handy, for lots of reasons."

"Yeah, I can see that. Good move, I say," was Alan's comment in a remorseful attempt at conciliation.

Over coffee, they again resorted to reminiscing on old times. Predictably, Helena contributed most and Gwynne least. However, to forestall having to reveal anything too personal when Alan queried her business expectations, she produced the photo of the scene Marek had set up with Merren's toys around the plate of chips. The delight on Merren's face was clear. As she passed her phone to Helena and Alan, Helena's gushing, if wistful, comment was, "Oh she looks lovely. What a bright looking little thing she is!"

It was Alan who, after looking at the photo, directed a penetrating gaze at Marek. Gwynne thought she could almost hear his brain ticking over while Helena directed her threatening, *don't say a word!* warning look at Alan.

"It's been a lovely night. Thanks, Gwynne," Helena proffered after a moment of silence. It was followed by general agreement and a move to begin clearing up. As they did so, Alan and Helena again complimented Gwynne on the meal, especially the *Cawl,* which Gwynne had varied from

Huw's mother's recipe book to make it a Welsh casserole rather than a stew.

Helena sidled up to Gwynne and asked, "What was that recipe variation you mentioned earlier?"

"Anchovy paste. But next time you're talking to Marek, slip 'seaweed gin' into the conversation."

Gwynne and Marek waved off Alan and Helena. It left them standing awkwardly on the footpath, not knowing what more to say or do. They turned and walked back to the front door. Marek tried to ignore the fact that it was the scene of previous romantic failures.

"I suppose I had better make a move as well. Can I give you a hand with cleaning up?"

"No thanks, I'll be right. I did some of it as I went. It's late and I have a busy day tomorrow." Ominously she added, "Mum's coming over early."

Unable to maintain his silent acceptance on the subject, Marek asked, "Can I ask if you're game for another day out? A picnic or whatever?"

"Yes, I think we'd like that. Give it a week or two though. And I'm not sure if Merren's up to another visit to the beach yet."

"I'll try to think of something for all of us. Thanks for all your hard work tonight. It was much appreciated, although I still can't place that unusual taste in the casserole."

"Helena seemed to like it too. Ask her; I gave her the recipe. Goodnight." Gwynne's voice sounded less than certain, as if there was something nagging in the background which she hadn't been able to voice.

"Goodnight, Gwynne." The downbeat inflexion of Marek's tone reflected his disappointment. *One step forward two steps backwards.*

Gwynne watched him walk to his truck. The words she hadn't said caught in her throat as she slowly closed the door. As the sound of his departing vehicle faded, she leant her back against the door, shut her eyes and took a deep breath.

Where's this all heading?

32

Was it becoming a habit? Again, he relied on physical labour to dull the disappointment after the dinner party. His frustration reminded him of a children's storybook he'd been given. It was an adaptation of a story by the Roman poet, Virgil, in which a disgruntled farmer, '... allayed his anger by shaking an oak tree in the woods.'

He was a disgruntled builder. And it wasn't because he had expected the evening to be a setup just to be with Gwynne for the night. Although, the possibility had crossed his mind. It was the cold dismissal he felt which was more than just a figurative slap in the face. It was like hitting a roadblock: *Wrong way! Go back!*

Where Gwynne was concerned, he didn't know which way to turn. 'Take refuge in what you're good at', he told himself: building with solid materials. Certainly not relationships.

Ross rang with another inspection job for which Marek was grateful. During the conversation, he also mentioned the seemingly never-ending saga about the land at Minmi. Ross told him that investigations into the burials had raised possibilities. The male body might have been either an Australian Agricultural Company employee, a miner, a ticket-of-leave ex-convict labourer, or a runaway convict.

Whoever he was, it appeared he had set up house with an Aboriginal woman on the fringe of the village.

Intrigued, Marek asked, "Where are you getting all this stuff?"

"That real estate mate of mine. He has an interest in Minmi's local history. He drinks at the pub there. Why don't you give him a call? His name's Harry Hays. I warn you though, he's a gold-medal talker on the subject of Minmi history." Ross added, "I'm pretty sure from what he said, that the official inquiry has just about reached a dead end! Get it? Dead end!"

In an expressionless tone Marek answered, "Yeah, hilarious. Stick to your day job if you want my advice. Thanks for the inspection jobs, Ross. It'll tide me over when I finish off this job. Talk to you later."

Settled on bar stools in the old Minmi Hotel, Harry Hays, just as Ross had warned, launched into the history of Minmi in mind-numbing detail before Marek could get him onto the topic of the burials.

"The area was dominated by the cattle grazing holdings of the Australian Agricultural Company. On the other hand, it was also possible he was one of the coal miners before the Brown Bothers took over the town in the 1850s. My guess is the bloke was an ex-con who shacked up with a black missus.

"She might have been one of the last survivors of one of the local Aboriginal mobs in the area. Nowadays we mostly refer to them as Awabakal people, but there were small clans within the tribe such as the Pambalong clan. Minmi is sort of on the edge of the Awabakal traditional lands, bordering with the Worimi people over the Hunter River. She may have been abandoned by her clan or possibly because her mob had died out or moved on. Or any number of reasons. She might also have been a leftover from the days when a missionary by the name of Threlkeld set up his Ebenezer mission in what's now Toronto. He sort of made the mission a safe house. She would have been very young, possibly even an orphan. Maybe it was simply a match-up by two outcasts from different societies," he had added speculatively.

All Harry's suggestions stirred Marek's interest. But he liked the idea that it might have been a love match. Such thoughts immediately brought him back to his own situation.

Good luck to them.

"Thanks Harry. Can you let me know if anything develops? It's got me thinking. Nice chatting, Harry."

On the drive home, he began to equate the plight of the Aborigines with the history of the Polish people. Both always living with the risk of dispossession, constantly living at the whim of foreigners threatening their way of life, changing boundaries and confusing allegiances. The decline in Aboriginal numbers he'd read about in both of Threlkeld's missions at Bahtahbah and Ebenezer was reflected in Poland's persecuted population and the Polish diaspora.

And the biggest coincidence politically was the resurgence in both races: Aboriginal land rites via the Mabo and Wik land decisions here, and Lech Wałęsa's Solidarity movement plus the breakup of the Soviet Union and the formation of the Third Polish Republic, the *III Rzeczpospolita Polska*.

Both sets of conditions opened the door to improved circumstances for each race; and at almost the same time. The main difference he could see was that Poland had international allies via the United Nations in 1945 and more recently NATO. The Aborigines seemed to be battling on their own.

Contemplating such issues was hardly going to lift his spirits. *Nothing was simple!*

Later that night his phone rang. He looked at the screen and saw Gwynne's name. After brooding on what was, or wasn't, happening in his life, his mood had not lifted. He was not in a happy frame of mind.

"Gwynne," was his single word response.

"Hi Marek, how are you?" she asked in what he chose to interpret as a cautious tone.

"Good," was his 'Queen's pawn to e4' guardedly safe chess move reply.

"What have you been up to?"

"Work."

"Is that all?"

"Yes."

In a light-hearted voice she said, "You know what they say, 'All work and no play ...'" She didn't complete the proverb.

"Yes, I know." Fleetingly, he felt as if he was channelling Conrad's Captain MacWhirr in *Typhoon* when the atmospheric conditions of the raging storm prohibited non-essential chatter.

"You're not saying much. Can't you talk? Are you alone?"

Marek hesitated for a few seconds and, ignoring her questions, continued the proverbial theme. "It might make Jack a dull boy, but it does help with other things."

"I'm not sure I follow. Anyway, I'm ringing on a business matter. A decision will have to be made regarding your registration for the GST and the Fringe Benefits Tax, given the likelihood of your impending property purchase. Last time we spoke, you were going to prepare some estimates. If there are any changes, we should go over them."

"Only a few, all relatively minor. Give me a time."

"Right. I'll send you a text when I get to work tomorrow and confirm my appointments. Is that OK?"

"Fine."

"Are you OK? You're not sounding your usual self. Can't you talk?"

"I tried being my usual self and I'm not sure where it got me. Now I'm focusing on work."

"You sound annoyed. Are you? With me?"

"You could say that. What else do you expect after the way we ended the other night? The dinner you prepared was lovely. I'm grateful you went to so much trouble on my account. I can't say the same about what happened after they left. You get an A-plus for knowing how to abruptly terminate an evening."

"What are you getting at?" Gwynne's tone was cautious.

"If you don't know then I really have been wasting my time. Oh, bugger it! I'll spell it out for you. You knew very well that I sought your company. You then proceeded to play me like a fish, drawing out the process to suit yourself. Well, to some extent, you were entitled to do that. You had other responsibilities and commitments to factor in. Instead, you factored me out! Sat me on the bench. Kept me at arm's length. To put it bluntly, I am fed up with that." He drew a breath.

"And don't go through your life's history again. I've heard it. You're scared to step outside the home-paddock you and your family have constructed around you, and you won't let anyone inside. You're like some institutionalised inmate, walled away, scared of the outside world."

"If that's the way you feel, I'll get another of the accountants here at Select to take over your file."

"Oh, bloody typical! There you go again, running away."

"I'm doing what I think is best for you." Gwynne's tone was lowered, conveying latent resentment.

"What's more, I don't want another accountant."

"Well, what do you want?"

"Oh, look it up in your customer relations manual if you can't figure it out for yourself! Send me a text message for our next appointment. I'll try to be completely objective and, as much as possible, impersonal."

"That doesn't sound like the world's best practice definition of a good business relationship."

"No, it doesn't. But it seems to be part of your modus operandi for a personal one."

"I'm *sorry*." Gwynne's emphatic tone totally contradicted her words.

"Not as sorry as me. But I'll get over it. There's always work. Maybe being dull won't hurt Jack after all. Or me."

"There was something else I was going to say but I'll leave it for now. Goodnight, Marek.

"Well, it doesn't feel like a good night. Goodbye." Marek ended the call and switched off his phone. He was in no mood to talk to anyone. He slumped onto his lounge chair with his book. The comparison of the title *Typhoon*, with his current frame of mind was on a par. He'd left off reading it for several days but now Joseph Conrad, and the travails of Captain MacWhirr, given the title itself, seemed the best distraction.

33

When he walked into Gwynne's office, neither could look the other in the eye. Gwynne again adopted her professional role and addressed each issue methodically.

The discussion was all business until they were packing up whereupon Marek asked, "What was the other thing you were going to say the other night?"

Gwynne stopped what she was doing, looked thoughtful, and then said, "It doesn't matter now. I hadn't made up my mind anyway so just forget about it."

"It's pretty easy for me to forget about something I didn't know about in the first place. I assume it was something not connected with what we have just been discussing."

"Correct." Tension in Gwynne's face and shoulders was clearly evident.

She took a breath and began: "It was to do with Merren's birthday on Saturday fortnight. I was going to invite some of her friends over for an afternoon backyard party. Usual kids' stuff: birthday cake, candles, balloons, streamers, games and so on. Just a few parents on riot duty to hang around and calm down anyone who gets too excited. It'll be mostly girls, but I know of a couple of boys in her day care group who'll probably come, possibly bringing their fathers."

"And ...? Where do I fit in? If at all?" Curiosity was getting the better of him. Gwynne faltered before speaking.

He watched as she tidied a few remaining papers as she spoke, not looking directly at him,

"I think Merren would like you to come."

"You *think*?" Marek's stomach churned.

In the ensuing silence his mind struggled with the ramifications of the whole idea.

Right from their first meeting he had felt a connection with Merren's *Pollyanna*-ish, '*everything is an adventure* view of the world.

Her response to his own childhood game of enacting how bees kissed the flowers had touched him more than he had expected.

Now the proposition was being considered whether he should be invited to attend her birthday party. He would meet her friends as well as other parents and it would cast a whole new light on his connection not just with Merren, but with Gwynne.

Or was it the other way round? He was confused.

Gwynne sensed his dilemma and tried to ease it. "Since I haven't sent out any invitations, the matter is sort of hypothetical."

Marek exploded. "Gwynne Alwen, I don't believe this. I've said it before, and I'll say it again. You are a grade one tease!"

He abruptly pushed back his chair, arms folded, and continued. "After our telephone conversation the other evening, you sit there and dangle an emotional carrot, without any reference to your own feelings, or mine. You know very well how I feel about Merren. Given what I said about you playing me like a fish, you're doing it again. What's my role in all of this? Am I just an accessory to whatever you decide?"

"I'm sorry I said anything. I shouldn't have." Gwynne's own confusion as to where their conversation was headed was evident.

"No, you bloody well shouldn't! Well, yes, you should, but only after you had thought about your own attitude and feelings. The question is, 'Do *you* want me there?' Because if you don't, that's the end of the matter."

After a long pause she murmured, "Yes,"

"Why? So, I can be a spare pair of hands if needed to move the furniture, or just stand around with any of the blokes and keep them out of your way while you run the party?"

"No."

"Why then? Get real! Come on, cough up. Why?"

"Because Merren likes you. You're very good with her. And you've been very good to … us."

"Except for the bit about Merren, that's a pretty small carrot. How will you explain my presence to the other parents? Don't you think their curiosity will be stirred up, just a bit?"

"I hadn't thought about that but you're right. Shall we drop the whole idea?"

"No, we damned well won't! Come on, spit it out before it chokes you. What's your real feeling about my role in this?"

Finally, Gwynne took a deep breath, looked him straight in the eye and said, "I'd like you to be there. I want us to be friends. I'm just not sure how. I'm cautiously feeling my way, but I feel blindfolded."

Marek realised his voice had been getting more strident.

He let Gwynne's words sink in. After a pause, spleen vented, he softened his voice almost to an undertone and said, "You can say that again, as far as we're concerned. But surely that blindfold isn't grafted on?"

Gwynne's whispered reply indicated a softening. "I have always enjoyed your company. I'm just not sure how to let things progress. I'm scared how things might snowball. What affects Merren, affects me, and vice versa."

"Has she suffered to date because of me? Other than getting bowled over by that wave at the beach that is?"

Gwynne couldn't suppress a wry smile at the recollection. "No, she hasn't."

"Well then, let's get to the practicalities of any proposed party. How will you introduce me? As your butler? Your gardener? Odd jobs man? Your not-so-secret admirer?"

"Somewhere close to the last two, I think. Although I concede, if you do come, tongues might wag."

"If you're worried about that last bit, let them. I only wish they had something to wag about."

"Be patient. It could be a slow process."

"Couldn't be any slower and bumpier than the ride so far. Personally, I'm looking forward to the smooth bits in between the bumps. Depending of course, on what sort of bumps we're talking about."

Gwynne dropped her gaze and shook her head at the innuendo. "You don't give up, do you?"

"I've thought about it a few times, but it didn't look to be an option leading to a happy outcome. Would it help you to understand if I reminded you my parents were Polish? They imagined a better life for themselves and sacrificed *everything* to achieve their happiness here in Australia." Almost as an afterthought, he asked, "Are you happy?"

"You're like a dog with a bone! What sort of question is that? Happiness is a comparative and changing state of being. Don't you agree?"

"It's also one of life's prime motivations. Not just an aspiration but a deep-rooted goal. In some places, pursuit of happiness is considered a human right. You didn't answer the question."

"It's a work in progress. Sometimes you don't help. Sometimes you do."

As if it was her last roll of the dice, she suddenly gave her thoughts free rein. "When I let myself think about us, I inevitably recall my life when I first met Merren's father. In retrospect, it was a scene out of a soap opera, but at the time it *was* real; I lived for, and loved, every moment. I let myself go and acted in response to my feelings and emotions. Then it turned into a Shakespearean tragedy. Something deep inside was killed off. I admit I have rebuilt my survival strategies to fend off any similar attacks."

"And you see me in terms of someone attacking or undermining those strategies! Look again. Can't you see that there is an opportunity to adapt, or at least modify those strategies in the light of new evidence?" He felt he had to acknowledge Gwynne's reference to Merren's father. "From the little I know, it wasn't a soap opera, it was a heartbreaking event. But that was over four years ago. Here and now, I'm offering a shoulder to lean on. I'm offering myself as a way that together we can make things better, if you give it a chance."

Tentatively Marek reached out and placed a hand over Gwynne's clenched fist.

Gradually he felt her tension ease and she returned the gesture by placing her other hand over his.

Those hands again!

As he drove to Merren's birthday party, he was still completely at a loss regarding his role. When he arrived it was Keith who opened the door. Relief was evident on both their faces. "Thank God! Someone sane. Welcome to the mad house. Gwynne and Colette are busy in the kitchen preparing the food. All party goo: sausage rolls, cocktail franks, fairy bread, lollies for each kid and cans of drink are just the start. It's bedlam, and the Munchkins haven't even arrived yet."

Marek had decided to come early, on the pretence of helping in the setting up, but really, to gauge the feeling in the room and possibly make his excuses after wishing Merren a happy birthday.

As he followed Keith through to the deck, Colette called out, "Hey, you two, there's a packet of balloons on the table. Can you blow them up and tie them in bunches of four? Vary the colours and use your imagination where to hang them around the deck."

"I know where I'd like to hang *someone*," Keith muttered as he picked up a balloon, drew a deep breath, and set to work.

Gwynne looked somewhat hassled as she appeared with paper plates and napkins. "Hi Marek, thanks for coming. *I* appreciate it and so does Merren." It was said with politeness tinged with gratitude … as well as some other unidentified quality. Could it be a smidgin of pleasure?

Despite everything he'd said on the phone, the sight of Gwynne in blue denim shorts and an apricot loose-fitting halter-top gave him a lift, which stirred his imagination. "Thanks. You look nice. Where's Merren?"

Right on cue Merren, wearing the Polish fairy costume he had given her, skipped up to Marek, pirouetted, and waved a wand at his head, chirruping, "La! la! la! Hello Marek. Isn't it exciting?"

"Hello princess, you look beautiful. *Wszystkiego najlepszego!* Or happy birthday! Or many happy returns, in Polish. Whichever you prefer."

Merren was determined to sit on his lap while he was blowing up a balloon, which proved to be more of a hindrance than a help, especially when she started pressing the balloon back onto his face and giggling. He and Keith eventually got the job done just as there was a knock on the front door.

Gwynne called from the kitchen, "Can you get that Marek or Keith or whoever?"

"You go Marek," said Keith, "I need to catch my breath. Arm yourself!"

Merren leapt off his lap and, leading the way, skipped to the door.

When Marek had half opened it, the door was pushed out of his hand as a stampede of party-crazed creatures hurtled down the hallway followed by several parents, mostly women. Some carried gifts for Merren, and a few held very suspicious-looking brown paper bags from which he thought he heard a clinking sound.

Merren, squealing with delight, disappeared with the children. Lastly came two men looking as enthusiastic as he felt.

"Hello there, I'm Ben," said the first.

"Come in Ben. Welcome. I'm Marek. Go through to the back."

The other, holding the hand of a boy who seemed uncertain of what was expected of him, stopped and said, "Pleased to meet you Marek. I'm Gary, and this is my son Noah."

"Come in. Pleased to meet both of you."

To his relief, none of the parents seemed terribly interested in why he was there.

Gwynne appeared carrying a tray of disposable cups and the sparkling contents from one of the brown paper bags. "Welcome everyone. You've met Marek? He dropped in to lend a hand."

When they had seated themselves, Keith introduced himself and they began a round of introductions, followed by the usual small talk about which child was theirs, work and sports results. When it was Marek's turn Keith interrupted saying, "Marek is the builder who did these additions." Marek gave Keith a grateful nod in appreciation for forestalling further explanation.

As they cast an eye over Marek's work, they were quite impressed and asked what sort of building work he generally did. They were soon joined by a few of the mothers and gradually Marek felt more at ease. It appeared they all presumed he was the father of one of the children.

As the party got into full swing, the music of a popular kids' group blared. The children danced, jumped or stomped, so it seemed, to some rhythm of their own. To Marek, they looked like a tribe of undersized Berserkers skipping over hot coals. However, no actual violence or injury was sustained, for which the parents were grateful. When the parents had had enough, a few organised games followed, from which Marek was content to be excused.

One such game was a competition to see who could do the best *Macarena*. When the music started and the children began dancing, the adults all but fell about laughing at the attempts of four-year-olds to keep in time and get the actions right. A couple of the mothers tried to lead but the children carried on regardless. The mothers continued for their own amusement. The best child dancer was Noah who obviously had talent, or had learnt the moves elsewhere, and who seemed oblivious to the shambles the other children were making of the dance.

After the dancing, some of the children sang – and shouted – a few songs, including *Bob the Builder,* in which Merren substituted *Bob* for *Marek the Builder.* Then, at Gwynne's request, everyone sat around the table waiting for the birthday cake to appear. Candles were lit and, with Gwynne leading, *Happy Birthday* was sung. Marek was moved to recall his own birthday celebrations at home when the song was sung in Polish by his parents and Helena. Quietly he sang the Polish birthday song, *Sto Lat!* despite the tune being different from the traditional song in English.

Only Gwynne seemed to notice the difference.

Next came the opening of the presents. Merren dispensed with any pretence of self-control and simply ripped off the wrapping paper of each with rapid enthusiasm. At the end, almost without being prompted, she had the kindness to go to each child and give them a hug and say, "Thank you."

While she was thanking one of the children, Marek put his present among the wrapping paper on the table. When she had completed the round Gwynne said, "Merren, you've forgotten this one."

Merren grabbed the unopened present and unceremoniously ripped off the paper. One by one she held up a set of animal glove puppets. She tried several, mimicking the actions and sounds of each animal. She then looked at the crumpled tag and looked questioningly at her mother, who simply nodded in Marek's direction.

She immediately skipped over to Marek and hugged him. Unnoticed by almost everyone except Keith, Gwynne moved around to Marek, slid her arm through his, and murmured, "Thank you."

The last activity was a treasure hunt in the back yard. The 'treasure' was an assortment of chupa chups, packets of sultanas and fruity sugar-free lollies. As the children gathered around swapping and sharing their spoils or playing with the presents, the parents started clearing up some of the party debris.

Children were sent to gather their belongings and say their goodbyes. The exodus trickle was almost complete except for Gary and Noah. Holding his son's hand as he walked past Marek he asked, "What's your connection to the family? Are you Merren's uncle?"

It was Gwynne who saved Marek from any embarrassment by answering, "No, Gary, nothing like that. Just a good friend of the family. Your son looks to have a promising future as a dancer. Thanks for coming Gary, and Noah's lovely present. G'bye".

Keith, the only one close enough to hear their conversation, shook his head. He turned and walked back to where he had left his drink.

Pulling teeth isn't even close!

34

All things considered, the house wasn't a complete shambles after the party. The damage was generally confined to spilt food and drink, scraps of torn streamers, burst balloons and shreds of wrapping paper. At present, the girl of the moment, 'Princess-for-a-day' Merren, was singing, or gabbling away to herself, while having her bath, without any apparent care in the world.

Keith was standing on the deck quietly content. In a moment of comparative calm, with his hands full of used disposable plastic cups, paper napkins and party debris, doing his bit for the clean-up, he asked, "Marek, have you made any headway on the purchase of that land you were considering in Minmi?"

"I got a bit of feedback from Ross on some of the legal aspects. The burials appear to be from well before 1900 but further details may never be known."

Marek stopped to sip the contents of his paper cup. "Why do you ask?"

Keith was in a ruminative mood. "Just being nosey. I don't know the legal details, but I've been reading a bit of the history of the Lake Macquarie area. I was intrigued to find out that Minmi was actually a privately owned town. I didn't know such a thing existed here, or anywhere, in Australia."

"Not you too? You're the second person to show an interest in the local history of Minmi. Alright, go on, what have you discovered?"

"The Brown brothers, James and Alexander, and later, James' son John, of Coal and Allied fame and fortune, owned the lot. They were granted various leases to mine coal in several locations around the 1850s and they bought the whole shebang. About five thousand acres worth. The coal was good steaming coal and they had over five hundred miners working at one stage. The population of Minmi was as much as seventeen hundred."

Marek was genuinely surprised. "I've never heard of that before. Sounds a bit medieval. 'Lords of all they survey', that sort of thing. So, what's the connection with the Minmi burials do you reckon? Any ideas?"

Keith stuffed his rubbish into a bin-bag and sat down, one hand around an almost empty bottle. "Only guess work from my readings. The area had been used for cattle grazing before the discovery of coal and allocating mining rights. At a guess our man in the ground may have been either a stockman or a miner."

Marek thought for a short while and said, "Yes, that fits with what I heard from a real estate agent who is a bit of an amateur historian. He also says the area was used as an access way from Maitland down past the western side of Lake Macquarie to the Central Coast by all sorts: Aborigines, the Mounted Police, drovers, timber cutters, even bushrangers. Ross reckons the investigation has reached a stalemate and thinks the land might come back on the market in the not-too-distant future."

Marek paused for a moment, sipped his wine, then asked, "But what about the Aboriginal woman? Where does she come into it, I wonder?"

Keith settled back in his chair sounding ruminative on the matter. "The book I read suggests a possible scenario that's worth considering. It involves a missionary character, a curious do-gooder with a complicated background who decided to try to convert the heathens of the Pacific south seas. He seems to have taken it as his life's work to spread Evangelical Protestantism to the natives.

"He eventually lobbed here in Lake Macquarie. Governor Brisbane allocated ten thousand acres at Reid's Mistake, north of the Swansea Channel, and a couple of years later, with the support of the London Missionary Society, he set up his mission. It was known as *Bahtahbah* where Belmont is now. Would you believe the site is currently occupied by the Gunyah Hotel and the old Infants School?

"Anyway, that endeavour failed, mostly because the Reverend spent too much money in establishing it, and a few years later he set up another mission in Toronto around 1830, which he named Ebenezer, after the chapel his father-in-law Thomas Arndell was instrumental in having built on the Hawkesbury River. Threlkeld's new mission was on the present site of the Toronto Hotel, but it fizzled out as well over a ten-year period."

In a typical Keith comment he added, "Curious, isn't it? That he chose two sites which are now occupied by pubs? Religion and booze, both great attractions to the masses."

Keith went on. "At one time, Threlkeld was his name, seemed to have been at odds with the dubious Reverend Samuel Marsden. Who, get this, was also known as, 'the flogging parson'. That nickname was disputed on account of him being the senior Church of England chaplain in the colony, representative of the London Missionary Society, Magistrate and wealthy land holder, offset by some supposedly good work he did in New Zealand. According to the book I read he, Threlkeld, not Marsden did a lot of work trying to help the Aborigines. Get this, he even learned and recorded their language and later, spoke up for them in legal disputes. He tried educating some of them, mostly only the boys. Part of the problem for the Aborigines was that there were reports they were being used as middle-men by ex- and escaped convicts and bushrangers, to steal from the settlers. The Aborigines were being caught and punished, but most of the ringleaders were escaping justice.

"In the end, by the early 1840s, the Ebenezer mission came to nothing. The Missionary Society big chiefs, either in London or the Colonial Missionary Society, thought Threlkeld's missions were a failure because he didn't succeed in converting any Aborigines to Christianity and he spent too much of their money while he was at it. Threlkeld himself returned to Sydney to do parish work. Funnily, the bloke at the Aboriginal Centre here in Newcastle reckons that at the time, the Aborigines thought the mission gave them a refuge from the white people taking over their lands. Alcohol also caused a lot of problems. No surprise there."

Keith leaned back in his chair, upended the bottle and draining the contents, without the least sense of irony, mused, "Sort of brings the whole history down to a human level, doesn't it?"

Marek contemplated his wine, tipped the dregs over the railing, and said, "We've got a lot to answer to for the plight of the Aborigines. The history of white contact has been deadly for them and reflects poorly on us."

Then, bringing history into his present predicament, he added, "Hmm, where I'm concerned, at the risk of sounding callous, those two bodies were a hindrance. In other circumstances I might have bought that land. Now I'm not so sure. Knowing it could be the subject of Aboriginal interest could be tricky." Marek concluded wistfully, "They got the rough end of the stick. Maybe the way things turned out did me a favour. It *was* a terrific site though."

Keith was obviously enjoying the speculation on the possible connections between the bodies in question. "The woman might have been a domestic worker; the bloke could have been anyone. It might have been romantic, or maybe they were just two lost souls, who looked after each other when the Ebenezer mission closed.

"I also got thinking about something else I read. There was a Welsh Congregational community in Minmi who attended what was known then as the Welsh Independent Church. However, when a mine flooded and the pit had to close for a time, many of the Welsh miners moved away to find work elsewhere. No work, no pay. They ended up in Lambton. Fascinating, don't you reckon?"

Marek rocked back in his chair; it all started to get too much. As if ridding himself of a problem, he dumped the paper cup into the bin-bag. "I'd prefer to think it was something mutually beneficial to both of them. It's obvious they didn't bury themselves. Someone else buried them together for a reason. I can't imagine that was a coincidence or even a convenience. I wonder who that person might have been? Curiously, there's something that I don't think I told you about, that was found with the bodies: a small wooden cross. It had a religious inscription carved on it: *LET to GOD*."

"What bodies?" Colette asked as she walked out onto the deck having heard snippets of their conversation. "Did someone mention something about the Welsh?"

"Oh, just something we were speculating about. I'll tell you the story later." Keith answered vaguely.

"We've just about finished putting the house back together again. Who would have thought that a dozen ankle-biters could turn the house upside down?" She asked rhetorically but sounding genuinely surprised.

"Where's Gwynne?" asked Marek. "I'd like to say goodnight to Merren and be on my way soon."

Keith raised an eyebrow as he and Colette glanced furtively at each other but said nothing.

Marek walked back into the house and met Gwynne coming out of Merren's room. "Is it alright if I say goodnight to Merren?"

"There you go again. Of course, it's alright. She'd be upset if you didn't. She's had a great time. And she loves your present. She's got them with her in bed. Very thoughtful of you. Thanks for coming and your help with the party."

"That's fine. I'll just pop in; I won't be long."

When Marek entered the room, Merren's smile told him how welcome he was. She immediately kissed her forefinger and held it up. Marek did the same and slowly the fingers met and each gave a "Bzzzzzz!"

Merren added her infectious giggle, which always drew a smile from him, and then held up her arms. He leant down and gave her a hug and, after a brief moment, a kiss on her cheek. "Goodnight, princess."

Marek stood and headed towards the kitchen, comforted by Merren's reaction to his visit. When he looked down the hallway, he saw Gwynne walking ahead of him.

When he reached the kitchen, he commented, "I'll be off now. The party was an interesting experience. It's a long time since I attended a kids' party. I never realised the mayhem a dozen pre-schoolers can generate."

Gwynne was confused about how she should react. She had been standing at Merren's door and watched them exchange their greeting and, even more importantly, Merren's seemingly unconditional acceptance of him. It was a telling moment for her.

She opened the door for him and stood, expecting … something. She heard him say, "Thanks for asking me. It worked out better than I expected."

"Maybe we both need to review our expectations." She said, obtusely.

She watched as he walked to his truck.

When she came back to join Colette and Keith on the deck, Keith asked, "Has Marek gone? We were having an interesting chat. I thought he'd hang around," he added suggestively, with eyebrows raised.

"Come on Keith, leave it. It's time we left as well," Colette said. "Four years old! Who'd have thought the time could go so quickly? Goodnight Gwynne." When they reached the door, she gave Gwynne a hug. "Be kind to yourself, you deserve it."

While she was pondering Colette's comment, Keith stopped to say, "He's alright, is Marek. Loosen up Gwynne. You two could do a lot worse."

As they drove away, the let down she felt was caused by more than the after-effects of the party.

On the way home Keith eventually broke the silence. "What did you make of that then?"

"Make of what?" Colette queried.

"Don't be coy. You know what I mean. Marek being there and then suddenly not. I thought he was set fair for the night. In like Flynn …"

"Stop it, Keith. Do you always have to look on the sleazy side of things?" By the tone of her less-than-harsh voice, Keith knew she had been thinking something similar.

"No, but I like to look at human behaviour and what I saw just now made me think that they are hiding behind a crusty old set of values. They look like two fish drifting around in the same bowl but not connecting with each other. I think Gwynne is unhappy and I'm not sure that we don't figure in that unhappiness to some extent."

"We've been through this before. We've left Gwynne to make her own decisions for months now. It's up to her. Stop second guessing her."

Keith couldn't let it go. "A couple of months doesn't wipe out almost four years. Another way of looking at it is that the family, me included, has been part of ring-fencing her. Sure, a couple of months ago we eased off. We might have loosened the sliprails, but we haven't given her *permission*." Keith's voice suggested real concern. "We could do more."

"Well, I for one don't feel further intervention, or 'permission' as you put it, is constructive for either of them. They'll just have to work it out for themselves."

"All I'm saying is that it's obvious Marek's got the hots for Gwynne and knows it. And Gwynne's got the hots for Marek but won't admit it, even to herself."

"You've got it all figured out, haven't you? Don't you have anything else to do?"

With the most innocent expression he could produce he replied, "What's more important than concern for your fellow man ... and woman? Especially when they're family. Or could be?"

35

As soon as Ross gave him the legal all clear, Marek focused on getting to work on the renovations of his new house. When he thought about it, he found it hard to take it all in. Technically he was the owner of two properties. However, a reality check showed one was mortgaged to buy the other which would not be liveable for up to two months and in the meantime, he needed an income to live on. He was reluctant to use the mortgage money for day-to-day living expenses because, if that ran out before the job was finished, he would have to go back to the bank, cap in hand.

He set about putting into practice the work schedule he'd laid out and spent long days on the job. One afternoon while driving home, his phone rang. He couldn't answer it and it rang out. When he got home, he checked and saw the caller was Keith. Curious as to why he could be ringing him, he returned the call. "Keith, sorry I missed your call. What's up?"

"Nothing really. We haven't seen you lately. Not since Merren's party. Everything okay?" Keith's voice didn't sound as relaxed without his usual dry, probing attempts at wit.

"I've been working flat-out on this job. The sooner I get it finished and on the market, the better. You don't sound your usual chipper self."

After a slight hesitation, Keith said, "Colette and I are fine, but I'd like to run a couple of things by you. Firstly, I thought you'd like to know Merren's been a bit off colour with a couple of bouts of tonsillitis. The doctor says it's common in children, especially if they have a cold, runny nose or a cough. That sort of thing."

"Right, okay. Thanks for letting me know. How's Gwynne coping with Merren sick, *and* work? Who's looking after Merren?" Marek knew he was rushing his questions, but he had begun to feel more of an affinity for Keith and thought he would understand.

"Audrey and Huw are helping out. Colette has also been recruited. It's being managed. I think."

Marek was not reassured by the lack of conviction in his last two words. "Do you think I should call in? I don't want to get in the way. I don't have any experience with sick kids."

Keith's reply came smoothly. "I don't think you'd be in the way. I'm sure Merren would love to see you. Gwynne too." He left it floating like a lure on a fly-fishing line in a slow-moving stream.

"You don't think so? Okay, I'll drop in, just to say hello. Thanks again."

"Oh, by the way, can we have another chat about that Minmi land? Some interesting info has come to light."

"Yes, but I haven't thought about it much. I'm focusing on this job. You know, one thing at a time."

"Fair enough. Another time. Good talking to you. Cheers."

"Hang on Keith. All this info about that land, where's it coming from? I didn't think you dabbled in residential land."

"And I don't. That doesn't mean I don't keep my ear to the ground about property in general. You're a builder. You know how construction works. I'm in property but the same applies. I talk to agents and listen to when and where property deals are happening. And I store that information away. For now, think about Merren … and Gwynne. Cheers."

It was only after Keith rang off that Marek realised how odd it was that Keith was the one to ring and tell him about Merren. His next thought was how annoyed, or worse, disinterested, Gwynne must be, if she had decided not to let him know herself. The thought put him in two minds: to visit or not?

Damn! Why did he always feel like he was on the back foot?

At work the following day Marek's thoughts kept switching between the job and Merren. He realised action was required to put him at ease. He thought he might get away with an unannounced visit on the way home from work on the pretext that he'd had to attend to some other business nearby. He'd take his chances and visit on the way home.

A car was parked in front of her house when he pulled up. There was no answer when he knocked and after knocking a second time, he was about to walk around the back when Gwynne opened the door.

"Oh, Marek, sorry if I kept you waiting. I think I need a doorbell. I've got a client. Can you stay for a few minutes? I'm nearly finished, and in the meantime … you can check in on Merren. She'd love to see you."

It wasn't the reception he'd imagined, but at least he hadn't been turned away.

"Sure, I was just on my way past to check on a job nearby." The lie sounded smooth and plausible. "I've got a few minutes. Where is she?"

"Watching television in the loungeroom. Go through. She might be a bit subdued; she hasn't been well. Don't worry, it's not catching. I'll be with you as soon as I can."

Marek quietly entered the room. He couldn't help noting the difference in her from when he saw her at her party.

She was lying on the lounge, tucked up in her pyjamas and dressing gown and not radiating her usual bright self.

Marek tentatively smoothed the back of his hand down her cheek not knowing what to say. other than: "Hello Princess. Not feeling well today?"

Her only response was a shake of her head and to clutch Squinty and Binko more closely to her.

Marek sat at the end of the lounge and said, "I'm sorry about that. Is it all right if I sit here with you while Mummy is busy? I'll try not to disturb you."

Marek felt out of place and didn't know what more he could do. He tried to relax while he waited. He found the cat glove puppet he had given her, squashed at the back of the lounge, and tried to put it on his hand.

He then felt Merren wriggle her way down the lounge to a new position with her head resting against him, still clutching Squinty and Binko.

He said nothing but gently placed his hand holding the cat-puppet across her hand, making patting motions.

"Well, don't you two look cosy? I'm sorry to disturb you." Gwynne's voice brought him back to reality.

He eased Merren's head onto a cushion as he stood to face Gwynne. "Not at all. I'm sorry. I was being quiet trying not to bother her too much."

"I think you succeeded."

Gwynne sat where Marek had been sitting and felt Merren's forehead. "Still a bit hot, but better than this morning I think. Have you eaten? Would you like to stay for dinner? It's only Spaghetti Bolognese."

"I only called in because Keith, of all people, rang me yesterday and mentioned Merren had been off colour. As I said earlier, I was in the area. I thought I'd …"

Gwynne gave him a sideways glance.

"Thanks Marek. I'm sure she appreciates it. As do I. You always seem to be on hand when something, or someone, is needed. Do you have a crystal ball?"

"Clearly not, given the hash I've made of some things recently. I just thought I'd see how she is for myself. Now I've seen her, I'll be on my way. I didn't mean to get in the way of your client or dinner time," he said matter-of-factly. With more feeling than he intended, he asked, "Why didn't you call and tell me?"

"I didn't want to worry you. And I don't think you've ever 'got in our way'. Quite the contrary. Now do you want to stay for dinner or not? It'll be ready in ten minutes. We'll eat in the kitchen. It's cosier."

Still feeling ill at ease as his stomach churned with mixed emotions he said, "If you're sure, that would be nice. Thanks. Can I give you a hand with anything?"

Gwynne's tone was firm. "It's Spaghetti Bolognaise, nothing fancy. The sauce is ready. I just need to cook the spaghetti. Ten minutes, fifteen tops. Wait here."

Marek looked around the room after watching Gwynne leave. He felt a surge from the pit of his stomach. He tried to ignore it by looking at her bookshelves. He was surprised by the number of classics: Austen, the Brontës, Dickens, a few modern works by Bryson, McEwan, Keneally, Follett and, unexpectedly, the complete Harry Potter series and most surprisingly, a Dylan Thomas book of poetry. *No Conrad!*

"Here we are then. Marek, can you clear the table please? Things are a bit untidy. Hope you don't mind. Merren, would you like to try some? It won't hurt your throat. It'll do you good. Come on, sit here between us."

The meal was eaten enthusiastically by Marek, less so by Gwynne and almost not at all by Merren. Halfway through she said she didn't want any more.

"Would you like to go back to bed or watch TV?"

Merren's response was to hug Squinty and Binko closely under her chin which Gwynne interpreted as her preferring bed.

"Come on then, I'll tuck you in."

Turning to Marek she said, "Do you want to finish Merren's? It'll only go to waste if you don't."

"If you're sure. Thanks. It's been a long day. For the both of us ... by the look of it."

"Yes, it has. You finish it off while I settle her down." Marek watched Gwynne as she left the room.

After finishing Merren's meal, he collected the plates, cutlery and glasses and went over to the sink. As he would have done at home, he rinsed them and placed them on the drainer.

When Gwynne returned and saw what he was doing she commented, "You're very unusual in lots of ways, particularly when it comes to being ordered and methodical. Is that a prerequisite for a builder?"

"Huh! I doubt it. You haven't seen the way some of my mates go about their work. Maybe it's something to do with my Polish training."

The reaction to the word wasn't what he expected. "What made you say that? Have you heard anything from Poland?"

"No! No, I was trying to be funny."

He looked at her saying, "I do think about Magdalena – and Ana – every now and then. I still can't believe what my father did. I never thought he could be with anyone else but my mother. It's a side of him I never imagined."

"Ana was very attractive."

"Er, yes. She and Magdalena both had a real depth to their personalities. Unsettling. *That* is definitely a Polish thing. It's probably locked into the national psyche by its history.

Mum showed it occasionally, but I never imagined Dad did. Maybe I was wrong. Maybe I only saw what I wanted to see in him. I thought his job with the men at Comsteel drained most of Poland out of him. I was wrong."

His train of thought took a branch line. "Do you think we really know our parents? Or anyone? Fully?"

The sombre twist in their conversation was taken up by Gwynne. "Maybe we construct the personality of some people to match our own wishes and expectations."

Marek gave a shrug. "It makes you think, doesn't it? Are our memories real or imagined? Or constructed by us?" He stopped himself.

"Sorry. Gwynne. This is all getting a bit heavy, I'd better go. Will you say goodnight to Merren for me? I don't want to disturb her any more than I already have."

"Yes, alright, but I have to say, any disturbance you cause where Merren is concerned is usually welcome on both her part and … I'll see you out."

When Gwynne opened the door, Marek stepped past. When she held his arm, causing him to turn, she reached up and kissed him gently. With sensitivity. On the cheek.

So unexpected was it that he was too slow to react. Completely caught off guard, he walked to his truck berating himself for not making more of the moment. He'd had to fight off the urge to go back and take her in his arms and … Then what? He berated himself again for even thinking of taking advantage of the circumstances of Gwynne having a sick child to care for. However, he couldn't help but think the night had ended on some sort of a high.

Gwynne felt buoyed. She stood at the window watching as he drove away. Was it only because she had loosened the bonds on her former emotional constraints? Or because Marek had?

Their conversation about really knowing the inner person had stimulated a train of thought about her relationship with Merren's father, David. Foremost in her mind was that she had only known him for less than two months. Could anyone really know a person in that brief time?

She had thought that she could, and had imagined, or constructed and accepted, a complete personality on that basis. Instinctively, she thought that she had got it right. It was a small sample on which to generate a life-changing event with seemingly life-long consequences.

But had she got it right?

On family advice, she had registered Merren's birth without naming the father and nor had she informed David's parents. That had been the beginning of her reinvented life. Now she began to look again at her present situation and sensed the notion of a change in her perspective. That included work with Select Accounting and the balance with her private clients at home and … *and what for herself? Had Lana been right?*

And why on earth did Keith ring Marek? She couldn't figure that out.

Seeing him sitting there on the lounge with Merren's head resting against him had been a sight to make her catch her breath. How many other single mothers could feel such confidence that all was well between their child and … and a what? A friend? Gentleman caller? Client? An acquaintance? Tonight, she had to admit that her feelings had moved on from the merely platonic.

But to what?

36

"G'day Ross. This is unexpected. What can I do you for?" Marek was genuinely surprised. As far as he knew there were no outstanding legal issues to for him to worry about.

"Marek, I just thought I'd let you know that the land at Minmi is coming back on the market. Everything seems to be resolved; up to a point."

"Up to a point? Sounds like there's a hitch somewhere. Go on, what is it?" The dubious tone in Marek's voice, though unmistakeable, didn't deter Ross.

"It's sort of complicated in one way but it isn't a deal breaker."

"Now you really are talking like a lawyer. What's the problem?"

"There's likely to be a covenant on the land. It doesn't look like it will interfere too much with the use of the land as far as your plans are concerned. It depends."

"On what? This sounds pretty vague Ross. Ambiguous legal-speak makes me nervous. Firstly, what exactly is a covenant? I've heard of them but what, specifically, does it mean in this case?"

"First, let me explain the *why*, then I'll try and explain the *what*. The burials are on the edge of the Awabakal tribal area covered by the local Aboriginal Land Council. Practices vary but Aboriginal people feel equally as respectful about old burials as we do about modern cemeteries. They are seen as part of a continuing culture and tradition as well as offering valuable archaeological information. The case of burials we're talking about is complicated because a white person is involved and the grave was accidentally disturbed, or exposed, through erosion. It is important that when a skeleton is found, it has to be reported to the police, to the National Parks and Wildlife Service and to the Local Aboriginal Land Council. These days remains are sometimes recovered and replaced in a more acceptable location.

"Firstly, the parties involved recognise that there seems to be a Christian element to the burials because a cross was unearthed. Secondly, the site is not intended to be developed beyond the construction of a house at some distance. Thirdly, the gravesite is adjacent to Crown Land which will allow separate access to the land you're seeking to buy. In short, the proposed covenant prohibits any construction within a five-metre radius of the burials. The agreement has been made with the best of intentions and the support of the local Land Council."

Marek's silence prompted Ross to ask, "Are you with me?"

"Yes, I was just calculating the area in my head. If my arithmetic is correct that could be up to seventy-five square metres. It seems a lot. I'd like to see a survey map."

"Of course. But it is near the boundary which reduces the area you're concerned with to a bit over half that. But a covenant is enough to put potential buyers off, especially given the reasons for it. Just thought you'd like to know. Let me repeat: being right on the boundary allows separate access to the burial site.

He added, "A cheeky offer might be worth considering. Give it some thought. It's less than five percent of a fifteen hundred square metre block. Anyhow, how's everything going with your new property?"

324

"Yeah, not bad thanks. If the weather cooperates, with luck, I could have it finished in a few weeks. Depending on contractors and supplies of course." Marek knew his optimism was getting the better of him. The thought of the land coming back on the market had side-tracked him.

"Hang on a minute, this information isn't exactly confidential. Any interested buyer could find out what you just told me, couldn't they?"

Using his 'official' voice Ross answered, "Only if they have a dedicated professional lawyer committed to the welfare of their client to the same extent you have."

"Bloody hell, I walked into that one, didn't I?"

Ross chuckled and replied, "All part of the service. By the way, have another word with Harry Hays when you've got time. He was telling me some interesting stuff about the Right Reverend Threlkeld. Did you know his were just about the first Aboriginal missions in New South Wales? Probably Australia? He was a real pioneer of the Lake Macquarie district. That's it for today. I'm looking forward to when you tell me you've got a buyer. More business for us. Cheers, mate."

"Hang on, I haven't been thinking about all this a lot since I got back from Poland. Being there reminded me of how resilient the Poles are despite being the punching bag of its neighbours for centuries. I can't help drawing certain comparisons with the plight of the Aborigines. Let me know of any other developments, will you? Thanks for the call. Cheers, Ross."

Marek was intrigued. Could Minmi be the location of his next project? It depended on some unknowns, such as the price he got for his current job. That was up to the market, which was reasonably buoyant at the moment. It also depended on the asking price of the land, which would undoubtedly require some tricky negotiations. He had to remind himself not to get too worked up about it until he had more information. It was a fascinating prospect, well worth considering.

For the first time Marek could recall, Gwynne rang him for no known reason. His initial concern was for Merren.

"Hello Gwynne, this is a surprise. Things are looking up unless this is a business call." He immediately thought of Merren and asked, "Is something up with Merren?"

"No, she's much better. Not quite back to her old self, but almost. The doctor doesn't think her tonsils will have to come out. They don't do that these days unless they have to. What are you up to?"

"Glad to hear about Merren. Me? I'm having a wow of a time. That's if you don't count keeping busy with this house from dawn till dusk. Some of the small delays frustrate me, but I have to remind myself everyone doesn't operate according to my schedule. I'm getting there. Thanks for asking. Was there something you needed to tell me?"

"Like what? I just rang to see how you're going. Well, now you mention it, I've been thinking, and I wondered whether you could take a day off next weekend so we could have another day out. Not the beach this time, but something along those lines. Perhaps that animal park near Williamtown? I'm sure Merren would like it. It will be a nice pick-me-up for her." Gwynne's voice was surprisingly upbeat compared to some previous conversations.

Marek's antennae were twitching at the thought of her taking the initiative for a change. "Nice idea. I like it, but I'm sorry, not this weekend. I've got a brickie coming in on Friday and Saturday and maybe some of Sunday. It took me ages to get him, and I don't want to put him off. How about Sunday week?"

"That sounds fine. How are you keeping up with the day-to-day stuff, like eating proper meals, shopping, washing and cleaning?"

"Nice of you to ask. Not so nice of you to hit a man in his weak spot."

He realised she was inquiring into areas never previously visited, but he felt some pleasure talking about such mundane things.

"Yeah, sort of. I'm managing, more or less, on a day-to-day, needs must, basis. I haven't been reduced to ratting through the washing basket to find the least dirty undies yet."

"Stop. Too much detail. Is that what you call managing?"

"Yeah, sort of. I'm hoping to see a glimmer of light in a couple of weeks. I don't want to rush it too much for fear of mucking things up. Some woman once told me to be patient. Not sure who it was."

"I've an idea I know. It was good advice at the time. Seems to be working. Would you like to come over for a take-away on Friday night? Only fish and chips, if you're happy with that."

"Wow! What's the occasion? Sounds good to me. And not just because it's one less meal for me to prepare. My shout. Same takeaway place as before? What time?"

Given Gwynne's radical change in attitude, he felt wrong-footed but warm and fuzzy all the same.

"We'll expect you around six o'clock. That's Merren's usual mealtime. All right with you?"

"Fine with me. I'll put a wash on and have a shower especially for the occasion. If I turn up in my work gear you might make me shower at your place and worse, make me wear some ridiculous item of clothing *again*."

"Clean clothes *and* a shower. We'll feel privileged. Six o'clock Friday it is. See you then. Goodbye."

"I can't help feeling I've missed something along the line but thanks for the call. G'bye."

The rest of Marek's week was a blur of activity punctuated by periods of wool-gathering on possible reasons Gwynne had called him. It was out of character for her but well within his flights of fancy.

It polarised his thinking, alternately wondering whether he was going to be abruptly given his marching orders *again*, or invited to stay the night. He almost succeeded in nipping that thought in the bud.

Early Friday morning he dutifully put on a load of washing that had accumulated over the last week, and then hung it out to dry. By 7:00am he was at the house, relieved to be watching the brickie setting to work. Progress!

By mid-afternoon he and the brickie decided to pack up for the day. Early start, early finish was the brickie's routine. That suited Marek but it meant another 6:00am alarm call.

On the way home he stopped for a haircut. When he got home, he brought in the washing.

It took ages to decide what to wear. None of his clothes were particularly fashionable, so neat and tidy was the next best option. He couldn't remember the last time he'd bought any new clothes.

He stopped off to get the food which gave him time to settle himself. On arrival, the usual greeting with Merren was exchanged but not so with Gwynne. Without being overly demonstrative, he sensed her smile seemed more welcoming.

Wishful thinking?

While the food was being re-heated, Marek was amused to see Merren putting out placemats and knives and forks. It reminded him of when his mother had asked him to do the same. Just as he had done, the knives and forks were mixed up in wrong positions.

"What a great help you are for your mum," he commented, with a bemused grin and a wink in Gwynne's direction.

After the meal, Gwynne put on a DVD for Merren in her playroom while they sat side-by-side on the lounge having coffee. He didn't know how but, before long, their shoulders were touching, and he felt elated. He gave Gwynne a progress report on the house and Gwynne chatted about work both at home and at Select.

Marek paused for a moment, took her hand and asked, "Have you thought about being at home alone with a client? It would worry a lot of women."

"I've been thinking about that and have decided to have a closed-circuit security system installed. How are you at that sort of thing?"

"Never done it before but following 'how to' sheets of instructions comes with the job. It depends on how serious you are and whether to go digital or analogue. Good home systems don't come cheap. Digital back-to-base are more expensive. If you know a good accountant, you might be able to claim it on your tax."

"I might be able to see to that. Do installation instructions come in Polish?"

"I hope not."

The sound of Merren calling, "Mummy, it's finished" interrupted their discussion.

"Duty calls. Back in a few minutes."

Marek tried to help by tidying up the kitchen while Gwynne got Merren ready for bed. He felt elated, but for some reason sensed it would be best if he went home. It was a dilemma. Should he try his luck? *Not this time!* Given his early morning start and Merren still in recovery, he wanted the occasion to be right on the night.

When Gwynne returned, he thanked her for the invitation and prepared to leave. He was pleased to see a fleeting frown when he told her, which was quickly followed by a wry smile. He liked to think she was a little disappointed.

At the door it was some consolation for him to take her by the shoulders for several moments, gently kiss her on her forehead and return the smile. 'Are we still on for that trip to the Wildlife Park next Sunday?"

"Yes. I'll text the details as it gets closer. I'm sure Merren will be fighting fit by then. She was almost asleep when I tucked her in. Goodnight."

"Thanks. Yes, it has been a good night. Thanks. 'Bye."

Gideon Owen Davis

Minmi, Lake Macquarie NSW

(six years later)

V

At dawn on a clear spring morning, he harnessed his horse to the cart Mr Threlkeld had given him. He set off on the three-hour drive to Maitland, just over eleven miles away, to get his monthly supplies. As usual, he would have to rest, feed and water the horse through the day to fit the journey into a single day, to return late that afternoon, still in daylight.

It was a rough track, but he found it a bearable, even pleasant drive.

On arrival, he bought what he needed, secured it in his cart and had a leisurely lunch at the Royal Hotel.

The trip home was uneventful and lulled him into a reflective state on the issues raised by Minister Lewis, particularly those referring to his future domestic arrangements.

As if by divine intervention, he returned home to a situation which transformed his existence. After stabling, feeding and watering his horse, he walked back to the cabin with the task of storing his purchases occupying his mind.

When he approached his cabin, he stopped and stared in astonishment. He was not alone! A vaguely familiar young Aboriginal woman appeared from around the corner. He stopped to take a moment to think.

"Ahlah?" he said hesitantly, using the Awabakal patois for 'hello'.

"Ahlah! Hello Mr Owen," came a whispered reply. She walked tentatively towards him, her head down, not making eye contact. She wore a dress which was obviously a carefully modified hand-me-down. Any ruffles on sleeves and hem had been removed and both had been shortened, clearly for practical everyday work.

Standing barefoot in front of him, she raised her head. He saw her eyes were glistening. Without saying a word, she raised her hands and gently stroked and brushed them over his shoulders, and down his arms. It was the traditional greeting he had seen performed countless times when tribal people had become reunited after an absence from the Ebenezer mission.

He raised his hands and hesitantly placed them on her shoulders. He was undecided whether to return the greeting or push her away. Forestalling further action from him, she stepped forward and rested her forehead against his chest and wrapped her arms around his waist.

He caught his breath as recognition dawned. In the six years since he had last seen her, she had matured into a young woman. Even without saying another word, and despite her welling tears, he recalled the aura of intelligence, dignity and serenity she had exhibited as a child. He immediately comprehended the enormity of her loneliness, the ravages caused by the deaths of her people from persecution, disease and dispossession. Long ago she had been isolated from immediate family. Now it was her traditions, her clan and lore of her country from which she was separated. He recognised from her behaviour the fundamentals of humankind. Someone made in 'His image'. He recognised she was the one person with whom he could share, even demonstrate, his Christian values. That girl, now a woman, had returned to Minmi, the place of her Awabakal language namesake.

She was the last person he had seen before leaving Ebenezer: Lily.

37

The *faux*-family theme continued Sunday week when Gwynne picked Marek up for the trip to the wildlife park.

Once within the park, in sight of the animals, the most entertaining feature for the adults was watching Merren's reactions. She particularly loved the younger animals: lambs, joeys, koalas, goat kids, chicks and ducklings. She squealed with delight at the sight of a baby koala clinging to its mother's back. Her look of amazement at watching a cow being milked and then being offered the chance to touch the cow's teat was worth the admission price alone.

On the other hand, she wasn't too impressed with the severe look a strutting emu gave her from its comparatively great height, or a salt water crocodile's exposed teeth as it drowsily pretended to ignore everyone.

Another highlight was hand-feeding the kangaroos and patting their joeys.

Next was an extended play on the playground equipment which gave Gwynne and Marek a little more time to themselves. To any observer, they appeared to be happy parents watching their child play on a family day out.

As they moved around to watch Merren on the different activities, Marek took a cautious hold of Gwynne's hand. It gave him enough encouragement to put his arm around her waist when they stopped to watch Merren climb the ladder to the slippery dip. When Gwynne allowed it to stay there, Marek felt an ego-boosting surge of contentment.

After lunching on hot dogs, they revisited some of Merren's favourite exhibits. As they continued to stroll between enclosures, Merren got between them and took a hand of each and tried using them as supports to swing back and forth, again with sound effects. This time there were no waves to spoil the fun.

By mid-afternoon, Merren was visibly tiring, and Marek asked her if she would like to sit on his shoulders as they had seen other children perched on their fathers' shoulders.

She looked up at him as if she was considering a major decision in her life and then quickly nodded her head saying, "Yes please!"

They stopped for Marek to swing her up into position and strolled back to the car. Once on their way, Marek asked, "Do you need any help to unload the car?"

"Thanks, but no. There isn't much. It's been a lovely day."

Without any other suggestion being offered, she drove to Marek's home.

"Would you like to come in and have a look at where I grew up?" he asked.

"I'd love to, but another time. Merren's looking drowsy and home will be the best place for her."

"Thanks for today. It was a welcome break from work."

"Is that all? No fun in it for you at all?

"I didn't mean it like that, and you know it. Don't twist my words. It was a relaxing and very enjoyable day and I'd like to have more like them. Give me a call if you get any more bright ideas. G'bye, Merren, goodbye Gwynne."

He stood and watched as they drove away. Sunday afternoon began to take on a depressingly empty aspect.

He spent the next five weeks working long hours six, and occasionally seven, days a week. As the end came into sight, it was with a sense of exhilaration mixed with mischief, that he rang Gwynne.

"Gwynne, I'm desperately in need of a woman's touch."

The response was a deafening silence.

"I think you had better explain yourself, Mr Benning! What exactly do you mean?" was the terse reply.

"I mean that I need the delicate touch of some woman."

"Yes, I heard that bit. Where, I mean exactly *what*, did you have in mind?"

"My place of course, where else? I need advice from a woman on some of the paint colours and tile selections. What did you think I meant?"

"Your choice of words could have been a little less ambiguous, smarty, and you know it."

"Now that you've put the idea into my head, I'm a bit flustered. The reason I rang is that I'm up to painting the interior and choosing tiles for the kitchen, bathroom and laundry. I might also take advice on curtains and possibly floor coverings. A woman's advice on what's fashionable and what isn't, would be greatly appreciated. What do you say?"

"Thanks for the clarification. I'd like to say yes, but it isn't exactly the sort of thing I'm best at, and nor is it something to which I can drag Merren along. She'd be bored in five minutes and be a distraction. I'd have to get someone to mind her."

She sounded disappointed with her own response.

"Hmm, I see your point. Sorry, I never thought it through. Although, I must say, I find your dress sense is always very attractive. It can't be that I'm the only one who appreciates it." In the most innocent tone he could manage he asked, "Couldn't your mother mind Merren?"

Before Gwynne could reply, he changed the subject.

336

"I've also decided to put the house up for a private sale. I'll get a sign up in the next day or so while I'm finishing off the job. I might get lucky and attract a buyer without using an agent."

Gwynne's voice reflected enthusiastic support. "Good luck with that. It sounds like a great idea. Getting exciting, isn't it? You know, when I think about it, the person you really need is Mum. She's much better at that sort of thing than I am."

After an ominous silence, Marek realised he had suddenly entered a minefield.

"Whoa! Would you be offended if I suggested spending that much time with your mother isn't at the top of my wish list?"

"Mr Benning, tread carefully. That's my mother you're referring to. I'll tell you what, I'll ask her. I'll phrase it so she has a choice: go with you to give advice, or mind Merren. I'll let you know what she says but I warn you, there's nothing my mother likes more than giving advice. Looking on the bright side, it could go some way to a détente. It could be the start of a beautiful new relationship."

That's exactly what I'm hoping for, but not with your mother.

Marek was almost lost for words. Choosing them carefully he said, "If she agrees to mind Merren, crisis avoided. We'll cross the next bridge when we have to. I need to measure up for specific quantities first. Have a chat with her about paint colours. Maybe we can decide the issue by correspondence."

"There you go again! Hardly the way to win the favours of a lady."

"Nothing new there then. I think I'm in over my head. Ask her and let me know when you've got an answer. I'd be grateful."

"How grateful?" The mischievous coyness of her retort was apparent.

"Gwynne, you're teasing again. But I like it! G'bye."

Marek followed up on his private sale decision and had a corflute sign made. As he erected it, he knew he was on the home stretch of the biggest project of his career to date. He also realised that if he was going to try and sell the house himself, he would have to do some smartening up of the yards to improve its kerbside appeal. Costs were a factor, but he considered it a case of having to spend money to make money.

On that subject, he now had to decide on a realistic sale price. He spent several hours that night going over the wholesale material costs, his labour costs and an allowance for extras. All had to be added to the purchase price he had paid. The final figure was over the guesstimate he had given Gwynne at the outset, but not by much. The most pleasing aspect was that his research on recent market prices indicated a trend there might be a healthier profit margin than he had anticipated.

He knew that, even after he had settled on a sale price, he still would not know the exact profit until he had consulted with Gwynne on the various taxes. GST, Capital Gains Tax if it applied, and allowable deductions made it almost impossible for him to know his exact financial position. Another business call to Gwynne was in order.

He was feeling optimistic as he sat back and calmed himself with the proverbial, 'every cloud has a silver lining'. He had been under a black cloud for some time and was due a silver-lined break. Now would be good.

He rang her next morning and gave her his costings.

"Well, it all depends on the sale price, doesn't it? I can't give any more than an estimate until we, sorry I mean *you,* have a buyer. I'll go over the numbers and get back to you. I should be able to arrive at a book figure sale price, or at least a narrow range, by then."

"Going over your figure sounds like something I'd like to do," Marek muttered under his breath.

"Pardon? I missed that. Oh, by the way, I asked Mum about what you wanted. I don't know who was more surprised: Mum, because you were indirectly asking for her advice, or me, because she agreed to accompany you. There's no predicting my mother!"

Barely concealing his misgivings, he replied, "Alright, I'll drop some colour charts in this afternoon to pass on. I want colours of a general nature. Nothing too bold or quirky. I need colours that appeal to a wide range of potential buyers. Does that sound too prescriptive?"

"Let's just see what she comes up with. Given the time and effort you've put into this, you should feel proud."

"I do, sort of, but I don't want to get ahead of myself. I've done that before and it led to disappointment." Marek hoped the comment wasn't too pointed and tried to gloss over it. "Thanks Gwynne, for everything. I'm looking forward to seeing your figures tomorrow. 'Bye!"

Marek ended the call musing on that equivocal, but attractive thought.

Events started to snowball. He rang Darren Merrigan to fill him in on the progress. He hadn't spoken to him for a few weeks and felt a bit guilty, given Darren had been his friend and boss for twelve years, and had helped him get to where he was in the trade. He owed him.

When Marek told him the renovations were almost complete and that he was advertising the house for sale privately, Darren congratulated him. "Well done mate. I wouldn't mind having a look over the job if that's okay. I sort of think I have a vicarious interest in it."

"That you do Darren, and then some. I couldn't have done it without your training and those years we worked together."

Darren then gave him a very hopeful bit of information. "You know, one of my colleagues here has been asking me about maintenance costs for investment properties. He is considering buying one. Is it okay for me to mention your job?"

"Are you kidding? That would be great. I need to know what potential buyers think, and what they want in a property."

"I'll let him know he can contact you. Can I call in if you're working this afternoon? I knock off at four o'clock. How about five or thereabouts?"

"Sure. See you then. 'Bye"

Marek knew not to get his hopes up. His year had seen more lows than highs and once again, despite his patience being tested to the max, he would have to wait and see.

When Darren turned up that afternoon, it was not to inspect Marek's work as his boss, although it was hard to believe he wouldn't do just that, but to see what he might be recommending for his workmate. They chatted broadly about aspects of the job amid comments from Darren about his own new job, particularly the lighter, less challenging physical work that was required of him. His most telling comment was, "I don't miss the heartburn, that much I can definitely say."

"Yeah, well, I know where that ended up," Marek replied with a wry grin.

Concerning the almost finished house, he was full of praise. "You've done well. You always showed you had a good eye for the work, and you've tested your skills and made the most of them. Well done."

Marek's chest expanded several inches. "That means a lot to me, Darren. You've taught me all I know and gave me the confidence to take on the job. Thanks, I won't forget it."

Two days after dropping in the colour charts to Gwynne, Marek was bemused when he answered a call from Audrey. Without any reference to her past obstructive role, she asked if they could meet to discuss his views and thoughts on what he wanted for the house. On the one hand, he was pleased to get on with the final decorations. On the other, he wasn't sure how the projected discussions would go. He suspected the diplomatic way forward was for Audrey to inspect the house for herself. When he suggested it, she immediately proposed the following morning. It made him think he might have a tiger by the tail. Or she had ulterior motives.

The following day, Audrey arrived as arranged but with Huw in tow. Marek had an unkind thought; whether it was the house or himself, Huw would be judging. True to form, Audrey took charge and with colour charts in hand, they went from room to room, with him making some suggestions and her commenting on what would be broadly appealing. He was impressed.

The thought struck him that her method was similar to Gwynne's business-like approach, but in a different discipline. In the end, after very few disagreements, Marek accepted most of Audrey's recommendations. They were practical and sensible and, he had to admit, he thought they would look smart.

Audrey then asked about tiles. Given the success of the paint colour selections, to his great surprise, she agreed to him picking her up in his truck the following day to check out a couple of tile suppliers' showrooms.

Just the thought of Audrey sitting in his work truck was enough to put a smug smile on his face.

Throughout the inspection, Huw had barely said a word. As they were about to leave, he asked, "Marek, do you mind if I ask if you have a price in mind yet?"

Marek, slightly puzzled, could only answer, "I'm waiting on advice from your daughter. She's possibly looking at the figures as we speak."

"Let me know when you've decided, I think I know someone who might be interested. Just might, I say, no promises."

"Thanks Huw. Yes, I'll do that." Turning to Audrey he said, "And thank you Audrey. You've been a big help. It's good to have a second opinion. I feel much more comfortable with your input."

Marek couldn't believe his good fortune: two expressions of interest in twenty-four hours. Maybe his luck was turning. Let the painting begin! It wasn't his favourite job by any means. but this was his own house, and he could save on the expense of contractors.

Gwynne emailed him the estimates which would allow him to set a minimum price. In the real estate market, he knew any house was only worth what a buyer would pay for it. He had to set the asking price, but the sale price would be a negotiated settlement.

He rang Darren and Huw and told them his decision on the asking price and tried to sound confident that he knew what he was talking about.

As they set off the next day, Marek cast sidelong glances at Audrey. The incongruity of her sitting there in all her *Vogue* fashion glory, as if she was being chauffeured in a Rolls Royce rather than a tradie's work truck, was huge. He was hard pressed not to ask outright, *'Why are you doing this?'* His suspicions were aroused, thinking it was another reconnaissance mission on her part, mostly intended to assess himself in preparation for her next move in her mind-games.

The choices for the tiles and decorations went as well as he could have hoped. He recognised that Gwynne was right, Audrey did have a good eye for decoration. Salespeople reacted positively to her ideas and, at times, his role was reduced to that of an observer. He had to admit credit where it's due, at least where this exercise was concerned.

When they finished and he had the truck loaded with the chosen tiles he said, in all sincerity, "Thank you Audrey. You've taken a load off my mind. At least I won't be second-guessing myself as I finish off the final stages. I also noted the responses of some of the staff we dealt with. I think they thought they were dealing with a professional."

"You're welcome," was her reply, accompanied by a self-satisfied smile. "I quite enjoyed myself, so thank you for asking me along.

Marek's curiosity finally got the better of him and he said, "Audrey, can I ask you, why did you agree to do this today?"

"Because Gwynne asked me."

"I know that. You know what I mean. Was it just an adventure for you to satisfy your curiosity?"

"Whatever you think of me, I know my daughter. And I'm not blind. Thanks for asking my opinion. That's all I'm saying."

"Well, I hope one day I get a chance to understand you better."

She turned to look out the side window so he couldn't see her face but, in a barely audible voice, he thought he heard her say, "I think you just might … one day."

That afternoon, both Darren's and Huw's interested buyers contacted him and arranged inspections. He informed them he was working on site, mainly just painting, and they agreed on times.

When Darren's colleague arrived two days later Marek tried to say as little as possible. He answered questions about the construction and materials with confidence but avoided offering opinions and advice.

Recent practice at being patient was evidently paying off.

Two interesting comments from Darren's colleague-come-buyer were that he didn't want any landscaping done because it was to be an investment property and he wanted to keep outside maintenance to a minimum. "Grass on a flat block only requires mowing."

His second comment was in the form of a question. "Are you generally available to do building maintenance on investment properties?"

Marek was careful answering, "That would depend on the workload, locations, agreed payrates and my availability."

He was wary because any landlord might only be interested in cheap patch-up jobs which wouldn't do his reputation any good. Or his ego. "I'll think about it. We can talk again when I've finished this job and sold the property. The fact is, I'm trying to specialise in additions and renovation projects and I'm waiting on some responses to some quotes."

Three days later, Darren's colleague dropped in again for a second look at the house. Most of the painting was finished and his few questions, mostly about the tiling selections in the bathroom, laundry and kitchen, indicated he really only wanted to confirm his decision. "I had another talk with Darren. He's a good bloke and he gave this job the thumbs up."

Finally, they got to the point of discussing money. Figures were mentioned and haggled over until agreement on a price was reached. Marek was at pains to conceal his pleasure. The man obviously felt he had negotiated a good deal for himself. Marek was pretty sure the price would give him a decent profit margin. Handshakes were exchanged and Marek gave him Ross' business details for the holding deposit and conveyancing process.

Two days later, Ross rang to let him know the buyer's solicitor had contacted him to say he was holding the deposit and to congratulate him on the sale. "I'll get to work on the contract. You'll have a five business-day cooling-off period after we exchange contracts. You're on the home stretch. Well done."

"Thanks Ross. I've got everything crossed there are no hitches. I'll be counting the days. 'Bye"

Marek then rang Huw to say a deposit had been made on the house. Huw thanked him for letting him know adding, "As it turns out, I was going to call you because the fellow I had in mind has decided not to proceed. He thinks the timing isn't quite right for him. Well done Marek on both the house and the imminent sale."

38

Marek saved the best call till last and rang Gwynne. As soon as she answered he asked, "When would it be convenient for me to take you and Merren to dinner?"

"What's happened? You sound pleased."

"I asked the first question. Do you always answer a question with a question? The fact is, a deposit has been made on the house! I can hardly believe it has all happened so quickly. A colleague of Darren's is buying it as an investment property."

"Congratulations. Is the price in the range we discussed?"

"Towards the top." Marek mentioned the figure, trying not to sound like he was gloating.

"Excellent! I'll start entering all the details against that figure and let you know how it ends up. Dinner, you said?"

"Yes, with you and Merren. This is something to celebrate. I thought of having a few beers with Darren and some mates, but their charms don't quite match yours … even on a good day. So, what do you say? When will you both be free?"

"I'm not sure we're too chuffed about being a second choice. Where did you have in mind? A counter lunch at your local? Merren isn't really restaurant savvy yet. Anything too upmarket might be challenging."

"Your choice where. Any Golden Arches outlet you like."

"Hmm! And you reckon I'm a tease. There's a little Italian restaurant in an arcade in Hamilton. It's popular but if we get in early, which would suit Merren, we should be fine."

Gwynn paused,

After a moment she asked, "Are you sure you want to include Merren?"

"Yeah, I am. The days we had at the beach and the wildlife park went well, not counting her being dunked. Let's stretch our luck. What's the worst she can do? Drum on the table? Smash the crockery? Start screaming? Throw up? She comes as part of a job lot."

"None of those, I hope. And 'job lot' doesn't sound too flattering. When?"

"Sooner the better for me. Your call."

"I'm working from home this Friday. Does Friday night suit?"

"Suits me fine. I'll book a taxi with a booster seat for Merren. We can have a bottle of something. Do you like Chianti? Is five-thirty too early for you?"

"Once you decide on something you really go for it, don't you? Yes, that will work. Thanks Marek, we'll look forward to it."

"Me too. G'bye, Gwynne."

By Thursday afternoon, Marek was able to look over the house and land, both inside and out, with a sense of pride and achievement. His mate with the tipper and bobcat had removed all the building debris and the house itself looked settled and comfortable on its block. It was no longer a construction site and fitted well with the other federation style brick houses in the street. Only this one had a modern interior and, when the bare patches in the yard were re-turfed, would even be a little more up-market.

The sense of accomplishment was accentuated by his realisation that the project had started optimistically, fallen into a black hole and then risen, almost Phoenix-like, from the ashes. That door was closing.

Was there another opening somewhere?

He dressed carefully in a new outfit of brown-check chinos, a close-fitting, cream cotton shirt with the sleeves rolled to his elbows, and brown boat shoes.

It was a long time since he had taken so much care of his appearance, but he was determined to look, and be, at his best. He had a trendy-looking men's shoulder bag out of which poked the tip of a bottle of Chianti in its raffia-woven basket.

Gwynne hurriedly opened the door after his jaunty knock and explained she was applying the final touches before quickly disappearing into her room.

While waiting, he joined Merren sitting watching television with Squinty and Binko, one in the crook of each arm. Her animal glove puppets were all placed in a line beside her facing the TV screen. After rearranging the puppets for space, he sat down next to her.

"Hello Princess, you're looking all dressed up. Going somewhere?"

Merren giggled and in a generous act of sharing, she offered: "Would you like to hold Binko while we wait?"

"How kind you are. Thank you."

Such was the sight Gwynne witnessed when she walked into the room. "Oh, very sweet, I'm sure. Is tonight going to be a threesome or a fivesome?"

Marek looked up to see Gwynne standing in the doorway wearing a dark red knee-length dress. It was a vision which sent his thoughts into a whirl. Form-fitting in an elegant way but with open lace sleeves, back and upper bodice, he could only stare.

Gwynne pirouetted for full effect. As she did so, the earrings he had given her sparkled. "Do you like it?"

Eventually he stammered, "I love it. You look stunning. Gorgeous!"

"Why thank you kind sir. You're looking pretty smart yourself. I hardly recognised you without my onesie. Perhaps you'd you like to keep it?"

"I hope that's not going to be the tone of conversation for the rest of the night."

"I hope so too."

The moment passed as the beep from the taxi sounded. They collected their things, checked they were all set to go, and walked out the door. Once Merren was buckled into her seat they set off. In different ways, it was a new experience for each one of them.

Being relatively early for most diners, the restaurant was practically empty. Marek produced the bottle of Chianti from his bag and placed it on the table. Between snippets of conversation about the finished house and other events in their working week, their order was taken. Entrée of mixed bread, a small spirelli pasta in a bolognaise sauce for Merren, plus a fizzy orange drink; avocado chicken for Gwynne, and Marek's favourite, veal *Saltimbocca*. The wine was opened and, in a more stress-free state of mind than Marek had experienced since he and Darren had dissolved their partnership, both seemed to relax into pleasant conversation.

When the food arrived, grated Parmesan cheese was offered and accepted as was cracked pepper. Merren was near her best behaviour and made a valiant effort with her meal. Gwynne and Marek ate slowly, relishing both the food and the moment. The level in the wine bottle gradually diminished and, by the end, they were all completely satisfied.

As a reward, Merren was allowed a banana split for dessert. It was more than she could manage so two extra spoons were requested and they all shared it in a playful spoon-clashing contest, arguing as to whether someone was taking more than a fair share.

With everyone feeling satisfied, Marek slung the bag with empty Chianti bottle over his shoulder and they left the restaurant. Standing between Marek and Gwynne, Merren raised her hands and started swinging their arms. Another habit had been created. They swung her between them as they set off on a short ten-minute walk along the vibrant main street. With its colourful street lighting, multicultural decorations, and tantalising fragrances from its mostly Mediterranean restaurants, it was a relaxing finale to their night.

At a time considerably later than Merren's bedtime, they arrived home. Marek had a nervous few moments after paying the taxi driver. His doorstep experiences with Gwynne at the end of their outings had been less than fulfilling. This time however, Gwynne invited him in for coffee and he willingly accepted.

While the coffee was brewing, Gwynne got Merren ready for bed. Marek amused himself with one of Merren's books. When Gwynne came into the loungeroom she pointed at the book saying, "That's one of Merren's favourites."

Tentatively, Marek asked, "Do you think Merren would like me to read it to her? Or another story?"

Gwynne gave him that look which she reserved for occasions whenever Marek said or did something completely unexpected. "Yes, I think she would like that. Let's ask her."

Together, they went into Merren's room. "Would you like Marek to read you a bedtime story?"

Merren's smile and nodding head gave them their answer. "That one please," she said eagerly, pointing to the book he held.

Marek sat on the edge of the bed and Merren snuggled up to him. He felt an unexpected glow of contentment as he read. From the first, Merren was engrossed but her reactions steadily became more muted, and her breathing settled into a gentler regular rhythm. He noticed her eyelids drooping. The story wasn't finished but he recognised time was up. He eased her back onto her pillow and pulled up the doona, gave her a light kiss on her forehead and crept out of the room to find Gwynne in the kitchen.

"She's just dropped off to sleep. I hope it wasn't because of my boring reading style."

"It's been a big night out for her. I'll just pop in and check on her. Sit in the loungeroom and I'll bring in the coffee in a moment."

A few minutes later, Gwynne returned with the coffee and sat next to Marek. "She's sound asleep. Thank you for a beautiful night. It was fun and at the same time, quite relaxing. Intimate, almost, for a first night out." In a more subdued murmur she added, "I liked it a lot." She leaned back and rested her head on the back of the lounge. "I think you win. Actually, I think we might both win. Perhaps all three of us." She continued pensively, "I think tonight has been a turning point. I've been worrying about all sorts of things for four years and now I wonder whether I got it all wrong."

"I don't know about that. There is nothing wrong between *us* that we can't make right."

"I don't mean wrong about us. I mean how I have been behaving."

"I know what you mean, but the way you have been behaving has ended up, here and now, with us sitting together enjoying each other's company. Perfectly satisfactory and natural as far as I'm concerned. In this case, the end justifies the means, or something like that. What I mean is, we have ended up in a good place. Let's not dwell too much on how we got here. Let's look forward to where we go *from* here."

"Agreed. I'll try to be more understanding. But don't rush things," was her muted reply.

"Would I be rushing things if I said you looked beautiful tonight?" He picked up one of her hands and examined it for a few moments and then lifted it to his lips.

After a slight adjustment, Gwynne removed her earrings, placed them on the coffee table and rested her head against his shoulder.

"Do you know, that besides your exquisite hands, you have very attractive ear lobes? I have an irresistible urge to kiss this one just here." He leant close and, after kissing it gently and without any complaint from Gwynne, thought … *might as well be hanged for a sheep as a lamb* and took it lightly between his lips while flicking it with his tongue.

"Ooh, that tickles. Now who's teasing?"

"Ah, sorry. I suppose the other ear is jealous, but I can't reach it." He continued. "Can I give this little part of your cheek a kiss instead? I'll dedicate it to Nonna's Kitchen. And this spot on your neck is positively crying out for attention. And there's this … sorry, I hope you don't mind, but there's something I have to do."

"What? You're not leaving now?" Gwynne said. "What do you have to do that's so urgent?"

He put his arms around her, drew her to him and kissed her with the passion he had bottled up over several months. One part of his pent-up frustration began to ease; another was reaching breaking point. When Gwynne broke the kiss, she again rested her head against his shoulder.

He pulled back. "Gwynne, I've been wanting to do that for so long. If it isn't obvious to you already, I'll say it straight out. I'm in love with you. I want to be with you. I want us to be together, and that includes Merren. We could all be very good for each other."

There was a long silence before he asked anxiously, "Don't you have anything to say?"

"Yes."

"Well?"

"Kiss me again."

This time it was Gwynne who clung to Marek as they kissed with mounting desire.

As her hands caressed his face and the back of his head, his own hands itched for more intimate contact.

Gwynne offered no resistance, and her response was to cuddle even closer, and in a wheedling voice said, "Marek, a couple of times you've referred to the time you wore my onesie. On one occasion I remember, after that lunch we had at Mum and Dad's, I asked why you wore it instead of the towel around your waist. You said, and I'm pretty sure these were your exact words: 'Maybe I'll tell you if we get to know each other better'. Do you think we know each other a bit better after our family outings and especially tonight? After all, we seem to be baring our souls to each other."

"Gwynne Alwen, you could tease for Australia in the Olympics. Did you have to bring that up?"

"I just want everything to be out in the open between us," she replied in feigned innocence.

"How can you say that with a straight face? After what you've put me through. Alright! I'll tell you. But promise me you won't laugh."

"I promise no such thing." Gwynne replied, pretending to be miffed.

"There's a cost if I have to tell you, payable in advance," he said, raising the stakes.

"Oh, yes? And what will that be?" Her pretence of 'calling and raising' à la poker-style, was unmistakable.

"This!"

He reached across Gwynne, gently turned her to face him and kissed her again, allowing his pent-up passion full flow. Almost.

Gwynne's physical response was unmistakable as the kiss and the embrace intensified.

His hand seemed to take on an independence of its own, starting on her back, edging lower, feeling, touching, stroking, caressing and eventually upwards and settling gently on her breast. He found her raised nipple through the silky-soft fabric and he gently stroked it with his thumb. That blissful moment turned to panic as Gwynne placed her hand on top of his, holding it steady. *Was it to be rejection again?*

He held the kiss and hand until the pressure of her hand increased, and then fell away.

When shortness of breath ended their embrace Gwynne, flushed and flustered, stood up and took a couple of steps back from him.

Uncertain what was to happen next, he asked, "Do I still have to tell you about the onesie?"

She took him by the arm and gently pulled him to his feet. Slowly, she began to walk down the hallway, saying, "Don't *tell* me, *show* me."

"Why, Miss Alwen, *that* will be my pleasure."

"Just your pleasure? Hmm. Selfish!"

"Sorry, *our* pleasure then. Better?"

"Selfish and perhaps somewhat … presumptuous?"

"Proof of the pudding …?"

"Mmm, promises! I'll wait and see."

"I'm right behind you."

"Ooh, something else to think about. As I said, prom …"

Marek came to a sudden halt and turned Gwynne to face him and asked, "Miss Alwen, do you always have to have the last word?"

"I'm an accountant. Our last word is always the bottom line," she retorted curtly.

"Yes, well, I've been checking it out and I like what I see, but I think it requires closer examination."

"Mr Benning, whatever do you …?

"Anyway, they say, the devil's in the detail. Sometimes the detail can appear quite minor."

"Let me be the judge as to whether the detail will stand up to requirements."

"Miss Alwen, that is a pleasure to which I can certainly look forward."

"Hmm! Your pleasure again! I think we're back where we started. Wait here!" Disengaging from Marek, she walked off down the hallway.

"Now what? Where are you going?"

"I'm just going to check on Merren. Don't go anywhere."

"Great timing! Not!" His sigh of frustration said everything.

Within a minute she returned, to stand directly facing him. Not once losing direct eye contact, she raised her hands and feather-lightly brushed them over his hair, forehead and face, then rested them gently on his shoulders.

Suddenly she smiled and drew a deep breath. She took him by the hand and led him onwards, asking over her shoulder, "Now Mr Benning, what were you going to show me about wearing my onesie?"

EPILOGUE

"Keith, what's up?" Marek was grouting the last of the tiling in the laundry and had to wedge his phone between his ear and shoulder.

"Are you sitting down?"

"No, I'm not. I've got my hands full with a fiddly grouting job." He tried to keep his exasperation out of his voice.

"Well, as soon as you can, ring me back. I've got some news you'll definitely want to hear – sitting down." Keith ended the call as abruptly as he'd started it.

Marek awkwardly pocketed his phone and continued to dress and clean the finished surface. He wiped his hands with a feeling of satisfaction, retrieved his phone and returned Keith's call.

"Ok, I'm sitting down, what is it?" It was a lie. He wasn't sitting down; he didn't want to lose any time and he was walking around inspecting various final touches of the job.

"You won't believe what I've unearthed. I was going over the story of the burials on that land in Minmi with Colette. I told her about the wooden cross that was found and that led to us talking about religion and stuff. I mentioned the Threlkeld mission, and she interrupted and said, 'How interesting! One of Mum's great uncles was sort of a Congregational missionary. I think he came out to Australia around the middle of the nineteenth century and, except for some letters over a few years, was never heard of again. Or so we were led to believe from the letters my grandmother collected.'

"I asked her, 'What sort of a missionary? What family letters?' You've never even mentioned this before."

"And she said, 'Well, I'm telling you now. Besides, you never asked. Grandmother Davis kept a few letters from the family, and they mentioned a Gideon who came to New South Wales and disappeared. In one of his letters, he wrote he had arrived in a place north of Sydney Town that was some sort of settlement run by a missionary.'"

Keith rushed on with the story. "Now listen to this Marek, and think about it. There's a distinct possibility this great uncle could have met up with Threlkeld and was befriended by him and the young Gideon Davis might have been persuaded, or volunteered, to join up with him. There'd be plenty of work, especially for a Welshman, who might know something about coal mining.

"Threlkeld's Ebenezer mission eventually closed but this Gideon character could have moved on to the Minmi area where there was a Congregational Church. I even looked it up. The pit got flooded and was closed for months afterwards. Perhaps this Gideon Davis was left behind because, just maybe, he had set up house with a black woman. Not the done thing in those days, not quite accepted, especially in strict missionary circles."

Marek interrupted Keith's flow, "Where's this heading Keith? You're talking in riddles again. Is it a family trait?"

"Patience lad. Bear with me. This great uncle's full name was Gideon Owen Davis!"

"Right. Got it. What's your point?" Marek's impatience was beginning to show.

"Gideon Owen Davis! G-O-D. Sound familiar?" Keith couldn't hide the 'eureka' moment from his voice. "Don't you get it? Think about it mate. Gideon Owen Davis' initials are GOD!"

"No, not really … Wait a minute … What was Threlkeld's full name?"

Keith interrupted, "Bingo! It's Lancelot Edward Threlkeld. His initials are L-E-T. Gideon Owen Davis' are GOD. 'LET to GOD'! That's got to be a connection!"

Marek's blood ran cold, and a shiver rippled over him. His voice almost failed him. It was a pivotal moment, comparable to that when he had stood in the Joseph Conrad Reserve in Zakopane at the time of his father's death. It took a few moments for the implications to sink in.

A goose has walked over my grave.

"Marek, are you there?" The pitch of Keith's voice had gone up a notch.

"Yes, I'm still here."

"Well? What do you think?"

"I'll tell you what I think. I think I have to put in an offer on a certain piece of land pretty damn quick."

BIBLIOGRAPHY

Adelaide, Debra, 1998, *Serpent Dust*, Random House.

Barnett, C.J., 29 March 2007, *address to Australian Parliament.*

Clouten, Keith H, 1967, *Reid's Mistake*, Halstead Press.

Grenville, Kate, 2007, *The Secret River*, Canongate U.S.

Hartley, Dulcie, *Reverend Lancelot E. Threlkeld 1788-1859,* 2004.

Hill, David, 2014, *The Making of Australia*, Penguin/ Random House.

Janson, Julie, 2022, *Benevolence*, HarperVia.

Johnston, Anna, 2011, *The Paper War*, University of Western Australia.

Karskens, Grace, 2020, *People of the River*, Allen & Unwin.

Karskens, Grace, 2010, *The Colony,* Allen & Unwin.

Lee-Talbot, Deborah, 2017, *Lancelot Threlkeld*, Colourful Histories.

Macintyre, Stuart and Clark, Anna, 2004, *The History Wars,* Melbourne University Press.

Metaxas, Eric, 2013, *Amazing Grace,* HarperOne (Harper Collins).

Michener, James A, 1983, *Poland*, The Ballantyne Publishing Group.

Murray, Peter, 2015, W*arners Bay: The Early Years*, 3rd edn, Peter Murray.

Murray, Peter, 2018, *Mission to Lake Macquarie*, Peter Murray.

Myers, Jeffrey, 2001, *Joseph Conrad: A Biography,* Cooper Square Press.

Pascoe, Bruce, *Dark Emu*, 2019, Magabala Books Aboriginal Corporation.

Schama, Simon, 2009, *A History of Britain,* The Bodley Head.

Shaw A.G.L. & Nicholson H.D., 1961, *An Introduction to Australian History.*

Smyth, Terry, 2016, *Denny Day: The Life and Times of Australia's Greatest Lawman - The Forgotten Hero of the Myall Creek Massacre*, Penguin, Random House.

State Library of New South Wales, *The Dictionary of Sydney.*

Zamoyski, Adam, 2015, *Poland, a History*, HarperCollins.

The following maps were redrawn and adapted by
John Franks using information
commonly available from various sources.

APPENDIX I

Awaba, Lake Macquarie, circa 1840s
(**known as** Awaba by the **Awabakal tribe**)

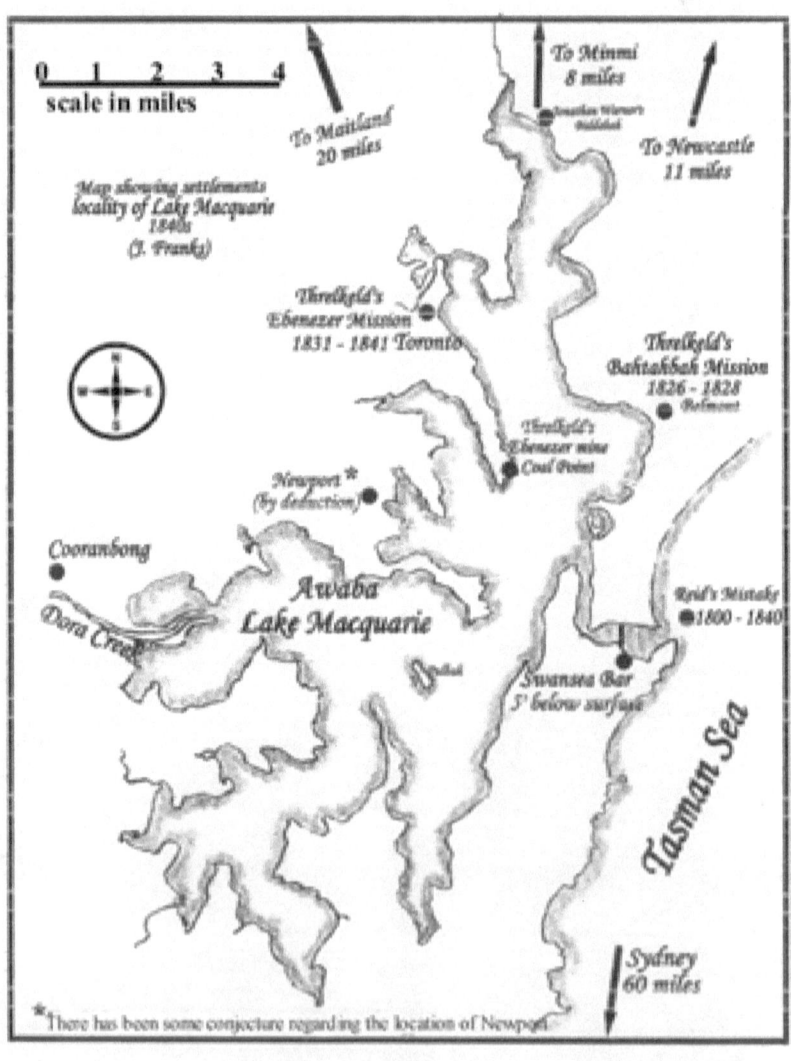

APPENDIX II

Milosz and Alicja's Journey
Zakopane to Genoa

ACKNOWLEDGEMENTS

ECHOES is a fiction. However, some names of real-life characters have been used, particularly in the historical flashback sections. To the best of my research abilities, events described in those sections are accurate but some minimal flexibility in chronology has been applied. This includes instances of the remarkable life of Lancelot Edward Threlkeld, a visionary Humanitarian and advocate for Aborigines in general and the Awabakal people. I am thankful to local authors and historians Keith Clouten for his book *Reid's Mistake* and Peter Murray for his books, particularly, *Mission to Lake Macquarie* for excellent books on Threlkeld and Lake Macquarie. I also thank Grace Karskens for her wonderfully informative and well-annotated book, *People of the River* which brought to life the plight of Aborigines, convicts and settlers in the early years of white settlement.

Where my story moves to Poland, I have referred to characters and events relating to Joseph Conrad (born Józef Teodor Konrada Korzeniowski) one of the great writers in the English language, despite not speaking English fluently until he was in his mid-twenties. There is a plaque in a 'Skwer' acknowledging him in Zakopane, a Polish town at the foot of the Tatra Mountains, which I visited.

Thanks go to the many people who helped with editing and factual details: Margaret Matheson for her editing skills and encouragement; Marek Zozworek, who first advised me to travel to Zakopane in Poland and mentioning the Goral people. Thanks also to Thelma and Bogdan Wawzonek for Polish language, historical and cultural background. I am particularly grateful to author Adam Zamoyski for his wonderfully readable book: *POLAND a history*. Most helpful was Anna Johnston's work *The Paper War*, detailing L. E. Threlkeld's correspondence with his supporters and adversaries as well as his published works.

Special thanks to Alison Hillier for her assistance with layout and presentation. I must also thank many of my friends, and acquaintances, whose good nature I imposed upon, to read various sections and give much needed advice. They include Leslie Wiles, Jeanette Abery, Mal Read and Stephen Oakes. For technical advice on taxation, I must thank life-long friends Bill Croker and David Gubbay. For building industry knowledge, Bill's son William Croker and Richard Oakes. My own building knowledge has been acquired through my good friend and tradesman extraordinaire, Bob Wiles, (deceased) under whose direction I laboured as a volunteer for almost five years.

I must also thank the critique group members of Lake Macquarie branch of the Fellowship of Australian Writers, especially Jan Mitchell, Alison Ferguson, Pam Garfoot and Linda Visman for much valued guidance and support. Thanks also to good friend Claire Williams who gave valuable editorial advice.

A special thanks to graphic artist Dez Robertson and his patience in responding to my suggestions for the cover design. Remarkably, he seemed to capture the essence of the story despite my help.

Special thanks to the state Library of New South Wales for confirming the 'out of copyright' status of the cover image of the Aboriginal girl I chose as my *Lili* character. The image, traced through *The Dictionary of Sydney*, was first published on 24th May, 1922 (p23) in the Sydney Mail under the heading 'ABORIGINAL GIRLS AS DOMESTIC SERVANTS'.

I apologise for any offence showing the image might incur. I can only say that I tried numerous times to get a comment on it's use from two local and Northern Territory indigenous authorities.

The two maps in the appendices have been adapted by me.

Having indulged my passion to write a novel, I then had to face the task of getting it published. For her professional assistance I must thank Sandra Boyd of Kani Consultants for leading me through the hoops and hurdles of that challenging task with her advice and publishing skills.

Having received so much help, I am obliged to declare that the final choices, including any errors, are mine.

Throughout this process, my greatest supporter has been my wife, Carolyn Franks. Without her advice, patience, reassurance, and constructive comments, I would have failed at the first hurdle – my confidence.

ABOUT THE AUTHOR

As a mature-age student, John Franks attained both bachelor's and master's degrees in education from the University of Newcastle. He has survived a forty-year career teaching in schools ranging from a one-teacher school in country NSW to large city schools in Sydney and Newcastle.

He and his wife Carolyn have travelled extensively within Australia and to forty countries, mostly in Europe but also to Ukraine, China, Russia, Morocco and three times to Turkey.

In 2020, John's first book, *Memoirs (warts and all) of a Baby Boomer*, was dedicated to his granddaughters, Nina Hillier and Rebekah Hillier. He credits that book's success to the numerous submissions to the Lake Macquarie City Library's Memoir Group's monthly meetings.

As a lover of the arts, one of his other interests is music, having studied clarinet at the Newcastle Conservatorium of Music. He has played in brass and concert bands, and the University of Newcastle Wind Orchestra.

Currently, he plays in a couple of small ensembles and conducts a small but enthusiastic U3A orchestra in Lake Macquarie.

John has been a long-standing participant in the vibrant Newcastle amateur theatre scene. In 2011 he was awarded life-membership of the Newcastle Theatre Company, having been secretary for nine years and president for two. He has performed with many local companies in over forty plays "without having troubled any talent scouts".

John has an abiding affection for Lake Macquarie, especially the lake itself, Awaba, as it is known by the local Awabakal Indigenous Australian people. He finds its natural beauty a source of inspiration. Despite its appearance, John takes a keen interest in his garden which was once described by a grandchild as "Pa's forest". (Out of the mouths of babes…) Like his writing, John and his garden are a work in progress.